The Restitution

LEGACY OF THE KING'S PIRATES | Book Three

M. L. TYNDALL

BARBOUR
PUBLISHING

Soli Deo Gloria
For God's glory alone.

ISBN 978-1-59789-361-9

All scripture quotations are taken from the King James Version of the Bible.

This book is a work of fiction. Names, characters, places, and incidents are either products of the author's imagination or used fictitiously. Any similarity to actual people, organizations, and/or events is purely coincidental.

Cover design by Müllerhaus Publishing Group

Published by Barbour Publishing, Inc., P.O. Box 719, Uhrichsville, Ohio 44683, www.barbourbooks.com

Our mission is to publish and distribute inspirational products offering exceptional value and biblical encouragement to the masses.

 Member of the
Evangelical Christian
Publishers Association

Printed in the United States of America.

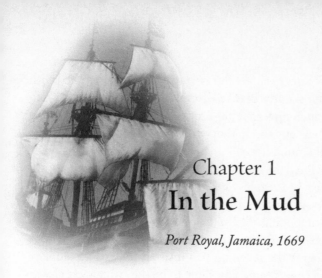

Chapter 1
In the Mud

Port Royal, Jamaica, 1669

Raising her chin in the air, Isabel Melody Ashton plodded through the muddy streets of Port Royal. All through the night, torrents of angry rain had pelted against the window of her room in the church. Each bolt of lightning, each bellow of thunder had sent her son, Frederick, screaming in terror, and although Isabel had tried rocking him in the rickety old chair Reverend Thomas had given her and singing Frederick's favorite lullaby, he would not be soothed. Now, he slept peacefully nestled against her chest in the sling Marlie had fashioned for him, while Isabel trudged forward, barely keeping her eyes open.

Isabel brushed the brown curls from his face and smiled, drawing him closer to her bosom. Taking a deep breath of the salty air still heavy with the sting of rain, she gazed over the churning sea that glistened in the mid-morning light. Fuming waves from the night's storm crashed onto the shore in a bubbling frenzy as dark clouds retreated on the horizon.

Tall ships anchored at bay tottered on the incoming swells, their bare masts jutting like ominous spires into the restless sky. Isabel shifted her gaze and swallowed hard, determined not to allow her terrifying memories to surface. By the grace of God, she would not have to set foot on one of those monstrous beasts again, save for the joyous moment when her father would summon her home.

Turning a corner, Isabel lifted her skirts and squished her way down the street, searching for dry ground. Her borrowed boots were caked with globs of mud, and she silently thanked Reverend Thomas for insisting she wear them. She much preferred her brocade slippers, especially when she ventured into town, but surely they would have been ruined in the black slime oozing all around her.

Brick warehouses lined the street on her right, and she glanced toward the Point, the main part of town just ahead. Fear pinched her heart. Even in the daylight, the taverns and shops that sprang up around Fort Charles appeared dark and foreboding, like a haunted village deserted by the living. She heard Marlie sloshing behind her and cast the young half-breed a quick look, happy the reverend had insisted the girl accompany Isabel. Port Royal had been deemed by some to be the "wickedest city in the world," and in the brief year Isabel had lived here, she had begun to believe it.

Squinting toward the sun, now just a handbreadth over the horizon, she knew most of the pirates and privateers would still be sleeping off their night's debauchery. She needed only to scale the outer edges of the main town in order to get to the mercantile where the reverend had sent her to purchase a bolt of linen fabric, and then she could return to the safety of the church.

Frederick gurgled in his sleep, and Isabel leaned down and kissed his forehead, breathing in his light, innocent scent. She adjusted the sling over her aching shoulders. At seven months, Frederick weighed nearly twenty pounds, and the strain of carrying him was taking its toll on her delicate frame.

Drawing her son closer, Isabel made her final turn to the shop. Only a few dockworkers and merchants labored across the avenues. A trickle of perspiration slid down her neck and under the bodice of her gown as the humidity and heat rose like steam from a cauldron of hot mud.

Snickers drew her attention to a group of filthy men loitering under the porch of a boardinghouse up ahead. They leered at her while whispering amongst themselves. A tall man emerged from their midst and swaggered toward her. His blue waistcoat, which stretched over a prominent belly, was richly embellished with gold braid that sparkled in the sun.

Isabel's heart froze. She grabbed Marlie's hand and averted her gaze as she hurried forward. The man halted in her path. "My apologies,

milady." He bowed, doffing his plumed bicorn, and waved it through the air. "May I trouble you for a moment?" Icy blue eyes froze her in place.

Coils of salt-and-pepper hair sprang from his cavalier tie. The pistol stuffed in his breeches and the cutlass hanging at his side sent spikes of terror down Isabel's back. Though his regal mannerisms and genteel speech indicated otherwise, Isabel had spent enough time in the company of pirates to recognize one when she saw him.

His degenerate minions swarmed up behind him.

Feigning a courage she did not feel, Isabel thrust her chin in the air. "Forgive me, sir, but I have not a moment to spare." She plodded forward, trying to skirt around him.

He blocked her way again. "I beg your pardon. I know 'tis rather imposing of me, but I saw you have a baby. It would mean so much to me if you'd allow me to gaze upon your child. You see, I have a son about your baby's age. Is it a boy?" He leaned down to peer at Frederick's face, and Isabel shrank back, hugging Frederick closer to her bosom.

"Yes. But really, I must be going."

Marlie slinked behind Isabel. A lot of help the young girl was.

"About seven months in age?"

Isabel eyed him with suspicion. How would a pirate be able to gauge the age of a baby? The men behind him pressed forward, their fierce, cold eyes shifting from her to Frederick. One of them smacked his lips and snarled at her.

The tall pirate ran a long, bony finger over Frederick's head. "May I hold him?"

Isabel jumped and nearly toppled backward over a rock. "How dare you? Absolutely not. Now be gone with you." Fear tripped through her mind, trying to find an explanation for this pirate's interest in her son. Clinging to Frederick, she backed farther away.

The man was not leaving. The smirk on his lips grew even wider, and he took a step toward her, reaching out for Frederick.

The crack of a whip and the snort of horses sounded behind her, and Isabel turned to see a carriage lumbering through the sludge. It was Abigail and her prudish friends, and they were heading her way. Relief softened the sting of her nerves—not her normal reaction when she ran across Abigail, but for once, the girl may be doing her a service.

The pirate looked up, and disappointment tugged at his smug features. Donning his hat, he offered Isabel a bow. "Another time, perhaps?" Then as quickly as they'd come, he and his band of men disappeared into town.

"Well, I daresay, look who the storm has dragged from her cave." A shrill voice jabbed at Isabel as the coach stopped beside her. She turned and glared up at the attractive, raven-haired girl leaning from the covered carriage. An icy smirk twisted Abigail's otherwise beautiful, rosy lips.

"And she dares to bring her illegitimate brat out with her." A girl next to Abigail chortled, sending her golden ringlets bobbing. The two girls sitting behind her giggled.

Isabel returned Abigail's stony glare and caressed Frederick's head, thankful he was too young to understand the insults flung his way. Anger fumed within her, but she offered her sweetest smile. "Coming home a bit early from your night's work at the tavern?"

Gasps sprang from the two women seated in the back. The blond-haired lady snapped open her fan and waved it in front of her red face, while Abigail's grin hardened into a firm line. "Yet it would appear that your clients"—she glanced in the direction the pirates had gone—"have the audacity to follow you out into the street."

Marlie gently tugged Isabel's elbow. "Come, milady. Let's go."

"Yes, by all means. Go with your little slave girl." Abigail sighed and fingered the sparkling ruby hanging around her neck. "Go purchase a proper push carriage for your—your—whose son is he?" She cast a playful gaze at her friends, igniting them in laughter. "Some pirate, wasn't it? But in any case, surely it is uncomfortable to carry him around like the slave women do while they work in the fields."

The muscles in Isabel's jaw tightened as tears burned behind her eyes. She could not afford a push carriage for Frederick or even proper attire. She was as poor as she had ever been in her life—nothing more than a beggar living off the mercies of the reverend. How far she had fallen from the wealth and luxury of her father's estate in Hertfordshire. Didn't these ladies know who she was? She was the daughter of Lord and Lady Ashton. Her father was an earl, giving Isabel a far higher position than a mere governor's daughter, which was all Abigail could ascribe to.

The biscuit and banana Isabel had eaten for breakfast rebelled in her stomach, and a sour taste rose in her throat. She had tried to befriend

these ladies when she'd first come to Port Royal, finding them the most suitable company for someone of her position. Since she'd been forced to live on this island for the time being, she'd hoped to at least befriend those of her kind, but to her deep chagrin, they had turned up their noses when they discovered her condition. Was it her fault she bore the child of a man who'd ravished her? They treated her as if she had sought out such a travesty, and they soon spread rumors of her wantonness throughout the city.

The rising sun cast a harsh light on Abigail's face, and she shifted back into the shadows of the covered carriage. Her gaze landed on Isabel's muddy shoes. "Wearing men's boots now? Have you no shame?"

"Look how dirty she is," one of the women in the back scoffed.

"Well what do you expect, Harriet?" the blond woman chimed in.

Isabel wanted to say something clever, but the fury churning in her stomach clouded her wit. The driver shifted in his seat, seemingly growing tired of his mistress's cruel banter. One of the horses slogged a hoof in the mud.

"Is there something I can help you with?" Isabel asked, quelling the humiliation rising within her.

"Help me? Why, I should think not. I only hoped to offer you a ride, but since you are as filthy as a farmer, I'm afraid I must renege." Abigail drew her handkerchief and dabbed at the perspiration on her throat. "Move on, Clive." She waved her hand through the air.

The driver gave the reins a flick that sent the horses straining against their bits. The coach wheels slipped in the muck and spun ruts in the dark slime before bounding forward and spraying black splotches of mud all over Isabel.

Jumping back, she stifled a howl of indignation, then shook the splatters from her arms and wiped the smudges from Frederick as she stared aghast at the retreating carriage. Abigail's jarring laughter filled the air.

Isabel stormed through the door and into Reverend Thomas's office at the back of the church. She tossed the bolt of linen onto his desk and braced her fists on her hips. He lowered his quill pen and raised his gaze to meet hers. A slow grin danced on his lips. He chuckled, clasped his hands above his head, and leaned back in his chair. "Pray tell, what happened to you?"

"I will not suffer it, I tell you." Isabel stomped her boot, splattering mud over the wooden floor. Frederick whimpered and opened his eyes, and Isabel began rocking him as she paced in front of the reverend's desk. "I will not go into town again. You cannot force me."

Marlie entered the room, panting and looking distraught. She glanced at the reverend, the whites of her eyes stark against her bronze skin.

The smile never left the reverend's lips, but instead spread to his blue eyes with a sparkle as he continued to watch Isabel. "Did you encounter a mud fight perhaps?"

"Yes." Isabel halted and glared at him, further infuriated by his patronizing look. "A mud fight with a carriage—Abigail's carriage."

"Ah, I see." He leaned forward, folding his hands on his desk.

Under his mop of wavy blond hair, his face glowed a healthy red from his years spent in the Caribbean, but it wasn't simply the salt air and sun that quickened his expression. There was a calm exuberance about him—a life that shone from within. Usually it soothed Isabel. Today, it angered her.

He scratched his head. "Why do you let her affect you so? Who is she to you?"

"It matters not." Isabel sniffed and swiped a tear from her eye. "But please, do not send me to town anymore."

"Since you won't lower yourself to do anything else around here, you leave me no choice. I must find some way for you to earn your keep."

"But, Reverend, the things you want me to do are not befitting my position. Surely you do not expect me to serve these people who instead should be my servants?"

"By these people, do you mean the poor and the hungry who come for our help?"

Frederick wailed, and Isabel removed him from the sling and laid his head on her shoulder. She patted his back, assailed by guilt for an attitude she knew was wrong. "I want to help the poor as much as you do, Reverend."

His brows rose.

Isabel kissed Frederick, trying to quiet him. "I'll give of my time and whatever I have to help them, but I will not do laundry and cook and sew—things only servants and slaves should do." She patted the silver and pearl combs pinned in her hair. They were the only remembrances of her past fortune.

She glanced at Marlie, whose normally cheerful face had sunken into a frown. The young girl had been nothing but kind to her. Half Negro and half Carib, she was much more of an outcast from society than Isabel was.

Reverend Thomas stood and circled the desk. "All God's people are equal in His sight, Lady Ashton. The sooner you learn that, the happier you will be." His tall, lanky frame seemed to fill the tiny room. Beams of sunlight rippled in from the window, grazing over the volumes of books lining the shelves against the wall and finally landing on the reverend, casting an ethereal glow about him. Isabel wondered if he weren't really an angel in disguise, and she felt even viler by comparison.

Frederick lifted his head, squeezed his eyes shut, and began to cry in earnest.

"Why don't you give the child to Marlie and let her put him to bed for his nap while we talk?"

Hesitating, Isabel debated discussing anything further with the reverend. He had a way of reaching into her soul and pulling out things she preferred to keep hidden. She no more wanted a lecture on the equality of men than she wanted to discuss what was really on her mind—her disturbing encounter with the man in town who'd wanted to hold Frederick. Finally handing her son to the young girl, her gaze followed him until he was taken from her sight. "I really have nothing more to say, Reverend."

"Come sit for a minute." Reverend Thomas gestured toward a bench in the corner.

Isabel plopped down with a sigh, and the reverend sat beside her, taking her hands in his. His familiarity didn't disturb her anymore. She noticed he behaved the same affectionate way with everyone. She gazed into his kind blue eyes. The fine lines etching out from their corners only made him appear more sincere.

"God didn't pick you because you were born into a certain family," he said. "This attitude displeases Him."

Isabel glanced down at the wooden floor, now speckled with mud from her boots. "I know, Reverend. My faith is so weak. I don't even know if God hears my prayers."

"Of course He does. He hears all His children's prayers." The reverend smiled.

Sitting so close to him, Isabel saw the gray hair just beginning to intermingle with the blond strands around his forehead. She guessed he was near her father's age, perhaps a few years younger. Yet Reverend Thomas had been more of a father to her, more of a friend to her, than either of her parents had been.

"Is it wrong for me to want to marry a man with title and money?"

"Not as long as that desire doesn't come before your love of God." He squeezed her hand. "If it does, you'll never find the true happiness you seek, even should you marry the king of England himself."

Isabel grimaced. She had seen King Charles II, and no amount of wealth or titles could force her to marry that grotesque man.

Reverend Thomas shifted in his seat. "Do you still cling to this dream even after deciding to keep your son?"

Her gaze shot to his. "Why can't I have both? Surely my parents will reconsider after some time has passed." Even as she spoke the words, she no longer truly believed them. She glanced toward the window. It had been six months since she'd last received word from them.

Cupping her chin, Reverend Thomas drew her head back to face him. "You made the right choice. God does not condemn you for what happened."

Isabel's thoughts skipped from her parents to Abigail and her pretentious friends. "No, but people do."

Reverend Thomas nodded, releasing her chin. "Are you still having nightmares?"

Isabel's hands grew clammy, and she withdrew them from his grasp. "Yes, nearly every night." Her thoughts sped to the strange encounter with the pirates in town earlier, and fear convulsed in her belly.

Leaning his elbows on his knees, the reverend peered into her face. "Do you wish to tell me about them?"

Isabel shook her head.

"Perhaps speaking of them would allay your fears."

Sighing, she stared into his caring, blue eyes and knew he would not allow her to leave until she told him. Maybe it would help to share her nightmares—to shine the light of day on how foolish they were. " 'Tis the same every night—the most terrifying vision you could imagine, Reverend. All dark and gloom and a mist that permeates my skin like icicles." She jumped to her feet and wrapped her arms about her chest, feeling Frederick's empty sling.

"Frederick is crying, and I am running through the fog, waving my hands before me. I cannot reach him. He stops crying, and I come upon his cradle. It is empty." She squeezed her eyes shut against the images that haunted her day and night. "A ship appears in the distance, dark and foreboding. Ashen showers spray over its bow. A pirate flag flaps from the mainmast. Then I see him." She opened her eyes and glared at the reverend. Somehow relaying the nightmare made it seem more real than ever.

" 'Tis Captain Carlton. He smiles at me with his twisted, salacious grin. Then he turns away, and I am alone." She began to sob. "Oh, Reverend, do you think he knows where I am? Do you think he knows about his son?"

"It is only a dream, milady." Reverend Thomas stood and drew her close to him.

"I could not bear to lose Frederick." She gazed up at him, tears streaming down her cheeks.

"Never fear." He grabbed her shoulders and leaned down, meeting her at eye level. "You belong to God. Nothing and no one can touch you, save by His permission. Rest assured in that." Tugging a handkerchief from his waistcoat, he offered it to her. "Besides, you are safe here under my protection. Who would dare harm anyone who resides within the house of God?" He offered her a warm smile.

Nodding, she took a step back, snatched the cloth, and dabbed her face. "How weak and silly you must think me."

"Not at all, milady. You have been through a great deal for one so young. Be patient with yourself."

She handed the handkerchief back to him, but he pressed it into her palm, closing her fingers around it. "Nevertheless, we must find something for you to do around here—something that you don't find too insufferable, perhaps?" His brows arched, and a slight grin upturned his lips.

"Of course, Reverend." She returned his smile, feeling a bit ashamed. "Now, I'd best see to Frederick."

Drying her eyes, she patted her hair in place and gave the reverend one last glance before shutting the door.

The tiny church seemed much larger when it was empty. The long wooden pews stretched back toward the front entrance like waves flowing toward shore. A chill pricked over Isabel's arms. Dream or no dream, she could not shake the eerie foreboding that had haunted her the past few weeks. And why had those pirates in town been so interested in her son? Surely it was nothing, but the incident only added to her unease. Rounding a corner, she flew up a set of stairs and bounded into her room, anxious to see Frederick again.

Marlie had put a fresh cloth around his bottom. The soiled one lay in the corner. The young girl bounced Frederick upon the tiny cot, and his giggles floated through the room like bubbles of joy. Isabel knelt beside the bed, and Marlie instantly stiffened and handed the baby to her. She stood.

"If you need anything, miss, I'll be in the garden."

Isabel reached up and grabbed her hand before she could turn to leave. Her dark brown eyes quickly shifted from Isabel to the floor. "Marlie, I beg your forgiveness if I have been rude to you."

" 'Tis all right, miss." The girl scuffed her shoes across the wooden planks and tugged her hand from Isabel's.

"No, I can be quite callous at times. I apologize. You have been so good with Frederick."

Marlie raised her gaze, and a twinkle flashed through her eyes. "He's a good baby, miss."

Isabel gazed at her son, who gurgled and played with his left thumb as if he had just discovered it. "That he is." She smiled at Marlie as the girl turned and started to leave.

Before she reached the door, Marlie swerved back around. "If I may be so bold, miss. . ." She bit her lip before continuing. "God loves all people just the same. We are all equal in His sight."

Isabel looked at the girl curiously. She nodded, unsure of what to say.

Shifting her gaze away, Marlie scampered from the room.

"You like her don't you, little one?" Isabel grazed her fingers over Frederick's chubby cheek, always amazed at how soft his skin felt. He looked at her and grinned, revealing two baby teeth jutting from his bottom gums. Saliva pooled between them. His eyes were dark, just like his father's.

But he wasn't like his father.

He had such a sweet disposition. She kissed his forehead and sighed. How could she ever have considered giving him up? Before he was born, she longed to be free of him—of any encumbrance and of any reminder of Captain Kent Carlton. Now, she could not imagine her life without her son.

Tears filled her eyes as Frederick grabbed her hair and pulled a strand of it loose from her pins. He tugged on it and squealed in delight. "You're all I have left, my son." Taking the handkerchief the reverend had given her, she wiped his mouth. "Oh Lord, please protect him."

After a quiet supper with the reverend, Isabel retreated to her room for an early evening. Frederick was unusually fussy, and it took quite a while before she was able to calm him enough to lay him in his cradle. Having put him to bed and washed her face, she donned her nightdress and ran a brush through her long hair as she stared out her window onto the moonlight-laced trees. Coconut palm fronds and rosewood leaves fluttered in the warm night breeze, casting dancing shadows onto the soil and plants below. The vegetable garden where Marlie grew tomatoes, sugarcane, and yams blossomed by the dirt road. The reverend's cottage sat snugly against a small hill to her left behind the church. Warm lantern light spilled from its windows, just like the warm love of God that spilled from the reverend's heart. Isabel envied his steadfast faith.

Taking a deep breath of the fragrant air, she tried to quiet the alarm that had been rising within her all day. The Lord had protected her and strengthened her through so many harrowing circumstances, why did she doubt Him now? Even though her future loomed before her like an uncertain shadow, she had no reason to mistrust the God who had seen her through troubles time and time again.

Frederick snorted and began fussing, and Isabel rushed to the cradle beside her bed. She rocked it until she heard his tiny breaths deepen, and then she lay down on her cot, her hand still gripping the cradle. Bunching a mound of pillows around her, she prayed for sleep to come.

After what seemed like hours, she fell into a chaotic slumber that kept jarring her awake. One hour she woke in a torrid sweat, the next, chilled to the bone. The third time she awoke, she checked on Frederick, tucked a blanket around him, and dozed off again.

The nightmare returned.

But this time the sounds rang in her ears, the smells stung her nose, and an icy mist pricked across her skin. Somewhere, a door creaked. Footsteps thudded toward her. Frederick murmured, but he didn't cry.

This dream was different.

Isabel waited for the ship to appear, waited for the face of the man who had ravished her to taunt her with his grin. But the images never appeared. Frogs croaked outside, and a breeze blew across her face.

She was not asleep. This was no dream.

The church's oak door slammed shut, trumpeting an ominous echo through the sanctuary.

Isabel bolted up in bed and glanced over the shadows in her room. Her eyes darted to the cradle beside her. It rocked back and forth. She peered inside.

Frederick was gone.

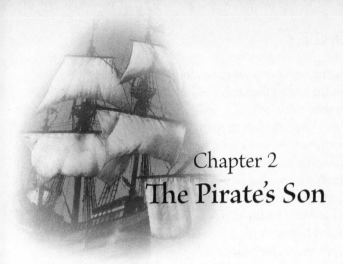

Chapter 2
The Pirate's Son

Isabel bolted down the stairs, stubbed her toe on a pew, and dashed from the church into the gloomy night. Save for the sliver of a moon that grinned at her from its perch atop the trees, no light graced the dirt pathway. Mud oozed cool between her toes, easing the pain shooting up her foot.

"Frederick!" she screamed.

A baby's wail pierced the humid air. "Frederick!" As she bounded down the street, her eyes scoured the dark shadows. Tangles of vines and shrubs framing the road clawed at her, slapping her face. Palm fronds quivered in the night breeze. Mist rose from the ground and crept over her feet and up her nightdress.

The black outline of a man darted around a corner up ahead. "Bring my baby back!" she cried. "Frederick!" Gathering all her strength, she rushed forward, the sounds of the night fading beneath the heaving of her deep breaths. She must not stop. She must get to her son.

Deep laughter echoed across the wooded path. She rounded a corner and saw the tavern lights flinging a hellish glow over Kingston Bay. Several ships dozed idly on the wave-tousled water as if nothing were amiss.

Isabel slowed. Her lungs strained for air amidst the heavy dew that seemed to weigh down every step. The road dipped and then ran along the shore by the warehouses. She scanned the buildings.

A baby cried.

15

Anguish shot through her heart. Forcing back tears, Isabel darted forward. Two dark figures bobbed up ahead. "Frederick!"

Footsteps pounded behind her. "Isabel!"

Ignoring the call, she kept her gaze upon the figures fading into the shadows of the town.

Storehouses raced by on her right. She stepped on something sharp, and searing pain lanced across her left foot and up her leg. Tumbling, she landed facedown in the mud, then pushed herself up and plodded forward. The men vanished into the murky night. Lifting the skirts of her sodden nightdress, she dashed down the road.

"Isabel!" the reverend beckoned.

Sounds of revelry spiraled around her as she plunged into the depths of town and into every kind of wickedness imaginable. Keeping her eyes forward, she sped onward.

"Hey, little missy!" one man yelled as she raced past a tavern.

Frederick wailed, and the man holding him glanced over his shoulder at her. The light from a nearby tavern illuminated his heinous features. That face. She'd seen him before. He'd been with that tall pirate. They'd wanted her son after all. How could she have been so careless?

A man stumbled in front of her. "Where's such a pretty girl off to in such a hurry?" The stench of alcohol struck her. He grabbed her arm, but she snagged it back and kicked him in the groin. He doubled over and groaned.

As Isabel tumbled through the filthy street, her eyes burned with tears, blurring her vision. She rubbed them and tried to focus.

The docks loomed in the distance. The two men had stopped and clambered into a boat. She trudged onward, summoning her remaining strength.

Frederick let out one of his unhappy sobs.

"Oh, my baby. I'm coming!" Her milk came down and saturated the front of her nightdress. "Mama's coming!"

Just another minute and she'd be upon them.

Just another minute.

"Hurry, ye fool, she's comin'."

The sound of paddles striking the water assailed her heart. "No!" Her feet hit the hard wood of the dock. "No!" She reached the end of the pier.

No boat was in sight. A thick mist blanketed the bay. The *swish* of water sounded. "Frederick!"

The fog parted slightly, and she saw the dark shape of a boat. Two figures sat inside, one of them clutching a small bundle.

"Isabel!" the reverend yelled behind her. His booted footsteps pounded down the dock. If he reached her, he would stop her.

Isabel plunged into the murky bay. Rising above the surface, she flapped her hands through the choppy waves. "Fred—" She gurgled as her head sank beneath the water. Gasping for air, she swirled her arms frantically about her, trying desperately to move toward the boat. A somber, smothering shroud of liquid silence settled over her.

She couldn't let them take her son. *God, help me.*

Strong arms grasped her waist and pulled her kicking from the dark water.

Isabel paced across the reverend's cottage all through the night, unable to keep even tea in her stomach. Reverend Thomas tried to comfort her, but neither his hopeful words nor the verses he read from the Bible nor even his persistent prayers brought her any consolation. Though she'd tried to pray, she felt only a callous chill where the warm presence of God normally filled her soul.

Jacob, a bulky man who lived near the church and who had helped the reverend pull Isabel from the waters of the bay, sat with them during the long hours. The kind farmer had wrapped her swollen, bloody feet in bandages and offered her what consolation he could.

She'd ventured back to her room only once. Perhaps she'd only had another nightmare. Perhaps Frederick wasn't gone, after all. Perhaps he still slept peacefully above the church. But as she stepped into the room, the empty cradle that met her filled her soul with chilling dread. After discarding the blanket the reverend had given her and removing her wet nightdress, she'd donned a simple gown and returned to the reverend's cottage, unable to face her room without her baby.

"How will I ever find him?" She sank onto the reverend's couch and looked up into his moist eyes. "What would pirates want with my son?"

The first rays of a new day trickled in through the windows, casting an unwelcome intrusion upon her misery.

"We must pray," the reverend said. "God knows where Frederick is. He will watch over him."

Isabel glared at the reverend, but thought better before replying. What good would it do to pour her fury and frustration out on him? Yet she didn't want to hear about God's care right now. Where had He been when her son was stolen? She needed to find Frederick. She must hire a ship and go after him. A thought sparked in her mind.

"What of Captain Merrick and Lady Charlisse? Surely, they can help me."

"I am most happy you asked, milady, for I have already written them a letter." Reverend Thomas patted the pocket in his vest. "No doubt they will make haste to aid you as soon as they receive it."

Isabel clasped her hands and thought of her good friends—the ones who had rescued her from Captain Carlton. They were more than capable of dealing with pirates.

"However," the reverend added with hesitation, "last I heard they were in the Carolinas. I'll send the letter to a relation of Merrick's who resides there. He may be able to locate him."

So far away. No sooner had her spirits risen than they tumbled back down again. But she mustn't give up. She searched the reverend's eyes for the comfort and faith she usually found there. He did not disappoint, and a new thought came to her. "I will write to my parents, too. Perhaps they will help rescue their grandson."

"Indeed, I'm sure they will."

Isabel busied herself for the next hour, composing a letter to her father, explaining the situation and pleading for his help. Then she and Marlie rushed into town and dispatched it, along with the reverend's letter to Merrick, on the fastest ship to New Providence. Even the quickest reply would take more than a week.

A week.

Isabel sobbed as she trudged back to the church. A week without knowing where her son was or whether he was still alive! *Oh Lord, help me.* She knelt by the side of the road, and Marlie stooped beside her and placed one arm over her shoulders. Instead of trying to comfort her with false assurances, the young half-breed wept right along with Isabel until

they were both out of tears. Arm in arm, they returned home.

Sleep was but a fleeting shadow for Isabel that night, along with all the other shadows that crept around her, haunting her. She rose from her cot and grabbed one of Frederick's blankets. Taking a deep breath of its fragrance, she sobbed.

"Where is Your justice, God? First You plant this life within me against my will and borne out of violence, and then just when I've given him my heart, You tear him away from me."

A cool breeze blew in from the window and swirled through the room. *Isn't that what you wanted? Now you are free. Now you can return home and marry a rich nobleman.*

Isabel dashed the tears from her face. She glanced around the room so filled with Frederick's things: his cradle, blankets, cloths, the little shirts and breeches the ladies in the church had sewn for him, a tiny doll stuffed with straw, blocks of wood he loved to gnaw with his new teeth. A sorrowful chuckle rose to her lips. "Are You punishing me for not wanting my son when I carried him?" She pressed her hand over her flat stomach. "But I kept him. I love him, Lord."

She fell to her knees and laid her head on her cot. She tried to pray, but no words formed on her lips or in her heart. She scratched her arms where a rash had broken out. The incessant itching only added to her agony and reminded her of Job, God's servant, who not only lost all his children but was struck down by a plague of boils, as well. "What will You do to me next?" she cried and crawled onto the cot, where she soon fell asleep, clutching Frederick's blanket to her bosom.

The next morning when the sanctuary filled with worshipers, Isabel remained upstairs, unable to face their comforting smiles and sympathies. After the service, Reverend Thomas tapped on her door and pushed it open. Wearing the reassuring smile that was beginning to grate on Isabel's nerves, he approached her and sat on the edge of the cot. He tossed a heavy sack onto the bed. It jingled when it landed.

"What's this?" Isabel asked, scratching her arm through her cotton sleeve.

"We took an offering to help you hire a privateer to seek Frederick." With arched brows, he shook the bag. A *clank* rang though the air, stirring Isabel's hopes.

"Truly?" Grabbing the bag, she fingered the coins through the burlap, amazed at the kindness of people who often did not have enough food to feed their own children.

"And not only that," the reverend added, his eyes snapping with excitement, "but two merchants—you may know them: Benson and Purdue—assure me they will keep an eye out for these pirates and an ear out for any word of a baby, and they will alert the Royal Navy should they hear anything."

Holding back new tears, Isabel folded her hands around the reverend's. "Thank you." She sniffed and drew the back of her hand to her nose. "I am quite astounded at everyone's kindness."

"But let us not forget to do the most important thing."

Isabel darted her gaze to his, worried she had forgotten some crucial task.

"To pray, my dear. To pray."

She sighed. "Yes, of course, Reverend."

Captain Kent Carlton eased his bottle of rum back onto the table and eyed the man who sat across from him. All he'd wanted was to be left alone—alone with his rum until he could down enough of the pungent liquid to dull the ache in his heart left by the graceful Lady Isabel Ashton.

He rose to his feet and pushed his chair back, its legs scraping across the wooden planks of the tavern floor. His hand gripped the hilt of his cutlass, and a hush fell over the unruly crowd. "Do you dare to challenge me?"

A stout, gap-toothed man with a black beard that hung to his waist planted both fists on the table and pushed his immense body up from his seat. With one flick, he sent the table crashing into a crowd of men whose curses filled the air. "Aye, that I do, ye slimy carp."

Kent glanced at his shattered bottle lying in a pool of rum at his feet. "I can excuse your ignorance in insulting my character, but now you've spilled my rum, and that is an affront I cannot ignore."

The man grinned. "Ye dare to fight me? D'ye know how many men I've killed?"

Kent knew. Captain Rand's fierce reputation sparked terror through-out the Caribbean. "Nigh two hundred, if I'm not mistaken." Kent brushed a speck of dirt from his waistcoat. He no longer feared this blackguard—perhaps because Rand was clearly drunk, or perhaps because Kent knew his own skill with the sword had vastly improved. Truth be told, Kent's dauntless courage sprouted from the fact that he really didn't care anymore whether he lived or died.

Rand spat onto the floor, and the left side of his mouth twisted in a snarl. "D'ye not realize I could kill ye where ye stand?"

"I never speculate on the impossible."

Chuckles filtered across the crowd of men who'd gathered around them. Rand's face burned a deep red. He snatched his cutlass from its scabbard.

In an instant, Kent's sword clattered against Rand's and forced it aside. The mob of pirates cheered, cursed, and punched their fists in the air as the two men parried. Rand lunged at Kent, striking his neck, before Kent could ward off his blow with his own thrust that sent Rand's sword tumbling from his hand.

The bearded pirate retrieved it amidst the cackles thrown his way. His eyes blazed with fury. He pointed his blade back at his adversary.

Kent swooped down upon him and, hilt to hilt, the two men fought, pushing the crowd back as they went.

Rand pulled back, panting. Beads of sweat littered his brow.

Kent rested his sword tip on the floor. "Come now. Is that all you have? You give me nothing to do."

Growling, Rand charged Kent again, but Kent, anticipating his attack, sidestepped the pirate's slash and, with two quick flicks of his own cutlass, sliced a bold *X* across Rand's belly, cutting off the bottom half of his beard. Rand doubled over, moaning. Two of his men came to collect him, and he scowled at Kent as they led him away. "You'll pay for this, mate." He grimaced around clenched teeth.

"I'll await the occasion with great anticipation." Kent bowed.

The crowd grumbled and dispersed while Kent sheathed his cutlass and turned around. Smithy, his first mate, righted the table and gathered his captain's chair, offering Kent an approving look. "By thunder. Ye beat ole Black Rand, Cap'n."

A man swaggered toward them from the back of the tavern. His modish blond hair fell loosely over his suit of black camlet, and Kent lifted his gaze to focus on him, hoping his senses had deceived him, then scowled when he realized they hadn't. Would he never be free of this vermin?

Kent huffed. "Why do our paths never fail to cross, Sawkins? It would appear you find it necessary to follow me all over the Spanish Main." Feeling a trickle on his neck, he plucked a handkerchief from the pocket of his velvet doublet and dabbed at his blood.

The man halted at the table and straightened the lace bounding from his sleeves. "Perhaps 'tis you who follows me?"

Kent plopped into a chair. "Fetch me some rum, if you please, Smithy." The scruffy pirate exchanged a sly glance with Sawkins before he sauntered into the crowd.

"Away with you." Kent waved a hand through the foul air. "I find your company cumbersome."

"Is that so?" Sawkins raised sleek brows and smirked. "Perhaps, but I'll wager all that I own you'll wish to know the news I possess."

"Last I heard, you possess nothing. All lost in a game of cards. Even your ship." Kent returned his handkerchief to his pocket and glanced over the room before his eyes landed again on Sawkins. "If it's money you want, I informed you the—"

"Nay, 'tis not that." Sawkins pressed his jeweled hand to his chest. "Must you always think so low of me?"

Kent snorted.

"It concerns your son." Sawkins lifted a chair from the floor. "May I?" He darted a questioning look at Kent but sat before he could protest.

Kent tapped his fingers on the table, wondering where Smithy was with his rum. "I have no son."

"Ah, but I have heard differently."

"You are mistaken."

"Is the name Lady Isabel Ashton familiar to you?"

Pain etched through Kent's heart, carving out sections he had long since buried. *Isabel.* He shot a fierce gaze at Sawkins and clenched his teeth before he allowed himself to speak. "You will tell me where you heard that name by the time my first mate returns, or on my mother's grave, I'll put a pistol shot through your skull." He clutched the butt of

the weapon housed in his baldric.

Throwing his hands in the air, Sawkins chuckled. "Your lack of civility does you no credit, my good man. I simply heard she was a. . .shall we say, a close acquaintance of yours?"

"What of her?"

"Did you not know?" Sawkins's eyes glinted with malicious amusement "Why, she bore a son nigh seven months ago. Word is you are the father."

Isabel lit a candle on a pedestal near the altar and draped herself over the wooden retable. She clasped her hands in front of her. "Oh God," she sobbed and dropped her head to the hard railing.

The agony of Frederick's absence seared her heart as if it were burning a part of her away each day. Tears streamed onto the wood and ran down the sides of the altar along with the last traces of her hope. Two weeks had passed, and no word of him had graced her ears, not from the privateer they'd hired or the merchants from the church or even from her old friends, Captain Merrick and Lady Charlisse. Even the Royal Navy ignored her constant pleas.

What else was there to do? Who else could she turn to? The hole left in her heart by Frederick's absence widened more each day into a cold void. How would she go on without him?

"Lord, help me."

Her pocket crackled, and she reached into it and withdrew the crumpled letter from her parents. Unfolding it, she turned it toward the candle light.

My dearest Isabel,

It was with great delight that we received your last correspondence, and although deeply saddened by the news of your recent loss, we are overjoyed to be able to offer you a passage home. There is now naught to keep you from us and from your proper place in society. Please make haste. We have sent our best ship to effect your safe return. Let us put behind us the tragic events of your recent past and begin anew. Our business ventures have prospered here in New

Providence, and we await your company with ardent joy.

Most affectionately yours,
Your dearest father,
Lord Brenton Ashton

Fury quickened Isabel's breathing, and she ripped the paper over and over until it floated to the floor in little pieces. She'd never considered that there had been a price on her parents' love and acceptance—not until she couldn't pay it. Now she felt truly and utterly alone for the first time in her life.

"Not alone, precious daughter. I am here."

"Are You, Lord?" Isabel wrung her hands together. "Are You really here?" Or was it simply her own wishful thinking?

The door creaked open, and a warm gust of wind wafted over Isabel, lifting the shreds of her torn letter into a chaotic dance before scattering them farther across the floor. It was most likely only Reverend Thomas coming to comfort her. Isabel remained where she knelt. Reverend Thomas had not slept well, either, since Frederick's disappearance, and his optimism had been the only thing that had kept her from going mad, but tonight, truth be told, she just wanted to be alone.

The deep *thud* of boots echoed behind her. Slow, methodical steps—heavy, not like the light gait of Reverend Thomas.

Isabel's heart clenched. Widening her eyes, she listened intently.

Heavy breaths reached her ears, the *clank* of metal scraping over the pews. *A sword?* Then a low cough, all too familiar, jarred her fears awake.

Isabel sprang to her feet and whirled, peering into the gloomy church. A towering black form lingered in the murky haze.

"Who goes there?" Her voice cracked.

The figure stepped from the darkness into a stream of moonlight. A cutlass hung by his side, and two brace of pistols clung to his massive chest. Dark waves of hair flowed from under a black head scarf.

His dark eyes perused her with amused recognition as a slight smile upturned one corner of his lips.

Kent Carlton.

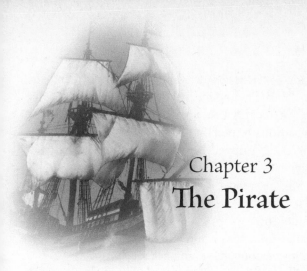

Chapter 3
The Pirate

Kent stepped slowly into the light and offered Lady Ashton his most comforting smile.

It did not have the intended effect.

Her eyes widened. She took a step back and tripped over the altar. Her hand flew to her chest, and she screamed. Kent grabbed her, forcing his hand over her mouth. All he needed was for her shrieks to awaken the priest or whoever ran this place and then have him alert the authorities.

Since Kent currently found himself in disfavor with not only the British Royal Navy but with most of Morgan's pirates as well, it would be best if his presence in Port Royal was kept as quiet as possible. His notoriety had forced him to venture here under cover of night, even though he knew the darkness would only make his sudden appearance more horrifying for Isabel.

"Egad, woman. D'ye think I came to harm you? Be still."

Thrashing in his arms, Isabel pounded his chest and moaned beneath his hand. The sweet scent of vanilla and coconut drifted past his nose. He breathed it in and smiled at the flood of memories that flowed over him along with it.

A sharp pain pierced his palm, and he jumped back, shaking his wrist in the air. "You bit me!"

Isabel bolted up two stairs toward the pulpit, but Kent was on her in seconds. "I wish only to speak with you."

"Let me go!" she cried, fighting in his grasp. Then she halted and faced him. Her expression of terror contorted into one of anger, and she kicked him in the shin. Pain spiked up his right leg. He grimaced.

"Where is my son?" She beat his chest with her fists. "Where is he? You stole my son!" Her screams turned into sobs.

"I did not take him." Kent gripped her shoulders and held her well away from him. "I assure you."

Jerking from his hold, she stepped back into the shadows, where he could not see the details of her face—that beautiful face he had longed to gaze upon for so many months.

Sobbing, she retreated from him again and seemed to sway in the darkness. Kent reached for her, but she sprang away.

"Don't touch me." She grabbed a nearby post. The flickering light from the candle cast its glow upon her. Her chest heaved, and her eyes fixed on his. She raised a hand to her nose. "You didn't take him?"

Kent flung his head back and snorted. Why did this woman persist in thinking him a scoundrel? "No. You have my word."

"Then how did you know where to find me?"

" 'Tis a long tale, milady, one I'll be happy to favor you with at another time, but for now, I came to tell you I know who took the babe."

"You do?" Isabel stepped toward him, then hesitated. Her glistening eyes searched his. A look of despair replaced the momentary hope. She turned away. "I don't believe you." Backing down the stairs, she slunk around to the front of the altar again, her gaze never leaving him.

Kent followed cautiously, his leather boots echoing through the church. Though clearly frightened, she faced him with more bravery than most of his crew. "I beg you, milady, listen to what I have to say. I have not come to hurt you or to take you captive again."

"Why should I trust you?"

The *creak* of wood echoed through the church, and the front door rasped open, allowing a warm breeze entrance. The candlelight fluttered.

Kent plucked a pistol and aimed it toward the door.

Isabel glanced over her shoulder. "No one is there. You left the door open, 'tis all."

Kent replaced the weapon in its brace and allowed his gaze to sweep over her. Moonlight from the window sparkled upon the silver combs that held her auburn hair in place. Her simple gown clung to her curves,

which seemed to have grown more voluptuous during the past year. How he had missed her. Just gazing at her soothed the ache in his soul.

Isabel pressed a hand to her stomach. "Still have enemies hunting for you?"

"More than I care to admit." He grabbed the hilt of his cutlass and sauntered toward her.

"That's far enough, Captain." She held up a hand and stole a glance at the door, which still stood slightly ajar. "One step closer and I'll run out that door and wake up Reverend Thomas." Her voice quavered.

"I think I can handle one simple preacher." Kent twisted his lips into a grin.

Isabel snickered and placed her hands on the swell of her hips. "Perhaps, but then there'll be Jacob to deal with."

"Jacob?" A spike of jealousy speared him.

"Never mind. What do you want?" She leaned one hand on the altar. "Have you come to gloat over my misery?" She sniffed, and a tear spilled down her cheek. "I do not know how you discovered where I was or that I had a child, but I'm appealing to whatever kindness exists in your dark heart to return him to me." She slid down onto the wooden floor and began to sob.

Kneeling, Kent reached a hand toward her, but she shrank back from him. He wanted nothing more than to pull her into his arms and protect her, but he knew she would never allow it. And why would she? Why would she ever trust his touch? His gaze landed on the altar, and he nearly chuckled. He hadn't stepped into a church in years, and here he was, kneeling at an altar, desperately seeking forgiveness, not from God, but from this woman before him.

"I didn't know you'd borne my son until just last week. The same time I heard he'd been stolen from you—'twas then I discovered your whereabouts. I've been searching for you for over a year."

Isabel glared at him, tears overflowing her shimmering eyes. "Why? So you could kidnap and ravish me again?"

Hanging his head, Kent let out a deep sigh. "Nay, I just needed to know you were well and happy." He looked up. Loathing burned in Isabel's eyes. He'd never had to fight for the affections of a woman—most succumbed to his charms easily enough. But not Lady Ashton. Yes, he had violated her, but only the one time, and after that he'd displayed only kindness to her. Still, she resisted him. Truth be told, he'd thought of nothing but Isabel since he'd sent her away with Merrick. The vision of her standing on the main deck of Merrick's ship, her long hair blowing in the wind behind her as their two ships separated, had consumed him day and night. Without her, without word of her, his soul had emptied, leaving him naught but a hollow shell. But how could he tell her that?

"Milady, I need your help."

"*My* help?"

"As I said, I know who took your—our son, and I need your help to find him."

Isabel studied him, doubt skipping across her eyes. "I never thought I'd see the day when the great Captain Carlton would need anyone's help—especially a woman's," she said between heavy breaths. "And why, pray tell, would I want to help you? I've sent word to Captain Merrick, and he should be arriving any day. If all you seek is female company, the many brothels in town should satisfy your debased needs."

Kent clenched his jaw and swallowed the fury rising in his throat. Edmund Merrick, his ex-captain, had a habit of rescuing damsels in distress. Would Kent ever be able to come out from under his overpowering shadow?

"If female affection is what I truly seek, d'ye think me daft enough to come to you for it?" He forced a chuckle. "Nay, I need your help because you are the only one who knows what the child looks like. How else am I to find him?"

Kent sat on the steps, hoping to allay her fears that he might pounce on her.

"Who took him?" she finally said as she slid farther from him.

Thumping his boots against the wooden floor, Kent draped both arms over his knees. "A pirate named Morris."

"Morris? Who is he, and what does he want with my Frederick?"

"Frederick? You named him Frederick?" A warm spark ignited within him. Frederick was Kent's middle name. Had he told her that? He couldn't remember.

"Yes." She averted her eyes. "But you didn't answer my question."

Kent rubbed the back of his neck and looked down. "John Morris

seeks revenge on me. He heard I had a son."

Jumping to her feet, Isabel glared at him. "My son has been kidnapped because of you? Because one of your enemies wants to get back at you for some hideous thing you've done?"

Kent eyed her, noticing the flare in her already reddened cheeks and the fury in her eyes. He stood. "I'm afraid so."

She rushed toward him and raised her hands to punch him, but he caught her wrists and restrained her, wondering if he shouldn't just allow her to pummel him and release her anger. God knew he deserved it.

Tearing away from him, she dropped her head and wept, keeping one arm outstretched against his advance. "Go away. Please go away." She raised her teary eyes to his. "Haven't you caused me enough pain?"

Agonizing sorrow swept through Kent, as unfamiliar to him as the remorse that followed in its wake. "It is not my intention to harm you further, but to help you."

"You care not for my son! You don't even know him."

" 'Tis true, I don't know him, but he is my son, too. And I can see how much he means to you. Let me help you find him."

Isabel scratched her arms and then wrapped them around herself.

Kent shifted his stance. "Come with me on my ship."

Terror darted across her eyes. She shook her head. "Never."

"As my guest this time."

She stared at him aghast, as if he'd asked her to walk the plank.

He took a step toward her. She flinched.

"Alas, milady. I will not force you to accompany me. I will not force myself on you in any way." The thought of endless nights, knowing she was but a few feet away from him, wrenched at his resolve. 'Twould be a hard promise to keep—perhaps too hard for the likes of him. "You have my word."

"Your word means nothing to me. You are a liar and a thief—a pirate." She raised her tiny red nose in the air.

"Perhaps." He bowed. "But if you wish to see your son again, this pirate is all you have."

Chapter 4
On Board
the *Restitution*

Isabel emerged from the mesh of soggy green vines. Her boots sank into the sand of the secluded shore—far away from the busy docks of Kingston Bay. No wonder Captain Carlton had insisted they leave at once. Obviously, he risked his life by coming to Port Royal. In her haste, she'd been able to write only a short note for the reverend, telling him where she went and to please pray. She drew a deep breath. The scent of moist earth and lush forest gave way to the sting of salt and rain.

The Caribbean.

With gaping mouth, it loomed before her, showering her with hot spicy breath, luring her into its depths. Waves sloshed upon the sand, but their gentle caresses were only a facade. She well knew the true nature of this vicious sea.

The sun winked at her as it peered over the horizon, firing spikes of ruby, lemon, and coral over the indigo water. Wiping a strand of moist hair from her forehead, she studied Kent's dark form marching in front of her. Despicable though he might be, he was truly her only hope of finding Frederick. He flung a glance at her over his shoulder, but his expression was lost in the shadows.

Her gaze took in the gloomy outline of a ship floating offshore. With the sun rising behind it, the three-masted frigate emerged like a fearless leviathan just risen from the deep. Isabel's empty stomach churned, and

her head swam. Raising her hand, she rubbed her temples and tried to steady herself against a sudden rush of blood.

A cockboat clung to the shore, surrounded by three men who, upon seeing their captain, scrambled to their feet.

"You brung her, I see." A man tipped his hat at Isabel. "Milady."

Smithy. She recognized him as the captain's first mate.

"Let's be off, then," Kent ordered, and the men pushed the boat off shore until only the tip of it remained on dry ground. He turned and offered Isabel his hand.

Ignoring him, she stepped into the tottering craft and nearly fell. Heat flushed her face as she stooped and clung to the sides, making her way to the back. Snickers rose behind her.

Kent leaped into the boat with ease, followed by his men. "Did you spot anyone while I was gone?"

"No, Cap'n," Smithy answered. "We've no' seen a soul since ye left us."

Nodding, Kent sat across from Isabel. She eyed him as the men gave the boat a shove and jumped in. A morning breeze toyed with the umber hair flowing from under his head scarf. He glanced toward his ship, shifting his broad shoulders—shoulders that carried the weight of command well. A few days stubble shadowed his firm jaw. He moved his dark eyes to hers, and a hungry regard shone in them. He neither smiled nor spoke, just absorbed her as if she were the last woman alive.

Isabel averted her eyes. A strange tingle warmed her belly. Then the massive frigate filled her vision, and the warmth gave way to a chill that threatened to freeze her heart.

Oh God, what am I doing?

Was she such a fool as to allow herself to be taken aboard this horrid ship again? Gruesome memories rose like bile slinking up her throat. She held her stomach and feared she would lose her dignity in front of these men.

Three bare masts jutted into the sky, their spires fisted toward heaven in defiance of God and all that was humane. Shrouds and ratlines climbed up the poles on all sides, creating a tangled web from which no victim escaped. Twenty covered gun ports lined the hull in deep slumber, but Isabel knew they could be flung open within minutes, their powerful cannons thrust out to belch a deadly blast upon their enemies. She could still hear the thunderous boom of those charred beasts and feel the tremor course through her bones. She closed her eyes and swallowed hard, chafing her itchy arms in an effort to ward off the chill that had settled upon her.

The water gurgled against the boat with each slap of the paddles. The soothing sounds of the jungle birds gave way to the creaks and groans of the encroaching monster.

Frederick. Oh, Frederick. If she kept her son in the forefront of her thoughts, she could do this. She had to do this—for him. *Lord, please be with me.*

"You have nothing to fear, milady."

Isabel snapped her eyes open to meet the captain's gaze. His voice carried a sincerity that matched the warmth in his eyes. Yet she knew she could not trust him.

The cockboat slammed against the moist hull of the frigate with a jarring *thud*, and two ropes dropped from above. While the pirates tied them to the boat, Captain Carlton stood and tugged upon a rope ladder. Turning, he held out his hand for Isabel. "Ladies first."

Raising her chin, she stood and refused his hand but quickly lost her balance again in the teetering vessel. He grabbed her elbow to steady her, a faint smirk on his mouth.

With a sigh, she gathered her skirts and clambered up the ropes. She'd forgotten how cumbersome they could be and nearly lost her footing, but one glance below told her the captain was quick on her heels, ready to catch her should she fall. Her skirts swished as she swung her leg over the bulwarks and braced her boots on the oak planks of the main deck.

Dozens of pairs of gaping eyes were there to greet her. Their salacious gazes bore into her, sending her heart thundering in her chest. A waft of rum and sweat assailed her, and her legs numbed. She turned away and gripped the railing, breathing heavily. *I can't do this.*

Captain Carlton jumped onto the deck and braced his hands on his hips. "What are you looking at, ye numb-brained apes? Get back to work." He glared at one stout fellow standing nearby. "Gibbons, weigh anchor. Smithy, hoist in the boat and have the men unfurl main- and topsails!"

"Ye 'eard the cap'n!" Smithy bellowed across the deck. "Be about it

or pay the price!" The deck swarmed with men as the pirates scurried to their tasks. Some flung themselves into the shrouds and scrambled aloft. Others circled the capstan and shoved it with grunting effort to hoist the iron anchor from the seabed.

The captain turned to face Isabel as the sun, peeking over the port-side railing, shot its fiery rays upon him. Like arrows of truth, they illuminated the uneasy sincerity in his eyes—so unlike the man she had known. He raised a brow. A tiny red scar etched a crooked line beneath it. She didn't remember it from before. "May I escort you to your cabin?"

After a last glance at the shores of Jamaica, Isabel drew a heavy breath and forced her trembling legs to follow him below. Each step down the companionway stairs brought back harrowing memories of her imprisonment aboard this floating hell.

"I hope it does not distress you, but I must place you in the same cabin as before." He swung the oak door open with a grating squeal and entered just as the ship lurched forward. "I fear we are short on space."

Isabel clutched the door frame to keep from falling and peered inside. The same tiny bed, leather chairs, desk, and bookshelves filled the room that was but three strides wide. Atop the oak-framed bed lay a lacy white quilt, and beside it, a vase bursting with exotic flowers graced a table. Gowns and petticoats spilled from a teakwood trunk. Dread sank its fangs into her soul. Had he expected her to come with him or did he lock other women in here as well?

"Is this where you keep all your mistresses?"

"No, only you, milady." He offered her a mischievous grin, then huffed and crossed his arms over his chest. "This is the master's cabin—normally shared by Smithy and one other of my officers."

"Somehow I don't see Smithy as the type of man to wear gowns and enjoy lacy quilts," she shot back and raised her chin despite the quiver racing up her back.

Kent's eyes sparkled in amusement. "Then you will appreciate the extra effort I took to ensure your comfort."

Disturbed by the affection she saw in his eyes, Isabel scanned the cabin again. She had spent months in this very room—months of anguish, months of fear—waiting to be summoned to the captain's cabin, waiting to be ravished. After the first night, he had not touched her, but how was she to know each time he sent for her he'd wanted only to talk? Now this baffling pirate stood before her, drawing her back into the same prison with his gallant talk and handsome smile. *I must be the daftest woman on earth.*

His gaze drifted over her. "I daresay I don't bite anymore. You may come in."

She stepped inside, hugging the wall, and scooted to the window. "I will enter your lair, Captain, but I don't doubt that your bite carries just as potent a sting as it always did."

"I hope to dissuade you from that opinion."

"I carry only the opinion you forced me to acquire—that you are a black-hearted scoundrel, an insolent knave, and a ravisher of innocent women." Isabel met his gaze sternly.

The man winced, and pain flared in his squinted gaze.

The ship lunged again, and the *snap* of sails filled the air as they caught the wind. A young boy appeared in the doorway. "Ye summoned me." He scowled at his captain.

"Yes. I'll have you attend to Lady Ashton's needs."

The boy stepped toward Isabel and smiled. The smoothness of his face betrayed his youth, which Isabel guessed to be no more than thirteen or fourteen years. He was short and a bit portly, with close-cropped brown hair. His cheerful gaze put her immediately at ease.

"May I introduce Hann, my quartermaster."

"Milady." Hann bowed.

The captain waved a hand in the air. "Bring her food, water, empty her chamber pot, whatever she needs. I want her to remain as comfortable as possible while she is forced to endure my heinous company." Pulling a key from his vest pocket, Kent handed it to Isabel. "I've moved the lock to the inside of the door." He cocked a brow. "To further allay your fears."

Shouts from above filtered into the cabin, and the clomping of boots thundered over the deck. "Now, with your permission, my attentions are required elsewhere." He headed toward the door.

"Captain?"

He spun around.

"May I ask where we are going? What is the plan to find Frederick?"

Isabel chided herself for not inquiring sooner—for not at least making sure he had a plan and wasn't just using her son to lure her back onto his ship. Everything had happened so fast, and the hope Kent had offered had clouded her judgment. She froze. Maybe he wasn't going to search for Frederick at all.

He must have sensed her suspicions for he let out a sigh and gave her a sideways glance. "We make sail for Charles Towne. I have an acquaintance who is gathering information on Frederick's whereabouts whilst we speak. I assure you my motives are pure."

He gave her a half smile and stomped out.

Hann's harsh gaze followed his captain from the room with a frown, and Isabel sensed the quartermaster didn't like the man anymore than she did. But when Hann faced Isabel, his features lightened. "May I get you anything, milady?"

Something odd struck her about the young lad, but truth be told, he was the only man, aside from the reverend, who Isabel felt immediately safe with. She glanced across the room. Visions of the nightmare she'd endured taunted her from every corner. "Do you have a Bible on board?"

Hann's features twisted for a moment, then his eyes lit up. "There might be one here." He grazed his finger over the scattered books upon the shelves and plucked one from its spot. " 'Tis the captain's, I believe. A gift from an old enemy of his, he once told me."

Isabel thought of Merrick and wondered if he were that old enemy. Grabbing it from Hann, she brushed off the dust and thanked him. "That will be all for now, Hann."

The boy turned. "I'll be checkin' on ye in a bit."

After he closed the door, Isabel took the key and locked the bolt. The clanking of the lock as it snapped into place scraped over her nerves, reminding her of all the times Kent had imprisoned her in this tiny cabin, terrified and alone. Now she had the key, but somehow, she felt just as much a prisoner as before.

Had the captain really changed, or would he come for her tonight? She found it hard to believe the lecherous rogue she once knew could possess an overwhelming concern for a son he'd never met. But what else could she do? He was her only hope. *Lord, keep me safe.*

Plopping on the bed, Isabel clutched the Bible to her breast. She'd give anything to have Reverend Thomas here with her. She'd not realized how much she'd come to depend on him for prayer, for comfort, for reciting the right scripture to her at the right time. Flipping through the pages of the sacred book, she searched for some words of hope but had no idea where to find them.

Charles Towne, New Providence. So, it seemed she would be going home after all. Perhaps while she was there, she could beg for her parents' help one last time. Yet the callous words of her father's letter still kindled anger in her soul. Frederick was their grandson. How could they harbor so little regard for their own flesh and blood?

Oh, Frederick. His screams still rang in her ears, tearing at her heart with each piercing wail. Where was he? Was he being harmed? Was he alone and afraid? Isabel fell onto the bed and clutched one of the pillows to her face to stifle her sobs.

The day crept along with the tumbling of the ship through the Caribbean. After dozing on and off, Isabel rose, washed as best she could with the water from the basin, and searched through the trunk of gowns for one that fit her. After donning it, she combed her tousled hair and pinned it up atop her head.

A tap on the door startled her, and she opened it to Hann's grinning face. "The captain requests your presence for dinner, milady."

Alarm spiked through her. *I'll bet he does.*

"He wanted me to tell ye that ye'll be dining with three of his officers, meself included."

Captain Carlton knew she would never come to his cabin alone, but did he think inviting other pirates would make his company more bearable or her fears less fervent? Yet she had so many questions that only he could answer—the main one presently on her mind being what sort of man had taken Frederick. Her stomach churned. Perhaps some food would help settle it.

"All right, then. Shall we?" She followed Hann out the door and down the hallway, and then turned toward the stern of the ship. The lad sauntered in front of her, but Isabel faltered with each step. The moist walls closed in on her, suffocating her, as the stench of decaying fish, rotting wood, and the bilge from below saturated her lungs and ignited her nightmares with vivid memories. Lanterns mounted on the walls flickered monstrous shadows

in front of her, almost taunting her to continue forward. Her legs began to quiver. How many times had she been forced to walk down this hall? "Please tell me this time is different."

"Milady?" Hann glanced over his shoulder.

Had she said that aloud? "Nothing."

Stopping, Hann opened the door and motioned for her to enter. A wave of dizziness whirled her vision. The captain stood with his back to her, gazing out the stern window. He turned, drink in one hand, the other behind his back. His eyes lit up as his gaze took in her gown. No hat or scarf sat atop his umber hair, which fell to his shoulders in neatly combed strands.

He straightened his leather jerkin and skirted the table that took up most of the small room. "Hann, summon Cutter and Smithy if you please."

Isabel darted a pleading gaze toward Hann before he shut the door.

Placing a hand on her gurgling stomach, she glared at the captain as he approached. His black, knee-high boots pounded over the floor. The hilt of a knife protruded from the right boot. How had she ended up alone with him in his cabin?

He halted a few feet from her. "I know you're afraid of me, and you have good reason. But it would give me great pleasure if you would not look at me as if I were the devil himself."

"And why would I desire to give you any pleasure?"

He grimaced and tipped his glass toward her. "Indeed." He took a sip.

Scanning the room, Isabel noted thankfully that the bed had been stowed in favor of the dining table, set with four places. Cluttering the middle were bowls of fruit, biscuits, and blocks of cheese.

"I take it you find your accommodations suitable?" Kent asked.

"No more suitable than the last time."

"Ah, but things have changed since then."

"Have they?"

He stepped toward her and leaned down. His lips curved into a dangerous smile. "Perhaps you should look closer."

His warm breath drifted over her—wood, spice, and rum. She felt his gaze wander from her face and down her neck, and she stepped aside, fear and confusion raking over her.

Clearing his throat, he took another sip from his glass and turned away. "Truth be told, I have come to loathe myself for what I did. I hope to make it up to you."

Relief swept through her. It would appear at least he had no intention of ravishing her again. She studied him, his wavy hair so much like Frederick's. "So you don't care about your son? This whole thing is only a form of selfish restitution?"

He swung around and gave her a hard look.

Fury overcame Isabel's fear at his threatening glare. "Do you think you can pay for what you've done? Do you know what I've been through this past year?" She began to pace, the rustling of her skirts filling the room. "And after you do me this great service of finding my son? What then? What do you hope for then?"

As he flung his head back, the captain's lips curled in a slight smile. "I hope you will find my company somewhat tolerable."

"I will not find myself in your company at all." She fired an angry glance his way, but instantly regretted her words. Why was she being so deliberately cruel to the only man who could help her?

Flinching, he downed his remaining drink and slammed his glass on the table.

She opened her mouth, hoping to say something that would soften her harsh outburst, but two men bounded through the door, silencing her. Hann followed behind them.

Kent reintroduced Isabel to Smithy, the first mate, and to Cutter, the ship's doctor, both of whom she'd met on her previous journey. Isabel nodded at Cutter and smiled. She longed to thank him for helping her and Lady Charlisse escape the last time she had been aboard the ship.

Winking at her, he took his place at the table. His left arm still hung withered by his side, and a hideous red and purple scar twisted his upper lip—both deformities caused by a prior accident unknown to Isabel. Her heart sparked with a glimmer of hope. At least she had one friend on board.

"Ye look a mite lovely in that gown, milady." Smithy took a seat and poured himself some apricot-colored liquid from a jug. "It be good to 'ave a woman on board again."

Snickering, Hann sat beside Cutter.

Kent motioned for Isabel to sit at his left and waited for her to take her seat before he took his at the head of the table. "And you'll keep both your eyes and hands off her or answer to me." He gave Smithy a sideways glance that held more mirth than petulance.

"Aye, Cap'n. Just payin' the lady a compliment."

Cutter plucked an orange from the bowl and began peeling it. "I've heard 'tis bad luck to have a lady on board a pirate ship."

"Only a foolish superstition," Hann said without looking up.

A thin black man entered, sparsely dressed in knee-length breeches and a torn shirt with a silver whistle around his neck. He carried a tray of browned meat and placed it on the table. Isabel's stomach vaulted as the smell wafted over her.

"Thank you, Caleb." The captain nodded toward the man. "Caleb is the best cook and steward I've ever come across." The black man's eyes grazed over Isabel as he backed out of the room. Memories of him chained at the ankles, swabbing the deck, sped through her mind. Hadn't he been a slave before?

The men pounced on the meal as if it were their last, snatching biscuits, fruit, and pieces of meat with their fingers. Rum and brandy flowed freely amongst them. Declining the alcohol with a smirk, Isabel sipped her tea and waited for an opportune moment to question Captain Carlton. She hoped her stomach would becalm itself enough for her to eat. She must keep up her strength.

The silver earring in Smithy's right ear glittered in the candlelight beneath his shaggy, wheat-colored hair that hung in strands down his back. The more he drank, the louder his guffaws bounded over the table. Though he was shorter than the other men, save for Hann, an untamed power surged beneath his massive shoulders.

Next to Smithy, Hann's frame shrank by comparison—like David's beside Goliath. Quiet, the young lad remained absorbed in his food, looking up or commenting only when Cutter addressed him.

The men conversed, sloshed their drinks about, and grabbed food at will—no more cultured than beasts in a barn. They spoke of wind and sails, ports and treasure. Every so often Isabel caught the captain's intense gaze upon her, and though she tried to return it with equal strength, she more oft than not shifted her eyes away. Her tattered nerves began to fray under the pirates' inebriant gaiety.

"Lady Ashton." Cutter pointed at her with his knife. "You've hardly eaten a thing."

Anger joined the bitterness in her stomach. "I'm afraid I've no appetite"—she glowered at the captain—"not knowing what has become of my son."

The men fell silent. "Understandable." Cutter nodded. "But 'twill do him no good should you die of hunger. Have some meat. It will settle your stomach." He lifted a tray and held it out toward her.

"What is it?" Isabel crinkled her nose.

"Turtle," Cutter said. "Good for whatever ails you."

Her stomach clamped. She turned aside. "No thank you."

Shrugging, Cutter replaced the tray.

Isabel turned toward Kent. "Captain, please tell me what you know of the man who stole Frederick."

He slapped down his cup and leaned back in his chair, folding his hands across his chest.

"Ah, good ole Morris." Smithy chuckled. "Quite an ill-tempered man, says I."

Hann looked at Smithy with disdain.

"Morris?" Isabel asked.

"Aye, John Morris." The captain eyed her and rubbed the back of his neck. "One of Morgan's Brethren of the Coast."

"A good man," Cutter added, grabbing another biscuit.

Isabel scratched the itch rising on her arms. "Pray tell, what did you do to this *good* man to bring such retribution?"

Sighing, Kent looked down at his boots. "I'm afraid I may have caused the death of his son."

Hann jumped to his feet. He hacked and banged on his chest, his face reddening. Grabbing his mug, he tried to lift it to his lips, then dropped it onto the table, spilling its contents. Cutter stood and slapped him on the back, and Hann spewed a chunk of meat into the air. It landed with a *plop* onto a plate of cheese.

Averting her eyes from the disgusting display, Isabel stared at the captain, alarmed at his declaration. *Killed his son?* Hope spilled from her like the liquor now dripping from the table. Surely the man would

execute quick retribution on Frederick—an eye for an eye. It was the law these pirates lived by.

Smithy belched and grabbed the pitcher of brandy. "Aye. He blew up the ship young Morris was on."

"Not just any ship," Cutter added. "Our illustrious captain had the audacity to blow up a British Royal Navy warship, the HMS *Oxford*."

Isabel furrowed her brow. "What was the son of a pirate doing on a British warship?"

Kent drew a deep breath. " 'Twas Morgan's flagship, commissioned by Britain for an attack on Cartagena. Nigh ten ships had gathered that night off the coast of Hispaniola to plan their strategy. I was privileged to be included." His voice glinted with pride but quickly fell in tone when he added, "Things got out of hand."

" 'Twas quite a party, if ye ask me," Smithy said.

With a scowl, Hann righted his mug and poured himself another drink.

Isabel tugged on a tendril of hair tickling her neck. "Why would you destroy one of Morgan's ships? Isn't he an ally of yours?"

"Not anymore, I'm afraid." The captain stared into the distance, agony wrenching his cloudy gaze. "I'm not sure it was I who caused the accident. That night remains a blur. We all had too much to drink." He leaned forward and looked down at his plate. "Shots were fired in celebration. The next thing I knew, I was thrown into the water and the ship was ablaze." He frowned. "Two hundred men died that night. John Morris's son was one of them."

"It was merely a mishap of fate," Cutter announced. "Who's to blame anyone?"

Hann tipped his mug to his lips and leveled a fierce gaze at his captain over the rim.

"Word spread that it was by my hand." Kent flung his head back. An unseen weight tugged upon his features.

"Sure ruined yer plans to take Morgan's spot as admiral, didn't it?" Smithy jeered. "Got ye banished from the brethren fer good."

The captain's smoldering eyes narrowed upon Smithy, and the conversation fell abruptly silent.

Isabel's momentary twinge of pity was smothered by a surge of fury.

"Your drunken foolishness has quite possibly cost my son his life!" Though she tried to force them back, tears filled her eyes. She sprang to her feet. "What's to stop this pirate from killing Frederick? Perhaps he's already done so." She pressed a hand over her stomach.

Kent rose slowly, a pleading look in his eyes. " 'Tis not in Morris's best interest to do that, milady. He wishes only to torment me. We will get Frederick back. You have my word."

"The word of a pirate means nothing." Wiping a tear aside, she glanced at the men. "If you'll excuse me, gentlemen." She spun around and marched from the room.

Footsteps sounded behind her. "I can find my way, Hann."

"I 'ave no doubt, milady." But still he followed until Isabel stormed into her room and slammed the door in his face.

The wind sang a mournful song against her window as the faint moonlight gave the room a hazy glow. Isabel locked the door, then paced, unable to sleep. The rush of water against the hull accompanied the shouts of men up late with their drink. A seedy ballad floated through the walls from a distant part of the ship. Wrapping her arms about her, Isabel felt consumed by emptiness. Her breasts ached, still full with milk. How she longed to hold her baby.

She knelt. "Oh Lord, please be with my son. Please protect him."

Nausea rose within her, and she turned and heaved into her chamber pot. After placing the key on the bedside table, she crawled into her bed, curled into a ball, and drew a pillow to her chest.

"Never fear. I am with you always."

Allowing the soothing voice to comfort her, Isabel succumbed to the exhaustion that finally shrouded her senses in slumber. Nightmares soon arose to disturb her peace. She was in the captain's cabin again. But this time, no table laden with delicious food stood in the center, no laughter or idle chatter filled the room, only Kent's muscular figure creeping toward her. His lecherous gaze scoured her. Her eyes darted over the room, searching for an escape. She screamed, but he only laughed. *This can't be happening to me.* Terror trembled through her in waves. He tossed her to the bed and pounced upon her, clawing at her gown. "No! No! I beg you!" she screamed and kept screaming until her voice cracked under the strain. Then his face loomed above her, his expression intent

and impassioned. He wiped the hair from her face and. . .

Isabel bolted up. She dashed a glance over the room, panting. All was still, save for the slight *creak* of the bolt on her door. The key still sat on the table beside the bed. Terror pricked up her spine. She tiptoed from the bed and grabbed a silver tray from the table.

The lock clanked open. With a jerk, the door snapped ajar.

Isabel rushed to stand behind it. She raised the tray above her head. Her heart pounded furiously.

The door creaked open, and a booted foot stepped inside.

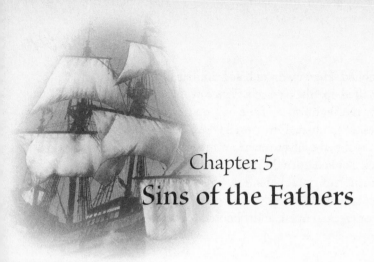

Chapter 5
Sins of the Fathers

K ent crept into the room, not wanting to alert the attacker. The empty bed glared at him in the moonlight sifting in from the window. Where was Isabel?

Clank!

Pain radiated through his head and down his neck. He tumbled to the floor and flipped over to face his assailant. A shimmer of silver filled his vision, propelled by a grunting force behind it. He lurched to his left before the oval platter clanged onto the wood where his head had been. A flash of white sped in front of him, and he threw out his legs and swept the attacker to his knees. He plunged atop the writhing figure and pinned his arms to the floor.

"Get off of me, you fiend!"

Isabel's sweet vanilla scent wafted over him as she struggled beneath his weight. Her auburn hair spread around her on the floor like a halo. Each thrash brought her curves crushing against Kent. Every muscle in his body tensed with heat.

"I knew you couldn't be trusted." Isabel's voice quavered. "You are still the lecherous cad you always were." Panting, she ceased struggling.

He knew he should release her, but he also knew he would most likely not have the opportunity soon, if ever, to be this close to her again. Perhaps he *was* the villain she assumed him to be.

Fear flickered in her eyes as they filled with tears, and Kent's passion shriveled. He jumped from her and offered her his hand. Trembling, she

scooted away from him, rose, and stood in the corner.

"Egad, woman, 'twas you who attacked me."

She wrapped her arms about her chest and hid in the shadows. "Whatever do you expect when you break into my room in the middle of the night?" Her stuttering voice etched furrows into his conscience.

Kent lit the lantern hanging on the wall and turned to face her. "I heard you scream." He sank into one of the leather chairs and rubbed his head. A knot rose on his scalp, and a lance of pain shot from his head down his back. "I thought you were being attacked, milady." He motioned for her to come forward. "I have not come to hurt you."

"As evidenced by you forcing yourself on top of me," she snorted.

Warmth showered over him as he remembered the feel of her beneath him. "I didn't know 'twas you."

"Who else would be here, you fool?" Sarcasm brought strength back into her voice.

"I don't know." Kent gritted his teeth. "That is why I came to your aid."

Isabel stepped from the shadows, grabbed a blanket from the bed, and tossed it over her nightdress, freeing her hair from beneath it. "Well as you can see, I have no need of your gallant rescue. You may go now."

He didn't want to frighten her further by staring at her, but he couldn't pull his eyes from the vision before him. Her silky hair flowed over the blanket to her waist like a waterfall of cinnamon, contrasted by the satiny skin on her face and neck—the color of pearls. She stared at him with wide, jade green eyes that never failed to melt his heart.

"May I ask what caused you to scream?"

She looked away, her eyes moistening. "This ship holds many vile memories."

Kent swallowed a burst of guilt. How could he ever have hurt such a precious creature? Would she ever forgive him? He wanted to say he was sorry, but the words did not come naturally to him. Being sorry was a sign of weakness—of subservience—a failing his father had never allowed.

"In this life, boy, all that is important is being the best, the strongest, to be in command of everyone and everything you see."

Hadn't Kent achieved that? Truly, he was the fiercest pirate in the Caribbean. Then why did he feel so weak whenever he was in Isabel's presence?

He tore his eyes from her, sensing her unease, and noticed the Bible sitting on the table by her bed. "Taken up religion, have you?"

She inched her way to the bedpost and clung to it. Her gaze took in his bare chest. In his haste to rush to her aid, he'd barely remembered to don his breeches. When his eyes met hers, she glanced away. "If you would be so kind as to leave me alone."

He knew he made her uncomfortable, but he couldn't pull himself from her company quite yet. "When my dizziness passes, I assure you I will depart." He rubbed his eyes, feigning lightheadedness. "But what of the Bible?"

Isabel sat on the bed and glanced at the holy book. "Yes, I believe God exists. I believe in His Son, Jesus, who came and died for me. And I believe He loves me. He's quite possibly the only one who ever has." Sorrow lowered the tone of her voice.

Kent didn't know about God, but he knew he loved this woman. He longed to tell her but knew she would not accept it. "This is Merrick and Charlisse's doing—this foolish notion of a loving God."

Isabel cocked her head slightly and seemed to be struggling with something. "They opened my eyes to the truth, to be sure, but it was God who touched my heart and revealed Himself to me."

The sincerity in her voice alarmed Kent. He'd thought her smarter than those uptight buffoons Merrick and Charlisse. Kent had no need for a God. That would require admitting there was someone stronger and better than he was. Unthinkable. He hadn't spent the past ten years defeating enemies and acquiring wealth to bend his knee to anyone, God or not. "And what has this God done for you? Seems you were better off without Him."

"The tragedies in my life of late are your fault, not God's," she snapped, clasping her hands together.

Kent stretched his bare feet out in front of him, ignoring the bite of her remark. "How powerful could this God of yours be if He cannot control one pirate?"

Isabel pinched her lips together and laid a hand over her abdomen. Her silence proved him right. God was not in control—especially not over him.

Kent noticed a greenish pallor rising on her face. "I'll send the doctor by tomorrow. It seems sailing still does not agree with you."

46

"The nausea comes over me only when you are present." She darted a chilled look his way. "If you would do me the favor of leaving, I can assure you of my quick recovery."

A twinge of pain plucked at his heart. Isabel's chest rose in rapid breaths. Kent thought of Frederick.

"Tell me of our son," he said, hoping to delay his departure. Not that he wasn't curious about the boy, but truth be told, his interests at the moment lay in proving to Isabel she could trust him. It was the first step in his plan to win her heart.

Isabel looked down and drew the blanket more tightly around her. "He is the most adorable creature that ever has graced the world." A tender smile alighted on her lips.

Kent studied her, delighting in the way her face lit up at the mention of their son. "What color is his hair?"

Isabel raised her gaze. "He has your hair, the same shade and texture." Disappointment tainted her voice.

Warmth settled over Kent. "His eyes—are they green like yours?"

"Nay," she sighed. "They are dark like yours."

Kent chuckled. "How daunting for you."

"But he is not like you in any other way." She raised her chin. "He has a sweet, kind spirit, full of joy. His laughter fills a room like sunshine." She smiled. "He makes gurgling noises in his sleep."

The glow from Isabel's face brightened the dim room and lightened Kent's heavy heart.

"He's big for his age and already has two teeth," she added.

"He'll make a fine pirate," Kent growled, enjoying the appalled look on Isabel's face.

"He shall be none of the kind," she raged. "He will be a gentleman, a nobleman. A man after God's own heart—like David in the Bible."

"Ha!" Kent raised his brows. "You forget, milady, from whose seed he sprang."

"How could I forget?" Her angry eyes snapped at him. "Yet it is from the heart that blooms the honor and integrity of a true noble, not by birth or fortune."

"As I recall, you require both from the men on whom you would bestow your affections."

"That is different."

"I do not see how."

"You wouldn't understand." Isabel gave Kent a sideways glance and squeezed her eyes shut. "I miss him so much. I cannot bear the thought that he may be suffering." Tears fell from her lashes onto the blanket.

Kent rose and approached her, wanting to take her in his arms, but she opened her eyes and thrust out her hand. "Please. Stay away from me."

Returning to his chair, he dropped his head into his hands. He would show her. He would find the boy and deliver him safely back into her arms. Then she would forgive him. Then maybe, just maybe, she would learn to care for him.

Grabbing a handkerchief from the table, she dabbed her nose. "How did you discover where I was? How did you know Frederick was taken?"

Kent leaned back in the chair and stretched his legs before him. "An acquaintance of mine, Richard Sawkins"—just saying the name put a sour taste in his mouth—"he heard Morris bragging about it in a tavern at New Providence."

"What did he hear?" Isabel scooted to the edge of the bed, hope widening her reddened eyes.

"Only that Morris had taken him. Sawkins is the man I spoke of earlier. We will meet him in Charles Towne." He wished he could give her more to hope for—wished more than anything he could bring joy back into those mesmerizing eyes. He dared not tell her that Sawkins, though one of her esteemed noblemen, was nothing but a reckless scoundrel not to be trusted with a single doubloon, let alone a child's life. But for now, he was the only informant Kent had, although Kent knew he would pay a hefty wage for Sawkins's services.

Isabel scratched her arms and sighed. "How long before we arrive?"

"Three days." Seeing her eyes fill with tears again, Kent leaned forward. "We will find our son."

"He is not your son." She stood and turned her back to him. "You had no part in him save one minute of violence."

A muscle began to twitch in Kent's jaw as rage stormed through him. How long must he endure this woman's impudence? He was the captain on board this ship. Rising to his feet, he took a step toward her.

She faced him.

Restraining himself, Kent bowed. "I will leave you to your rest, milady."

"Captain, before you leave. . ."

The sweet tone of her voice lifted his hopes. "Yes?"

She held out her hand. "The key, if you please."

"The key?"

"The one with which you gained entrance to my cabin. The one that counters your statement that I had the only copy." She glanced toward the key lying on the table and smirked.

With a roguish grin, Kent pulled a key from a pocket in his breeches. He'd hoped she wouldn't notice. After all, he'd kept a copy only for her protection. Dropping it into her hand, he marched out.

Kent stormed up onto the foredeck and clutched the main railing. Thrusting his bare chest into the wind, he braced himself against the plunging of the ship as she forged through the ebony seas. Frustration, shame, and anger surged within him like the turbulent waters of the Caribbean. How he'd longed to be near Isabel again. For a year, he'd searched for her across this dark expanse. Yet every moment he now spent with her threw his insides into a riotous brawl. He'd envisioned her naught but grateful for his aid in rescuing her son and willing to forgive him, willing to give him another chance. Yet her attitude and demeanor proved to be the opposite. How dare she? Did she know what he could do to her now that she was once again under his dominion? Her sudden belief in this invisible God only made matters worse. Now she'd have even more reason to toss her impudent little nose in the air.

Footsteps sounded behind him. Had she come to her senses and sought him out to make amends? Nay, the tread was too heavy to be a woman's. A whiff of tobacco tickled Kent's nose, and Cutter emerged from the shadows. The tall, lanky man halted beside Kent and stared out over the sea, saying nothing for several minutes.

He glanced at his captain. "The woman keeps you up at night, eh?"

"There are many things that disturb my sleep." Kent crossed his arms over his chest.

"Yet I have never seen you patrolling these decks at so late an hour."

Kent grimaced. "I'll not deny the woman is an added distraction." A gust of wind tore up from the sea and blew his hair into his eyes. He flung the strands back behind him.

Lifting his pipe to his mouth, Cutter took a few puffs, then withdrew it. "I fear she is more than that. You've not quite been yourself since she came aboard."

Kent's stomach clenched. Cutter's biting philosophy was not what he needed to hear at the moment. "What is it you want, Doctor?"

"I seek nothing save company on a lonely night."

"I'm afraid I'm not much company."

"Which is precisely what I've been saying."

Pride charged his anger, and Kent gripped the railing again. "She shuns my every kindness."

Cutter took a puff from his pipe, then lowered it. "Violation is not an easy thing to dismiss—especially when the act produces a child. Perhaps you are not considering what her life has been like this past year?" He gave Kent a questioning glance.

"And what of my life? Why I've done naught but search for her, my only concern being her wellbeing. And all the while I carried the weight of guilt for what I had done, like a heavy burden upon my shoulders—a burden only she can lift. Yet she refuses to do so."

"Was it truly just for concern that you sought her out? Then why is your ire so kindled when she does not react according to your expectations?"

Cutter's calm demeanor belied his sharp words—words that penetrated deep within Kent to a place he preferred to leave untouched. "Only you, good doctor, can make me feel ashamed for doing a good thing."

Cutter let out a deep chuckle.

Kent fisted his hands on his hips and braced his feet upon the deck as the ship rolled over a lusty swell. A flash of lightning spiked across the sky. "Truth be told, I'm doing this woman a grand service, and if she insists on spitting upon my graces, we shall see what will happen." He drew in a deep breath, relishing the scent of salt and the sting of rain that tickled his nostrils. The milky crests of waves bowed before him. "For I am determined to have her one way or another."

Thunder roared in agreement, shaking the ship beneath his feet. Sprinkles of rain showered over the two men.

Drawing his gnarled lips into a straight line, Cutter eyed Kent. "Then I shall leave you to your musings, Captain."

Kent nodded as the doctor sauntered away, leaving behind a cloud of

disapproval that nearly smothered him. He raised his head and allowed the rain to wash it away, as his father's words filled his thoughts.

"Failure is for weaklings. You must take what you want from life, be it money, power, success, or women." He had struck young Kent across the jaw, sending the boy to his knees. *"Why can't you be more like your brother? Never let anyone rule you, you feeble ox."* The burly man's scarred features had twisted into a swollen lump of hate, and he spat onto the ground near Kent before he grabbed his cane and limped away.

Isabel flew to the window and peered out. A sudden burst of rain pelted the glass, and she backed away. The captain's intrusion upon her evening had aggravated her nerves, sending them teetering with each toss of the ship. Had he really changed? He seemed to be the same haughty, ill-tempered ruffian she'd known before. Yet she detected a hint of warmth lingering behind his impertinent stare.

Confusion scurried through her, spinning her emotions into a whirl-wind. Sometimes his gaze raked over her as if he were peering through her gown. Yet at other times a true concern and affection flickered in his eyes and tugged upon her heart. She glanced at the chair where he'd sat, and a vision of him, bare-chested, appeared in her mind. It did nothing to calm her. She'd hardly been able to keep her eyes from the muscles bulging in his chest and arms, and her shameless attraction to him frightened her almost as much as his strength did.

She paced across the cabin, searching for the rest she so desperately needed.

"Oh, Reverend Thomas, I need you. I need a word from God."

"I am here, daughter."

Isabel swung around and gazed over the room. Her eyes landed on the Bible. Reaching for it, she sank to the bed and flipped through the pages. They opened to Isaiah 41:10: *"Fear thou not; for I am with thee: be not dismayed; for I am thy God: I will strengthen thee; yea, I will help thee; yea, I will uphold thee with the right hand of my righteousness."*

As she drew the Bible to her chest, Isabel's eyes burned. "Yes, You are with me, Lord."

Replacing the holy book with care onto the table, she knelt down beside her bed and clasped her hands together. "Thank You, Father, for Your unfailing mercy. Forgive me for my doubts."

"You must also forgive, beloved."

The words flowed over her with the sweetness of honey but soured when they reached her heart. Ignoring them, she continued, "And please take care of Frederick, Lord. Please watch over him."

She rose and wiped the tears from her cheeks, wondering why the sense of peace she'd felt only moments before had dissipated. After blowing out the lantern, she crawled into bed.

A blast of thunder sent a quiver through the ship. Dread tiptoed across her hopes, and she clutched her pillow. She would play the captain's game until they reached Charles Towne. After she discovered Frederick's whereabouts from Kent's informant, she would make her escape to her parents' estate and beg them for their help. Surely she could persuade them to rescue their only grandson.

The rain slapped against the window, filling the cabin with the sound of its laughter. She deserved the taunting. What a fool she was to put herself back in the hands of this pirate. Instead of groveling at her feet begging her forgiveness, he grew bolder and angrier each time she saw him. No, he hadn't changed. He couldn't be trusted.

What have I done?

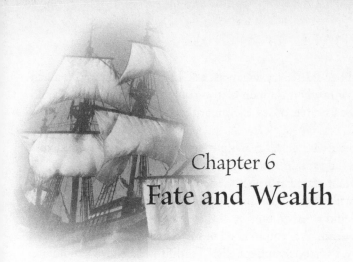

Chapter 6
Fate and Wealth

Isabel pried her eyes open. The Bible stared at her from the table next to her bed, and before her mind fully awoke to the grimness of her situation, a feeling of love surrounded her. God was with her. He would never leave her.

Rubbing her eyes, she sat up. Her breasts ached, reminding her of Frederick, and instantly, terror swooped down upon her, snatching away the momentary peace.

The ship lunged and nearly tossed her to the floor. Clinging to the bedpost, she stood and gathered her wits and courage for another day. Rain pelted against the window, and though only a gloomy haze drifted into the cabin, Isabel suspected she'd slept long into the morning.

After donning a gown, she washed her face and combed her hair. As she was pinning up the unruly tresses, a knock sounded on the door.

"Who is it?"

"'Tis I with the doctor." The captain's deep voice bore through the oak.

"I told you I have no need."

"Allow Cutter to decide that, milady."

With a huff, Isabel snatched one of the keys from the table and unlatched the bolt. Before she could open the door, the captain forced his way in with the doctor on his heels. A burst of humid air spiced with rain surged in behind them. Kent bowed, and a waterfall cascaded from his hat. Doffing it, he swung the saturated strands of his hair behind him and gave her one of his dangerous smiles. "I trust you slept well?"

Isabel tilted her chin up and glanced at Cutter. "Doctor, my stomach seems to ail me only when Captain Carlton is present. Perhaps you could save yourself the trouble of an examination and simply order him to leave."

Cutter's eyebrows rose, and a slight smile curved his lips. But one stern look from the captain and his features fell stoic again.

Scowling, Kent stared at Isabel. "Then so be it. I will take my leave, but the doctor will stay to make sure you are well." He slapped his soggy hat on his head and stormed out.

Cutter shrugged. "Are you in need of my services, milady?"

Isabel pressed a hand over her belly. "Truthfully, I believe I could use something to settle my stomach. It has never agreed with sailing, I'm afraid—nor with pirates."

"Yes, quite so." Cutter dropped a satchel onto the table and opened it with his right hand. He drew out a small pouch. His fingers were strong and slender, so unlike the ones on his left hand that hung withered by his side. "Cinnamon and myrrh." He handed it to Isabel. "I'll have Hann bring some chamomile tea. Add this to it. It should help you regain your appetite, milady." He smiled, and despite his mangled upper lip, Isabel noted the genuine concern in his eyes.

"I never properly thanked you for helping Lady Charlisse and me escape the last time I was on board this ship."

"Yet I find you've returned of your own free will." He regarded her with humor in his gaze.

Isabel shook her head. "You know as well as I 'tis concern for my son that has dragged me here."

Cutter's lofty bearing and gentlemanly demeanor gave Isabel the impression of an intelligence and strength hidden behind his deformed exterior. He studied her with eyes the color of the sky in the aftermath of a thunderstorm.

Isabel scratched her arms. "I seem to have developed a rash as well."

"Hum," Cutter grunted. "Let's have a look, shall we?" He motioned for her to roll up her sleeves.

"I'm ashamed to say this rash may be evidence of my lack of faith in God." Isabel groaned as Cutter examined the red bumps littering her skin. "It began when Frederick went missing. I've had it before—the last

time I was on this ship."

"Do not waste your thoughts on such a trifling pursuit as faith, milady." Cutter released her arm. "We shall treat the rash for what it is, a nervous reaction and nothing more. There is no God, at least none that cares about humanity."

"What makes you say such a thing?" Isabel studied the doctor as he withdrew a jar of ointment from his bag. Though she did not expect such a declaration from Cutter, she understood it all too well. Not too long ago, she had believed the same thing.

He shifted his gaze to hers. "I fear 'tis the only logical conclusion."

" 'Tis the only *irrational* conclusion, Doctor. There is a God, I can assure you. I have spoken with Him, felt His warm presence, seen His mighty hand perform miracles."

"You are young and susceptible to foolish notions." He handed her the jar of ointment. "Rub this on both arms twice a day."

Isabel squeezed the glass between her fingers. "May I ask what happened to foster such cynicism in your heart?"

Cutter's lips flattened. "Fate happened. She is the only controller of this world—and a rather unjust one at that." He tied his satchel and flung it over his shoulder. "It comforts me knowing I cannot pray to her, nor do I need to please her or appeal to her mercy. She does not listen to men but does as she pleases. Once I accepted that, I felt at peace."

Isabel's heart sank. She liked Cutter and didn't want to see him so unhappy and alone—especially when he didn't have to be.

"Did you ever believe in God?"

He grinned. "Yes, many years ago." He raised his withered arm. "And see how I was paid for my devotion?"

Isabel's eyes burned at the agony and bitterness in his gaze. "Please forgive my boldness, but may I ask what happened to you?"

He crossed his arms over his chest, placing the withered one beneath the stronger one, and regarded her, a battle brewing behind his stormy gray eyes.

A tap on the open door drew their attention. Hann stood with a tray of food. He stared at Cutter as if he'd never seen him before, and his tremble reached the tray with a clatter of cup, saucer, and spoon.

Shifting his stance, Cutter darted his gaze back to Isabel.

Hann stumbled to the table and set the tray down. "I'm sorry, milady. I did not know you had a guest. With the captain's compliments, your lunch."

"Can you bring Lady Ashton some chamomile tea, Hann?"

Hann shifted his gaze from Cutter to the floor. "I 'ave some right here, sir." A pinkish hue blossomed up his face.

Cutter furrowed his brow and scratched his head, then faced Isabel. "By your leave, milady. I have other duties to attend to."

"Of course. Thank you, Doctor."

As soon as Cutter left, Hann let out a deep breath.

Isabel studied the boy curiously. "Something troubles you about the doctor?"

Hann's wide-eyed gaze darted to hers. "Nay, milady. What makes ye say that?" He poured some tea and handed the steaming cup to Isabel.

"You seem quite uneasy in his presence. Has he hurt you?" Taking the cup, Isabel took a sip and set it down on the table.

Shock sparked across Hann's eyes. "No, never. T'aint nothin' like that, milady. Now if that be all, miss. Captain suggests ye stay in yer cabin during the squall. He says fer me to come get ye for dinner when the time comes."

"You may tell the captain I have no intention of dining with him tonight." Isabel threw her shoulders back.

Hann crinkled his nose, and a tenuous grin flickered on his lips. He turned to leave.

"And Hann?"

"Aye, milady?"

"Do you perchance have any more pillows on board? These two will not suffice."

"Them's the only two we got." Hann gave a disapproving chortle. "And those the captain had to purchase special at New Providence."

Isabel nodded, and the young boy left, closing the door after him.

Kent had remembered she loved pillows. He puzzled her. An uncomfortable feeling of being cared for came over her as she locked the bolt and sat in one of the chairs. Opening the pouch Cutter had given her, she sprinkled some of the mixture into her tea and prayed it would not only sooth her stomach but her whirling emotions, as well.

Hours later, Isabel sat by the window and watched the sun set upon a sea that seethed and frothed just like the raging of her heart.

Dinnertime came and went, and Isabel thanked God that Captain Carlton had not summoned her, although she received no food, either. She devoured the two buttery biscuits Hann had brought earlier, lit a lamp, and opened her Bible.

"I don't know what to do, Lord. I feel so alone and surrounded by enemies."

No voice came to reassure her, but as she scanned the scriptures, comforting words fell from the pages into her heart as if they were meant just for her: *"I will say of the LORD, He is my refuge and my fortress: my God; in him will I trust. Surely he shall deliver thee from the snare of the fowler, and from the noisome pestilence. He shall cover thee with his feathers, and under his wings shalt thou trust: his truth shall be thy shield and buckler. Thou shalt not be afraid for the terror by night; nor for the arrow that flieth by day."*

"Thank You, Father." Yet no sooner had she closed the holy book than a black shroud fell over her window and fear slithered back around her heart. Isabel lit another lantern to stave off the encroaching darkness. The wind howled an eerie chant as it rushed against the hull in a violent dance accompanied by the creak and groan of the ship charging through the churning sea.

As night fell, the sounds of evening reverie arose. Shouts, curses, challenges, and risqué ballads bombarded her through the cabin's thin walls. A pistol shot rang through the air. Isabel jumped from her chair.

After checking the bolt on her door three times, she settled on the bed and dissolved into a fitful sleep.

The wail of a baby filled her cabin—at first a low, distant whimper, then pulsating into a grating whine, louder and louder.

Isabel sprang from the bed. "Frederick!"

Hann crept up behind Kent, careful not to make a sound. Although he had removed his boots, the wood beneath his feet creaked with every step. The captain drew another swig of rum and leaned the bottle down on the barrel he sat upon. *That's it, keep drinking. Cloud your ears and your head to boot. It will only make my job easier.*

The ship lurched over a wave, sending a spray of sea over them. Regaining his balance, Hann hesitated. He gripped the knife and positioned it above his head. He was almost there. Two more steps, a quick plunge of the blade, and then overboard with the murdering scoundrel—to the depths of the sea where he belonged. Finally it would be finished, and justice would be served.

Grabbing a key, Isabel thrust it into the keyhole and jiggled it in the lock. Her hands trembled.

The scream of a child filled the air.

The lock wouldn't catch. She pulled the key out, and it slipped from her hand, clanging to the floor.

The howling grew louder. Sobbing, Isabel knelt, retrieved the key, and inserted it again. This time, the lock caught, and with one turn, the latch fell. She yanked the door open and darted outside. She glanced down the dark hall, craning her ear. The wailing continued. It came from the deck above. Isabel flew up the stairs. Her bare feet slapped against the cool, moist wood of the main deck. A burst of warm air struck her, nearly shoving her off her feet.

"Frederick!"

Squinting, she scanned the ship, trying to focus in the darkness. A band of pirates huddled by the port railing. She felt their eyes upon her but didn't care. The wail chimed through the night air.

"Frederick!"

Kent tipped the bottle to his lips and poured a full draught down his throat. The tangy liquid burned his mouth and warmed his gut. He plopped onto a barrel near the foremast and sighed, scanning the black expanse. He loved this sea. And he was her master. Though wild and unpredictable, he had tamed her, had made her his slave, and stolen her treasure. If only he could do the same with the tempestuous woman below.

"See, dear Father, I am not the failure you thought me to be." He thrust the bottle into the midnight sky. A gust of heavy air smashed into him. Though the storm had passed, a strong wind still toyed with

the ship. Sails snapped above him in the lingering tempest as the blocks creaked and groaned. The rush of wind through the tackles whined like a siren's song. He chuckled. He'd always considered the sailors in that story foolish to be so easily lured to their deaths by feminine wiles, yet now he found himself under the same spell—that of Lady Ashton.

Tossing back his head, he raised the bottle and downed another gulp. He hadn't meant to drink tonight, but after the infuriating woman had denied his request to dine with him, he'd been unable to stop himself—especially when Smithy and some of the other pirates had enticed him to join their party. He'd done so for a while, if only to dull the pain and the anger brewing within him. Lady Ashton. The last person who'd treated him with such disrespect had found himself tied to the keel of the ship.

A chill swirled around him. *Are you in command or not? Go down and take her. You've done it before. You can do it again.*

"Frederick!"

Kent shook his head. Now he was hearing the blasted woman's voice. Could he not shake her from his thoughts for one night?

"Frederick!"

Kent sprang from the barrel and turned. Something moved behind him and he peered into the shadows. "Hann, is that you?"

The lad emerged into the sparse light from the foremast lantern, a sheepish grin on his lips.

"I didn't hear you, boy," Kent chided him. "Don't be sneaking up on me again."

A woman screamed, and Kent glanced down on the main deck. Isabel darted frantically across the ship, her gown billowing in the wind. A group of pirates were closing in on her.

Isabel raced up onto the quarterdeck, her gaze dashing wildly over the frightening shadows. The mizzenmast loomed above her, its tip lost in the darkness. A dark figure stepped out from behind the whipstaff.

"Where's my baby?" Desperation swallowed her fear.

A deep chortle drifted to her on the wind. "I dunno, miss, but I'll be yer baby, if ye wants." A pirate groped at her shoulder.

The howling rang like a chime across the deck. Isabel glanced up. It came from above. "Frederick!" She bolted back down the stairs, tripped over a hatch coaming, and crashed to the deck. Pain spiked up her arm. She crawled to the railing and clutched the wood, sobbing. "Frederick, where are you?"

The shuffle of boots sounded behind her. "Can we help ye with somethin', young missy?"

Snickers followed, and Isabel recognized Smithy's voice. Tainted with rum, however, it did not seem as solicitous as it had before. She dared not look around but kept her gaze on the inky sea foaming below her. How could she be so close to her crying child yet unable to find him?

The *thump* of another set of boots joined them, and Isabel heard the pirates scramble away, groaning.

Strong arms reached from behind her and lifted her to her feet. Struggling, she swung around and glared up into the captain's darkened face. Though his eyes were obscured in a shadow, a slight smirk sat upon his lips, evidenced by the gleam of his teeth.

"If you longed for the pleasure of my company, you might have joined me at dinner," he said in a mocking tone. The tangy scent of rum flooded her nostrils.

Pushing against him, she backed away. "I do not seek you, you fool." She wiped the tears from her cheeks. "I heard Frederick crying. You have him here, don't you?" She charged him and beat her fists on his chest. "Why do you keep him from me?"

"Milady"—he grabbed her arms— "I do not have him. Do you think me so cruel?"

She tried to free herself from his grasp, but his firm grip tightened. The crying pierced the air again.

"See, do you not hear him?" She yanked her arms free. "Let me go to him!" Her voice cracked as tears gushed down her face.

Kent sighed and clutched her shoulders, forcing her to face him. " 'Tis only the wind whistling through the tackles, milady." He glanced upward, then loosened his hold on her. "Though I admit it does sound a bit like a child. I assure you, your son is not on board. I may be many things, but I am not a man who steals babies from their mothers."

Hesitating, Isabel listened as the whimpering eased and finally ceased along with the wind. Despondency once again weighed upon her heart.

Her stomach lurched, and she hung her head and sobbed. Indeed, she'd heard the sound many times before.

The captain pulled her to him in a strong embrace. For a brief moment, the strength and warmth of him soothed Isabel, but his spicy odor sent fury and fear clamoring through her. She shoved away from him.

"How dare you? Trying to take advantage of my weakness. Trying to comfort me when you are the one who has caused me this pain."

He growled. "Woman, you try my patience. Have I not assured you I will make amends? Where is your faith?"

"My faith is in God, not in a pirate."

"This pirate can bring you more happiness than any God." A cloud dislodged its hold on the moon, allowing light to filter down upon the ship. Kent waved a hand in the air. "Do you not see what I have accomplished? Success, power, and"—he leaned toward her, showering her with the sting of rum and sweat—"I have a vast amount of treasure I have saved for us. Once we find our son, we can live out our days in wealth and luxury." His voice rose in excitement.

"All I see is a drunken fool, a man without honor." Isabel jutted her chin in the air.

"Aye, yes, I did have a drink. May Your Piousness forgive me." He bowed mockingly. "I was informed I would not be seeing you this evening, but alas, you have surprised me. Now what of my offer, milady? 'Tis what you've always wanted—wealth, success."

Isabel sneered. "Wealth without title, without position, is meaningless. Honor and integrity cannot be bought, and you, sir, are without both."

A cloud obscured the moonlight again, shrouding the captain's face in shadows, but not before she saw moisture glisten his eyes. All was silent save for his deep breaths and the groan of the ship. Guilt pricked at her conscience. Had she been too cruel? Was this the way a true Christian woman behaved? She could almost feel his pain leeching through the darkness. Then he growled, and in one swoop, hoisted her over his shoulder. "Swounds, woman, I would that it did not come to this, but your impudence is not to be borne."

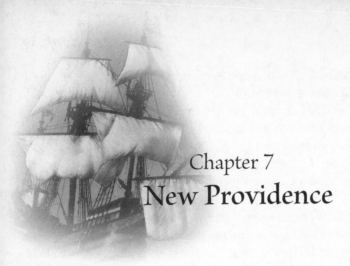

Chapter 7
New Providence

Kent staggered, nearly dropping Isabel, before marching across the deck and down the companionway stairs.

"What are you doing? Put me down at once!" Isabel pounded her fists on his back; then her voice softened. "Please, I beg you."

"Ah, now you beg me, but 'tis too late. You need to be taught who is master aboard this ship."

He kicked open the door to her cabin and swung inside.

Isabel began to sob; then her struggling ceased and she instantly fell silent.

Kent laid her limp body gently on the bed and took a step back. Blast, the woman had swooned. He hadn't meant to frighten her so badly—scare her into submission perhaps—but he'd had no intention of hurting her. Didn't she realize he could never force himself on her again? Kent rubbed the back of his neck and thumped his forehead against the bedpost with a groan as the rum cavorted in a lawless dance in his head. The woman's sharp tongue had lit the fuse of his liquored mind and blasted his reason to bits—once again.

Sinking into a chair, Kent planted his elbows on his knees and stared at the beauty who had caused him more pain than any enemy had. Would she ever see him for the man he longed to be, not the man she remembered? Even with a noble title, he knew he would always fall short of what she desired—and deserved.

Dizziness overtook him, and he bowed his head. "Am I truly the vile

rogue she believes I am?"

Silence echoed his answer, and he grunted. What God would answer him?

Regardless of whether she forgave him, he would help her find their son. Then if she wished, he would leave her be. How could he do any less?

Standing, he allowed his gaze to peruse her—something he dared not do so boldly while she was awake. Silky auburn hair cascaded over her shoulder and sparkled like rubies in the lantern light. Long lashes cast shadows onto her creamy cheek, still stained with tears. His pulse rose at her nearness and vulnerability. Grabbing a blanket, he covered her and retrieved a key from the table before forcing himself to leave.

Boom!

Isabel shot up, clutching the blanket to her chest.

Boom!

A tremble ran through the ship, threatening to tear its timbers asunder.

She dashed to the window, craning to see who they fired upon. No ship was in sight, at least not in the small angle of vision afforded her.

A knock and Hann's voice summoned her to the door.

"The captain wishes me to inform ye that he's testin' the cannons this morning and that we will arrive at New Providence within the hour." Hann entered and set a tray of tea on the table. He hesitated, glancing across the room before his dark violet gaze rested on Isabel.

Relief spread through Isabel. "Thank you, Hann." She regarded the lad, sensing an unusual empathy in his eyes. Dirt smudged his chin and cheeks. Isabel couldn't recall ever seeing the boy's face clean. He looked down under her scrutiny. "I best be goin'." He shuffled his boots.

"Was there something else, Hann?"

He shook his head, gave her a sly look, and scurried out.

Isabel couldn't wait to get out of this tiny cabin. For two days, she'd been cooped up within its confining walls, trying to remain calm amidst the stifling air. Where was the peace God had promised to those who followed Christ? Hers had been chased away by the fear and anxiety that hovered over her like monsters ready to pounce. With her faith so weak, she wondered whether God heard any of her prayers.

After donning a fresh gown and washing her face, Isabel braved to venture up on deck, excitement squelching her fears. So far, none of the other pirates had paid her much attention. The only one she had cause to fear was Captain Carlton, and now she believed he would not hurt her. He'd had the perfect opportunity the other night, yet he'd not touched her. Perhaps he *had* changed.

Isabel darted across the deck to the railing as warm, moist air rose from the sea and showered her with its salty sweet fragrance. Off in the distance, land sprang from a shimmering turquoise mirror, an oasis beckoning her to safe shores. She recognized the shape of the island. New Providence—her home.

Smithy stomped across the deck, barking orders, and stopped to tip his hat in her direction. The gleam in his eyes disquieted her.

Her gaze scoured the ship. Men swayed in the ratlines and shrouds, adjusting sails. Others scurried about, hauling ropes and measuring depth. Some loitered, their glances snaking her way. The helmsman gripped the whipstaff in one hand, but in the other he held a squirming white rat. Isabel cringed and averted her eyes to where the captain stood, perched up on the foredeck with spyglass to his eye. He'd left her alone for more than a day. Perhaps he'd given up on winning her affections.

"We are nearly arrived, milady." A loud voice startled Isabel, and she looked over to see Cutter standing beside her, pipe jutting from his mouth.

"My apologies," he said, the smoking tube flapping with his lips. "I didn't mean to frighten you."

Isabel tried to smile. "I didn't hear you approaching." She looked toward the island and rubbed her arms. "I'm quite excited to finally be here."

"Aye, 'tis been a trying voyage for you, to be sure."

"And it isn't over yet, but at least I should receive some news of Frederick soon."

"Your family comes from New Providence, do they not?"

"Yes, how did you know?"

"The captain searched for you here after you left him."

So Kent had looked for her. She couldn't remember telling him of her family but must have disclosed that information during the long hours she'd been forced to endure his company.

"My father is Earl Brenton Ashton." She heard the pride in her voice, and a burst of nausea rose in her throat. How could she still esteem the man who'd so cruelly rejected her child? "We had a grand estate in Hertfordshire. But after the plague took my baby brother and the fire ravaged London, we lost all our holdings and made the crossing to the West Indies to start anew."

Cutter grabbed the rail with his left hand. Only two fingers clutched the wood; the other three lay inept on the railing. Red and blue patches of skin curdled over his hand and up under the lacy sleeves of his shirt.

He glanced at her. "You were not pleased with the move?"

Isabel flinched, remembering the agony of those years. "I would have preferred to stay in England. These islands are most uncivilized." She patted the combs in her hair. "And I was to be married to William Herbert, earl of Pembroke." Embarrassment warmed her face at the personal disclosure. She gazed into Cutter's gray eyes, so filled with unfeigned regard that they seemed to lure from her the intimate details of her life. Perhaps she simply longed for a sympathetic ear aboard this frightening ship.

Cutter puffed his pipe. The sweet, musky smell clouded over her, reminding her of her father. She missed him, missed his strength and protection. He was a strong, commanding man both in stature and personality, and he guarded and coddled the women in his family as if they were precious jewels. Though from time to time Isabel feared his wrath, she had always felt cherished and loved. Maybe that's why she found it so easy to talk with the doctor.

"What happened with your engagement?" Cutter asked.

"When my father lost everything, including my dowry, apparently, I was no longer of value to William."

Cutter leaned on the rail and gave her a sideways glance. "Then why do you mourn such a shallow man?"

"I do not mourn him." She glanced away and raised her nose.

"I beg your pardon." Cutter grinned.

"I mourn only the loss of our status." Isabel closed her eyes and

65

allowed the warm breeze to caress her skin. "But my father has done well in Charles Towne with his shipping business."

"Yet you do not live with him."

"Nay, he does not approve of Frederick."

"I see." He nodded. "I, too, am quite familiar with being rejected for something I could not avoid—for something I once had but lost against my will."

Isabel gazed at Cutter, shielding her eyes from the sun. A lonely shroud hovered over him, yet he hid his sorrow well. She tried to picture him without the scars and realized he had been a handsome man once. How he must have suffered. "Yes, I believe you do understand."

Pulling a locket from his waistcoat, he flipped it open to reveal a tiny portrait of a woman. Curly blond ringlets surrounded an angelic face, sparkling with blue eyes.

"My fiancée," he said. "I had this painted just before we were to be married."

Isabel examined the picture. "She's very beautiful."

"Yes, but apparently I was not so to her—not after my accident." He uttered a bitter laugh.

Although no sheen of moisture tinted his gaze, Isabel could feel unshed tears burning behind her own eyes. She offered him what she hoped was a comforting smile. "It seems we have more in common than we thought."

Cutter's attention flickered behind her, and he straightened his stance.

A shadow crept over her, bringing first relief from the heat and then a waft of leather and salt.

"We should arrive in Charles Towne in less than an hour." Kent's deep voice sent a strange tingle fluttering in her stomach.

The doctor bowed. "Milady." He nodded toward Kent. "Captain." With a puff of his pipe, he strode off.

Isabel did not turn around. She hoped the captain would leave.

He slid beside her, dropped his elbows onto the railing, and gazed at her. A heated gust toyed with the strands of hair flying out from under his black scarf. Coarse stubble peppered his chin and neck. "Does my news not bring you joy, milady?"

"My apologies." She gave him a curt smile. "I dared not presume you

addressed me, since you've not said a word to me in nigh two days."

"Missed me?" His lips curved in a half smile.

Darting her gaze out to the island, Isabel chortled. "Your insolence is ever a source of humor."

"Well, at least I provide some service to you." He stood, straightened his vest, and clamped a hand over the hilt of his cutlass. "I'll leave you to your reflections, then." He spun on his heels and sauntered away. With his departure, a sudden chill came over her. She glanced over her shoulder. A horde of pirates clustered across the deck. Shaggy, unkempt, and adorned in stained, mismatched attire of varying degrees of style, they leered at her through rotting teeth. Her gaze shifted to the captain's retreating form on the quarterdeck. As long as he was present, she'd be safe—from them, at least.

The first small cays that led the way into the harbor at Charles Towne popped up from the sapphire sea. Isabel tensed, whether from nerves or excitement, she didn't know.

"Lower tops and gallants." The captain's commands echoed across the ship. "Bring her about, Hoornes. Steady."

Smithy repeated his orders, adding his own colorful obscenities, and the filthy men rushed to their duties.

Shielding her eyes from the noonday sun, Isabel watched the bare-footed pirates climb like monkeys up the ratlines into the shrouds and nearly disappear amongst the billowing sails. Her gaze dropped to find the captain standing on the quarterdeck next to the whipstaff, hands fisted on his hips as if he owned the world. She still found it difficult to believe he was Frederick's father.

A blast of heat blowing in from the land struck Isabel, and she plucked a fan from the sash of her gown and snapped it open. Perspiration dampened her neck and slid down her back, and the fluttering of her fan did nothing to assuage it. She sighed, wishing the ship would move faster, but she knew the entrance to the harbor with all its reefs and cays held many hidden dangers for even the most skilled seaman. Captain Carlton navigated it with ease.

Coming into view off the port side were the golden shores and green fields of Hog Island, named so for the farm animals that were allowed to roam freely there until they were butchered to feed the settlers. The stench of hog and cow dung roasting in the sweltering heat crashed over Isabel, nearly choking her.

Holding a hand to her nose, she turned to see the rows of wooden docks punching out into the harbor from the center of Charles Towne. Memories washed over her—agonizing memories of a difficult farewell. As the ship glided past the first dock, visions of her mother weeping as she clung to her father's arm passed through Isabel's mind. Her father had handed Isabel a sealed envelope. His face remained stoic. He'd paid for her passage to Port Royal, sending with her a letter to a woman at a boardinghouse with enough money to support Isabel until she bore her child. Afterward she could return home—alone.

Isabel forced back tears and surveyed the masts. All the sails save the fore and main courses had been lowered and furled. Beyond the ship, sloops, schooners, brigs, and other vessels rocked at their anchors in the simmering bay. She wondered how many of them were pirate ships. Her eyes landed on Kent, and hatred burned within her. Because of him, she'd had to forsake home, family, and her dignity.

Of course, she hadn't gone to the boardinghouse. Lady Charlisse had given her directions to Reverend Thomas Buchan's church in case she ever found herself at Port Royal and in need of help. She'd shown up at his cottage—dirty, shabby, in tears, and pregnant. She would never forget the comforting smile on his face as he escorted her inside.

"Lower all courses!" the captain bellowed. "Anchor away!"

Isabel glanced over the city. Crowds of people mobbed around the docks and scurried along the streets, weaving around horses and drays loaded with goods. Brick and wooden buildings of varying width and height cropped up behind them and littered the hills beyond.

"Oh, Frederick," she whispered. Perhaps he was here. She knew it was too much to hope for, but at least she could finally leave this horrid ship and make some progress in the search for her son.

The frigate glided to a near stop, and the huge iron anchor struck the water with a *splash*, its enormous chain clanking against the hull as it sank.

Cutter approached Isabel with a smile and led her aside while the cockboat was hoisted from its cradle amidships and lowered overboard. The captain disappeared below. He reappeared shortly in a fine satin

doublet with silver-laced buttonholes. Atop his head perched a plumed bicorn. After he issued orders to the men, assigning them shifts onshore, he swaggered toward Isabel.

"I understand your family lives here. Do you wish to see them?"

Taken aback at his concern, Isabel studied him, then surveyed the city. Truly, she wasn't sure she could face another rejection by her father, but as soon as she obtained information on Frederick's whereabouts, she had to take that risk. "Yes, perhaps, but we must first speak with your informant."

"Then, shall we?" Kent gestured to the rope ladder that one of the men had flung over the bulwarks.

A sudden quiver raked over her. She was putting herself once again at the mercies of this pirate. She turned toward Cutter. "Will you be joining us?"

"I'm afraid not." He winced and glanced over the city. "I rarely expose myself to the public. There are women and children to consider." Bitterness tainted his short chuckle.

Isabel replied with an understanding nod but felt abandoned by her new friend. When she faced the captain again, his jaw flexed. "You may stay on board if you prefer." He raised his brows.

"Of course not," she snapped.

Grinning, the captain flung himself over the railing and climbed down into the boat. After a wary glance at Cutter, Isabel followed, clumsily scaling the coarse ropes. Kent grabbed her waist and placed her in the boat before she could protest. Smithy and two other pirates joined them.

The pungent odor of brine, rotting wood, and fish viscera steamed from the shallow water, assaulting Isabel. She pulled out her handkerchief, dabbed at the moisture dotting the back of her neck, and then held the damp cloth to her nose.

After shoving off the hull, the men snapped the oars in the locks and began rowing toward shore. The sun reflected off the placid water in sharp rays that pierced Isabel's vision. Squinting, she gazed over the scene. Workers swarmed the docks. Bare-chested Caribs and slaves, their bronzed backs glimmering with sweat, unloaded crates and barrels from boats and hauled them to nearby drays. Isabel marveled at their strength and perseverance in the sweltering heat.

The captain sat across from her. Though she tried to avoid his gaze, occasionally their eyes met. She found his silence as unnerving as the sharpness of his tongue. The hilt of a large knife jutted from one of his black Cordovan boots. Through the folds of his doublet, she saw the butt of a pistol stuffed into the waist of his breeches. The tip of his cutlass pointed over the side of the boat. Was he expecting trouble? Isabel did not recall Charles Towne being nearly as dangerous as Port Royal.

Squelching her dismal thoughts, she allowed her hope to rise with each stroke of the oars. The man they were supposed to meet knew where Frederick was. She could feel it. But other feelings vied for her attention—feelings resurging from the familiar scenes surrounding her. She was returning home. Her father and mother were but a few minutes' carriage ride from the city. She missed them and longed to feel their love and approval once more. Agony swept over her.

The cockboat slammed against the dock and splashed water over Isabel's shoes. One of the pirates leaped onto the wharf and tied the boat. Captain Carlton followed him and turned with hand outstretched for Isabel. After a slight hesitation, she accepted it, for she knew if she tried to lift herself from this teetering boat, she'd surely end up in the bay.

Clamping his warm, strong hand around hers, he gently brought her beside him. His dark brown gaze drifted over her. Tiny flecks of gold sparkled in their depths. Had they been there before? She hadn't noticed. Snatching her hand back, she averted her gaze, but not before seeing his expression fall. He turned and led the way.

Though she knew he slowed his gait for her, she had a hard time keeping up with him as the mass of people swarmed at her from all directions. She glanced over her shoulder and saw Smithy and the other two men following at a distance. Unease churned in her stomach.

As they marched down Bay Street, Isabel recognized the familiar shops and taverns. Would she cross paths with anyone she knew? Her gaze halted on one of the stores. The wooden building seemed to jump out at her from amongst the rows of shops lining the street. Heat sizzled off it in distorted waves that sent Isabel's head spinning. Feral images blazed through her mind—images of Captain Carlton and his band of miscreants barreling into the mercantile, wielding weapons and bottles

of rum. With but one glance upon her, he'd tossed her over his shoulder and dragged her to his ship.

Kent glanced at her, guilt staining his brown eyes.

A chicken squawked and scampered across her path, pulling Isabel from her memories. She shrieked, barely avoiding it, and stepped into a pile of horse dung.

"Ugg." She plucked her shoe from the fetid glob and held her handkerchief to her mouth, gagging. Kent stopped only long enough to glance at her over his shoulder and chuckle before continuing on his way.

"Insolent cad," she sneered, lifting her skirts as she ran to catch up to him.

Harpsichord music twanged into the street from a tavern to Isabel's left. Merchants and sailors with ale in hand crowded the porch, ogling her as she passed by.

"Where are we going?" she shouted.

Grabbing her hand, Kent dodged a wagon as he crossed the street. "To meet Sawkins, the man I told you about."

Abruptly, the captain froze. Isabel followed his gaze to a handsome, modishly dressed man standing beside a gilded carriage.

Isabel recognized the family crest engraved on the door. Her heart lurched.

It was her father's carriage.

Chapter 8
Home Sweet Home

Kent marched toward the carriage, gritting his teeth and eyeing the familiar man standing beside it. Sawkins. A wide grin sat upon his insolent lips, revealing sparkling white teeth. Ignoring Kent, he bowed, reached for Isabel's hand, and raised it to his mouth. Ash-colored hair was slicked back from his face and gathered in a cavalier tie down his back. "You must be Lady Ashton."

A blush consumed Isabel's creamy skin, and she pulled her hand back.

Kent stepped between them. "We were to meet at the Ship Tavern."

"Plans have changed." The man smirked and shifted his icy gaze back to Isabel. "Since the captain hasn't the manners to introduce me, I shall take that liberty. Lord Richard Sawkins, at your service."

Isabel glanced at Kent. "Is this the man you spoke of?"

He nodded, disgust curdling in his belly.

Biting her lip, she stepped toward Sawkins. "I beg you, milord, what news of my son?"

"He is well, milady." Sawkins clasped one of her hands and engulfed it between his.

"Thank God." She raised her other hand to her bosom and began to sway.

Kent took the opportunity to wrap an arm around her waist to steady her and wrench her from Sawkins's grip. Just seeing the man's hands on

hers sent rage searing through his gut.

Twisting from his grasp, Isabel's eyes flared toward Kent. She faced Sawkins. "Where is he?"

"That is what I must discuss with Captain Carlton. I know the direction the villain has taken. We must plot our course directly."

"Then he is not here?" Isabel wrung her hands.

"I'm afraid not, milady. But I know where they are taking him." Sawkins straightened the lace at his sleeves.

Isabel turned away. A shudder ran across her back.

"This is my parents' carriage, milord." She faced Sawkins again, wiping a strand of hair from her forehead. "How did you come by it?"

"They sent me to escort you home. I informed them of your arrival, milady. They are most anxious to see you."

A foul stench wafted over Kent, and it wasn't just from the rotting fish in the bay. "You did not inform me you were acquainted with Lady Ashton's parents."

Sawkins twirled his greased mustache. "I wasn't until yesterday. The meeting was quite accidental, I assure you. You can imagine my astonishment at running into the grandparents of the child I am seeking."

"Astonishing, indeed," Kent snarled.

Sawkins raised his elbow toward Isabel. "I promised your parents I would bring you home."

Recoiling, Isabel glared at him. "I cannot see them. Not yet. Please tell me where my son is."

Apprehension swarmed around Kent. Were Isabel's parents now willing to assist her? If so, she'd have no further need of him. He squinted at Sawkins. The rogue seemed quite taken with Lady Ashton, and how could he blame him? Kent bunched his fists, longing to be rid of this buffoon. "Why delay, Sawkins? As the lady requests, give us the information now, and let us be on our way."

Sawkins sighed with annoyance, then gazed at Isabel. "The captain and I need time to discuss our strategy. Why not take this opportunity to greet your parents and refresh yourself from your long journey. I can only imagine how grueling it must have been for you." His voice dripped with feigned concern.

With a sigh, Isabel raised a hand to her neck. "You have no idea."

Kent crossed his arms over his chest. "She was treated with utmost courtesy."

"My apologies, Captain." Sawkins bowed. "I only meant that a *pirate* ship is no place for a lady."

Smiling, Isabel placed her hand inside Sawkins's outstretched elbow and raised her chin toward Kent.

Was the woman so daft as to fall for this insolent man's charms?

"We will return my parents' carriage to them," Isabel huffed. "This will allow me to make one final appeal for their help." She glowered at Kent. "But I have no wish to linger. We must be after Frederick immediately."

"My sentiments exactly." Sawkins patted her hand and led her to the carriage.

Groaning, Kent released Smithy and the other men, ordering them to meet him back at the ship by nightfall. When he turned back around, he watched Sawkins fondle Isabel's hand as the lecherous cur assisted her inside the carriage. Wiping sweat from his brow, Kent marched toward them, fuming.

He had no desire to meet Isabel's parents, but he also had no desire to leave her alone with Sawkins. When he climbed into the carriage, Sawkins had already taken the spot next to Isabel. Plunging onto the seat across from them, Kent's insides boiled as the rogue inched his way closer to her. The urge to draw his sword and plunge it into the knave's heart tensed the muscles in Kent's arms. But that certainly wouldn't speak well of him to Isabel, nor aid in the search for their son. And finding the boy was far more important than Kent's contest for Isabel's affections. Restraining himself, he listened to the clamor of Sawkins's voice oozing its venomous charm over Isabel. Thankfully, the ride was a short one.

A servant swung open an iron gate as the carriage approached. Kent poked his head out the window to see a two-story white house beaming in the bright sun. Rays of blinding light bounced off the multipaned windows that sat above wide balconies on the second floor. Below, a huge porch covered with cushioned furniture angled out from a broad, paneled door. Flowers of all shapes and colors surrounded the house like dabs of paint on a white canvas. Cedar and rosewood trees dotted the landscape. A large barn and grazing land spread out to the right. The family's shipping business must be doing well indeed.

Envy burned within Kent. His father had been a merchant with high hopes his son would take over the family business, but Kent found the work grueling and dull, and he had no mind for numbers—another failure in his father's eyes. So the old man had given the business to Kent's half brother, the product of one of his father's many affairs. Kent directed a squinted gaze at Sawkins, still blubbering over Isabel. What great pleasure it had brought Kent as he'd watched his lame-brained brother run the business into the ground with gambling debts.

The carriage jolted to a stop in front of the house. A rare fear constricted his throat. He was about to meet the parents of the woman he'd ravished. Would she tell them? If so, he must be prepared. He hoped her father would not be so foolish as to challenge Kent to a duel. Kent did not wish to kill him.

Isabel patted her hair in place and took a shaky step up the stairs to her home. What would be her parents' reaction to seeing her face-to-face? Perhaps they would reconsider and be willing to help her. Just the sight of the huge house where she'd once lived revived a tempest of emotions within her—relief and comfort, confusion and heartache.

Home.

Why hadn't her parents met her in town if they'd been so anxious to see her? Could they truly have had a change of heart? With Sawkins's information and one of her father's ships, she'd have no further need of Captain Carlton. She glanced at him as he came up on her left. His brown eyes swung toward hers, and he seemed to smile at her without even a lift of his lips. Somehow she didn't think he'd be easily put aside.

The front door swung open, and in a swish of silk and lace, her mother glided toward her. "Oh, my darling."

Joy and uncertainty bubbled within Isabel. Yet she couldn't help but grin at the gleeful expression lighting up her mother's flawless face. Truly, she must love her after all, despite the shame Isabel had brought to the family.

The need to feel safe again in her mother's embrace overwhelmed her, and Isabel rushed and flung her arms around her mother's neck. The sweet fragrance of rose and lavender blanketed Isabel with warm memories of love and sanctuary. Closing her eyes, she released a sigh.

With a huff, her mother pushed her back, then leaned in to whisper, "My dear, you know ladies never run nor display such affection in public. 'Tis most improper."

Isabel glanced down, suddenly feeling like a little girl all over again.

Her mother wiped wayward strands of hair from Isabel's face. "Oh, look at you." Disappointment stained her voice. She stepped back, placing her hands upon her hips. "You are an absolute disaster." She clicked her tongue. "Filthy, and"—she tugged at Isabel's gown—"this horrid rag. Wherever did you get it?"

"I'm quite well, Mother, thank you." Isabel met her gaze and grimaced. "I didn't expect to see you so soon."

"Not see your parents? Absurd."

Isabel glanced over her mother's shoulder to see her father standing in the foyer. His satin crimson doublet glistened in the rays of light coming in from the windows. Ruffles of lace trimmed his spotless breeches, beneath which silk stockings extended to his boots. Below his brown periwig, his ruddy face glowed not with joy but with perspiration and annoyance.

Booted footsteps sounded behind her.

Isabel had forgotten about the captain. Kent stepped beside her, his mouth set in a firm line.

Her mother shrieked and tugged Isabel away.

"Never fear, Mother." Isabel pulled back and patted her mother's hand. "The pirate is with me."

Her mother's face twisted in horror. "With you?"

Toiling with the white cravat bounding from his throat, the earl approached and halted before Kent, studying him with disdain. "A pirate. I daresay. Daughter, what has become of you?"

"Hello, Father." Isabel shuffled her feet and darted her gaze to Kent. Heat swarmed up her face and neck. "May I introduce Captain Carlton? He's assisting me in my search for Frederick."

"Frederick! Who the blast is Frederick?" The earl adjusted his periwig.

Isabel's heart sank. She tried to speak, but a burst of sorrow stuck in her throat.

Kent must have seen her agony. " 'Tis your grandson, milord." He doffed his plumed hat and swept it before him in a bow. But the flexing of his jaw and twitching of his upper lip gave Isabel pause to wonder at the deeper feelings he hid behind them.

"Humph," the earl snorted. "I should have you arrested and hanged."

"On what charge?" Kent smirked.

Sawkins inched up the stairs and took his place next to the earl, a cavalier grin on his lips.

Isabel's heart pounded. She gave Sawkins a pleading look, hoping he would step in. All she needed was for Kent and her father to break into a sword fight. If her father knew the captain was the pirate who'd ravished her, he would abandon the sword and simply fire a pistol shot through Kent's skull. The thought disquieted her. If her parents wouldn't help her, she still needed the captain's ship to search for Frederick.

Sawkins did nothing save stare at her from behind a silly grin.

Clutching her stomach, Isabel stepped between her father and Kent. "Father, please, he is a friend."

Kent's warm whisper drifted onto the back of her neck. "Have I stepped up a notch from scoundrel, then?"

The earl clutched Isabel's arm and pulled her to his side. "No matter. His company is unbefitting someone of your status. You are home now and have no further need for pirates."

Turning toward Kent, he waved his jeweled hand in the air. "You are dismissed."

Kent's dark eyes smoldered as they shifted from the earl to Sawkins.

Isabel wrenched from her father's grasp. "No, Father, your refusal to help me caused me to look elsewhere for assistance. I *do* need the captain." She hoped her declaration would prod her father into offering his help. Instead, the earl's face ballooned into a purplish red.

"Is it not enough that you brought shame on this house? Now you disrespect me!"

Her mother wove her arm through Isabel's. "Come now, Brenton, please do not quarrel. Isabel has just arrived home."

As she stared up into her father's fierce eyes, a tremor ran through Isabel—the same tremor she'd always felt when she faced his stubborn wrath. But more was at stake this time than simply purchasing a gown or attending a ball. Her son's life teetered in the balance betwixt her will and her father's. She swallowed hard and looked at her mother. "Alas, Mother, I have not come home to stay. I thought perhaps you might. . ." She gazed up at her father. "I have returned your carriage. Now, I must go with these men and rescue my son."

Isabel turned to leave, but her mother clung to her arm, desperation pooling in her eyes.

The earl stiffened his jaw and glowered at Isabel.

Sawkins cleared his throat. "Milord." He bowed toward the earl. "If I may offer a suggestion. . . I do need to discuss plans with"—he pointed a slender finger at Kent—"this man. And while we are thus engaged, perhaps Lady Ashton would like to refresh herself within?"

"Brenton"—Isabel's mother touched her husband's arm—"please let these men come inside to discuss whatever business they must. At least we shall have our Isabel back for a brief time."

Raising his chin, the earl gazed off into the distance. "Lord Sawkins may come in, but not the pirate."

Isabel stomped her foot. "His name is Captain Carlton, and 'tis his ship which he offers to help find your grandson."

The earl's green eyes narrowed as he glared at the captain.

"Brenton, please, Isabel is home." Her mother cast a surly glance at Kent. "Surely you can accommodate this. . .this. . .man for a few moments."

Kent peered through the door, then nodded toward Isabel's mother. "How kind of you, but I would much prefer to conduct my business on your porch"—his gaze snapped to the earl—"if you don't think my presence here would defile it overmuch."

The earl's burning glance scoured from Kent to Sawkins, who gave him a reassuring nod. "Very well, but be quick about it." He turned to Sawkins. "And you, my good man, are welcome inside when you are done."

"I will stay out here as well," Isabel stated. "I also wish to hear the news of my son."

Ignoring her, Isabel's mother squeezed her arm. "I'm sure you've not been formally introduced to his lordship, my dear. Lord Sawkins," she cooed, leaning toward the blond gentleman, "may I introduce my daughter, Lady Isabel Ashton? Isabel, this is the Lord Richard Sawkins of Colchester.

He's the son of an earl." She chuckled as though they were just meeting over tea.

"Please forgive Isabel's appearance," her mother continued. "I'm afraid she's just come from a long voyage."

Isabel cast her mother a peevish glance.

"Quite the contrary." Sawkins curled a strand of his hair behind his ear and swept her with his gaze. "The sun and wind become you. You are the picture of beauty, milady."

Isabel's face warmed under his perusal. "Why thank you, milord."

Kent snorted.

With his gaze riveted on Isabel, Sawkins gestured to the earl. "Perhaps you should listen to your father. Go inside, rest from your journey, and I will meet with Captain Carlton here on the porch."

"Ah, at last, the voice of reason," the earl said. "Now come along, Isabel."

Her mother pulled her through the doorway.

Isabel yanked her arm back. "No, Mother. I want to hear about my son." She spun around and thumped into her father's wide chest. He pushed her back into the house, but Isabel slunk around him.

"Isabel!" His harrowing voice roared through the foyer, halting her.

Kent stared at her through the open door, and she gave him a pleading look.

He gestured for her to go in. "I will tell you everything later. You have my word." He nodded.

Her father's arm stretched out before her, grabbed the door, and flung it shut. The sound shook the walls and echoed through the house like the sealing of a tomb.

Isabel turned around. Her glance took in the Italian tiled floor, the wood-paneled walls, the glittering chandelier suspended high above her. Carved oak doors surrounding the foyer led to the study, the library, and the sitting room. A curved staircase ascended to clusters of rooms on the second floor.

Nothing had changed.

Numb, Isabel allowed her mother to escort her upstairs and tried to drown out the wearisome drone of her mother's voice as she chattered on, relaying the recent town gossip.

"Isn't Lord Sawkins charming?" She unlocked the door to Isabel's room and swept her inside. "And so handsome and wealthy. What luck to run into him on this savage island."

"What luck indeed, Mother."

Isabel scanned the room and released a deep breath. Toiletries sparkled on her vanity, the armoire in the corner overflowed with colorful gowns, a white coverlet billowed on her bed beneath mounds of pillows. All the comforts and luxuries she had missed so much. She plopped onto the plush feather bed and spread her hands over the soft silk.

"I'll have a bath brought up, my dear. Refresh yourself and get out of that hideous rag." Her mother rolled her eyes and gave her a maternal smile. "I'll return shortly. Oh, 'tis so good to have you home." She headed out the door, her laughter ringing through the hallway as she left.

Isabel crinkled her brow. Didn't her mother understand she must leave soon? Hadn't she heard any of what Isabel had said?

Soon, two servant girls brought up pail after pail of water and poured them into a white tub in the corner of Isabel's room until the bath was filled. After they left, Isabel tore off her dirty gown, kicked it in the corner, and stepped into the bath. The hot, steaming water splashed on her chin as she plopped into the porcelain tub, expecting the warmth to soothe her nerves like it always had—but today it only seemed to aggravate her further. Hours and hours she used to spend soaking in this very tub, dreaming of a grand future, without a care in the world. Now, though her home, her parents, and this very room had remained the same, Isabel realized with a start that she had changed. All she wanted to do was get back downstairs as soon as possible and discover the plan for Frederick's rescue.

After a quick scrub, she jumped out of the tub, raced a towel over her body, and snatched one of her gowns from the armoire, donning it hastily. She combed and pinned her hair up and sprayed herself with perfume, then leaned to glance at her reflection in the mirror of her vanity. She barely recognized the woman who glared back at her—no longer the innocent girl who'd last graced this room.

Isabel scurried to the window and scanned the lush green lawns and gardens. Her father had done well since she'd been gone. If she stayed now, surely it wouldn't be long before she'd enjoy all the luxuries they'd once had in Hertfordshire. Or perhaps he'd even make enough money to move them

back to England. That had been her dream when they'd first been forced to New Providence. Now that she saw it coming to fruition, it no longer seemed important. All Isabel could think about was what Lord Sawkins and Captain Carlton were discussing below. She would not wait another minute.

Darting to the door, she flung it open and crashed into her mother, nearly knocking her over.

"Dear," her mother stammered as Isabel steadied her, "where are you going in such a hurry?" She took a step back. "You look absolutely stunning. Lord Sawkins will be so delighted," she cooed, ushering Isabel back into the room.

"Why would I be concerned with delighting Lord Sawkins?" Isabel glanced out the open door.

"Why, he's everything you've ever wanted. He's what you've dreamed of. He seems quite taken with you, my dear." She clasped Isabel's arm and leaned toward her. "And he doesn't seem to mind your little indiscretion."

Isabel stomped away, feeling her heart wrench. "I would hardly call my son an indiscretion."

Isabel's mother pursed her lips. "You seem different, dear."

"I *am* different, Mother. I have a child."

Her mother flung her gaze away and busied herself with straightening the pillows on the bed. Isabel studied her, an ache in her heart forming for the woman she had once admired above all others. Her chestnut hair was curled and pinned elegantly at the back of her head, circling a beautiful creamy face. Only the tiny lines around her eyes and the slight sag of the skin on her neck gave away her age. Isabel's heart went out to her, for she now understood the agony of having one's only child kidnapped. How horrifying it must have been for her mother when she'd had no news of Isabel for months. But many good things had happened to Isabel during that time as well. Should she tell her mother about her newfound faith? Isabel wrung her hands and glanced out the door again. The baritone sound of male voices lured her downstairs. She hated to delay even another minute her quest for her son. Her mother's sweet face swung to hers, nothing but love and adoration flickering in her gaze.

Isabel rushed to her mother's side and grasped her hands. "And I've found God, or I suppose He found me. I've given my life to Jesus, Mother, and it's been so wonderful." She longed for her mother to do the same, knowing it would make such a difference in her life.

"Well, yes." Her mother tucked a loose strand of Isabel's hair into her bun. "We took you to church when you were young."

"I don't mean church, Mother. I mean a real relationship with God."

Her mother furrowed her brow. "Never mind that now, dear. You are home. Let us forget the past few years and begin where we left off."

Sorrow swept through Isabel, and a huge sense of loss. At one time she'd been so close to her mother. Now she felt as though she were talking to a stranger. She gave her mother's hand a squeeze and smiled. "It's good to see you."

Tears moistened her mother's eyes.

"Shall we go see what Father is doing?" Isabel tugged on her mother's arm.

Down in the sitting room, the earl sat in his padded leather chair by an immense fireplace that he'd insisted on building but never used in the tropical heat. With pipe in hand, he spoke pointedly to Lord Sawkins, who stood with one hand draped over the mantel.

The spicy scent of tobacco drifted over Isabel as she and her mother entered. Lord Sawkins turned, and his eyes lit up.

Isabel scanned the room. "Where is the captain?"

"On the porch where he belongs," her father said, taking a puff from his pipe.

Ignoring him, Isabel approached Lord Sawkins. "I beg you, milord. Please tell me what you told Captain Carlton."

"I'd be happy to, milady."

Isabel's mother wrinkled her brow. "Surely you aren't encouraging her in this preposterous trek, milord."

"Mother, how can you say that?" Isabel sobbed. Her gaze shifted to her father. "Every minute I linger here is one more minute Frederick is lost. If you won't help me, Father, I must leave immediately with the captain."

Isabel's father rose. His immense frame swallowed her up in his shadow. "I forbid it, Isabel. I thought perhaps a bath would not only clean you of your filth but wash away these foolish notions as well. You are home now, and home you will stay."

Taking a deep breath, Isabel stepped toward him. Her knees quivered.

"I cannot do as you say, Father. I must find my son."

"Nay, I will not have it. You will—"

"Darling." Her mother clutched Isabel's arm, but her pleading gaze landed on her husband. "Perhaps these men could find the boy and bring him back here."

"I'll not have that son of a pirate in this house!" Her father flung his pipe against the marble fireplace.

Clutching a hand to her stomach, Isabel coughed as her eyes filled with tears. "He is your grandson, and he always will be." She yanked her arm from her mother's grasp and ran out the front door.

Kent jumped up from the bottom step, concern warming his eyes. Sawkins stomped down the stairs after Isabel and onto the gravel pathway.

"If you sail off with this pirate," her father bellowed from the doorway, "and bring further disgrace to the Ashton name, I will disown you as my daughter!"

Isabel halted and turned around. Her mother gasped. The earl's gaze hardened in his reddening face.

A warm breeze blew in from the sea and fluttered the leaves on the gardenia bushes surrounding the porch. Isabel glanced over the immaculate house, the beautiful gardens, the wealth that seeped from the very ground beneath her feet. Her eyes met her mother's beseeching look. All Isabel had to do was walk back in that house, back where she would be safe and cared for and where all her dreams would come true.

Even as she stared at her father, moisture glistened in his unbending gaze. He loved her in his own way. She knew that. How could she turn her back on her family? How could she turn down her only chance at happiness? If she left now, she'd be nothing but a desolate commoner with no money, no husband, no title, and no future.

Isabel gazed into the pleading eyes of her parents, her heart crumbling in her chest. Then she turned her back to them and forced her quivering legs to walk down the gravel pathway. She skirted the carriage as Kent and Sawkins fell in step beside her. By the time she reached the gate, sobs burned in her throat, but she swallowed them as the servant swung the iron lattice open with a grinding screech. It clanked shut behind her, locking her forever from all that mattered to her in this world—all save Frederick. And it was his call alone that beckoned her onward.

Chapter 9
The Deception

Sawkins checked his pistol for the third time and returned it to its holster on his baldric. He paced the dirty alleyway, careful to avoid the puddles of slop that had been heaved from the windows above. His nose curled at the stench of human waste and rotting food. Bawdy music and roaring laughter blared from the tavern next to him. He rubbed his sweaty fingers over the hilt of his cutlass.

A splash and the crunch of sand alerted him, and he squinted into the shadows. Captain John Morris emerged into the scattered rays of the moon, a twisted grin on his lips. "You sail tonight?"

"That we do." Sawkins caught movement behind Morris and reached for his pistol. The slight whimper of a baby reached his ears.

"Calm yourself. 'Tis only the babe." Morris fingered his own pistol. "You're as skittish as a ship mouse."

A dark-skinned woman lingered behind Morris, holding a wrapped bundle to her chest.

"You brought the child here?" Sawkins found Morris's audacity invigorating. "What if she hears her baby cry?"

" 'Tis all part of the fun of it." Morris chuckled. "We have an accord then?"

"Yes, as planned." Sawkins hesitated, his thoughts drifting to Isabel. "The woman—she's quite delectable. I had no idea Captain Carlton had such exquisite taste."

"Do not underestimate him. He is a formidable foe." Morris turned

and spat onto the ground. "And don't allow your weak sentiments to dissuade you. I know what a fool you are for a comely face. She must go, along with the child."

Sawkins nodded. "I'll see you in a week."

Morris grunted and strode away.

Clutching Kent's outstretched hand, Isabel stepped into the cockboat once again. This time, she stepped in no longer a lady, no longer with title or wealth. Even when she'd been living in Port Royal, she'd always fostered the hope of coming home and regaining her status someday. Yet an hour ago, she had turned her back on her sobbing mother and the beseeching eyes of her father and walked away.

But how could she do any less?

Captain Carlton had been silent on their walk back to the docks. Her parents had treated him miserably, perhaps no more shamefully than she had, but she knew who *he* was—the wretched pirate who had ravished her. They had only judged him by his appearance. He had taken their insults with an honor she was unaware he possessed.

Sitting down in the tottering boat, she drew her shawl over her shoulders against the chill rising from the water and the vulgar gazes of Smithy and the other pirates. The captain jumped in and sat next to her just as Lord Sawkins clomped down the wharf.

"My apologies. I was delayed." He leaped into the boat, out of breath.

"We nearly left you." Kent's voice seeped with disappointment.

The soft cry of a baby floated on the evening breeze.

Isabel jumped to her feet. "Frederick!" She knew that wail anywhere. She started toward the dock, but the captain held her back.

"Milady, there are many babies in town."

"No. It's Frederick." She struggled. "Let me go." Wringing from his grasp, she scrambled over the men to get out of the boat.

"Lady Ashton"—Sawkins grabbed her hand as she passed—"it cannot be your son. I passed a young mother and her baby just moments ago. Besides, I know where your son is. He is not here, I assure you."

The strength of his hand comforted her. Concern tightened the lines on his face. He was right. She was overreacting. "Of course." She sighed, disappointment sapping her sudden burst of energy. "I'm afraid 'tis been a most trying day."

Sawkins patted her hand and led her back to her seat.

The captain's dark gaze followed her, a pained look flowing from it. Did he realize he was the cause of all her agony—the loss of her innocence, the loss of her child, and now the loss of her status and wealth? Hatred filled her heart, though she knew it was wrong to give in to it. She gazed over the dark water shimmering in clusters of silver flung upon the bay from the city lights.

Smithy shoved off, and soon the dark hull of Kent's ship loomed above them. A lantern hung from the taffrail, casting its spooky glow upon the stern of the frigate. Isabel examined the ornate carvings decorating the ship. The name RESTITUTION stood out in bold black letters. She glanced at Kent. "I thought your ship was the *Vanquisher*."

His expression was lost in the shadow of his hat, all save his lips, which flattened into a thin line. "I'm done with vanquishing."

The cockboat bounced against the hull of the frigate in a muted thud of moist wood. Isabel huffed. Did he think he could make amends by merely renaming his ship? "Restitution begins in the heart, not on the side of a ship." She stood and grabbed the rope ladder.

"I had to start somewhere." He grinned, clutching her elbow against a sudden wave that lifted the boat. "After you, milady."

Once aboard, Isabel delayed returning to her cabin until she had spoken with Lord Sawkins. While Captain Carlton stormed across the deck, shouting orders for the unfurling of courses and mainsails and the weighing of anchor, she waited by the railing for the nobleman to swing himself over the bulwarks. He planted his boots firmly on the deck, straightened his doublet, and scanned the ship with an imperious gaze.

"Lord Sawkins, may I have a word with you?" Isabel took a step toward him.

He turned, his features rising into a noble air. "Why of course, milady. Whatever are you doing unescorted on the deck of this pirate ship?" He glanced toward the captain. "I should have realized a ruffian such as Kent would not know the proper way to treat a lady."

Isabel's heart fluttered at his protective attitude. Here was a true gentleman. "I remained above only to question you concerning Frederick's

whereabouts. I hope you don't mind my forwardness, but I'm sure you can understand how anxious I am for any information. I inquired of the captain, but all he was able to tell me was that Frederick is headed toward Cartagena."

"Indeed." He placed her hand inside the crook of his elbow and led her away from the pirates scurrying over the deck. "My sources in town have informed me that Cartagena is Captain Morris's intended destination."

Cartagena. So far away. Isabel's thoughts raced. "I don't understand. Why would he take Frederick there?"

Lord Sawkins let out a deep breath, leaned on the railing, and looked out over the small town. As night fell, the warehouses, taverns, and shops blurred into an indistinct clump of gray from which blazed gleaming lights. "I am not sure. But it matters not since we will most likely reach him before he arrives there." He gave her a reassuring smile and patted her hand.

Isabel glanced across the deck and found the captain's piercing gaze upon her. He was a good seaman, and her hopes soared, encouraged as well by the strength of the man beside her. "And Captain Carlton knows how to find him?"

"Yes. Never fear."

Shouts from above drew her attention up to the masts and riggings as the barefooted pirates, clinging to thin ropes, unfurled and set the sails. Some of them climbed so high that Isabel could no longer see them as the night swallowed them up. She wondered at their bravery—or was it foolhardiness. Down on deck, five pirates encircled the capstan and heaved it, groaning, until the anchor lifted and the ship lurched forward.

Isabel fell against Lord Sawkins, who caught her in a tight embrace—one far too familiar. She wrestled from his grasp and took a step back.

He ran a finger over his shiny mustache and grinned. "My apologies, milady. I thought you were falling."

Warming under his perusal, Isabel patted her hair and averted her gaze to see the captain storming across the deck. From the fiery look in his eyes, it appeared as though he intended to push Sawkins overboard.

Kent halted before them, every muscle in his jaw flexing. His eyes grazed over Isabel and landed on Sawkins in a sharp squint. "I'll have Smithy show you to your berth."

"My berth?" Sawkins chuckled. "Surely you don't expect me to sleep with the other men?"

"You'll sleep where I tell you to sleep."

Animosity saturated the air, and Isabel wondered what history existed between these two volatile men.

Moments passed as Sawkins glared at the captain. "Very well, but I'll escort Lady Ashton to her quarters first, if you please."

"Nay, I do not please." Kent grabbed Isabel's arm. She winced, and he loosened his grip as he led her down the companionway stairs.

"You're hurting me."

"Forgive me." He released her after they stepped inside her cabin. "It was not my intention." He shut the door and glared at her, flicking his head back. A spark of alarm fired through Isabel. "I must insist you stay away from Sawkins," he added sharply. "Do not allow yourself to be alone with him."

Isabel shot him a venomous look. How dare he demand anything of her after what he'd done? "You may insist whatever you please, Captain"— she thrust out her chin—"but I happen to find him quite charming."

Kent snorted.

Isabel searched his face. "Why do you hate him so?"

"I don't hate him. I know him, 'tis all. He is not what he appears."

"What he appears is every bit the gentleman you are not," Isabel spat, rubbing her itching arms. "You're jealous."

"Ha!" He gave her a sideways glance. "Of that arrogant halfwit? He's naught but a pompous, spoiled boy who fancies himself strong and clever enough to play the pirate."

Fury raged within her as she stared at the man who'd ruined her life. "Why would a man of title and wealth wish to lower himself to the likes of you?"

Kent's upper lip twitched. He narrowed his eyes and approached her.

Isabel flinched and backed away, stumbling into the bed.

Halting, he studied her, and the cold shield fell from his gaze. "Do you not know by now I will never hurt you again?" He turned away momentarily before he glanced back at her, a sheen glistening in his eyes.

The hatred that had burned within her only moments before cooled beneath his tender look. She glanced down and wrapped her arms around

her chest. Confusion battled against her resolve. When she lifted her gaze again, it was to Frederick's eyes—those brown yearning eyes that dove into her soul, wrapping it with cords of love.

"Your son resembles you." The words flew from her mouth before she realized their kind intent. Oh how she wanted to hate this man, but at the moment, his resemblance to Frederick forbade her.

The captain's lips curved in a grin that reached his eyes.

A moment of silence passed, then Isabel cleared the emotion from her throat. "Are we sailing toward Cartagena?"

"For now, yes." He gave her a cynical look, then glanced away.

"You don't believe Lord Sawkins?"

Kent planted his fists on his hips. "Let's just say I've found it necessary to use caution when dealing with his *lordship*."

At the mention of Sawkins, the captain's demeanor had instantly hardened, and Isabel found she missed the gentle compassion he had so recently shown.

"Rest assured, milady, I can find Morris. There isn't a ship in these waters that I cannot locate when I set my sights upon her."

His confidence enlivened her hopes, but at the same time, it reminded her that he was a man accustomed to getting what he wanted.

Turning, he clutched the door handle and glanced at her over his shoulder. "Pray, would you grace us with your presence at dinner?"

The warm appeal in his eyes, coupled with the growling in her stomach, hastened Isabel's quick acceptance. Besides, she hoped to see Lord Sawkins again. He intrigued her now more than ever.

The captain ordered her to lock the door, and then he left.

Crack! The wind filled the sails, sending the ship lunging forward. Isabel clung to the bedpost and listened to the purling of the ocean against the creaking hull. Out into the unknown dark waters the ship sped—dark and unknown like her future. Plopping on the ledge by the window, she smoothed her skirts around her and watched as the flickering lights of Charles Towne dissipated like candles snuffed out by one by one. Grief overcame her, and she forced back tears. She would not cry. She'd made her choice. *Oh God, what have I done? I can never go back. I am truly an orphan now.*

Words poured over her from the Bible—words she'd heard Reverend

Thomas often quote: *"Behold, what manner of love the Father hath bestowed upon us, that we should be called the sons of God."*

A comforting warmth flowed around her. *"You are My child. I have adopted you."*

"Thank You, Lord." Isabel sobbed, finally freeing the tears from her eyes.

An hour later, when she entered the captain's cabin, her mouth watered at the bounty spread across the table: pineapples, guavas, peanuts, maize, yucca root, and steaming crab. Sweet, savory scents filled the air. Her stomach grumbled. A pot of baked pudding sat near the end of the table. She glanced toward the captain as he spoke with Hann. Had he remembered pudding was her favorite food? She shook the thought from her mind.

Lord Sawkins stepped beside her, brushing against her arm.

Isabel backed away to a more proper distance. "It pleases me to see you here, Lord Sawkins. I feared I would be forced to suffer only the company of pirates again."

"You poor dear." He curled a strand of hair behind his ear. "I don't know how you have endured such hardships."

The captain finished his discussion with Hann and turned to face them as Smithy, Cutter, and the helmsman bounded through the door. Cutter winked at Isabel, but when she turned to introduce Lord Sawkins, the nobleman had taken a step back. The features of his face twisted in repulsion.

Cutter glared at him.

"Lord Sawkins, are you all right?" Isabel asked.

The captain's deep voice interrupted. "Never mind him. He's always been a bit squeamish. He finds scars grotesque, don't you, Sawkins?" Kent slapped him on the back.

Sawkins coughed, then straightened his stance. "Forgive me. I was not expecting—"

"Lord Sawkins," Isabel interrupted, "this is Cutter, the ship's doctor. Cutter, Lord Richard Sawkins."

Sawkins gave a brief nod while keeping his eyes glued on Cutter.

"A pleasure, milord," the doctor sneered, eyeing him with equal suspicion.

Hann squeezed through the crowd. "His scars would be well earned, milord." His violet eyes stormed as they peered at Sawkins. "I see *ye* 'ave none to boast about."

Smithy chuckled from the table, where he was pouring himself a drink, and Sawkins raised one brow at the short boy.

After the men drifted to their seats, Isabel turned to Cutter. "I'm sorry."

"Ah, 'tis nothing, milady. I'm used to it."

The captain insisted Isabel sit next to him while he placed Sawkins at the other side of the table. Smithy sat on Isabel's right, a rank odor emanating from him, and the helmsman took the next chair.

No sooner had they sat down, then Sawkins shot to his feet, horror etched on his face. "I will not dine with a rat!" He withdrew a handkerchief and held it to his nose, pointing at the helmsman sitting across from him.

Leaning forward, Isabel spotted the rodent poking its twitching black nose through the helmsman's long straggly hair. Pressing a hand to her stomach to ease her rising nausea, she sat back with a sigh. What did she expect on board this vile ship?

"Stinking, filthy beast," Sawkins hissed.

"He's no dirtier than ye are!" The helmsman cupped the creature in his hands and stood. His chair scraped across the wood like a challenge.

Fingering the hilt of his cutlass, Sawkins glared at him, still holding the cloth to his nose.

The captain gave the helmsman a judicious look. "Hoornes, I realize there are indeed other beasts present at this table"—his eyes flickered to Sawkins—"but haven't I asked you not to bring that particular one?"

"But he needs to be eatin', too, Cap'n," Hoornes replied, running his fingers down the rat's back.

"Faith, there's a lady present." Sawkins waved his hand toward Isabel as if he just remembered her.

Smithy chuckled. "I don't see 'er making as much a fuss as ye are."

Hann slapped the table and laughed.

Kent cleared his throat, and Isabel got the impression he suppressed a smile. "Regardless. Let us not enhance the barbaric opinion I'm sure the lady already holds of us."

Too late, Isabel thought.

He gestured toward Hoornes. "Grab some food and be gone with you then."

"With pleasure, Cap'n." Hoornes placed the rat on his shoulder and snatched a handful of peanuts and a chunk of bread before turning to face Isabel.

"Beggin' yer pardon, milady." Hoornes nodded, then narrowed his eyes upon Sawkins before marching out the door.

When all were seated again, the men began plunging into the food.

Isabel cleared her throat and scanned the group with a harsh glare, drawing their attention toward her. She'd let their lack of thanksgiving slide before, but no more. "Shouldn't we give thanks to God for His provision?"

All eyes landed on her with brows raised. Smithy's chunk of meat halted in midair on its way to his gaping mouth. One by one, each man dropped his food back onto his plate.

"I see no point in that," Smithy said with a guffaw. "We done provided for ourselves."

"Did you, Mr. Smithy?" Isabel glared at him. "Did you create yourself? Did you give yourself two legs, two arms, and a brain so you could acquire what you need?"

"We aren't sure about the brain yet, milady," Hann chimed in with a snicker. Chuckles burst from the other men, and Smithy grunted.

"By all means"—Sawkins gestured toward Isabel—"we should bless the food."

Cutter gave her a sideways glance. "Though you'll be speaking to the air, if it brings you some comfort, I'll agree to it."

"But what if I'm not speaking to the air, Doctor. What if you're wrong?"

"Then I would insist upon giving thanks where thanks are due, milady." He nodded.

Isabel allowed her gaze to wander over each man, finally landing on the captain, who, with arms crossed over his chest, merely grinned at her.

"Shall we then, gentlemen?"

After a few mumbles, they closed their eyes.

With a grin, Isabel shut her eyes as well and bowed her head. "We thank You, Lord, for watching over us and for this food. Amen."

"Amen," the men parroted and dove back into their meal.

With her appetite restored, Isabel enjoyed sampling each of the delicious fruits and the succulent crab as she listened to the men talk.

Hann, quiet as usual, poured himself another drink—or was that his third?

The captain, however, merely sipped his rum. Isabel caught his warm gaze scouring over her more than once, sending her pulse quickening each time. *Am I still afraid of him? Or perhaps 'tis just anger that sets my head to reeling when he looks at me that way.*

"May I ask your forgiveness, sir"—Sawkins directed his question toward Cutter, but his glance made sure he had Isabel's ear as well—"for my earlier behavior? If you'll permit me to explain myself."

"There's no need, milord." Cutter continued eating without looking up.

Sawkins took a drink. " 'Tis quite all right. You see, my father fought in the war with the Spanish in '54 and was severely injured—crippled for life. It was quite difficult for me to see him suffer so miserably."

The captain coughed and pounded his chest.

"I'm sorry to hear of it, milord," Cutter said, the look in his eyes belying his words.

"When I saw you, it brought back those painful memories." Sawkins dropped his gaze and seemed unable to speak further.

Hann snorted. "Cutter is not a cripple, your lordship. He is more of a man than most on this ship."

All fell silent, eyes agape toward Hann, including Cutter who, with furrowed brow, seemed unsure how to respond. Ignoring the comment, he scooted his chair slightly apart from his young friend.

The lad let out a sigh and returned to his meal.

"What is your real name, Doctor?" Sawkins broke the awkward silence. "If I might ask."

Hann set down his fork. "He is John Barnard Preston of Canterbury."

"Seems ye got yerself an admirer, eh, Cutter?" Smithy chuckled, then studied Hann and instantly shrank back into his chair "Ye aren't no catamite, are ye?"

Hann sprang to his feet. His chair tumbled to the floor behind him. "Of course not, ye old blubbering fool." He fingered the hilt of his cutlass.

93

"And I'll have ye take that back before I run ye through and carve ye up for dinner."

"Run me through, ye little squeaky varmint? Ha." Smithy plucked one more piece of meat from his plate and shoved it into his mouth, then stood. "I dares ye to come over and try."

Isabel's heart flipped in her chest. Hann had been nothing but kind to her, and he was just a boy. By size and cruelty alone, Smithy would surely best him in a fight.

"I'm sure Mr. Smithy did not mean what he said, did you, Mr. Smithy?" She widened her eyes toward the first mate.

Hann stepped back and weaved around the table, heading toward Smithy. "Naw, I'll be thinkin' he meant it all right."

The captain jumped up. "There'll be no fighting at my table." He faced Smithy, eyes flaring. "Take the insult back or deal with me, not the boy."

Smithy scowled, lowered his head, and mumbled, "Mebbe ye ain't what I said ye were."

Halting, Hann remained standing.

"Have a seat, Hann." The captain motioned toward the table.

"I've lost me appetite." With one glance toward Cutter, Hann left the room, slamming the door behind him.

Sawkins grinned.

All eyes were upon Smithy. "What?" He scratched his bushy sideburns and belched.

The stench of sour rum and decaying food drifted over Isabel, and she held her hand to her nose.

Kent leaned on the table. "You forget yourself, Smithy. There is a lady present."

"Beggin' yer pardon, miss," Smithy recited with disgust and shifted a sly glance toward Sawkins.

Holding her stomach, Isabel slowly rose. Perhaps she had eaten too fast, or perhaps the company and the conversation had curdled the food in her stomach. "I believe I shall retire, gentlemen."

Kent, Sawkins, and Cutter sprang to their feet. Cursing, Smithy joined them, swayed, and teetered against Isabel.

With a shriek, she pushed him away. He grabbed onto the table to keep from falling.

Kent raised his elbow. "I'll escort you." Though his voice was commanding, a gentle invitation beckoned from his eyes. It was the first time he'd offered her his arm and not taken hers by force.

Hesitating, Isabel studied him. He widened his eyes as if to reassure her of his intentions, but she did not wish to give him hope for any affection between them. Refusing his arm, she turned and headed toward the door. The sound of his boots thudded behind her.

Slowing his pace to match hers, he frowned as they strolled to her cabin in silence. Much to Isabel's surprise, no fear rose to grip her along the way. His warmth and strength coupled with his scent of leather and spice seemed to have the opposite effect.

In the doorway, he paused. His gaze drifted to her lips, remained there for a moment, and then rose back to her eyes. She wondered whether he thought of kissing her, and alarm coursed through her. He gave her a sorrowful smile before he bowed and closed the door.

Taking the companionway stairs in one giant leap, Kent burst onto the main deck, having no desire to return to the heinous company below in his cabin. The hot, heavy wind blasted over him, and he took a deep breath and closed his eyes, trying to quell his thunderous passions. Sparkling jade eyes stared at him in his thoughts, so often firing hatred his way, but tonight he'd seen something soften behind their harsh gaze. As she'd stood there in the cabin, looking so vulnerable, it was all he could do to stop himself from taking her in his arms and covering those full pink lips with his. But he didn't want to frighten or repulse her with his actions and felt certain he would have done both.

Nodding at the watchman up on the foredeck, Kent pounded to the railing and crossed his arms over his chest. The moon, nearly full now, hung low in the sky. Like a lighthouse in a storm, it sent fingers of light across the raging sea, offering guidance through the dark night until a new day dawned.

He chuckled, remembering how the pirates with morsels of food nigh lifted to their lips had been halted in their tracks with Isabel's insistence that they say grace. What tenacity. And they'd done it! Her faith remained strong amidst all the tragedies in her life. And what courage she must possess to leave her family and everything she valued. It baffled him. He knew what she'd given up for her son—their son. She loved Frederick, despite her feelings for his father. Somehow the thought warmed his soul but also saddened him. No one had ever loved him that way. He had never been worthy.

Deep guffaws interrupted his thoughts, and he turned to see Sawkins and Smithy emerging from the main hatch. Kent wondered at their acquaintance. Like attracted like, he supposed. They were suited for each other.

Sawkins posed another problem. Kent regretted taking him on board, but the insufferable man had withheld the exact location of Morris's expedition as payment for his passage. Cartagena was the only name he'd disclosed, with a promise to offer further details on arrival.

Blast! Kent gripped the railing. He had vowed never to take that devilish, lying scoundrel on board his ship. Now that he was here, Kent determined to remain sober and alert at all times, especially with Isabel on board.

He saw the way Sawkins looked at her, like a wolf licking his lips at his intended prey. Lord Sawkins was a nobleman, yes—by his mother's blood only. But nothing noble existed in his dark soul. Rumor had it he'd left a trail of broken women across the Caribbean. Kent thought of his own conquests, and shame tugged at his soul as he realized he'd done the very same thing. Hadn't he also pounced on Isabel as if she were just another prize—another trophy to add to his collection? Hanging his head, he swallowed a burst of guilt.

Sawkins would no doubt dangle his position before Isabel like a mesmerizing charm. Kent must warn her before she succumbed to his wiles, for she had no idea that beneath the gallant facade lurked a poisonous viper.

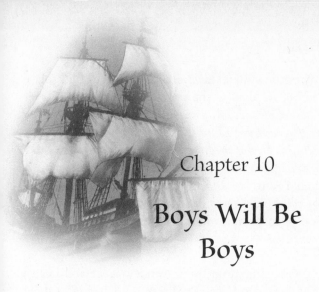

Chapter 10

Boys Will Be Boys

Isabel's eyes popped open. She bolted up in bed. Focusing her sleepy gaze over the bright room, she tossed off her quilt, allowing air to cool her body, damp with perspiration. The heat had risen along with the sun that now glared in through the window. She chided herself for sleeping so long and wondered why Hann had not woken her with breakfast. No doubt the young pirate was embarrassed about the incident at dinner. She couldn't blame him. It was a terrible thing to be accused of, especially if it weren't true. Yet she had wondered herself what affections existed between Hann and Cutter.

Flinging off her nightdress, Isabel took a cloth and dabbed cool water from the basin over her body. The red bumps littering her arms had not disappeared, though she'd applied the ointment Cutter had given her. The hot, humid air seemed only to irritate them further, and Isabel found it difficult not to be continually scratching them. With a sigh, she opened the jar and rubbed more of the salve upon her arms, then chose a fresh gown and pinned her hair atop her head in a loose bun, allowing tiny curls to tickle her neck.

The Bible beckoned to her from the table, and she sank into one of the chairs and skimmed through its pages. "Father, speak to me this morning. I need Your wisdom." She longed for Reverend Thomas. He had this book nearly memorized and always knew where to find solace within. A sudden puff of wind blew the pages over, and Isabel's eyes landed on Isaiah 49: *"Shall the prey be taken from the mighty, or the lawful captive delivered? But thus saith the LORD, Even the captives of the mighty shall be taken away, and the prey of the terrible shall be delivered: for I will contend with him that contendeth with thee, and I will save thy children."*

Those last incredible words rose from the pages and dove into her heart: *"I will save thy children."* Where had that wind come from? No windows or doors were open. A warm shimmer passed over her, and she knew God had spoken to her.

"Thank You, Lord."

Closing the book, she bounced on to the window ledge and looked out, soaring on wings of hope. The Creator of the universe had assured her Frederick would be saved. What else had she to fear? Who else had she to fear? Certainly not Captain Carlton. She no longer believed he would assault her. And with Lord Sawkins—a true gentleman—on board, another assurance of safety settled on her heart.

Excitement bubbled within Isabel as she gazed over the placid sea and thought of Frederick. "Mother's coming to get you, darling."

Yet not a foamy wave in the distance or a toss of the ship confirmed her declaration. The brilliant turquoise sea stared back at her like shimmering glass. No snap of sails, no creak of the rolling hull reached her ears, no sound save the clanking of swords. The unusual silence that snaked through the ship threatened to crush her newfound hope.

Grabbing her key, Isabel unlatched the door, traveled quickly down the hallway and up the companionway stairs, and burst onto the main deck. A wall of scalding air assaulted her along with a multitude of ribald gazes. Her glance took in the deck roasting beneath the sun. Clusters of pirates huddled in patches of shade afforded them beneath fore- and quarterdeck stairs and next to masts, crates, and barrels. Her eyes locked with those of the captain who, with sword leveled upon another pirate, had also stopped to glare at her when she'd emerged.

His bare chest heaved as his imperious gaze raked over her. Clad only in breeches, he shook the hair back from his face and let it fall to his shoulders in wild disarray. The other pirate—Gibbons, she thought his name was—froze, sword in hand, beneath the pointed tip of Kent's blade.

"Milady." The captain bowed. "To what do we owe the honor of your presence?"

Shielding her eyes, Isabel pulled her gaze from his muscular chest to Cutter, who was perched upon a barrel, playing cards with three pirates beside the foredeck. One of them was Logan, the master gunner. The other two she didn't know. "Why aren't we moving?" She snapped her gaze back to the captain.

"The wind has left us. There's naught to be done."

Isabel glanced over the glassy sea and then up to the quarterdeck, where Lord Sawkins sat in the shade of an old sailcloth strung betwixt the mizzen mast and its shrouds, sipping a drink. She dabbed at the perspiration forming on her neck and let out an exasperated sigh. "But we must catch Morris."

The captain offered her a playful grin. "If I could, I would move heaven, earth, and even these seas for your ladyship, but alas, even *I* cannot control the wind and tides."

Snickers rose from the pirates.

Isabel pursed her lips, feeling the familiar hopelessness claw its way back into her soul. "Well, at least we have discovered you are not truly master of all you see."

Cutter flashed a smile at her from behind raised cards, and Smithy's chortle was instantly silenced by the captain's stern gaze.

"Lady Ashton," Lord Sawkins called from the quarterdeck, "won't you join me?"

Throwing her nose in the air, she twirled around and climbed the stairs, casting a haughty glance over her shoulder.

The smirk on Kent's face soured.

Sawkins rose, hand extended, as Isabel reached the top of the stairs and led her to a stack of crates beside his. The hard wood chafed the skin through her dress. Tickling beads of perspiration slid down her back, but at least beneath the covering, the bite of the sun's heat was not as sharp.

Modishly dressed in a ruffled Holland shirt, Sawkins wore no doublet, giving Isabel a chance to survey his handsome frame.

"Hann!" he bellowed to the boy who stood against the quarterdeck railing, looking down upon the main deck.

Slowly, Hann turned his head.

"A drink for Lady Ashton, if you please." Sawkins snapped his fingers.

Hann crinkled his nose and narrowed his eyes into tiny slits before he faced forward again, unmoving.

"Humph," Sawkins snorted. "If I were captain of this ship, I'd have such insubordination flogged." He stomped his boot upon the deck, his face twisting in rage. But as soon as he turned toward Isabel, his features softened.

Isabel gave him a gentle smile. "I fear you are mistaken, milord. Hann is neither a slave nor a servant, but a quartermaster upon this ship."

"Never mind. I shall go below and get you a drink myself." Leaning over, he placed a moist kiss on her hand and left.

The sharp *clang* of swords drew her attention below to where the two men had resumed parrying.

Kent lunged toward Gibbons, who raised his sword and met his blast with a vibrating ring. With a quick step to his left, the captain spun around and slashed across his opponent's waist. If Gibbons had not jumped back, the captain would surely have drawn blood.

Isabel raised a hand to her mouth. Were they fighting or only practicing? She'd never seen anything quite like it. Hilt to hilt, they pummeled each other. Kent drove Gibbons back with forceful slashes of his blade, the pirate barely able to stave off the captain's powerful blows. A thrust toward the pirate's thigh caught Gibbons off guard and sliced his breeches before he could swing his sword about.

Isabel found she couldn't pull her eyes from the battle—especially not from Kent. He fought with such skill and ferocity, his strained muscles swelling across his chest and arms, his face set in grim determination.

When Sawkins returned, his large frame blocked her view, and she craned her neck to see around him. After easing onto his seat, he handed her a mug and followed the direction of her gaze. He spoke, his voice dripping with disdain.

Isabel heard his murmur but was unclear what he'd said. "I beg your pardon?"

He leaned toward her, and the sharp scent of cedar oil from his mustache stung her nostrils. "Savage beasts, I said." He nodded toward the sword fight.

She returned her gaze to Kent, who had just swung to his right and brought his sword from behind him in a clever move that sent Gibbons reeling backward. "Yes." Isabel feigned a smile. "Brutes." Yet the word floundered in effect as it fell from her lips.

Sawkins shifted in his seat. "However, I cannot help but perceive your interest in the game."

"Interest?" Isabel raised her hand and swatted nonexistent wind over her, wishing she'd not left her fan below and wondering where the blast of sudden heat came from. "Not at all. I merely am curious how they can exert themselves in such torrid weather." She gave him a lopsided smile.

Sawkins sipped his drink. His blue eyes scoured over her.

One more strike and Kent knocked Gibbons's sword from his grasp, sending it clanging onto the deck. Bending over, Gibbons held a hand up, with chest heaving and sweat dripping from his brow. "I concede, Captain."

Kent mopped his brow. "Then I believe you owe Lady Ashton an apology."

"An apology?" Isabel glared at the defeated pirate and then at Lord Sawkins. "Whatever for?"

Sawkins dabbed the perspiration on his neck with his handkerchief. " 'Twas naught but a trifling squabble amongst savages."

Kent pointed his sword at Gibbons, who stood, grunting, and glanced up at Isabel. Drops of sweat glistened in the coarse hairs of his chest, and he squinted at her from beneath thick, dark eyebrows. "Me apologies, milady," he muttered. Kent's sword poked deeper into his side. "Fer callin' ye a trollop."

A trollop? Indignation lifted Isabel's shoulders. She glared at Sawkins. "A trifling squabble? You call this degradation of my character a trifle?"

Sawkins shifted his gaze uncomfortably over the deck. "You must consider the source, milady. There is no honor amongst pirates."

"Indeed, but I fear it was not their honor which needed defending," Isabel huffed and returned her gaze to the deck below where Kent's sly grin indicated he was enjoying their banter. If she had expected anyone to come to her defense at such an insult, it would have been Lord Sawkins, not the captain.

Flinging his saturated hair behind him, Kent scanned the pirates loitering over the ship. "Anyone else have an opinion regarding Lady Ashton?"

Grumbles emanated from the mob, but no one stepped forward.

The captain's squinted gaze landed on Sawkins. "Lord Sawkins, perhaps you would do me the honor of engaging me in swordplay?" A sardonic grin twisted his lips. "Purely for sport, I assure you."

Sawkins's face paled. "In this heat? Surely you are mad." He waved his jeweled fingers through the air.

"Nay, I suppose we wouldn't want to strain your delicate, *noble* frame." Kent chuckled and swiped the sweat from his brow with his forearm. "By all means, stay in the comfort of the shade where you belong."

Chortles echoed across the ship, and a few pirates prodded Sawkins to accept the challenge.

Fingering his mustache, Sawkins drew in a deep breath and rose to his feet. His hands twitched as he unbuttoned his shirt and flung it over his head. Isabel wondered at his hesitancy. He seemed most content to lounge in the shade and sip his drink while others worked. Perhaps he feared defeat, yet certainly as a nobleman he'd be well trained with a sword and most willing to use it when the need arose. He cast a regretful glance at her before jumping down to the main deck.

Drawing his sword from its scabbard, he stood to face the captain.

Kent swaggered around him as the pirates began to cheer.

Sawkins attacked at once with a ferocious lunge that the captain quickly tossed aside with his blade. Kent then swung about and drove his cutlass in from the left. Sawkins dipped his sword in defense, and the two weapons crashed with a resounding *clank*. Chuckling, the captain lengthened his arm in a riposte that forced Sawkins backward to avoid the point.

His face purpling, Sawkins increased the ferocity of his onslaught, but it spent itself idly against the captain's skill, for each thrust, each blow, each assault was met with a calm, defensive maneuver and an immediate counterattack that sent Sawkins reeling. His body, though tall and lithe, carried not the strength and power that Kent's did, and he suffered immensely under each blow.

Fear and embarrassment mangled Sawkins's handsome face, and Isabel realized if the captain did not relent soon, the poor man would be utterly humiliated in front of the pirates. Alarm spiked her heart. What if the captain hurt him or, worse yet, killed him? No affection existed between these two men, to be sure. But this was just a playful parry, was it not? Isabel scratched her arms as she continued watching.

The captain met Sawkins's low thrust with a counter-parry that sent him stumbling to the railing, where he labored to catch his breath. The captain studied his opponent, then glanced over the pirates who circled the brawl, wicked delight flickering in their eyes. Slowly and deliberately, he lowered his point to the deck and cocked his head. " 'Tis enough. I grow weary."

Sawkins glanced up, confusion storming in his eyes before they brightened. He lengthened his stance and returned his sword to its scabbard with a *snap*. "Had enough, have you?" Still winded, he ran a hand through his sweaty golden hair.

"Finish 'im off, Captain." Moans of disappointment rose amongst the crowd.

"I said I was tired." Kent gritted his teeth, and Isabel got the impression of a bull penned inside a corral. Why would he end a fight he was clearly in command of?

"Let your captain be, men, if he cannot handle a simple skirmish with a nobleman." Sawkins smirked.

Tossing his cutlass to the deck with a clatter, Kent barreled toward Sawkins, who scrambled white-faced to retrieve his sword from its scabbard. His fingers fumbled over the hilt.

Isabel's heart jumped, for it appeared as though the captain intended to push Sawkins overboard. She leaped from her seat. "No!" Sawkins was the only one who knew where Frederick was, and he was the only gentleman aboard to whom she could entrust her safety.

The pirates began to cheer, and even Smithy and Cutter looked up from their game of cards. Wide-eyed, Sawkins backed against the railing, holding up both hands as the captain bore toward him.

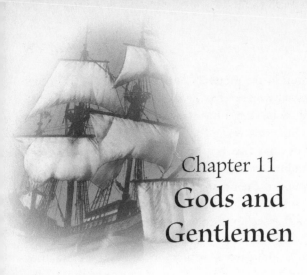

Chapter 11
Gods and Gentlemen

Isabel raced down the quarterdeck stairs. She must stop the captain before he pushed Sawkins to a watery grave.

His lordship cringed, eyes agape as Kent stormed toward him. The captain halted just inches before Sawkins. He flashed an insolent grin, then sidestepped him, jumped up onto the bulwarks, and dove into the sea with a resounding *splash*, leaving a flurry of chuckles behind him.

Isabel darted to the railing and combed the surface of the water, not knowing whether it was fear for the captain or annoyance at his action that propelled her. A burst of bubbles cracked the surface of the porcelain blue, but he was nowhere in sight. She gripped the railing, desperate for a glimpse of him. Squinting, she gazed up at the sails and saw them drooping listlessly with nary a wisp of wind to stir them. At least the ship would not sail away without him.

"Egad, what a fool." Sawkins composed himself and turned, looking down upon the glassy sea.

A group of chortling pirates approached the railing.

"Don't be worryin', miss." Hann stepped beside her. "The captain be a good swimmer."

Instantly, Kent's head popped above the surface.

"I wasn't worried." Isabel released a breath.

He grinned and dove back into the azure waters.

Several pirates flung off their vests, shirts, and belts and tossed them to the deck. They clambered over the railing and dove into the sea, splashing and frolicking like a band of dolphins—or rather, sharks, to be more accurate.

The captain swam with strength and confidence, and Isabel envied his ability. Thoughts of her frivolous attempt at Port Royal to rescue Frederick weighed upon her. If she had known how to swim, she would still have her son and wouldn't be on this pirate ship.

Soon Smithy, Cutter, and Hoornes joined the others overboard. Truthfully, their merry amusement grated on Isabel. She longed to be on her way to rescue Frederick, but she knew there was nothing to be done about the wind. *Lord, give me patience.*

"Seems the captain disapproves of me." Sawkins grabbed the railing.

"Whatever happened between you to cause such discord?"

Sawkins opened his mouth, hesitated, then snapped it shut. "Ah, you know the captain." He shrugged. "I should rather suppose he finds my presence a threat. I've had the opportunity to best him on land and sea on many occasions."

Isabel wondered. She'd seen no indication that Sawkins could outwit or outfight Captain Carlton in any way. "Do you captain your own ship, milord?"

"That I do, Lady Ashton, or *did*, I should say. She went down in a fierce storm while I was attempting to rescue a merchant vessel."

Isabel regarded Sawkins with curiosity. "How noble, milord."

"Yes, 'twas a risk I was willing to take to save lives." His shoulders rose as he spoke. Plucking a handkerchief from his pocket, he dabbed at the moisture on his face and neck. The poor man seemed to be suffering far worse than she was in this heat.

"Come in, Hann." Cutter splashed another pirate and beckoned to the young lad who stood beside Isabel.

Hann took a nervous step back. "Nay, I don't feel like a swim."

"Come on, lad," another pirate motioned toward him. "The water'll cool yer humors."

Releasing a deep sigh, Hann gave Isabel a nervous look and sauntered away.

She turned to Sawkins. His hairless chest glistened with perspiration as he stared with envy at the pirates cooling themselves in the water below.

"Why don't you join them?" she asked, tugging at her clinging gown. "If I were a man and knew how to swim, I'd jump in as well."

He grinned, his cool eyes the same color as the sea. "It thrills me to no end that you are not a man, milady, and I have no intention of leaving you unprotected on board this ship."

Isabel dropped her gaze, warmed by his concern. "I cannot tell you how grateful I am for that assurance, milord."

He laid his hand over hers and gave it a squeeze. Cringing at his familiarity, she allowed it for now as they stood for several minutes in silence.

The doctor swung his legs over the bulwark. His bare feet landed with a splash on the deck. Isabel caught his gaze wandering to Hann, who was draped over the larboard railing. Cutter had not removed his shirt, and the sopping white cotton hugged his chest, accentuating the purple scars beneath rather than hiding them. He sat down on a barrel.

Isabel detected a shiver running though Sawkins as he averted his gaze.

"You mentioned your father was injured in the war?" She withdrew her hand from beneath his.

"Yes. He lost one arm and a leg, and burns much like the doctor's covered most of his body."

"I'm truly sorry." Isabel studied his eyes.

Sawkins gave her a wary smile. "Though still young, he was nothing but a cripple and people looked at him as such—with pity. He could no longer wield a sword, protect his family, nor manage his own business— all because of the Spanish mongrels."

"He blamed Spain?"

"Yes. 'Twas them he fought. He cursed them to his dying day." Sawkins lowered his head and clutched the railing. His hair fell in light strands around his strong jaw. "He died a cruel, lonely death, and I vowed never to end my days as he did."

"Perhaps, milord, it was bitterness that killed your father. Sometimes God has plans for us that seem harsh at the time but are for our ultimate good." Even as she said the words, Isabel thought of her own situation.

But what good could possibly come of Frederick's kidnapping?

The muscles in Sawkins's face pinched. "No, I fear God is not to be depended upon. We must make our own way in life."

Isabel cringed at his hopeless philosophy. "And what is your way?"

"To live life to its fullest, milady—to take every risk, pursue every adventure." Sawkins pressed a lock of hair behind his ear and scanned the horizon. "For 'tis better to die young and full of life than to end up a miserable cripple. Should I find myself in such a disadvantage, I would end my life immediately."

Isabel blinked, taken aback by so easy a dismissal of his own life. "This adventurous life you seek, I assume, is what brought you to the Caribbean?" Isabel scanned the pirates below as they dove into the deep waters and dunked each other like little boys on a summer afternoon. Her eyes locked upon the captain, holding another pirate in a playful headlock.

"Yes, adventure, fame, and"—Sawkins clenched his jaw—"revenge against Spain."

"Forgiveness goes a long way to heal the soul, milord. Perhaps if your father had forgiven his enemies, he wouldn't have died in so miserable a condition. If God has forgiven us so much through the sacrifice of His only Son, who are we not to forgive others?"

"God is also a God of judgment." Sawkins mopped his brow. "And 'tis that aspect of His divine nature to which I aspire."

"Only God can—"

"Why didn't ye go swimmin', Hann? Yer lover boy was callin' to ye." A raspy voice slithered behind her. Isabel wheeled around. One of the pirates who had remained on deck, a short, corpulent beast with a prominent nose, stalked toward Hann.

"Why, yer as pretty a boy as e'er I seen." The pirate snickered and flashed a glance over his shoulder at his comrades, who chortled in agreement.

"That'll be all, Mr. Wolcott." Cutter rose slowly from his seat and moved toward him.

Wolcott plucked the pistol from his breeches and held it to Cutter's head. "Stay back, ye jackal. I'm talkin' to the boy here."

"What do ye want?" Hann gripped the hilt of his sword, glancing at Cutter.

Isabel gasped. Fear coursed through her—fear for the lad who had been so kind to her—and for Cutter, who stood, frozen in place by the pistol pressed upon his forehead.

Two more pirates swaggered toward the group, their yellow-toothed grins dripping with mischief.

Leaning over the railing, Isabel darted her gaze over the pirates in the water, searching for the captain. His head popped above the blue surface, but he did not look her way before he dove beneath the water again. Isabel turned back around.

"Methinks ye favor men." Wolcott spit a black glob onto the deck. "And 'tis bad luck to have one of yer kind on board, says I." Wolcott's vile glance raked over Hann from head to toe, then over the pirates standing nearby. "Ain't that true, boys?"

"Aye, I says he's the cause of the wind leavin' us, to be sure," one pirate said.

"Har, tie a cannonball to his boots and toss 'im overboard!" another shouted. "Then the wind'll fill our sails again!"

Hann's face blanched. Drawing his cutlass, he swung it out in front of him. "I'll slice the first man in half who touches me."

"Leave him alone." Caleb's head popped up through the main hatch. He jumped onto the deck and took a hesitant step forward.

Isabel let out a breath. Finally, someone to stand up for Hann. She gazed down at the water again. Still no sign of the captain.

"Well, if it don't be the cap'n's personal slave." Wolcott grinned, showing no fear at the intruder. "Ye don't have the cap'n to protect ye now. Mebbe we should toss ye over wit the pretty boy."

Caleb grimaced but remained where he stood. His breeches and vest hung loose on his tall, skinny frame. He carried no weapons, and Isabel sensed his fear from where she stood.

Chuckling, the other pirate drew his sword, and both he and Wolcott advanced toward Hann. "Go ahead and fight us, boy. Either way yer goin' over."

Cutter flinched, but the man cocked his pistol and held it firmly to his head.

Isabel glanced at Sawkins. "Aren't you going to do something?"

Sawkins's gaze took in the proceedings with no more interest than if he were watching a play. He fingered his mustache. " 'Tis none of our

business, milady. These barbarians will work it out amongst themselves or die in the attempt. What is it to me?"

The pirate lunged toward Hann. The glare of the setting sun gleamed off his sword and nearly blinded Isabel. She squinted as the *clank* of metal rang in her ears. Hann swung his cutlass up, his face bunching with the strain, and met the other pirate's slash with a feeble thrust. The force knocked him back into the railing. As he bumbled, attempting to regain his footing, the pirate attacked, this time slashing Hann's wrist and flinging his cutlass to the deck with an ominous *clunk*.

Terror squirmed on the young boy's features. He glanced over the railing as if he contemplated jumping.

In a burst of courage that faltered with each step, Isabel marched toward the pirates. "Leave the boy alone at once, you—you repugnant fiends." Her heart pounded in her chest, sending a gush of blood to her head. "You should be ashamed of yourselves."

The startled men gazed at her for a minute before breaking into wicked chortles.

Incensed by their insolence, Isabel stomped her foot and threw her hands to her hips. "How dare you?" She glared at them, but with each passing second, their leering grins only widened. *What am I doing? Why can't I keep my mouth quiet?* Straining, she listened for the sound of Sawkins's footsteps behind her. Surely he would come to her rescue.

Fear skipped across Cutter's wide eyes as they met hers. Beads of perspiration formed on his forehead and slid down to the muzzle of Wolcott's pistol digging into his skin. Hann stepped forward. The tip of a sword held him in place.

"Do as the lady says!" Caleb bellowed, coming up behind Wolcott.

Ignoring him, one of the pirates made a move toward Isabel. "Ye've a bit of pluck in ye, don't ye?"

Isabel's heart seized.

Wolcott's fat lips lifted in a wicked sneer. "Murdock likes his women with a bit o' fire in them, littl' missy. Now stand off, or by the powers, I'll let him have ye." He glanced nervously toward the railing. Sounds of splashing bubbled up from below. "Be on wit' it. Toss the boy overboard," he ordered his men with a stern glance.

Isabel gazed over her shoulder at Sawkins, who, clearly flustered, seemed to be searching for a weapon. The pirates slunk toward Hann, cannonball in hand.

A *thump* sounded from the other side of the ship, and out of the corner of her eye, Isabel saw the captain's muscular, dripping form bounding on deck behind Wolcott.

The pirates instantly halted. Wolcott's eyes darted to the powerful, half-clad form of the captain.

Kent marched toward them, stopping only to pluck a pistol free from a belt one of the men had tossed to the deck. He cocked it and pointed it at Wolcott. "Drop your weapon and stand down."

Wolcott's rum-glazed eyes focused on the barrel of the captain's pistol. He flexed his jaw.

The captain glanced at the other two men. "You'll be next, Zeke, Murdock, if you don't lower your weapons forthwith."

With great effort, Isabel tried to back away from the ensuing battle, but her legs would not move. Trembling, she surveyed the three men, two with pistols drawn and the other with a sword, and wondered how Kent would handle them if they all decided to disobey him. Yet the only fear she detected was bristling in their gazes. None emanated from Kent's hardened glare.

Slowly, the two men dropped their weapons. "We's just havin' a bit o' fun, Cap'n. No harm done," Murdock said as they both backed away.

Caleb snatched Zeke's weapon out of his hand and shoved him forward.

Wolcott lowered his pistol. "Aye, Cap'n. Thar's naught to concern ye."

"I believe there's much to concern me when you dare to challenge my quartermaster without cause." Kent motioned with his gun for them to drop theirs. "And then you insult our guest, Lady Ashton, with your crude threats."

Hann eyed the captain, his brow wrinkling, as the three pirates tossed their weapons to the deck.

Commotion below drew Isabel's attention as pirates began climbing up the rope ladder. One by one, they swung on deck, shaking themselves like wild dogs.

The captain glowered at Wolcott and motioned to two of his men. "Lock them up below. Two days in the hold without food should give

them a new perspective." In a rush, they swarmed the three pirates, disarmed them, and escorted them out of sight.

Feeling returned to Isabel's legs, and she glanced at Cutter. The doctor approached Hann, but in a heated rush, the lad fled down the companionway stairs and disappeared below.

Kent turned to Isabel. "I'm sorry they frightened you, milady." He raised a mocking brow. "But were you planning on taking on the whole crew by yourself?"

"If I had to, Captain." She fanned herself with one hand. "I will not stand by and watch another person be attacked aboard this ship."

Searching his eyes, she expected to see pain from her snide quip, but only regard shone from their depths. He gazed over the sea, and Isabel found her own admiration rising for this fierce pirate captain, despite her ardent attempt to quell it.

Sawkins glanced up to the foredeck where a pirate had confiscated his ruffled shirt. "No. No! You there!" Sawkins yelled, then turned to Isabel to excuse himself. "Put that down! Don't you know what that costs, man?"

Isabel watched him race off to confront the pirate, then she faced the captain. "Why did you stop your parry with Lord Sawkins?"

He ran both hands through his slick hair and gave her a sideways glance. "There's no honor in disgracing another man."

Isabel searched his eyes for a hint of sarcasm, enjoying the way the sun lit up golden flecks floating in the dark pools. Only sincerity rested within them. His drenched breeches clung tightly to his firm waist. Disturbed by an unusual tingle in her belly, she pulled her eyes away.

Though beginning its descent, the sun still shot its unflinching rays upon the ship. Isabel didn't have to look up to know the wind had not risen, for no respite from the heat cooled the sting of her skin. Tugging at her dress to admit a breath of air, she sighed in frustration. Was she destined to remain endlessly on this godforsaken pirate ship with a band of deviant rogues?

"Where is the wind, Captain? The longer we float idly, the farther Frederick sails away."

Instead of the sneering comment or sarcastic look she'd expected, concern warmed his gaze. "Believe me, milady, I am as anxious to be on our way as you are."

She heard footsteps and turned to see Sawkins descending from the quarterdeck, having retrieved and donned his Holland shirt. Cutter leaned on the railing to her right, smoking his pipe.

The captain scratched the stubble on his chin. "Perhaps you should pray to your God to send us wind. If He exists and cares for you as you say, perchance He would prove it to all of us."

Isabel huffed. She patted her combs and wiped the perspiration from the back of her neck. Cutter, Smithy, Gibbons, and some of the other pirates glanced her way. Her gaze passed over each of them. They loved a challenge, and she had just been passed one, or rather God had. She remembered the incredible miracles she'd witnessed while on board the *Reliance* with Lady Charlisse. Would God answer her prayers as well? Lady Charlisse possessed the faith of a saint. But where did that leave Isabel? *Oh Lord, please help me.*

"Very well." She stormed to the starboard railing in a swoosh of skirts and leaned over the bulwark. One glance over her shoulder told her all eyes were upon her as she bowed her head and clasped her hands together. "Oh Lord, please send a wind to fill these sails—for my darling Frederick and to prove to these men that You are indeed all powerful."

Opening her eyes, she raised her head and scanned the deck. The same eyes that had swarmed over her now shifted to the sky, the sails above, and over the calm seas. Moments passed. Nothing save stagnant air surrounded them.

Shrugging, Smithy grunted and turned away. Some of the other pirates chuckled and returned to their cards or their drink. The captain crossed his arms over his chest and stared out over the Caribbean, refusing to meet her gaze.

Facing the sea again, Isabel hung her head.

Cutter drifted over to her. " 'Twas a noble effort, milady, but as I have told you, there is no God, only fate." He puffed upon his pipe and gave her a lopsided grin.

Sawkins eased beside her and grabbed the railing. "Perchance there is a God, good doctor, but He does not suffer Himself to be concerned with petty human affairs."

Isabel remained silent, chiding herself for her weak faith and for making a fool of God in front of these men.

Forcing back tears, she wondered if any of her prayers would be answered. A light breeze danced amongst the tendrils of her hair, cooling the perspiration on her neck. She sighed and squinted toward the fiery orb now dipping below the ruffled sea. Well, at least the night would bring some relief from the blistering heat. A draft swirled around Isabel, and closing her eyes, she wrenched her sodden gown from her skin, hoping some of it would find its way beneath.

Her eyes sprang open. *Wind?*

The slight flap of a sailcloth drummed over the ship.

"Hmm." Cutter glanced up.

"I daresay," Sawkins added.

A blast of wind struck them, and Isabel lifted her gaze to watch each sail fill to brimming with a series of billowing snaps. The ship lurched to the port side as mountains of white canvas rose above them. The captain studied her with crinkled brow before he turned and began firing orders to his crew.

Isabel clung to the railing as the ship plunged forward through the rippling sea. Sawkins and Cutter stood beside her, jaws agape, staring up into the sky. She gave them a patronizing grin before darting down the companionway stairs, feeling as if she were floating upon the fresh breeze God had sent her way.

Bursting into her cabin, she closed and locked the door, then lifted the latch on the window and pried it open. A cool breeze raced through the room, sweeping aside the stifling air. Giggling, she tore through the buttons and lace on her gown, desperate to remove the sticky garment and feel the wind upon her sweltering skin.

"Thank You, Lord. Oh, thank You for answering my prayer." She felt giddy with delight and praise. Stripped down to her petticoat, she twirled through the room and allowed the cool air to dance over her. Finally, she lowered her petticoat and reached to splash some water from the basin onto her skin.

It was then that she heard the scuff of boots on the wooden floor behind her.

With her arms flung across her chest, she spun around. Hann rose from a crouching position behind the desk and pressed a finger to his lips.

Isabel screamed.

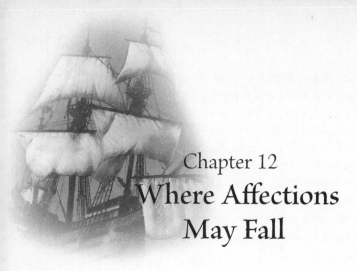

Chapter 12
Where Affections May Fall

Isabel screamed—a loud, piercing scream she knew would bring the entire crew to her door. The pounding of boots sounded across the deck and echoed down the stairs. She stared at Hann, aghast, unsure of what to do. The young lad made no move toward her. His eyes held neither malicious intent nor lust as they shifted from her to the door. A quiet appeal reached from them as he took a step toward her and shook his head.

"Do not fear me, milady," he whispered.

"Why should I not?" Isabel held her petticoat tightly to her chest. "Clearly you are no better than the rest of the licentious pirates on board this ship."

Amusement flickered in Hann's eyes. "I am a woman."

Isabel backed away. *A woman?*

Bam! Bam! Bam!

"Lady Ashton! Are you all right?" the captain shouted through the oak door, distress blaring in his voice.

Holding up a hand to silence her, Hann flung off his baldric, removed his vest, and tore off his soiled cotton shirt, dropping it to the floor. Beneath it, a coil of cloth was tightly bound to his chest.

Bam! Bam! Bam!

"Milady?"

"Yes." Isabel heard the unease in her own voice but thought it better to respond before the man broke down the door.

Hann turned to his side, revealing the slight curves of his figure confined by the tight fabric.

"I intend to break through this door if you do not assure me you are safe, milady."

Isabel continued to stare at Hann, the reality of what she was seeing finally blanketing her fears. Throwing her arms into the sleeves of her petticoat, she drew it over her chest and nodded toward Hann. "I'm quite safe, Captain. Thank you."

Staggering to the bed, she clutched her stomach and sank onto the soft quilt.

Hann gave her a sheepish grin, picked up his—her—shirt from the floor and quickly donned it.

A *thump* sounded on the door as if a head hit it. "Did you not scream, milady?"

"Aye, 'twas but a mouse, Captain. Forgive me." Isabel raised a hand to her mouth to stifle a giggle. Hann gave her a playful look and did the same.

Grumbling emanated from the hallway. "Shall I come in and defend you against the vicious beast?" The sarcasm in his voice oozed through the wood.

"Nay, Captain." Isabel grinned, then straightened her stance. "Why add one vicious beast to another?"

He growled, and Isabel heard the shuffle of his boots fade away.

When she no longer heard sounds coming from the hallway, she turned toward Hann and let out a huge sigh. "You gave me quite a start."

Grinning, Hann donned her vest and plopped into one of the leather chairs. "My apologies, miss. I had no idea you would return to your cabin so soon. Nor that you would strip down to your petticoat within seconds." She rolled her eyes.

"I was hot." Isabel defended what could be perceived as risqué behavior. "But you are a woman?" The truth still sailed across her mind, unwilling to anchor into anything solid.

"Aye, 'tis been my misfortune my whole life."

Shaking her head, Isabel scanned the young lad—or young lady— noting the soft, brown hair that curled slightly as it touched her collar, the large violet eyes framed by lashes much too long for a man's, the delicate lift of her nose, and the lack of stubble on a face always smeared with dirt. "Why didn't I notice this before?"

"People tend to see only what they want to."

Water gurgled against the side of the ship. Familiar creaks and groans of the timbers, tackles, and booms returned, and with them, Isabel's hope, for once again she felt the gentle forward heave of the ship around her.

She glanced back at Hann. She'd never felt uneasy in the boy's presence—even when she'd found herself alone with him. "Who are you? And how did come to join a pirate ship?"

Hann flung her an uneasy gaze, hesitated, then stood and turned her back to Isabel. " 'Tis a woeful tale, and a long one at that." She strode to the window and peered out before turning back around. "Let us just say that I did not flourish as a woman in a man's world."

Hann's words trampled over Isabel's reason. She'd never considered such a thing—never thought she'd had a choice in the matter. Before Kent's assault on her, she'd rather enjoyed being a woman and all the privileges and lack of responsibilities that accompanied the weaker sex. It thrilled her to find herself under the protection of honorable men—still did, in fact. But no man had come to rescue her from Kent that night. She'd been forced to rely on her own strength and cunning—and found herself lacking.

Her curiosity rose, and she patted the bed beside her. "Please favor me with your story, Hann. I'd love to hear it. That isn't your real name, either, I suppose."

"I am Lady Anne Milissa Bovie." Hann grinned and curtsied, making the feminine gesture look rather silly in her pirate regalia.

Isabel giggled, then raised her hand to her mouth. "A lady—a pirate lady?" Her thoughts drifted to Charlisse. "I knew another pirate lady once."

Hann approached the bed. "I thought I was the only fortunate one."

Isabel took Hann's hand in hers and noticed how slender and long her fingers were despite the roughness of her skin. "How did I not see it?" She gazed over the delicate features of Hann's face and saw beauty within. "You've hidden your gender well."

"Not so well today, I fear."

TheRestitution

Isabel gave her a coy look and chuckled. "Though the pirates certainly thought you a catamite, I don't believe they ever suspected you were a lady."

"I should have been better able to defend myself," Hann huffed. "I've put much practice into my swordplay of late."

"That you stood up to three of those knaves at all astounds me— especially now that I know you are a woman."

"But not when I was a man." Hann gave her a taunting grin.

"No, though I feared for your safety."

"Aye, I appreciate your stepping in for me, though 'twas a foolish thing to do. If the captain hadn't entered at that moment. . ." Hann crinkled her nose and looked away.

"Well, he did, and that's the end of it."

Hann cocked her head. "Perhaps you have more manly courage within than you give yourself credit for."

Isabel smiled, warmed by the compliment, but recalled the over-whelming fear that had halted her in her tracks. "Come sit, my new friend, and tell me what tragedy or providence has forced you to a pirate's life."

Hann glanced anxiously at the door. "The captain may be looking for me."

"I can handle the captain." Isabel grinned, then furrowed her brow. "May I ask what you were doing in my cabin?"

"Searching for something."

Isabel remained silent but gave her a questioning look.

Hann sighed. "The captain stores an extra pouch of tobacco from Peru in this desk."

"I've never seen the captain smoke," Isabel said.

"Nay, he keeps it for Cutter when the two of them have one of their late night discussions." Hann glanced uncomfortably around the cabin. "I overheard Cutter saying he missed the sweet flavor, and I thought he might enjoy some—especially after nearly being shot on my account."

Isabel gave her a sideways smile, finally understanding the strange attraction between Hann and Cutter. "Does the doctor know?"

"That I am a woman?" Hann's brows shot up. "Nay, milady. No one but you knows." Kneeling, she retrieved her baldric and cutlass and strapped it on as a blush rose up her neck.

"Please stay awhile, Hann." Isabel pleaded. " 'Tis been too long since I've talked to another woman." Truth be told, Isabel found herself fascinated by this pirate girl and wanted to know everything about her.

Nodding, Hann jumped into one of the chairs, and answered Isabel's questions, at first with hesitancy, but as the evening progressed, with much more ease. The longer they conversed, the lower Hann's tense shoulders dropped and her manly facade with them, until Isabel easily saw the feminine gestures she'd entirely missed before.

"Your father arranged the marriage?" Isabel patted the combs in her hair.

"Aye, to Phillipe Alain Bovie, Comte de Gimois—the rat," Hann spat. "A good match, my father had assured me—to wealth and title."

"French?"

"Aye. *French*." She spoke the word with contempt. "Since no noble blood runs through our veins, 'twas a beneficial union for our family."

"But you did not love this Phillipe?"

"Love him? I didn't know him. All I ever wanted was to work with my father on his sh—" Hann froze and darted a cautious gaze at Isabel. "He was a beast." She scooted to the edge of her seat. "An old tyrant who berated me with his tongue and hounded me with his lecherous, bony hands."

Reaching over, Isabel laid her hand on Hann's leg. "I'm sorry."

Hann flattened her lips. "It matters not. I ran away at the first opportunity."

A breeze wafted through the darkened window, carrying with it the fragrance of the sea—salt and spice and the pungent scent of fish. It played with a tendril of Isabel's hair, and she tugged upon the curl, pondering Hann's story. "But to what did you run? You left your only chance at wealth and title." Isabel shook her head and realized she'd done the same thing but with good reason—for the life of her son. "Could you not tolerate his company for that recompense alone?"

Throwing her shoulders back, Hann frowned. "Once I had those privileges—the silk gowns, the fine delicacies, the respect of society—I found them to be empty and frivolous, mere trifles for the rich to fritter away their lives with."

Isabel gave her friend a puzzled look. "But without them, you are nothing in this world—a commoner destined to trudge through life with naught but the clothes on your back. 'Tis a hard life you've adopted when all you had to do was tolerate the company of an old man—though horrid he may have been—who would have surely died long before you." As the words flowed from her lips, Isabel realized they could have easily come from her mother's lips, as well. She held her stomach, suddenly nauseated.

"Phillipe did die, six months after I left him, or so I heard. Natural causes. But still, I am not sorry I left him when I did. I've had six months of a far better life. And now that I play the part of a man"—Hann's eyes flickered with excitement—"I am no longer dominated by anyone save myself. 'Tis a man's world, milady. If you want to live life to its fullest, you must become one."

Isabel sighed and studied her new friend. She'd never met another woman with such preposterous ideas, a philosophy that threw itself in the face of everything Isabel had ever valued and believed. Though she certainly didn't agree with her, she liked the girl. Admired her for her courage, her resourcefulness, her pluck. She was everything Isabel had been taught not to be, and the way she'd forged into a man's world—a *pirate's* world of all places—deserved much praise. Could she truly deny her gender forever? Isabel thought of Cutter, and she smiled. "Yet you still are a woman with a woman's desires. I see the way you look at the doctor."

Hann's face blossomed like a rose, and she shot to her feet. "I don't know what you mean."

"Oh, come now, 'tis obvious you have affections for him."

Hann's shoulders sank. "Is it really?"

"Even the men noticed it. 'Twas why they thought you a catamite."

Hann knelt and took Isabel's hands in hers. "He's such a kind, generous man, isn't he? And so wise." Her violet eyes sparkled.

"I like him, too."

"But what difference does it make now?" Hann released Isabel's hands and stood "He thinks I'm a boy and a rather odd one at that."

"You *could* reveal yourself to him."

Hann's brows raised. "And lose my position on the ship. If the captain knew I was a woman, he'd drop me off at the nearest port. Or worse, confine me to the hold." Anger spewed from her lips.

Isabel doubted the latter. Kent liked Hann. "Why do you hate the captain so?"

"I don't hate him." Hann turned away. "Why do you say that?"

"Just something I've observed."

Hann marched to the door and braced her hands on her waist, and Isabel thought better than to pursue the subject. "But what of Cutter? Would it not be worth it to have his affections?"

"Nay." Hann shook her head. "I never want to be a woman again. I don't understand why anyone would. We are considered weak and ignorant, pretty dolls for men to dress up in silks and lace and place on display until their desires require our services. I will never submit myself to another man, no matter how gallant he is. No, 'tis a pirate's life I've chosen. I need only keep my sentiments at bay."

Isabel doubted the success of Hann's plan. "Well, your secret is safe with me, *Anne*." She winked.

"Thank you, milady." Hann reached out and gave Isabel's hand a squeeze.

Isabel's eyes moistened. "I must admit, 'tis a comfort to have a friend to talk to on this ship full of boisterous men."

"For me as well." Hann glanced at the door. "Now, I must be off. If the captain finds me here alone with you, he'll lash me and hang me from the yardarm, to be sure."

"Then be off with you, and be safe, my friend."

The young girl nodded and left.

Isabel lay on the bed, hoping sleep would overtake her, but the exciting events of the day—the sword fights, God's miraculous answer to her prayer, and Hann's fascinating story—skipped through her mind, keeping it from slipping into rest. Finally, she crept up onto the deck, searching for a peaceful spot where she could gaze upon the ocean and pray for Frederick.

Darkness huddled in corners, under stairways, behind masts and crates, hiding from the newly risen moon that shone its liquid light upon the ship, casting the sails above into shimmering silver.

Two pirates marched up on the foredeck, and another group clustered

to her left by the port railing. Behind her, several more of the crew crowded around the whipstaff. A song drifted on the breeze along with laugher and the scent of rum. She focused her eyes on the band of men to her left, and the glitter of a gold button caught her eye. Sawkins, in his satin doublet, stood next to Smithy and Gibbons. Their whispers twirled around her but would not form any recognizable words.

Ignoring them, Isabel turned, took the stairs up onto the quarterdeck, and reached the aft of the ship. Leaning over the taffrail, she watched the pearly wake churning off the stern—the froth matched the bubbling anticipation within her. At last, they were on their way to rescue her son. She scanned the horizon but could not make the division betwixt sky and sea. It was as if some giant monster obscured it—not allowing itself to be seen on this dark night. No matter. She would not let the gloom dampen her hopes. As she bowed her head and began to pray, footsteps tapped over the wooden planks and halted beside her.

"What a pleasure to find you on deck this evening, Lady Ashton."

Isabel looked over to see only a sliver of moonlight angle across Sawkins's firm jaw and glisten in his loose blond hair, normally neatly combed, but tonight tousled by the wind.

"The pleasure is mine, milord." Isabel returned his smile, disappointed that her privacy had been intruded upon.

Sawkins slid a finger over both sides of his thin mustache and gazed off the stern. "Quite a coincidence earlier when the wind returned."

"I beg your pardon." Isabel snapped her eyes to his. " 'Twas no coincidence. God answered my prayer."

"Forgive me, milady. I did not mean to distress you." Sawkins bowed, then gave her a look of concern. "All that matters is that we are on our way to your son."

Drawing a deep breath of the night air, Isabel studied the man beside her: tall, vigorous, dashing. He was handsome, indeed. He brushed an arm against hers and leaned on the railing. His warmth flowed over her along with his scent of mustache oil and cedar that mingled with the fragrance of the sea. Yet she wondered at his concern for a child he'd never met. "What truly brings you along on this voyage, Lord Sawkins?"

"It would mean so much to me if you would call me Richard."

"I hardly know you, milord."

"I'd like to remedy that," he whispered in her ear.

Glancing back over the sea, Isabel raised a hand to her throat, flustered at his sudden boldness. Her breath quickened. "You did not answer my question."

His gaze turned thoughtful, and several moments passed. "As I have said, I live for adventure, milady, and I hate to see a mother and child separated. When I discovered I could be of some service, I offered myself to Captain Carlton, despite his ill feelings toward me."

Isabel laughed. "I perceive there may be another reason as well, milord? 'Tis a rare thing to find a heart so completely chivalrous."

Sawkins studied her for a moment. "Alas, you have caught me." He gave a nervous chuckle. "Since I am without a ship at the moment, I need passage to the Spanish Main, where I have plans to procure a vessel and join the Brethren of the Coast."

"But aren't they common pirates, milord?"

"Nay, privateers, milady—commissioned by the governor of Jamaica. I assure you, 'tis legal."

"You must have more than enough fortune to purchase your own passage and buy another ship as well?"

"Yes, my inheritance is quite vast, I assure you." He brushed dirt from the shoulder of his doublet. "You suggest a more reasonable approach to be sure, but where would the fun be in that?"

"Ah." Isabel smiled. "Where indeed?" From his mannerisms, his modish and costly attire, and his eloquence, Isabel had assumed what he now confirmed was true—he *was* wealthy. Her mother had said he was the son of an earl. *Wealth and title.*

"Yet there is another reason for my presence here which I feel obligated to divulge, one that had not revealed itself until lately." He clutched her hand and placed it gently between his. "By now you must have noticed my extreme regard for you."

Isabel widened her eyes.

With a sigh, he leaned toward her. His warm breath showered over her cheek. "Milady, I find myself quite taken with you."

Isabel stepped back, plucking her hand from his grasp. "Alas, milord we have been acquainted for only a few days."

"Bewildering, isn't it? Yet my feelings cannot be denied. I know this

is sudden," he continued, "but I'm a man who takes risks, as you know, and I could not let another moment pass without informing you of my fervent ardor."

Aware of Lord Sawkins's attraction to her, Isabel had brushed it off as flighty male infatuation. She'd seen it many times before. But this declaration of his affections had taken her by surprise. She'd never expected any true nobleman to take a serious interest in her again. Surely she misread him—or had he some other motive? Joy fluttered through her as she considered the possibility of his sincerity. "Milord—"

"Richard," he interjected.

"Richard, I am flattered by your affections, but I wonder if you have thought. I'm sure you realize that I have a child, an illegitimate child whom I love dearly and intend to keep."

"I am fully aware of that."

"A match between us would certainly not meet the approval of your family."

"It would meet my approval, milady. My family would come to accept you in time." He ran a finger over the sleeve of her gown. "I pray you'll take the time to get to know me better. Perhaps in time you may return my affections. It is all I hope for."

"I don't know what to say, milord. . .Richard."

Leaning toward her, he grazed her cheek with his lips.

Isabel flinched and jumped back, unsure of how to respond to his familiar actions. When she looked up at him, the moonlight lit a sneer that curled on his lips, giving her pause.

"I shall leave you to your musings, milady." He raised her hand and placed a moist kiss upon it. "Until tomorrow." Bowing, he swaggered away. Isabel watched him until his blond hair descended below the quarterdeck.

She swung her gaze back out across the ebony seas. A nobleman wishing to marry her? Could it be so? It was a dream come true. She could have everything she'd ever hoped for. His name would wash away the stain of her violation and the illegitimacy of her son. Frederick would be raised the son of a lord, not the son of a pirate. Truly there were things that troubled her about Sawkins, and she certainly didn't know him very well, but what had she just said to Hann? Much could be tolerated for wealth and status—especially for the sake of her son and his future—one which she could never provide for him on her own. Indeed, what harm could there be in acquainting herself further with Lord Richard Sawkins?

Sawkins bounded down onto the main deck and crept back into the dark shadows under the foredeck, where he'd met with Smithy and the others earlier. Grabbing a leftover bottle of rum from beneath the railing, he wiped the head with his sleeve and took a full swig. Things were going his way. Upon hearing his declaration of love, the beautiful Lady Ashton had nearly melted into his arms. He'd seen the way she gazed at him—the way all the women gazed at him. His handsome looks coupled with his innate charm, wealth, and status caused all the women he'd pursued to swoon at his feet. And he'd conquered them all, one by one. Of course, none had kept him satisfied for long. It wasn't his fault their charms faded after time. But he had a feeling Lady Ashton would be different. Here was a woman with courage and tenacity to match his own.

He growled as he remembered how she'd retreated from his kiss. How dare she? She should feel privileged he chose her to lavish his affections upon. After all, dismissed as she was from her family and raising an illegitimate child, what decent gentleman would have her? It didn't matter. He would work his charms on her as he had his other conquests, and in time, she would give herself willingly to him.

Soon he would possess not only this ship, but Captain Carlton's vast treasure and his woman as well. Yes, things indeed were going his way.

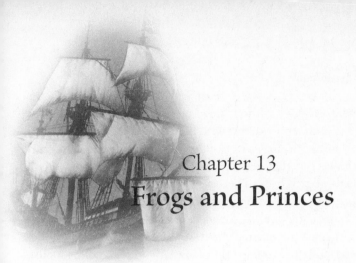

Chapter 13
Frogs and Princes

Kent spread the charts out on his desk and noted the *Restitution*'s current position. They'd been at sea for five days. They'd cleared the treacherous Windward Passage between Cuba and Santo Domingo. Now it would be smooth sailing to Cartagena. With favorable winds and no unforeseen enemy to halt their progress, they'd reach their destination in another ten to fifteen days.

Hann cleared his throat, reminding Kent the lad was still in his cabin, combing through the lists of supplies and navigation equipment. Kent had to give the boy credit. His skills as a quartermaster were superb, and his insistence at ensuring they had enough provision for the trip to Cartagena was to his credit.

Kent glanced over his shoulder. Hann sat on the window ledge. The boy quickly dropped his gaze to the papers in his hand. He was a good pirate, yet something in Hann's violet eyes gave Kent pause.

Shrugging it off, Kent leaned back in his chair and allowed the sun penetrating the window behind him to warm his back. His thoughts floated to Isabel—as they always did. For a year, he'd thought of nothing else. Like a man dragging himself over a parched desert desperately seeking a cool drink, he'd searched for her all across the Caribbean. Now that he'd found her, all he wanted was to drown himself in her presence. Yet he'd been forced to accept only the small sips she offered him—her coy glances, the occasional smile, a glimmer of admiration in her eyes— wonderful, quenching sips.

But his thirst remained.

He sighed. Simply to have her near was enough for now, for he doubted he could ever live without her again. Life without Isabel was nothing but a farce, an empty desert with no oasis in sight.

Kent's eyes shifted to his cot in the corner of the cabin. His heart dropped as memories of that night pounced upon him. As soon as he'd left the bed and turned his back to her sobs, regret had clamped his soul—that new and uncomfortable feeling that had taken him by surprise. He'd donned his breeches and done all he could to console her, but the damage had been done. As he remembered the terror and hatred flashing in her eyes, he cringed. What he wouldn't do to erase that look and his foolish actions that had caused it.

Gently placing the papers down, Hann eased herself from the ledge and slid her knife from the sheath on her thigh. From the way the captain stared off into the cabin, she knew his mind was far away. He would not hear her slink behind him—would not hear the swish of the blade until it was too late and the cold steel severed his heart. A chance like this would not likely come again for quite some time.

She swallowed hard and moved into place. The floorboards creaked slightly, but he did not stir.

Hann raised the knife. Something held it in check. Kent had been naught but kind to her since she'd signed on with his crew. Hadn't he stood up for her, rescued her from the other pirates, and trusted her as his quartermaster? No matter. She must do what she came to do.

A knock on the door broke through Kent's dismal thoughts. He turned at the shuffling sounds behind him. Hann's back was to him.

Kent swung back around. "Enter."

In swaggered Lord Sawkins, wearing a foul grin that matched the stench of the cedar oil he doused himself with. Kent had forgotten he'd summoned the knave. Closing the door, Sawkins adjusted the lace bursting from his violet damask waistcoat and glanced across the room, taking a step inside. "You wanted to see me, *Captain*?"

Pushing out his chair, Kent circled his desk. *Want* was not exactly the word he would use. "Have a seat." He gestured toward a wooden chair, but Sawkins shifted his boots and remained standing.

Hann skirted the desk. "I'll just be takin' these lists down to the hold, Cap'n, to double check what we have."

"Thank you, Hann," Kent said as the boy passed Sawkins with a sneer.

Sawkins watched him leave, then faced Kent. "If this is in reference to Morris's location, I have already told you I will not disclose that until we are nearly there."

Leaning back against the top of his desk, Kent crossed his arms over his chest. "You have made that quite clear."

Sawkins would not meet his gaze. Instead, he slithered to the bookshelves lining the wall.

Kent cleared his throat. "I want to know what you're really doing on board my ship." He watched for Sawkins's reaction, but the man held his back to him as he glanced over the books.

"Why, 'tis just as I have told you. I need passage and. . .of course I wish to help you find your son."

Kent grunted. He doubted the veracity of either reason, just as he doubted Sawkins was capable of telling the truth. "Allow me to give you a fair warning, then. I will not tolerate your antics aboard my ship. Whatever mischief you are about, you had better call a halt to it immediately."

Sawkins turned and raised a cultured eyebrow. "Whatever do you mean?"

"Come now." Kent flung him a knowing glance. "You forget to whom you are speaking."

Plucking a book from the shelf, Sawkins opened it and flipped through the pages. "Still trying to improve upon your meager education, I see?"

"I did not have the privilege of England's finest schools as you did."

Sawkins grinned. "You still hold that against me."

Amongst other things—many other things. Kent's insides bristled, but he maintained a look of indifference. "Truth be told, I rarely give you a moment's thought."

Sawkins grimaced and replaced the book. "Lady Ashton is quite lovely."

Kent shot to his feet. "You will leave her be."

"I assure you I wish only to help her find her son."

Kent chuckled. " 'Twould be a first for you to do anything that didn't appease your selfish desires."

"Ah." Sawkins laid a hand over his heart. "So harsh. But can't a man change? Haven't your own cruel tendencies softened?"

Kent crinkled his brow. Had he become soft? Was it so evident? Perhaps that explained why Sawkins had come in for the kill—like a predator, he'd sensed wounded prey.

"May I?" Sawkins sauntered to the desk and grabbed a bottle of rum. Kent eyed him.

Pouring a drink into a glass, Sawkins lifted it and tossed it down his throat with a flick of his neck. "I must say you've done better for yourself than I would have expected."

"I would be doing even better if I hadn't been forced to pay off your debts." Kent glared at Sawkins and braced his hands on his hips.

"Oh, pish." Sawkins waved a hand through the air. "That again. I never asked it of you."

Hatred fumed within Kent. No, he hadn't asked, nor had he appreciated it. "I saved you from the hangman's noose on more than one occasion, and still I find you have frittered away your fortune on cards."

" 'Tis my right to do so."

"I will not bail you out again."

"As you have told me."

Kent eyed Sawkins with disdain. Once—many years ago—he had looked up to him, admired him even, but no more. "Stay away from Lady Ashton."

"That would be quite impossible." Sawkins's eyes twinkled. "You see, I'm quite taken with her, and I believe she feels the same way toward me."

A blast of jealousy drove its sharpened teeth into Kent's heart.

Sawkins pressed his greased mustache. "I've asked her to marry me."

Blood surged to Kent's fists. He fought the urge to punch Sawkins. "She would never be that foolish."

"Ah yes." Sawkins shook his head and feigned a look of disappointment. "I suppose that makes two women I've stolen from you. But wait, stolen is not the best term. It would appear that when faced with

the choice between us, the ladies see the obvious one." He poured himself another drink. "I offer her everything you cannot. She'd be a fool to turn me down."

Kent lunged at Sawkins, grabbed his neckerchief, and twisted it, tightening it upon Sawkins's throat. Coughing, Sawkins stumbled backward, eyes agape. He clutched Kent's hands and fought to dislodge them. With a grunt, Kent flung Sawkins backward and dropped his arms to his sides. Panting, he twitched his head back and gritted his teeth, trying to regain control. "You don't love her."

"Love?" Sawkins took a ragged breath, straightened his neckerchief, and backed away from Kent. "Overrated, as are most sentimental emotions. But that has always been your downfall."

Visions of Elizabeth, sweet Elizabeth, with her strawberry curls and innocent smile flashed through Kent's mind. He'd been so young. They'd both been so young. But oh, how he had loved her. She'd agreed to be his wife, until—until Sawkins came along and swept her away with his flatteries and empty promises. After he'd taken what he wanted from her, he'd left her, devastated and despoiled. Shortly thereafter, her family had moved her back to England.

"You destroyed her."

"Elizabeth?" Sawkins waved his hand through the air, the lace at his sleeve fluttering. "You know how easily I become bored."

Kent's thoughts sped through the myriad of women he'd known. Hadn't he done the same thing—lured them into his bed with his charm, only to abandon them in the morning? And Isabel, hadn't he destroyed her as well? Kent bunched his fists and glanced out the window. No, he loved her. And he would not let this cruel libertine steal the woman he loved.

Not again.

He glared at Sawkins. "I'll throw your scrawny carcass overboard before I allow you to lay a finger on Lady Ashton."

"Tisk, tisk, Captain. Such jealousy does not become you." Sawkins glowered, rubbing his neck. "Why don't we let the lady decide who the best man is?"

Fury tore through Kent, constricting his throat, forbidding him to speak or move lest he throttle the buffoon into a nondescript lump of flesh.

Sawkins dropped his gaze beneath Kent's intense glare. "Now if that will be all?" Shifting his boots on the wooden floor, he peered back up at Kent and, with a nervous twitch, scuttled from the room.

Leaning against the main head rail on the foredeck, Isabel drew her shawl tighter against the morning chill floating up off the fog-laden sea. A breath of light glazed the horizon in a pink glow, announcing the sun's arrival on a new day—a day that would carry her closer to Frederick. Though bereft of milk, her breasts still ached for her baby. She knew they would until he was back in her arms again.

She'd come up on deck before the pirates stirred, hoping for a moment of peace in which she could worship her Father and lay her petitions before His almighty throne. Somehow it seemed much easier to bow before Him with the majesty of His creation sprawled out before her rather than in her stifling cabin below. She thought of Reverend Thomas and smiled at how pleased he would be if he could see her reading her Bible and praying on her own—and receiving answers as well.

"Father, I know You are with me, and I know You are with Frederick. Please help me during those times I doubt You and when I allow fear to consume me."

The *Restitution* lurched over a white-capped swell, showering her with a spray of salty water. Despite the chill, she smiled, sensing it was naught but a playful splash from God. Did He play with his children like earthly fathers did? She liked to think so.

"Lord, regarding Sawkins. Thank You for his offer of marriage. You truly do give us the desires of our hearts. But is this from You? Something about him disturbs me." Isabel held her stomach, trying to quell a sudden curdling.

As if in reply, a shifting boom groaned above her, and a blast of wind flapped the sails. A bell chimed eight times, echoing across the sea like an ominous toll that sent a shiver across her back.

She thought of Hann. "And thank You for Hann, but please protect her from these men."

A dark shape moved beside her, and she jumped.

"Beggin' yer pardon, ma'am." Caleb bowed and clasped his hands

together. He turned to leave.

"Caleb." Isabel beckoned him. "Please stay for a moment. I'd like to speak with you." She'd been curious about the black man ever since she'd come aboard.

"Yes'm." He faced her but did not raise his gaze.

"Weren't you a slave on this ship?" Isabel pulled from her memory a vision of a man chained at the ankles, swabbing the deck—a man she'd hardly given notice to the last time she'd been aboard.

"Aye, ma'am." Caleb shifted his bare feet across the hard wood.

"You are no longer in chains?"

"No, ma'am. The cap'n freed me." He fumbled with his hands, and Isabel noticed how large and bulky his fingers were compared with the rest of him.

Isabel could not imagine the captain performing such a kind deed. "Freed?"

"He made me his steward." Pride lifted the tone of his voice.

"Indeed." Isabel drew a deep breath of dewy air. Why would Kent do such a thing? "Caleb, I wanted to thank you for stepping forward in Hann's defense the other day. It was quite noble of you."

"Ah, 'twas nothing, ma'am." Caleb looked down. "I didn't hep much. The others don't listen to me right well."

"That you risked your life at all was more than enough." Isabel studied the tall, skinny man. She sensed a strength in him, squashed and trampled by years of abuse. "You are no longer a slave, Caleb. Don't let the other men bully you around. You must command their respect."

"Aye, that's what the captain tells me." Caleb grinned, and his white teeth lit up the morning.

"For once I agree with him." Isabel smiled, noting the twinkle in Caleb's dark eyes. She got the impression he waited to be dismissed. "Thank you, Caleb. That will be all."

"Yes'm." He bowed and ambled off into the mist.

Facing the sea again, Isabel returned to her prayers, her thoughts in turmoil. "Lord, can I trust Captain Carlton? He baffles me, frightens me, yet he has shown evidence of genuine kindness. I don't know what to think."

Heavy footsteps thudded behind her. They halted, approached, then halted again before growing louder.

The sun peered over the horizon in a brilliant arch of yellow, casting its rays over the sea, dissipating her fears along with the fog.

A tingle coursed through Isabel as the captain eased beside her, brushing his arm against hers. For a moment, he said nothing. A wisp of air fluttered over them, showering her with his scent of leather and spice.

"Milady." His deep voice slid over the salty breeze.

"Captain."

He placed a gentle hand on the small of her back as the ship rolled over a swell. She flinched.

"If I make you nervous, I'll leave."

"Nay," she snapped. "I mean. . .leave if you wish, but you no longer frighten me."

"That gives me great pleasure." He bowed.

She looked at him, studying the flecks of gold flickering in his dark eyes. Sincerity warmed his gaze, and something else, something sad. She knew he thought of that night, and she shifted her glance away. She'd been so terrified of him then. Which of them had changed?

He scratched the stubble peppering his chin. "Did I interrupt your prayers?"

Isabel tossed him a curious look. "How did you know?"

"Your face carries a glow about it when you pray."

"Indeed?"

"Aye, there is something different about you. Perhaps Merrick's God serves you well."

Isabel couldn't help but smile. "He is everyone's God, not just Merrick's, and He does not serve me. I serve Him." The captain returned her smile, the curve of his lips matching Frederick's so exactly, it sent a burst of longing through her.

"Yet when you call to Him, as with your appeal for the wind"—he waved a hand through the humid air—"He answers."

Isabel studied the man. Was he truly interested in God or just sneaking his way into her sentiments? "He answers those who love Him and know Him, but still 'tis His will He does in the end."

"Hmm." Taking a deep breath of the morning air, the captain glanced out over the sea. "It pains me to dampen your humors, but—"

"Not even you can destroy my good mood, Captain." She raised her chin in the air.

"I must speak to you of Sawkins."

"What of him?"

"I'm afraid he has deceived you."

Alarm spiked through her. Hadn't she suspected something was afoot? "How so?"

Squinting toward the sun, now sitting just above the horizon, he sighed. "He is not sincere in his affections, milady."

Isabel huffed.

"He offers you his hand, when in reality he will do naught but take advantage of your feelings and leave you with nothing."

"You know about his proposal?"

Kent nodded.

"He doesn't need your permission, Captain, nor do I." Isabel patted her silver combs. "Besides, he offers me more than mere marriage. He offers wealth and title for Frederick—a chance for him to grow up with honor, not as the illegitimate son of a pirate."

A pained look sank the captain's expression. He wrenched the railing. "Lord Sawkins is not what he seems, milady. His nobility is fleeting at best. His wealth is nonexistent. He ran his father's merchant business into the ground with gambling debts. Why do you think he needs to steal passage aboard this ship? He is a charlatan, and he will use you and toss you aside when he tires of you."

Pain and fury lanced through Isabel's heart. "Do you think no man would desire me for more than to warm his bed?" Tears sprang to her eyes. "Do you believe me nothing more than a common trollop?"

Kent laid a hand over hers. "Nay, milady, of course—"

"Don't you have everything you want, Captain?" Isabel snapped her hand away and faced him. "Your ship, your treasure, power? If I recall, that was all that was ever important to you. You take what you want from life, as you did me. You had my body. What is it to you if I give my heart to another?" She raised a hand to swipe an escaped tear before he saw it.

"Are you giving your heart or selling your soul?"

Raising her hand, Isabel swung it toward his face, hoping to slap the smirk from it and ease the pain in her heart.

He caught it in midair and raised his brows, a sardonic grin on his lips.

"You're jealous, 'tis all." Isabel jerked her hand away, and scratched the sudden itch on her arms. She faced the sea, forcing back tears. "Lord Sawkins can give my son what you never could."

Clenching his jaw, Kent lengthened his stance. Rage twisted his handsome features, and Isabel once again longed to take back the words that so carelessly flew from her mouth.

The ship pitched over a surging roller, and Isabel's legs gave way beneath her. In a flash, the captain grabbed her and drew her to himself. Heat rose up her body. Looking up, she gazed into his eyes, his rage replaced by a warm affection.

"When are you going to forgive me, milady? Doesn't your God require it?" His spicy, hot breath wafted over her.

"I have forgiven you." She searched his eyes, feeling her heart quicken, and pushed back from his chest. "But I find it much more difficult to forget."

When she freed herself from his embrace, the sudden loss stole all warmth from her.

"A sail, a sail!" The shout came from above them, and the captain shifted his gaze toward the sea.

Isabel rushed to the railing.

"How stands she?" he yelled.

"Off the starboard beam!"

Excitement set Isabel's hopes alight as she swung her gaze to the right. The captain plucked his spyglass from his belt and marched to the starboard railing.

"Is it Morris?" Isabel asked.

Before he could answer, a flash caught her eye in the distance, and a thunderous *boom* sent the air aquiver.

The round shot splashed into the sea just yards off the starboard quarter, sending a spray of seawater onto the deck.

Chapter 14
Slaves and Masters

Taking a step back, Isabel gripped her qualmish stomach. Horrifying memories blazed through her mind: cannon shots blasting through the ship; flaming spikes of wood spearing across the deck; gaping, blackened holes in the hull; fire and smoke filling the air; and the screams of injured men. Terror held her in place.

Angry shouts and boot steps thundered over the deck as pirates emerged from below, rubbing the sleep from their eyes.

The captain lowered his glass. "Gibbons!" he yelled aft. "Hard aport!"

"Hard aport, Cap'n."

Marching to the foredeck railing, he scanned the crew below. "Smithy, set all studding sails. Bring her full into the breeze."

"Cap'n, why is we runnin' like snivelin' dogs?" Murdock shielded his eyes and studied the ship in the distance. "Could be a fair prize, says I."

The pirates grumbled in agreement as the ship lurched to the left, sending Isabel stumbling to the port railing.

Kent flung a glance over his shoulder and reached out for her, hastening her beside him. "Fair prize or not," he bellowed, "we have other business to attend to!"

A tall, shifty-eyed pirate with a jagged scar circling his neck glared up at Kent. "We been tending to yer business fer too long. This ship is fer piratin', not escortin' yer lady friends and huntin' their babes."

Isabel felt the tension fill the air around the captain's taut body. "Since this is my ship," he spat through gritted teeth, "I'll be the one saying what she is for and not for. Haven't I done well for you gentlemen? Aren't you the richest pirates ever to sail these waters?"

Hoornes jumped onto the deck, his rat perched on his shoulder, followed by Hann, who smiled at Isabel before glancing toward the horizon.

The crew grumbled, and Isabel feared a mutiny brewed. Where was Lord Sawkins? A lump formed in her throat. What would happen if the crew took over the ship? What would they do with her? She glanced at the captain. No fear etched his features, only annoyance.

Cutter popped on deck, his sandy hair flopping in the breeze. His gaze found Hann over by the rail and then landed on Isabel.

Letting out a frustrated sigh, Kent tossed his hair back, turned, and squinted behind him at the ship fading in their wake.

Isabel darted an anxious gaze at him. "Perchance it is Captain Morris."

"Nay, 'tis a sloop. Morris sails a frigate."

"Beggin' yer pardon, Cap'n," Smithy squawked. "But we's of a mind to take her. By thunder, 'twill only take a few hours to capture and plunder her." The first mate's stern expression made his statement more a demand than a request. His short, skinny legs seemed barely able to hold up his prominent belly and beefy chest.

Grunts issued from the raucous crew, reminding Isabel of a troop of apes beating their chests in defiance. Some of them towered well above their friends; others could barely be seen amongst the mob. Some were lanky, others corpulent, some had long stringy hair, others were bald, some were bearded, some smooth faced, and they all wore an assortment of flashy colors and mismatched, ragged apparel that made them resemble a band of roving gypsies. Respect and fear gleamed in their gazes cast toward their captain. Yet something else—an emotion even more formidable: greed.

The captain faced Isabel. "Go below."

She shook her head. "Surely you aren't going to attack that ship?"

"What would you have me do? Even I cannot fight the whole crew single-handedly."

"But it will delay finding Frederick." Frustration bubbled within Isabel. "You said you were done with vanquishing—or was that a lie like everything else?"

Shoving off from the railing, he crossed his arms over his billowing

shirt. "*I* am done, but as you can see, my crew is not of the same mind." He shrugged. "I am a pirate, after all, and until I formally retire and set these men ashore, I must abide by the articles they signed when they joined my crew."

"Humph. I doubt you will ever retire." Isabel thrust her chin in the air. "Once a pirate, always a pirate."

Turning from her, he scanned the crew. "Hoornes, bring her full about. All hands on deck. Let's be about our prey, men!"

Cheers and howls echoed across the ship as the men disbanded and scurried in all directions. Some hopped down the hatch, others flung themselves into the ratlines and clambered aloft like monkeys.

Isabel clung to the railing as the ship came about on the windward side. With taut ropes whining in the wind and masts groaning, the huge frigate turned toward the sloop—naught but a shimmering mirage on the horizon. The breeze shifted, and a blast of torrid air struck Isabel from behind, loosening her hair from its combs.

"Now will you go below?" the captain asked, giving her an imploring half grin.

She thought of her stifling cabin and how terrifying it had been to be locked below during a battle, hearing the cannons roar and the clash of swords and screams of men and not knowing what was happening. What if the ship sank and she were trapped? Or worse, what if the ship were boarded and the marauders found her alone in her room? She threw back her shoulders. "Nay, I will not."

The captain flattened his lips. His brown eyes flickered in concern. " 'Tis dangerous for a lady to be on deck."

"Not if you are the pirate you claim to be." Isabel tightened her jaw against the fear that spiraled through her.

"I could have you escorted below and locked in your cabin."

Isabel gave him a brazen glance. "You wouldn't dare."

"Do not try my patience, milady." The tiny scar beneath his right eyebrow rose. He flexed his jaw. "You may stay above for now, but rest assured I will have you locked below if I deem it necessary."

Ignoring him, Isabel glanced away.

The captain roared a series of rapid-fire orders that pierced Isabel's eardrums. In response, his men bustled over the deck to do his bidding and arm themselves with pistols, knives, and swords—the hilts and handles of which stuck out like spikes from every part of their bodies.

Shielding her eyes from the sun, Isabel pitied the poor ship, its silhouette growing larger on the horizon. They were making their best attempt at outrunning the pirates. She wondered what type of ship it was—merchant? Perhaps one of her father's ships?

As if answering her thoughts, Kent lowered the scope. "Slaver."

"A slave ship?"

He nodded. "A Spanish slaver. They carry Africans and Indians from the Spanish Main to the other islands."

Isabel cringed, and her thoughts drifted to the slave families Reverend Thomas helped back at Port Royal. "Then there won't be any treasure aboard." Hope sprang through her. Perhaps they would abandon the chase and get back to looking for Frederick.

"Nay. The Spanish always carry treasure."

"Surely not on a lone, undefended ship." Isabel heard the desperation in her voice.

"Zeke, run up our colors!" the captain shouted as Hann approached. He turned toward Isabel. "They often hide their treasure aboard slave ships, milady."

Isabel huffed. "If they did not wish to engage us, why did they fire upon us?"

"As a warning." The captain flashed a haughty grin. "But it would appear they had no idea whom they fired upon." He nodded toward Hann. "Watch her," he ordered before gripping the hilt of his cutlass and swinging himself down the stairs onto the main deck.

Isabel's gaze followed him as he marched amongst his crew. He commanded them with authority and confidence. She'd witnessed his skill in sea battle, but fear still clawed its way up her heart. People would no doubt die in this foolish clash, not to mention the time it stole from finding her son. And for what? Fortune? Memories of the huge estate in Hertfordshire where she'd spent her childhood stung her: the lavish food, the expensive gowns. Hadn't she put as much importance on possessing wealth as these pirates did on stealing it?

She shot a tremulous glance at Hann and grabbed her hand, then quickly released it before anyone noticed. "Whatever will you do?"

"What do you mean?" The girl seemed oblivious to the ensuing danger.

"Surely you won't fight?"

Hann chuckled. "If I play the part of a man, I fear I must play it in all their vile ways."

Isabel wrung her hands, then scratched the rising itch on her arms. "You could be wounded or worse."

Hann's violet eyes twinkled. "Your concern warms me, milady, but never fear. I have been in many such fights."

"Truly?" Isabel could not imagine it. Dressing like a man was one thing, but to possess the strength to fight like one was quite another.

"Aye, milady. How could I escape it? 'Tis part of a pirate's life, to be sure. Besides, despite what you witnessed the other day, I'm quite proficient at swordplay."

With a sigh, Isabel gazed above her as the sails swelled into snowy mountains. A blast of salty air filled her lungs. "You are much braver than I am."

The captain's deep voice howled over the deck, and growls and cheers emanated from the pirates. Isabel feared for the sloop and her captive passengers as the ship made a desperate plunge through the sea.

Hann grew quiet, and Isabel followed her gaze to Cutter, standing next to the captain. "He's a very wise and kind man."

Red blossomed on Hann's tanned cheeks, and she looked down. "Like no other I've met."

Isabel's eyes shifted to the captain as the two men talked, noting his imposing stance, his striking frame, and the courage and confidence that surrounded his every move.

"But it escapes me what you see in the captain." Hann spat with contempt.

"What do you mean? I see nothing," Isabel snapped, a sudden warmth rising up her neck. "I'm just intrigued at how he commands the ship."

"Of course." Hann crinkled her nose.

Sawkins lumbered onto the deck from the hatch, brushing a speck of dirt from his velvet doublet. His pale hair reflected the sun with a shimmer. He smiled her way, and Isabel nodded in return. All the horrid things the captain had said about him instantly sailed through her thoughts. How could such a finely chiseled face harbor the mind of a deviant scoundrel?

Hann snorted when she saw him.

"Don't be too hard on him, Hann. He meant no insult to Cutter."

Hann regarded him with a harsh gaze. "I wonder."

The *Restitution* swooped down a surging roller. Kent steadied his gaze upon his fleeing prey. Under a full crowd of sail, the sloop made a good run for it, but she sat low in the water. Although her crew members tossed crates and barrels overboard to lighten her load, their efforts would be futile. Hot wind swarmed over him, igniting the excitement of the chase. He braced his boots as the ship thrust boldly into the next swell, sending a spray of foam exploding over the bow. He shook it from his hair.

With Isabel aboard, he'd hoped to avoid attacking any ships, but he would certainly put her in more danger should he not keep his voracious crew appeased. He saw the way some of them looked at her. With him out of the way, they wouldn't hesitate to pass her amongst them like a common trollop.

Hann stood next to her on the foredeck, grinning like a pirate who'd just found treasure. The lad leaned in to whisper something in Isabel's ear, and she giggled. Jealousy oozed green in Kent's heart. Must the woman lavish her affections on every man on board—every man except him?

Sawkins slunk up next to him. "What is the meaning of this, Captain?"

Kent eyed the man with disdain. "Did we disturb your sleep, your lordship?"

"Yes, in truth, you did." As Sawkins studied the sloop, the *Restitution* crested a massive wave, then canted, nearly tumbling him to the deck. "Egad, do you plan to engage her?"

"That I d—"

The crackle of a hundred whips filled the air, and a rain of deadly small shot blasted over them. Ducking, Kent peered over the larboard railing to see a cloud of gray smoke hovering over the sloop's swivel gun.

Kent gave Sawkins a knowing look. "I would arm myself if I were you." Then he stood with fists planted on his hips and surveyed his crew. "Clear the deck for battle. Logan, prepare the larboard battery."

"Aye, aye, Cap'n." The master gunner disappeared below.

"Caleb!" Kent yelled across the deck. "Distribute the boarding axes!" The black man nodded with a grin and sped off. Kent had high hopes for Caleb. He'd shown a keen intellect and unusual courage, but he had to overcome the subservient mentality that had been pounded into him. With enough confidence, Caleb would make a far better first mate than Smithy, whom Kent wasn't sure he could trust anymore.

Kent's eyes locked with Isabel's. Was that fear in their green depths? Her delicate brow wrinkled, and she did not glance away as she usually did when their eyes met. He hated to pull his gaze from her, but he had a crew to lead and a ship to plunder. Fear hooked his heart. Not fear for him or his crew, but fear that Isabel would be injured.

He started toward her across the deck. "Lady Ashton, get below at once!"

With a slight upturn of her dainty nose, she squared her shoulders and glanced away.

"Osborn." Kent turned to his bosun, infuriated at her insolence. "Escort Lady Ashton to her cabin."

"But, Cap'n, we're almost in range."

"Do it now, man!"

With a snarl, Osborn dashed up the foredeck stairs.

Kent snapped his gaze back to the sloop. Close-hauled, the *Restitution* had come abreast of her starboard beam. In minutes, and with one swift turn to their port side, they would overtake her.

"Sparks, lead your musketeers to the tops!" Kent roared to his sharp-shooter. The brawny lad with the eye patch replied with an "aye," then led his men aloft. Kent shook his head. The boy had only one eye and an uncontrollable twitch in his right arm, but he could hit a cockroach square betwixt the eyes at one hundred yards.

Osborn returned, and one glance over the ship assured Kent that Isabel was below. "Fire when ready, Smithy."

"Fire!" Smithy yelled down the main hatch, and in seconds the ship rumbled with the blast of her broadside. A violent shudder swept her from stem to stern, testing each creaking timber. Choking plumes of smoke drifted over the deck. Coughing, Kent peered through the acrid fog toward their enemy.

Musket and pistol shot cracked the air. The pirates drew their swords and knives and growled like starving beasts scenting prey. Kent scanned the deck for Sawkins. He was nowhere to be seen.

The sound of splitting wood drew his attention back to the sloop, visible now through the clearing smoke. Her foremast toppled in shattered fragments of spiked oak, the yards and shrouds hanging in a snarled web on the deck. One of the fourteen-pounders had crushed her larboard timbers just above the water line. A ghostly silence yawned across her deck as a white flag rose on her mainmast. Not a living soul was in sight.

Kent studied his salivating crew, thankful the other ship had given up so quickly. "Hoornes, put the helm down and bring us alongside her bow. Men, prepare to board. Grapnels ready."

Positioning themselves, the men swung the iron claws over their heads. With a quick simultaneous release, the grapnels flew through the air and clanked into the deck of the sloop. Grunting, the men wrenched the two ships together. Their hulls thudded, then ground together as the pirates lashed them in place.

Drawing his sword, Kent leaped onto the bulwarks. "To the fight!" He pounded over the railing and stomped onto the sloop's main deck. Shouts and curses cut though the air as behind him, pirates scaled the bulwarks and poured into the vessel like rats.

Where was the usual thrill of battle that always coursed though Kent's hot blood? Perhaps it was Isabel's presence and his concern for her wellbeing that stifled his lust for conquest. His gaze took in the sloop from prow to stern. Empty.

Smithy came up beside him. "They've gone to closed quarters, Cap'n."

"So be it." Kent marched to the center of the ship. "Men!" he roared, drawing the attention of his crew. "Boarding axes to the forecastle bulkheads and hatch combings! Beware of the loopholes, gentlemen! Wolcott, Hoornes"—he faced two of his men standing nearby—"chop up that foremast and use it to ram the roundhouse."

Hoornes kissed his rat and tossed him into his coat pocket before following Wolcott.

"Smokes." Kent located the pirate with the blackened face and wild eyes. An expert at explosives, the man's attire hung in singed, black shreds. Apparently, he'd tested his inventions out on himself more than once. "Go fetch some of your grenades, if you please."

The men scrambled to do his bidding, bloodlust glinting in their eyes. Soon, hacks and chops and thunderous booms vibrated over the ship as the pirates slashed and pounded their way through the barricaded doors. Musket and pistol shots bombarded them through loopholes in the bulkheads, sending the men diving across the deck. With luck, he'd suffer no casualties.

A piercing scream—Kent spun to see Dorsey tumble to the deck, clutching his bloodied stomach. A jet of gray smoke spewed from a loophole on the main hatch coaming.

"Get the doctor!" Kent yelled, though he knew from the location of the wound, Dorsey would be dead within minutes. Blood and smoke bit Kent's nose, and disgust trampled his gut. He'd seen plenty of death. Why should the sight disturb him now?

A crunching *thud*, the splintering of wood, and the victorious huzzahs blaring from a band of Kent's men at the forecastle drew his attention, and he stormed toward them. Weaving his way through the crowd, he reached the wooden door, now a jumble of shards and spikes at his feet. He stepped through it, followed by his men. The stench of sweat and fear assaulted him.

The Spanish sailors backed up into the gloomy shadows of the forecastle, prodded by the tips of cutlasses and barrels of muskets leveled upon their chests. A large explosion from the aft shook the ship, and one by one they tossed their weapons to the floor and raised their hands.

Kent strode forward. "Where is your captain?"

A dozen pairs of nervous eyes stared at him from within shaking heads. From their attire and the terror skipping across their gazes, Kent knew they were naught but common sailors.

"Su capitán!"

A tall man with a pointed black beard and twisted mustache plowed through the crowd and stepped forward. "Capitán Nicklas Manuel Estiban, at your service." He bowed.

"Do you surrender, sir, or do you require more blood to be spilled?"

Adjusting the Castilian lace that trimmed his Spanish suit, the capitán peered down his nose at Kent. Then drawing his saber from its scabbard, he extended its hilt.

Kent accepted it with a bow and handed it to one of his men.

"Caleb." Kent turned toward the black man. "Take Murdock. Go below and free the slaves."

"What 'bout the treasure?" Smithy whined.

"See to the slaves first, then seek your treasure."

Smithy snorted.

Facing the captain again, Kent grinned. "Now, Captain, I beg you to suffer our presence for but a short while longer. Then, I assure you, we will be on our way."

"Do you not care for treasure, Doctor?" Isabel had not stayed long in her cabin—would not be dismissed like a common servant. As soon as she'd felt the ships collide and heard the pirates thundering over to the sloop, she'd come on deck and inched her way closer to the larboard railing where Cutter stood, pipe in hand.

"It holds no value to me. I was once a wealthy man." Cutter gave her a wary look. "Ah yes, I see the surprise in your eyes. But 'tis true. Wealth brought me no happiness then. Why should I expect it to now?"

Isabel cocked her head and examined him. She'd never heard of anyone who did not aspire to wealth, save Hann, who had left all she'd had to become a pirate. What a strange breed of people. Yet as she studied the greed dripping from the pirates' faces as they blasted their way into the hold of their enemy's ship, she had to admit riches had an ill effect on some.

It is not the money itself, but the place it holds in one's heart, beloved.

The revelation blossomed from deep within her, and she turned to relay it to Cutter but found his intense gaze locked upon Hann. The girl, looking like the fierce rogue she pretended to be, hefted the end of a thick pole also held by three pirates and bashed it into the door of the roundhouse with an ear-crunching *thump*. Isabel longed to tell him that the ardent affections that gleamed from his eyes were not misplaced as he indeed must be thinking, but she had promised Hann to keep her secret.

Lord Sawkins appeared at her side, looking rather distraught. "I cannot tell you how happy I am that you are unharmed, milady."

A sharp *crack* spiked through the air, followed by a scream. Isabel's heart jumped as her gaze shot to one of the pirates who'd dropped to the deck of the sloop.

"Doctor!" A harrowing shout roared in their direction.

With an anxious glance, Cutter darted over the bulwarks.

Isabel said a quick prayer for the injured man and glanced at Sawkins. "I did not see you with the rest of the men."

Looking bored, Sawkins waved a hand through the smoky air. "I do not get involved with these trifling pirate squabbles. I warned the captain against it, for it will take time away from finding your son. But you know pirates and their lust for treasure. He would not relent."

Isabel pursed her lips and ran a hand over the sudden churning in her stomach. The captain had said he preferred *not* to attack the sloop. She gazed at Sawkins as he pressed a strand of his blond hair behind his ear and grinned. Did he truly care for her and her son? If so, since he did not participate in the fight, why had he not sought her out to offer her his protection?

Dozens of dark-skinned, half-naked, emaciated men clambered over the railings onto the *Restitution*. Purple and red scars circled their wrists and ankles, and thin bloodied strips marred their backs. Squinting in the bright sun, they scanned their new surroundings with eyes devoid of hope and life. Isabel's heart fell into a deep sorrow.

Drawing a handkerchief from the pocket of his doublet, Sawkins held it to his nose. "What on earth compels the captain to bring these savages on board?"

"They are slaves, milord." Isabel's nerves pricked with indignation even as the rancid smell made her eyes water. "No doubt they have been held captive in the bilge of that ship for God knows how long. I daresay you would not fare so well."

"Come now, 'tis what they were bred for, as well you know. Some men must serve. It is their lot in life, and they enjoy it."

Isabel crinkled her brow and studied Sawkins. Nearly the exact words had been touted by Isabel's father. Hadn't she believed them as well? Why did they sound so appalling to her now? She thought of her time at Port Royal. A picture of sweet, beautiful Marlie formed in her mind. The young slave girl had been kinder to Isabel than most of her highborn friends had been. Marlie's words drifted through Isabel's mind, stinging her conscience: *"God loves all people just the same. We are all equal in His sight."* Isabel gazed back at the tortured slaves. "It would appear, milord, that these men find no pleasure in their current lot."

With raised brows, Sawkins frowned, then turned away. "I agree, milady. To starve and abuse them is inhumane."

Insincerity tainted his pretentious tone, and Isabel gave a sarcastic snort.

When the pirates had nearly completed the plundering of the sloop, several climbed back over the railings of the *Restitution*, arms bursting with glittering trinkets, chortling with glee. Straining, four of them hoisted an intricately carved chest over the bulwarks. Bottles of rum were passed amongst the celebrating vandals.

Searching the crowd, Isabel found Kent speaking to a pirate over on the sloop. He turned and with a single leap scaled the bulwarks and landed on the deck of the *Restitution*. With a commanding air, he ordered some of the crew to escort the slaves below and find places for them to sleep. His hair had escaped the cavalier tie and blew around him in a wild dance, making him appear even more threatening. She could not pull her gaze from him.

Something flickered in the corner of her eye. A stick of a man, dressed only in frayed breeches, dragged himself over to Isabel and knelt at her feet. He clasped his hands together and gazed up at her with pleading eyes. The stench of sweat and human excrement assailed her.

"Food, ma'am?"

Isabel's eyes pooled with tears as she gazed at the gaunt man. He swayed and clutched her gown to keep from falling. She flinched at his sudden forwardness; then shame flooded through her. She glanced at Sawkins, hoping he had a morsel to give him, but his eyes blazed with fire.

He plucked a knife from his belt and aimed it at the man's bare chest. "How dare you touch a lady, slave!" Spit flew from his angry lips.

The tip of the blade pierced the man's flesh, and blood trickled from the wound. He froze, the whites of his eyes stark against his dark skin.

Grabbing Lord Sawkins's arm, Isabel wrestled to pull him away. "He wasn't hurting me. He only wanted something to eat." But Sawkins wouldn't budge, nor did he appear to hear her.

He brushed Isabel aside and raised his blade over the slave. "You will die for that."

Boots pounded over the deck, and the tip of a cutlass landed upon Sawkins's chest.

Isabel glanced up to see the captain, narrowed eyes fixed upon Sawkins. She looked back at the slave. A tremble ran through him. *Lord, please do not let Sawkins hurt this man.*

Slowly, Sawkins raised his gaze to meet the captain's, a sneer cowering on his lips. Several pirates stopped what they were doing and gathered around as the two men glared at each other.

"Stand off," Kent ordered.

"Or what?" Sawkins grinned. "Are you going to kill me, brother?"

Brother? Shock jolted through Isabel. Her confused gaze drifted between them.

A flurry of angry Spanish words blared from the sloop, tugging all eyes away from the captain and Sawkins and onto a sailor who stormed across the deck of the enemy ship. Crazed, he waved two pistols in the air and continued his tirade, threatening them with his unknown words and the fury shooting from his eyes.

Isabel raised her gaze to watch him.

Crack!

Warmth stabbed Isabel's shoulder, and she glanced down to see a burgeoning circle of red staining her gown.

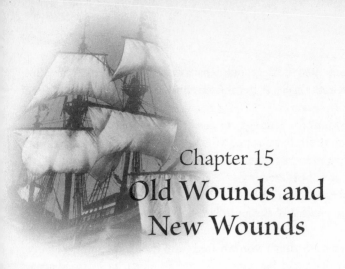

Chapter 15
Old Wounds and New Wounds

A scorching throb drove spikes into Isabel's consciousness. She raised a hand to her brow, praying it would stop.

"She's awake, Captain."

Isabel didn't want to open her eyes, afraid the pain would only increase if she did. Something poked her shoulder—something hot and sharp. She cried out.

Boot steps scuffed toward her. With difficulty, she pried open her heavy lids and peered around her. The captain leaned toward her on the left, concern tightening his handsome face, while Cutter ardently searched through a black satchel on her right. Hann grinned at her from the foot of the bed.

"What happened?" Her gaze took in the familiar details of her cabin. Afternoon sunlight penetrated the dirty window and set floating dust particles aglitter. Isabel searched her memories. The last thing she recalled was Sawkins attacking the poor starving slave—but wait. Something else tried to shove its way through her jumbled thoughts.

"Never fear, milady. 'Tis but a flesh wound. Ah." Cutter withdrew a vial from his bag and turned toward Isabel. "The pistol shot went clean through you."

Fear gripped her. "Pistol shot?" Isabel shifted her elbows back in an attempt to raise herself, but a spire of agony pierced her shoulder and sped down her arm, and she fell back onto the bed.

Captain Carlton wrapped his strong hand around hers, the familiar action quickening her breath despite her pain. She gazed at him. Fear flickered in his dark brown eyes—an emotion she'd never seen in them before, not when he'd faced battle, or a duel, or even death. The warmth of his thick fingers gave her comfort. His lips lifted in a half smile. "Try to be still, milady. Cutter will dress your wound." He let out a pained sigh. " 'Twas my fault. I thought all the Spanish sailors were confined."

The Spanish sailor. Visions of the mad Spaniard strutting across the deck of the sloop, brandishing his pistols through the air appeared vividly in Isabel's mind. But why her? Why had he shot her?

Cutter poured liquid from the vial onto a white cloth. "This may sting." He placed it over her shoulder. Pain radiated in pulsating waves. She squeezed her eyes shut as tears filled them.

"You're hurting her." The captain's grip on her hand tightened.

The cloth fell away, but her pain did not.

"I must clean the wound, Captain."

Tears slid into her hair. Opening her eyes, she tried to focus on the captain through the blurry moisture. " 'Tis all right, Kent." *Egad, did I just use his familiar name?* Too late, the rising of his brows and flicker of delight in his eyes revealed his pleasure. Warming under his sensual grin, she dropped her gaze. Red blotches stained his white shirt, and a sudden terror rose to join her pain. "You're hurt?" She gave his hand a squeeze and instantly realized he still held hers, and she snapped it from his grip.

"Nay, milady. 'Tis not my blood." Sadness stole his handsome smile, and Isabel cringed at the thought of the blood that must have been shed earlier that day.

Her gaze landed on Hann, thankful the young girl had not been hurt. "I suppose now that I've been injured in the plundering of a ship, I'm a real pirate?"

Hann chuckled. "That ye be, miss."

Rubbing the stubble on his chin, Kent regarded her with admiration. "You certainly possess enough courage to be one."

Isabel's heart fluttered at his compliment, and she lowered her gaze. As Cutter peered into the wound, she strained to see how bad it was but saw only a glimpse of red. The metallic smell of blood pricked her nose, and she turned her head away.

"I cannot dress this wound unless I cut her gown from her shoulder," Cutter announced, wiping his hands on a towel. "You men will have to leave or turn your backs."

"Swounds, man." Kent crossed his arms over his chest. "I've seen a lady's bare shoulder before."

"I trust you have, Captain, and"—Cutter gave him a judicial look—"no doubt this lovely shoulder, but you will not see it today, nor you, Hann." He gestured for them to turn their backs. "About with you now."

Grunting, Kent swung around, and Isabel smiled as Hann winked at her before turning around also, but when Isabel glanced back at Cutter, his urgent expression alarmed her. "What must you do?"

"Milady, I need to stitch up the opening." He grimaced. "I can offer you naught but liquor to dull the pain."

She drew a deep breath. How bad could it be? Worse than giving birth to a child? She nodded her assent.

Isabel's body tensed as the doctor cut her gown away from the wound. Grabbing a flask, he doused her shoulder with rum. Fiery pan gripped every nerve, and she lurched from the bed with a shrilling wail.

Kent flinched and flung a glance over his shoulder. "Confound it, man, what are you doing to her?"

Ignoring his captain, Cutter held the bottle out to Isabel. "I beg you to drink some, milady."

Eyeing him, she hesitated, never having partaken of the vile liquid, but the pain coursing through her convinced her to give Cutter an agreeing nod. Lifting her shoulders, he poured a draught into her mouth. The torrid liquid scorched a trail down her throat that spread out to her whole body in flames. She coughed and hacked and thought for certain she would lose what little she'd swallowed.

Cutter lifted a needle and thread from his bag and leaned over her, a sober expression on his scarred lips. The tiny metallic spike shook in his withered hand and loomed larger the closer he brought it. Isabel's head grew light, and the room began to spin. Darkness stole the corners of her vision and crept inward, absorbing everything until only the doctor's receding form remained, before he, too, was swallowed in black.

Kent propped his head in his hands and closed his eyes, allowing himself a brief repose from the harrowing events of the day. The familiar creak and moan of the ship as she soared through the dark sea becalmed his frenzied emotions. Opening his eyes, he watched the lantern light arch across the floorboards as it swayed with the movement of the ship from the hook above him. He raised his gaze. Only an inky darkness stared at him from outside the oval window, like the shroud that hovered over his heart.

A slight groan touched his ears, and his eyes drifted to the bed where Isabel slept. A red splotch marred the white bandage wrapped tightly over her right shoulder. Cursing himself, Kent stood and paced across the cabin. How could he have allowed her to be shot? A few inches to the left and he would have lost her. The thought sent ripples of agony through him. He rubbed the back of his neck. *God, if You are there*—he cast a tentative glance upward, half expecting a bolt of lightning to strike him—*thank You for sparing her.* He wasn't sure God would incline His ear toward someone like him, but if so, Kent wanted Him to know how grateful he was. A warm tingle showered over him, and he glanced around the cabin.

Shrugging it off, he leaned against the bedpost and watched the sleeping beauty. Her full lips pursed, and a sigh escaped them as her head tossed over the pillow. She seemed to be having a bad dream, and he hoped it wasn't about him. Her auburn hair cascaded like silk around her head. Even from where he stood, the sweet scent of coconut and vanilla encircled him, inflaming his senses. Another moan escaped her pink lips, and Kent flew to her side. He took her hand in his. Warm. But when he laid his palm on her forehead, her skin was not hot. He let out a sigh of relief. Cutter had warned him of a possible fever should infection set in.

Her eyelids fluttered and slowly opened. Sparkling green eyes found his, and though recognition flickered in them, fear did not follow. His heart leaped at the amorous glow pouring from them before her shield rose to block it from his view.

Her gaze took in the room and then returned to his. "Am I dead?"

Kent chuckled. "Not unless you expect to find *me* in heaven."

A slight smile alighted upon her delicate lips. "I thought perhaps I'd ended up in the wrong place." She raised a hand to her forehead. "It would seem this girl you deemed so brave passed out at the sight of blood."

"When 'tis your own blood, it is allowed." Kent smiled.

A moment passed in silence. He could not tear his gaze from hers. What he wouldn't give to know what she was thinking.

Tugging her hand from his embrace, Isabel shifted her gaze away, and Kent felt the loss like a knife in his gut.

He cleared his throat. "Would you care for some water?"

Isabel nodded and strained to sit, pain etching her face.

With arms outstretched, Kent moved toward her. "Allow me?"

She stared at him wide-eyed, then nodded.

Easing his arm behind her back, he leaned toward her, his face just inches from hers. Her sweet fragrance danced around his nose. Pounding heat throbbed in his blood. He lifted her and allowed his gaze to wander over her face. She looked up at him, confusion and yearning in her eyes, and he felt a tremble course through her. The air grew warm and heavy between them.

She has some affection for me, I know it.

It was there in her eyes, in the quiver of her body, the heat of her touch. He longed to take her in his arms, but instead, swallowing his passions, he propped her pillow behind her and laid her gently back down.

She averted her gaze, and Kent turned away to retrieve the pitcher of water and calm himself before facing her again. Pouring a glass, he handed it to her. She raised her right hand to take it, and winced. A cry escaped her lips. Kent moved the glass toward her mouth to assist her, but she snatched it from his grip, trembling, and took a sip. "How long have I been sleeping?" Her voice hardened.

Kent glanced toward the window, saddened by the gulf widening between them again. "For half a day. 'Tis about midnight, milady."

Her brows pinched. "What are you doing here?"

"The doctor said someone must watch over you in case a fever arises. Hann sat with you until nightfall, and then I took over."

"As you can see, I am quite well." She ran a hand over her stomach. "I won't burden you further."

" 'Twas my pleasure, as you well know." He felt his ire rising. Why the sudden change in her manner? Did she blame him for her being shot? Or was it still the past between them that stole her affections so quickly? The past. Kent hung his head. He made it sound so unassuming and guiltless, when in reality what he'd done to her was unforgivable.

She took another sip and handed the glass back to him. Her fingers shook, making the water slosh. "What of the hungry slave?" Her features softened as if she remembered something nice about him.

"He's below with the others, and being well fed, I assure you."

She stared at him for a moment, and then her eyes widened. "Lord Sawkins called you *brother*."

Kent marched to the desk and pretended to sift through the charts spread across it. He'd hoped she hadn't heard the knave's admission. But what could he do now? If he didn't tell her the truth, she'd inquire of Sawkins, and God only knew what twisted tales he'd weave for her. He swung about and leaned back against his desk.

She studied him. "How could you be brothers when he is a nobleman, and—"

"I am not?" Kent raised his brows. "When he is a lord, and I am not?" Anger thundered within him. "When he is a gentleman, and I am not?" He crossed his arms over his chest and clenched his fists. "Truth be told, milady, we are half brothers. He is the illicit product of one of my father's many conquests. Only this mistress was a countess, wife to Earl Nathaniel Sawkins."

Isabel stared at him, her green eyes reflecting shock and something else—sympathy?

Gripping the hilt of his cutlass, Kent stomped to the leather chair beside the bed. "The earl thought Richard was his son and gave him his name and title. But alas, to my great misfortune, when both the earl and his wife were killed in a fire, young lord Sawkins came to live with us."

He grabbed a bottle of rum from the table. Lifting it to his lips, he took a huge gulp. The hot liquid bit at his throat and sent its numbing waves across his chest and into his belly.

Isabel cleared her throat. "Did he not have any other family who would take him in?"

Kent shook his head. "None save a great-grandmother who could no longer care for herself. Besides, his true parentage was being questioned even then."

"But his name?" Isabel asked in a tentative voice.

"Is Lord Richard Sawkins Bristol."

Kent plopped into the chair, noting the confusion crimping her face. "And my full name is Kent Frederick Carlton Bristol."

"Why do you keep your relationship a secret?" Isabel asked.

"Our mutual abhorrence for one thing, but alas, I have grown tired of his creditors seeking me out to settle his debts." He gave her a wry smile.

"You are nothing like him." Isabel wrinkled her brow, then dropped her gaze.

Kent studied her, wondering if that was indeed the flicker of a smile he'd seen on her lips. "Though I know you did not mean it as such, I will take that as a compliment."

She gave him a coy gaze, then glanced toward the dark window. "Did he lie to me about his father being injured in the war?"

"Nay, milady." Kent leaned the bottle on his thigh. It was probably the only thing the villain hadn't lied to her about. "Our father was indeed maimed."

Isabel clasped her hands together and looked down. "Truly, I'm sorry."

"No need to be. 'Twas not my father's outward deformities that caused him to fail in life, but his inward ones."

Isabel looked at him curiously. Her cinnamon hair spiraled down around her face, over her shoulders, and tickled the lacy quilt on the bed. Kent swallowed. He'd rarely seen her hair out of those blasted combs, and he longed to run his fingers through the silky threads.

"Was he cruel to you?"

Her question and the concern warming her voice drew his focus back to memories of his father—a subject he much preferred to avoid. He took another swig from the bottle, hoping to dull the pain, and suddenly remembered his vow to remain sober while Sawkins was on board. He slammed the flask on the table. Isabel jumped.

"My apologies, milady." Kent sighed. "Yes, my father was a hard man to please."

"Yet Lord Sawkins speaks well of him." Isabel raised her chin.

"Richard was the favored son." Kent gritted his teeth and leaned forward, planting his elbows on his knees. He tried to force back all the sordid memories that clambered from the corners of his mind, but they shoved their way forward despite his efforts. His father's endless bragging about Sawkins, praising his intelligence, his strength, his nobility, all the while belittling Kent for not being more like his brother—blaming Kent for everything that had gone wrong in his life. When Sawkins stole money from his father, Kent was whipped for it. When Sawkins did not complete a chore, Kent was sent to bed without supper. He looked up at Isabel. "He was spoiled beyond measure. My father worshipped him, gave him everything—his business, his ships, his fortune—and Sawkins trampled them under his boots."

Isabel gave him a skeptical look. "He seems quite successful to me."

"Have you seen this wealth he boasts about?" Kent raised his brows.

Isabel looked away.

"He has not two doubloons to warm his pocket, no property, no ship."

" 'Twas not his fault he lost his ship in the storm on a rescue mission."

"Egad!" Kent laughed. "Is that the tale he told you?"

Isabel crossed her arms over her chest, then cringed and shifted her injured shoulder. "Are you saying he didn't lose his ship?"

Kent shook his head and leaned back in the chair, amazed at the ease with which Sawkins could entrap women with his bewitching charm. "No, he lost it, but 'twas in a game of cards, not a rescue mission."

"I don't believe you." Isabel huffed. "A nobleman would do no such thing." Gathering her silken hair in a bundle, she laid it over her left shoulder. "Why do you hate him so?"

"I pity him more than I hate him."

Isabel's eyes snapped to his. "As I have said before, I daresay you are merely jealous of him."

"Is that so?" Kent jumped to his feet, fury seething a hot trail through him. He started toward Isabel, then halted. "Insufferable woman," he spat.

"Me? Insufferable?" Isabel raised her nose in the air and sniffed haughtily. "You're the pirate."

"Then what of your precious Captain Merrick?" Kent sneered. "He is a pirate, too."

"Captain Merrick is a man of honor, while you are naught but a lecherous dog. He does not plunder for gain, but for the glory of the crown. He does not torture and kill innocent people but values all life. Nor does he ravish women, but cherishes and respects the weaker sex. So my apologies, Captain." Isabel flashed a superior grin. " 'Tis not that your trade makes you insufferable. Your character alone does that quite well."

Grimacing, Kent swallowed the burning searing in his throat. He turned away.

"Please leave." He heard her stern voice behind him.

Releasing a sigh, Kent regained his composure and faced her. "Very well." He bowed and slammed out the door before she could see the pain in his eyes. Slinking into the shadows, he flattened himself against the adjacent wall and lowered his head. Why had he disclosed so much of himself to this woman? Now, she had more than enough poison darts to do away with him for good. He could still feel their sting in his heart. Though he thought he'd sensed her attraction to him, it must have been naught but his own foolish wishes. She seemed quite taken with Sawkins, no matter what he'd said. But why would she believe the word of a pirate anyway? He must make her see the truth. He would not let his scandalous brother have her—not as long as he had the power to prevent him.

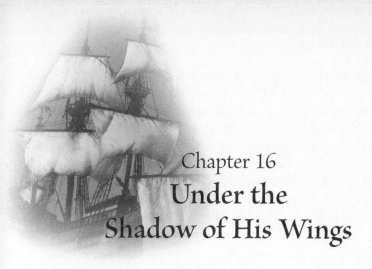

Chapter 16
Under the
Shadow of His Wings

Isabel drew her shawl tightly about her shoulders against the chilly mist billowing up from the sea. Leaning over the railing littered with tiny droplets, she peered into the gray haze, searching for the familiar turquoise of the ocean, but only the purling rush of water against the hull assured her the ship maintained its speed. Cool moisture soaked through the sleeves of her gown, and she stepped back from the rail.

Oh, Frederick. How long had they been at sea now—ten days? And no sign of Morris. Was he truly going to Cartagena? Would they find him there? *Father*—she glanced up into the silent ashen sky—*please keep him safe.* A burning ache formed in her throat, threatening to rise and fill her eyes with tears. She wanted to trust God, yet as each day passed, her faith waned. *Lord, I believe. Help me in my unbelief.*

Hugging herself, she closed her eyes and tried to remember the feel of her baby in her arms, the gurgle of his playful babbling, his innocent scent. A dull pain spiraled out from her shoulder, and she reached up and rubbed it, easing it in a semicircle. Three days had passed since the pistol shot had pierced her skin, and although still sore, Isabel had recovered quickly. She'd spent most of that time sleeping. Her only visitors had been Hann, who'd come to bring her food, and Cutter, who'd periodically checked her bandaging. She'd not seen the captain since she'd tossed him from her cabin. But what did she expect? She'd been horribly cruel to him. She remembered the pain leeching from his eyes, and guilt raked over her. It was no way for a Christian woman to behave. Her thoughts drifted to the way his strong arms felt on her back as he lifted her from the bed. A warm blush crept up her neck and onto her face.

"What makes you smile this early in the morning?"

Jumping, Isabel looked up to see Hann grinning at her. Two pistols hung tied to a scarlet ribbon draped over her shoulder. Her tight leather vest, topped with brown waistcoat, well hid her gender. Taller and thicker boned than Isabel, Hann indeed could pass for a pirate, save for the rosy blush that graced her cheeks and the lush dark lashes framing her violet eyes.

"Was I smiling?" Isabel let out a nervous giggle. "Perhaps I'm just happy to be out of that stifling cabin."

"I'm glad to see you so improved, milady. You gave us all quite a scare—especially the captain."

"I'm sure he did not trouble himself overmuch." Isabel raised her chin. "I have not seen him for three days."

Hann leaned one arm on the railing and cocked her head. "On the contrary, he inquired after you several times each day and ensured that you were well fed."

Shifting her gaze away, Isabel tried to still the sudden leap of her heart. No reason existed for Kent's kindness save that he hoped to make restitution for what he had done to her. He must learn that no amount of good deeds could ever erase his horrendous actions of that one night. "Surely Lord Sawkins was also concerned?"

"Difficult to say, milady, since he has spent most of his time drinking and gambling." Hann crinkled her nose and glanced over Isabel's shoulder. Her eyes lit up, and before Isabel could turn around, she knew the doctor had come on deck.

With a tip of his hat, Cutter nodded to Isabel, but his eyes lingered on Hann.

"It must be quite difficult for you." Isabel looked with sympathy at her friend and longed to give her hand a squeeze.

Hann shrugged. "Truth be told, I'm happy just to be near him." She continued to gaze at Cutter, who stood across the deck, puffing a pipe.

"Then you are fortunate indeed." Isabel gave a sorrowful smile. "I

long to feel so passionately toward a man."

Hann snorted and raised a brow. "Perhaps you already do?"

Boot steps pounded on the deck, and several more pirates emerged from below, scattering to their stations. With a quick nod, Hann darted off before Isabel could ask her who she'd meant. Sawkins?

The pirates on watch up on the fore- and quarterdecks were relieved of duty. The groan of wood drew Isabel's glance upward where the masts, which had been shrouded in fog when she'd first come on deck, now poked their tips into the grim blanket hovering above them. Sails floundered in the light breeze, and Isabel spotted the red- and white-checkered shirt of a man perched in the crow's nest.

Gibbons trudged up beside her, gave her a surly glance, and tossed the lead line into the water to measure the depth. The tiny *splash* bounced off the mist and echoed across the ship.

Clutching the rail, Isabel gazed out over the fog—so thick it seemed as though she could reach out and grab a hold of it. She wondered how the pirates were able to navigate the ship.

The clanging of a distant bell sounded, followed by a string of muffled foreign words. Squinting, Isabel peered out into the fog. She darted a glance over her shoulder to see if the pirates had heard anything, then back out to sea. The sound had not come from their ship but from beyond in the haze. Alarm quickened her breath.

Thick, masculine fingers gripped the rail beside her hand, sending a warm tingle down her arm. "Milady, it pleases me to see you looking so well." The captain's deep voice blanketed her, allaying her fears for the moment.

Isabel looked up at him. His dark hair was pulled back in a cavalier tie, revealing his firm, stubbled jaw. He narrowed his gaze upon her and gave her a roguish smile.

Gulping, Isabel opened her mouth to relay a sarcastic quip, but the words clumped in her throat. *What is wrong with me?*

"Perchance, your wound has affected your voice, milady?" He winked.

Isabel's anger dissolved the knot in her throat. "Don't be a fool, Captain."

He bowed. "I shall take that under consideration."

A bell chimed again, this time off the port side of the ship. Kent turned and squinted into the mist. A flurry of indistinct words in a foreign accent drifted over them.

Kent's gaze latched upon Isabel's.

"What language is that?" she asked, noting the unease flashing in his eyes.

Kent grimaced. "Spanish—flawless Castilian."

Smithy lumbered up to them. "Cap'n," he yelled. "T's—"

"Shh. . ." Kent raised both hands, marched across the deck, then slowly lowered them. "Quiet, everyone."

Terror coiled around Isabel.

Chattering ceased as the pirates stared at their captain.

Laughter blared from a group of men up on the poop deck.

Smithy flew up the quarterdeck stairs. "Hush, ye daft loons," he blurted in a loud whisper, immediately silencing them. They glared at him, eyes agape, then glanced down at their captain, who held a finger to his lips.

Plucking his spyglass from his belt, Kent leaped up on the foredeck and lifted it to his eye. Hann and Smithy joined him on either side.

Minutes passed as the pirates crept across the deck, staring out into the fog on both sides of the ship. Leaning over the railing, Isabel strained to hear. The *creak* of moist wood and the gentle *groan* of a hull filtered over her from the distance. A ship sailed nearby—a large one.

Fear pinched her nerves. Inching her way up the foredeck stairs, she joined the captain, longing to feel safe. She brushed his side as she made her way to the main head railing and peered through the gray soup. A torrent of Castilian flooded over her from up ahead. Suddenly, a huge wall of cracked brown wood broke through the murky haze.

Alarm rang through Isabel. Jumping, she slowly retreated from the rail as the leviathan glided by the bow of the ship. She backed into something hard. One strong arm encircled her waist while another covered her mouth to stifle her scream. She squirmed.

"Raise the flag of Spain," Kent whispered above her. "And gather all the Spanish uniforms you can find." Footsteps sped off.

Moaning, Isabel writhed in his grasp. Pain etched through her shoulder.

"Be still, woman, and I will release you."

With a sigh, Isabel froze, and he let her go. When she turned, she found herself pressed against his broad chest.

Looking down at her, he grinned, and instantly she stepped back. "Pray tell, Captain. What ship was that?"

"It appears we have sailed into the middle of a Spanish fleet, milady."

Isabel raised a hand to her mouth. "But when the fog clears. . ."

"Aye, then we're done for," Hoornes said, cupping his rat protectively in his hands.

Sawkins appeared behind Kent. "What goes on here?" he bellowed, turning his nose up at the sight of the rat.

"Shh." The captain, Isabel, and two other pirates turned toward Sawkins.

Halting, he scanned their faces, brow wrinkling, then gazed off into the mist. Smithy and Hann returned, arms overflowing with velvet Spanish waistcoats, corselets, and high-crested helmets.

Cutter appeared behind them, pipe braced between his teeth.

"Have the men put these on," Kent whispered to Smithy, "and send the rest below out of sight."

Hann glanced at Cutter before rushing after Smithy down the stairs. The woodsy smell of pipe smoke swirled around Isabel as the doctor approached her. "How does your shoulder fare today, milady?"

Isabel gave him a curious smile and gazed upward as a patch of bright blue winked at her through the fog. "I fear we have bigger problems at the moment than my shoulder, Doctor." Dashing to the railing, she peered over the side. The azure water frothed up against the hull and could be clearly seen several yards out from the ship. Speck by speck, the cold mist dissipated as the hot Caribbean sun gained dominance over the day.

Above her, the red and white flag of Castile flapped against the head of the mainmast. She gazed at Kent, who stood arms crossed over his chest, surveying the fog. His eyes met hers—unease stirred within their dark depths.

Two more bells clamored, one up ahead and one off their port side. The rustle of water and moan of wood drifted over them. Turning slowly, Isabel squinted into the gray mist all around them. The sounds came from every direction. Her legs began to tremble.

They were surrounded.

As if just waking up from a shocking dream, Sawkins sauntered to Isabel and possessively stood between her and Kent. "Faith, Captain, have you sailed us nigh into the gaping mouth of the lion? What foolishness! What danger you have placed upon this lady and your whole crew."

Kent turned a granite stare upon him.

Osborn, standing on the far side of the deck, turned and spat onto the deck. "D'ye know what Spaniards do with pirates?" He lumbered toward them and raised his upper lip in a sneer that revealed decaying teeth. "They flay 'em alive and hang 'em by the yardarm." His lecherous gaze raked over Isabel. "And they don't be treatin' a lady no better—that is, after the whole crew has a turn with 'er."

Isabel swallowed hard and felt the blood race from her heart. She grabbed the railing to keep from stumbling. Sawkins's face turned as white as the fog that surrounded it.

"That will be all, Osborn." Kent's low, commanding voice was enough to send the aged pirate scampering away with a moan. The captain faced Isabel. "Perhaps you should go below, milady."

Sawkins took a step forward and darted an anxious glance around him. "Captain, if you intend to pursue this ruse of being a Spanish merchant, wouldn't it be better to keep the lady on deck?" he whispered and clasped his hands together. "Spanish captains often travel with their wives." He glanced at Isabel with a nervous grin. "And Lady Ashton makes a lovely *señora*."

"You would put her at risk?" Kent shook his head.

"Nay, please, Captain," Isabel pushed past Sawkins. "I want to stay on deck. Perhaps I can be of help."

"Let her stay above, Captain," Cutter interjected between puffs of smoke. "If we are captured, we are all done for anyway." The calm tone of his voice drew all eyes to him, Isabel's included. His stolid acceptance of whatever fate brought his way put Isabel's own faith to shame.

Kent flexed his jaw and gazed down upon her, then nodded his assent.

Smithy and Hann flew up the stairs and stood before their captain.

"Have Logan ready both batteries," Kent ordered his first mate, "and tell the men to hide their weapons beneath their coats."

"Aye, aye, Cap'n." Smithy spun on his heels.

With a quick glance of concern toward Isabel, Hann handed the captain a Spanish coat with silver embroidery. He slipped it over his white shirt, then donned a Spanish helmet.

"How do they wear these blasted morions?" He twisted it atop his head.

A beam of sunlight struck the deck and blossomed outward, grazing the tip of Isabel's boots. She glanced out to sea and saw similar beams striking the rippling water, chasing the fog from their midst. Blotches of blue sky invaded the haze above them. Isabel's heart slammed against her ribs.

The pointed masts and square hull of a massive galleon emerged from the haze off their port side.

A bell tolled.

Isabel turned to see another ship appearing on their right. Following Sawkins's groan and the point of his trembling finger, Isabel faced forward. The high flat stern of another galleon rose not fifty yards off their bow. Through the dissipating haze, the bright red of a cross painted on the high arching sails soared above them like an omen of death.

Isabel's breath stole from her. Was this the end? What would become of Frederick? And her? She'd heard of the horrifying tortures inflicted by the Spanish on those who did not follow their faith.

"*Quién va allí?*" The words flowed to them from one of the ships.

"What are they saying?" Sawkins retreated from the railing, ashen-faced.

"I believe they are asking who we are." Kent leveled a gaze upon Isabel. "If ever there was a time for prayer, milady, this would be it."

Cutter snorted.

Hann eased beside the doctor, who looked down upon the lad with concern.

Of course. Isabel shook her head and chided herself. 'Twas the first thing she should have done. Why did it always seem to be the last? Shamed at her own weakness, Isabel knelt on the deck, all propriety aside, and bowed her head. "Father, I need You. We need You. Please rescue us. Please deliver us from our enemies. Show these men who do not believe in You Your might, power, and glory. Cover us in the shadow of Your mighty wings. In the name of Your Son, Jesus, I thank You. Amen."

Opening her eyes, Isabel stared at the sodden wood of the foredeck, examining the cracks and lines and listening for the thunderous booms of the cannons that would end her life. *Where is my faith?* Her back warmed under the glaring sun that now brightened the deck around her. Visions of Frederick sailed through her mind: his playful grin—so much like his father's—his curly umber hair and dark eyes alight with innocence and love. Her heart ached.

Gasps sounded from the men above her.

"Egad!" she heard Sawkins exclaim.

Isabel lifted her gaze. Kent offered her his hand, and she took it, rising to her feet. Following the men's gaping glances, she looked out across the water. The morning fog had disappeared, hammered back into the sea by the sun's rays. In its stead, as far as her eye could see, Spanish galleons dotted the horizon.

Raising a hand to her mouth, Isabel slowly turned to see several more ships behind the *Restitution*. Her gaze met Kent's, and he raised his scarred brow.

"I hope your God heard you."

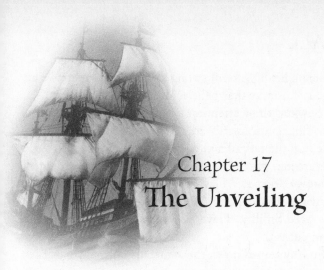

Chapter 17
The Unveiling

Terror consumed Isabel. "Where did all the Spanish galleons come from?" Her voice quavered. "Why are there so many?"

"More'n likely a treasure fleet, miss," Smithy offered without a glance. "Transportin' their fortune to Cadiz. Pearls from Rio de la Hacha and silver and gold from Peru." Eyes gleaming, he rubbed spittle from his lips with the back of his hand. "They grow tired of us pirates stealin' their gold." He gave a coarse chuckle.

"Identifíquelo y su barco!" The Spanish demand blasted over them from a man standing on the galleon off their port side.

Cutter withdrew his pipe from his lips. "I hope you remember your Spanish, Captain."

Amazed at his calm demeanor, Isabel shifted her gaze from Cutter to Sawkins, who kept shaking his head and repeating the same phrase. "Sheer folly. Sheer folly."

Hann stared at the towering, square-shaped galleon veering toward them. She cast a glance over her shoulder. "They're opening their gun ports, Captain."

Adjusting his helmet, Kent marched to the railing and cupped his hands around his mouth. *"Somos la Restitución,"* he shouted. *"Comerciantes Españoles."*

Surprised at Kent's command of the language, Isabel watched as the soldier leaned and spoke to a man next to him. The harsh angles of his corselet and morion gleamed in the sun.

Planting his fists on his hips, Kent swung about. "I told them we are Spanish merchants. Let us pray they believe me."

A moan from Sawkins drew attention to another galleon just thirty yards off their bow. Spanish soldiers had taken their posts behind two swivel guns mounted on the taffrail and were preparing to fire.

Lord Sawkins's anxious gaze swerved to Kent. "We must surrender."

"Nay." Kent's brow darkened. " 'Twould be better to die than to fall into their hands. I will not have Lady Ashton subjected to their cruelty. We will fight." He faced Smithy. "Have Logan stand by with the guns, but do not run them out yet."

"Aye, Cap'n." Smithy leaped down the stairs, his normally hardened gaze spiked with fear.

" 'Tis madness!" Sawkins spat.

" 'Tis fate, your lordship," Cutter retorted.

Father, are You there? Please help us. Isabel hugged herself in an effort to stop trembling. Kent moved closer to her, concern warming his eyes. He raised an arm as if to place it on her shoulder, then hesitated and dropped it to his side.

Isabel's heart sank. At that moment, she longed for the strength of his touch. She looked up at him, no longer trying to shield her feelings. Bewilderment tinted his gaze as he examined hers, and a sad smile played on his lips.

Confusion tripped through Kent as he stared into Isabel's eyes. Was that affection in their depths? He wished he could lengthen the moment and find out. He wished her display of emotions had not come so late, but at least she had given him a token of tenderness before he died.

He glanced at the galleon sailing off their port side. A cluster of soldiers lined the railing of the Spanish warship. The Spaniard who had conversed with him lifted a glass to his eye and scanned the length of their ship, then lowered the scope and turned to talk to his men. The muttering of Spanish words drifted to them over the expanse of water.

Surely the Spaniards had seen past their deception, especially now that Kent had ordered their guns to stand by.

Isabel looked up at him. "What are they saying?"

"I cannot make out the words." Kent glanced at her, trying to mask the growing fear within him. He did not wish to alarm her, but truth be told, a few of the captain's words—words such as fire, capture, and sink—had wrangled their way from Spanish into English and spiked into his mind.

At the thought of what would happen to Isabel should they be captured, an unfamiliar feeling of terror clamped Kent's heart. Grimacing, he hung his head. He had let her down again.

Soft hands gripped his arm. Startled, Kent turned to see Isabel, her eyes tightly shut, clinging to him as she braced herself against the oncoming blasts. So brave. Warmth poured through him, despite the dire circumstances. She could have reached for Cutter or Sawkins for comfort, yet she had embraced him. He cupped a hand around hers and patted it gently. She did not pull away.

Kent glanced at the galleon in front of them. One of the men manning the swivel guns held a glowing linstock in his hand and was lowering it to the touchhole to ignite the charge. So, this was it. At least he had Isabel by his side. Thoughts of Frederick burst into his fears. Kent didn't even know what his son looked like. What would happen to him now?

Muttering, Sawkins stumbled to the foremast and gripped it with one hand. " 'Tis my folly to have sailed with you, brother. You always were a failure."

"And what would you suggest, your lordship? By all means"—Kent raised a hand toward him—"favor us with your wisdom."

With a snort, Sawkins looked away. "I had not thought to die aboard your ship, but upon my own—perhaps in a glorious sea battle, a fitting end to my resplendent career."

Kent raised a brow. "If you are ever able to retain a ship of your own, do contact me. I'd be happy to oblige you."

Sawkins's eyes darted about in a frenzy. "We are about be slaughtered, and you continue your insolent jests." His lips quivered. "Indeed, I hope we die and are not left maimed for life." He glanced with disgust at the doctor.

Taking a puff from his pipe, Cutter glared at Sawkins. He pulled the brown tube from his lips and blew a cloud of smoke toward his lordship before turning to face Kent. " 'Tis been a pleasure and an honor to have sailed with you, Captain. No one could have foreseen this."

"Aye, that goes for me, too," Hoornes added, approaching them.

Hann dashed to Cutter's side.

Logan popped up from the main hatch.

"On my order, run out the guns and fire at will," Kent instructed him.

A loud Spanish voice blared from their left. *"No encienda los cañónes. Permítalo pasar."*

Shock jolted through Kent. He peered toward the Spaniard on the galleon and ran the words through his limited Spanish vocabulary. Surely he had misinterpreted what the soldier had said, yet when he glanced at the ship in front of them, the two men who'd manned the swivel guns withdrew the linstock and backed away from the cannons.

Opening her eyes, Isabel tugged on his sleeve as Cutter, Hann, and Sawkins showered him with questioning looks.

Kent rubbed his chin. "I believe he just ordered them not to shoot and to allow us to pass."

"Nigh impossible." Cutter swung his gaze back out toward the galleon.

Hann crinkled her nose. "But why would they? 'Tis obvious we are not Spaniards."

Still clinging to the mast, Sawkins opened his mouth as if to say something, but merely coughed instead.

All eyes darted to Isabel. She quickly released her grip on Kent's arm, her face reddening, then broke into a beaming smile. "My prayer has been answered, gentlemen."

"Are you saying this is God's doing?" Cutter's eyes widened.

Kent returned his gaze to the galleon off their larboard side. The soldiers had dispersed and were raising their topsails to catch the full wind.

Pirates scrambled to the railings and stared aghast at the galleon as it slammed shut its gun ports and sped after its compatriots. Flurries of Spanish echoed over the sea as the warship lumbered past the *Restitution*'s larboard bow.

The abandoned swivel guns peered at them like two gaping eyes. The mighty vessel shrank to join the others that speckled the horizon, spitting a frothy wake at the *Restitution*.

Kent studied Isabel's calm face. She raised a hand to shield her eyes

from the sun as she examined the retreating galleons. A gentle smile graced her lips.

Releasing a sigh, he scanned the horizon, reason still clambering in his mind for anything solid to hold onto. There must be another explanation, but as he watched the enemy ships withdraw without so much as a shot fired, he could think of none. Isabel's God had answered her again. A deep longing welled within Kent—a desire to know this powerful God, to meet His approval and be valued by Him as Isabel seemed to be. But what would a God so holy and almighty find worthy of regard in Kent?

Hope drowned beneath a resurgent flood of shame. Bunching his fists, Kent forced his focus back to what he did best, captaining a ship, and at the moment, his frigate was not out of danger. Scanning the pirates remaining on the foredeck, his gaze landed on Hann. "Furl all sails."

With a nod, Hann started on his way, but Kent clutched his arm and stopped him. "Do it quietly, and. . ." The captain cast a quick glance behind him. "Alter our course twenty degrees south southeast. We'll let them sail right past us." He released Hann, and the lad disappeared down the stairs.

Kent turned to Isabel. "I don't know what is happening, and I'm not sure I believe it, but the fortune that has come upon us is not of this world."

Isabel's eyes sparkled as her lips rose in a grin.

Cutter shot Kent a curious look from the railing, then continued to smoke his pipe and gaze out over the Spanish fleet.

"Ye hear that, little fellow?" Hoornes plucked his rat from a pouch hanging at his belt and perched him upon his shoulder. "We are saved." He smiled at Isabel. "Now I best be gettin' to me post." And he scrambled down the stairs.

With all sails taken in and the yards nearly bare, the *Restitution* eased into a slow, clumsy drift. One by one, the massive ships of the Spanish fleet sailed past them on both sides. The only indication that they knew the *Restitution* sailed amongst them was an occasional hail by one of their captains—to which Kent replied appropriately. As the galleons parted the sea with their heavy frames, the *Restitution* rolled and quaked over each burgeoning wake but otherwise remained untouched.

Gaping at their enemies, the pirates who had donned Spanish uniforms took turns shouting reports to those of the crew Kent had ordered to remain below. Miracle or not, he did not intend to take any chances by allowing any of his less-reputable-looking men on deck—not until they were well out of range of the Spanish cannons.

The last galleon rose like a menacing beast off their starboard side. She sailed so close to the *Restitution* that Kent could see the expressions on the Spaniards' faces—no shock, no alarm flickered in them, no indication that they saw the pirate ship drifting in their path. He shook his head in continued disbelief.

Finally stepping away from the mainmast, Sawkins brushed the specks of wood from his doublet and balled his hands on his hips. He cast an imperious glance at Isabel. "What devilry is at work here, milady?"

" 'Tis no devilry, I assure you," Isabel answered with a tilt of her head. "Quite the opposite."

Cutter raised his scarred lips in a pretentious grin. "I'd still my tongue, Sawkins, if I were you. Or perhaps the Almighty will change His mind. The ships are still within firing range."

"What of fate, good doctor?" Isabel regarded him with a faint smirk.

"Fate cannot do this, milady." He bowed.

Smithy popped up on deck, and Kent leaned over the foredeck railing. "Bring the helm hard over, Mr. Hoornes. Smithy, begin to lower all sails. Let's put some distance between us and our Spanish friends."

Hoornes sped to the whipstaff.

"Aye, Cap'n." Smithy scratched his thick sideburns, then turned and like a mad dog barked orders that sent a dozen men leaping into the ratlines and clambering aloft.

Leveling his spyglass to his eye, Kent steadied himself as the ship lurched to starboard.

Sawkins clutched Isabel's elbow to keep her from stumbling. "This is not God," he stammered, then stormed toward Kent, flashing angry eyes. " 'Tis some clever trick you are playing upon me—to make me appear the fool."

"Ah, but you do that so well without my assistance." Kent lowered the glass.

Sawkins clenched his fists. "God cannot create such an illusion."

As if agreeing with his declaration, the roar of a cannon thundered across the sky. Round shot crashed into the deck amidships in a blast of

splintering wood that sent a shudder through the frigate. A scream sliced the air.

Dashing to the railing, Kent raised the spyglass. A plume of smoke jetted from the stern of the galleon that had just passed. Why had only the last ship fired upon them? And why now?

Cutter gave Sawkins a smug look. "Look what you have done."

"Egad, you dare blame me, sir?" Sawkins snorted. "I knew 'twas not God."

Kent glanced aloft. "Spread all canvas to the wind, gentlemen. Tops and studding sails up." The *Restitution* had nearly completed her turn, and the sails began to swell with the warm Caribbean air. Behind them, the pursuing galleon fumbled in its tack as shifting sails floundered in the breeze. A plume of gray smoke shot from the Spanish ship's starboard battery, and Kent grabbed Isabel as a roaring *boom* hammered the air. This time, however, the round shot splashed into the sea several yards aft of their starboard quarter.

Tugging from his grasp, Isabel gazed toward the galleon. "They won't catch us."

"Nay, milady. We are windward and have the sailing advantage," Kent answered, unsure whether she asked a question or merely made a statement. He studied her eyes, but no fear burned within them.

Turning, he leaned over the foredeck railing. "What damage?" he yelled below.

A crowd of pirates huddled on the main deck. One of them looked up. "It be Hann, Cap'n. He's hit."

Isabel gasped and raised a hand to her mouth.

Kent's stomach lurched. He darted his gaze to Cutter's.

Dropping his pipe, the doctor flew down the stairs, raced across the deck, and shoving the pirates aside, knelt beside his friend.

Kent tightened his grip on the railing. Hann was more than a quartermaster. He was a good pirate and had been kind to Isabel. He did not want to lose him.

Isabel snatched up the smoldering pipe, lifted her skirts, and darted down the stairs, ignoring Kent's beckoning call behind her. Terror raked over her, prodding her forward. The only thought racing through her mind was that Hann was hurt, possibly dead.

A blackened, smoking hole gaped at Isabel from the starboard bulwark. Spears of charred wood littered the deck. Two pirates grabbed Hann's legs and arms and lifted her. Isabel peered between them to see a blotch of deep red creeping across Hann's waistcoat. At its center, a wooden spike at least one inch thick protruded from her side. Droplets of blood marred her face and neck.

"Easy men, easy," Cutter admonished, fear quaking in his voice.

Isabel flew to his side. "Will she—he—be all right?"

"I don't know yet." He nudged her out of the way and assisted the men down the companionway stairs.

Isabel followed them into the darkness below, down two flights of stairs, past the gun deck, and into the berth where the crew slept and ate. A chill swept over her despite the stifling heat. She'd never ventured this deep into the bowels of the ship before, and the stench of rot, filth, and urine suffocated her. Hammocks swung from beams overhead. Rats scurried across tables littered with rotted food and spilt grog. The faces of a throng of pirates drifted her way, their expressions made more hideous in the shifting shadows. Toward the aft of the ship, slaves huddled together in the darkness as if unaccustomed to the light.

With a frenzied sweep of his arm, Cutter cleared one of the tables in the corner, sending bowls, mugs, and utensils clanking to the floor. The pirates laid Hann's unconscious body across the filthy slab of oak.

"Get my satchel!" Cutter yelled to one of the pirates as he tore off his doublet and rolled up the sleeves of his shirt. The skin on his left arm curled in a weave of purple and red. "And some water and rum!"

Isabel rushed to Hann's side and grabbed her hand, so cold and lifeless. "Hann," she sobbed, forcing back a flood of tears.

Cutter leaned his head over Hann's mouth and hesitated, his eyes closed. "He's alive," he announced with a sigh of relief. Then, stepping back, he began unbuttoning Hann's bloody waistcoat.

Isabel gasped and Cutter lifted his gaze to her as if he'd just noticed she were still there. "You should go. This is a bloody business and no place for a lady."

Isabel shook her head, but no words came to her lips. She must tell him Hann was a woman before he found out for himself. But as her eyes shifted from the blood spurting from Hann's wound to the white pallor of death shrouding her friend's face, Isabel thought it best to allow the doctor to work undistracted.

"Very well. If you're staying, make yourself useful." Cutter ran a bloody hand through his hair, lifted the lantern from its hook above them, and handed it to Isabel. "Hold this over him."

The pirate returned, and Cutter plucked a knife from his bag and began slicing Hann's clothing from around the spike that still protruded from her body. Layer by layer, he peeled back the bloodied waistcoat, vest, and undergarments, flinging each saturated piece to the floor.

Isabel held the lantern above her friend's bruised and bloodied body, fighting the nausea that rose in her throat. Raising her other hand to her mouth, she groaned.

"If you are going to be sick, please leave." Cutter eyed her sharply. "I have no need of another patient."

"Nay, I must stay." Isabel swallowed and squared her shoulders, praying for strength. She had to stay—for Hann's sake.

With a shake of his head, Cutter returned to his task. "Odd." His brow suddenly wrinkled.

"I beg your pardon?"

"Looks like sailcloth." Cutter yanked a strip of blood-soaked cloth from Hann's wound and held it up to the lantern. "But how would sail-cloth get inside his clothes?"

Isabel coughed and peered into the bloody mess as Cutter pulled out the rest of the material with a pair of tongs. Then, dipping a sponge into the bucket of water, he dabbed at the blood surrounding the spike. Hann let out a strangled moan, and Isabel gave her hand a squeeze.

"Hold his legs," he ordered the pirates. "And his shoulders."

Grabbing the flask of rum, Cutter poured it over Hann's side. One of the pirates skirted Isabel and clutched both of Hann's shoulders while the other grabbed her ankles.

The ship lunged and Isabel nearly lost her footing.

"Hold the lantern closer!" Cutter yelled as he flung a white cloth over his shoulder and grabbed the spike with both hands. "And say a prayer." The desperate look in his eyes caught Isabel's breath in her throat.

She moved the lantern toward the doctor, her shoulder aching from the strain, and turned her face away. *Oh Lord, please do not let Hann die.*

Grunting, the doctor pulled the spike from Hann's side in a gurgling smack of flesh. Hann writhed in the pirates' grasps and let out an ear-piercing scream. Isabel turned to see a red pool surging from the wound. Cutter dropped the spike to the floor and pressed the white cloth against the puncture, panting. Sweat beaded on his brow. He held the cloth there for several minutes, a troubled look brewing in his stormy gray eyes.

The pungent, tangy smell of blood joined the other foul orders of the hold, and Isabel shoved the lantern into a pirate's hand, darted to the corner, and vomited.

Chuckles sounded behind her.

Wiping her mouth with her handkerchief, she took a deep breath and returned. With a nod, she grabbed the lantern back from the pirate and resumed her duties.

Cutter flashed her an approving look. He pulled the rag away and peered into the wound. The bleeding had stopped, but Hann had slipped back into unconsciousness.

"Will she live?" Isabel could wait no longer for an answer.

Confusion crossed Cutter's face. "I believe he will, yes. I must sew up the wound, but it appears no major arteries or organs were struck." He tossed the bloody rag to the floor and grabbed the sponge. "He's lost a lot of blood."

Relief surged through Isabel, restoring her strength. "Thank God."

"Yes, thank God." Cutter gave Isabel a wink and proceeded to clean the wound. Then, after dousing it with rum again, he threaded a needle and began to suture the laceration.

The pirate holding Hann's feet released them. "I knews ye could do it, Doc—especially for this one."

Cutter snorted and continued to work. "I thank you for your help, gentlemen. You may go now." Lifting his hands from Hann's shoulders, the other pirate lumbered around Isabel and joined his companion. "Inform the captain, if you please!" Cutter called after them. Grunting, they shuffled off into the darkness.

When he'd completed the stitching, Cutter took the lantern from Isabel and replaced it on its hook. "Would you help me remove the rest

of his coat and shirt?" He clutched his knife and began cutting Hann's waistcoat from her chest.

Isabel gasped. "Nay." She stayed his hand with her own. "You cannot."

"Of course I can." Cutter gave a humorless laugh and flung her hand away. "I need to clean the boy and bandage him." He continued peeling back layers, then reaching Hann's shirt, split it down the middle with one swipe of his blade. Underneath, frayed sailcloth coiled in a bundle of blood-stained ribbons.

"No, please." Isabel dashed around the table. "Allow me to do it." She tripped over a stool and nearly fell. Should she tell him? She'd promised Hann she wouldn't.

"More sailcloth," Cutter said curiously, lifting the ragged pieces from Hann's chest.

Isabel dashed around the corner of the table and reached out to stop him, but he'd already snatched the last threads away.

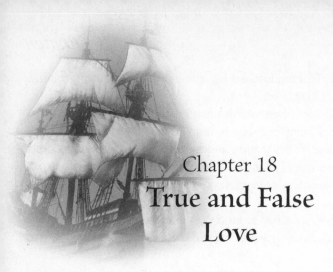

Chapter 18
True and False Love

Alarm spiked through Isabel.

"Oh my." Cutter's hand froze in midair. "Egad." He swerved his face away, his wide gaze landing on Isabel. "Oh my." He cast a quick glance over his shoulder, then turned around again, his face blossoming into a rosy red.

"Now will you allow me to do it?" Isabel placed both hands on her hips and gave him a lopsided smile.

Cutter took a step toward the wall. He bent over, bracing his hands on his knees, and gasped for air.

Sidestepping him, Isabel covered Hann with the other half of her waistcoat. "If you're going to be sick, please leave," she teased, but instantly her smile faded as her foot slipped in a puddle of blood—so much blood. Fear gripped her heart again. "Cutter, tell me what to do."

Cutter's breathing settled, and he stood. "He's a woman—all this time."

"Doctor?"

"Yes, wash him—I mean her. Wash away the blood and grime as best you can. I'll get the bandages." He knelt and dug in his satchel while Isabel removed the rest of Hann's coat and shirt and eased the sponge over her pale skin.

"The water is too bloody." Isabel held a hand to her stomach and

176

took a deep breath. Red streaks snaked across Hann's stomach and side.

"Do the best you can." Cutter darted off into the darkness and returned within minutes with a shirt in hand. "Put this on her." He handed it to Isabel while averting his gaze. "Then I will bandage the wound."

Tossing the sponge into the bucket, Isabel heard a frightening *drip-drip* and glanced at Hann. Blood trickled from her wound onto the table, and then slid onto the floor. The room spun, and Isabel raised one hand to her head. "She still bleeds."

"Not to worry, milady. It will stop presently."

Shoving Hann's right arm into the sleeve of the shirt, Isabel grunted as she reached behind the girl's shoulders and lifted her from the table long enough to push the shirt behind her. Then dashing around to the other side, Isabel placed Hann's left arm into the other sleeve and buttoned up the shirt, leaving only the girl's stomach and side exposed. "I'm finished. You can look now."

Cutter slowly turned around, careful to avoid looking at Hann's chest. His normally tanned skin had grown ashen—even his scars paled from their normal purple hue. But once he saw the girl had been modestly covered, he got to work, finished cleaning her, and bandaged the wound. Plopping down onto a stool, he crossed his bloodied, scarred arms over his chest and gave Isabel a look of reproach. "How long have you known?"

"A few days." She brushed the hair from Hann's forehead and clutched the table, feeling suddenly weak. "She will recover?"

"Aye, with proper care." Cutter gazed at Hann, then shook his head and chuckled. "I thought I'd gone mad or perhaps had been too long at sea."

"You care for her, then?"

Cutter stood and grabbed Hann's hand, pressing it between his. "That I do."

Isabel smiled.

Grumbling voices and the pounding of boots echoed through the dark berth as some of the pirates wandered below. Kent approached the table. Concern burned in his gaze.

Cutter released Hann's hand and shifted uncomfortably.

"How is he?" Kent's glance wandered from Isabel to Cutter. His eyes narrowed when he saw the blood covering the floor and the blotches of red splattered over their clothing.

Cutter cleared his throat and gave a knowing glance toward Isabel. "He will live, Captain."

With raised brow, Kent regarded them curiously.

Isabel took a step toward him and patted the combs in her hair. "What of the Spanish fleet?"

"We have outrun them." He grinned. "Thanks to you."

"Thank God, not me." Isabel blinked away the sparks of light that flashed in her vision.

"Lady Ashton has been very brave." Cutter grabbed a towel and wiped his hands. "I never thought a lady would fare so well in the midst of so much blood."

Kent eyed her with regard. "Yes, she's quite exceptional."

Isabel warmed under his perusal, yet the room began to spin and she sighed, raising her hand to her head.

"Steady now." Grabbing her arm, Kent drew her near, and his scent of wood and leather spilled over her. " 'Tis been a trying day. Allow me to escort you to your cabin, milady."

Without protest, Isabel took Kent's arm, no longer concerned with propriety, for she feared she would topple to the floor without his support. She cast one last glance at Hann and then at Cutter and knew her friend was in good hands.

"You never cease to amaze me," Kent said as they ascended the stairs.

"How so, Captain?" Isabel was anxious to hear his answer, but quickly chided herself for asking. Why should she be concerned with the opinion of a pirate?

"Your bravery, your faith in God, and now your overwhelming concern for a pirate boy."

They stopped before her door, and Kent opened it, allowing her to step inside. "Would that you cared as much for me."

The forwardness of his words shot through her, and where they should have piqued her indignation, they only touched her heart. They had been uttered so softly, she wondered if he'd meant to say them aloud. Had she encouraged his boldness by clinging to him up on the deck when she'd thought their lives were over? Why had she done that? She gazed into his dark, expectant eyes and tried to remind herself that this was the man who'd ravished her.

"You are ill advised if you believe flattery is the way to my heart." Isabel thrust out her chin.

"Then pray tell, show me the way." Kent raised his lips in a sensuous grin that sent a warm shimmer through her.

"I fear, Captain, that for you, the route is impassable."

"Alas, that you fear it gives me some hope."

Frustration pricked at her nerves. Did this man never quit?

"I'll have some hot water delivered so you can refresh yourself." He gave her a sad smile before closing the door.

Kent strode onto the deck, taking a deep breath of salty air. Tossing his hair behind him, he leaped onto the quarterdeck and planted his boots firmly on the wood. High above, the sun hurled its searing rays upon him, but he didn't need further warming, not after Isabel's gentle grip on his arm and the soft feel of her beside him. Though her sharp tongue denied it, he sensed a softening within her—in the look in her eyes, in her touch. Perhaps she was beginning to forgive him. Dare he hope for more than that?

Kent grunted. He must be fooling himself. She still longed for the wealth and title that he could not give her.

He scanned the ship. Sawkins, Smithy, Wolcott, and Murdock squatted on barrels up on the foredeck. They surrounded a small table where they played a hand of Truc. What would his father think of his favored son now—a penniless milksop, tossing what little he had left to the fickle winds of a card game? Remembering Sawkins's cowardice earlier that day and his defiance of Isabel's God stirred fury within Kent. How he longed to rid himself of his brother's company. He hated the way he looked at Isabel. Was she still taken in by his charm? Did she still think giving their son his name would be the best thing for the boy? Closing his eyes against a blast of hot wind, Kent gritted his teeth.

Isabel. Her close proximity became an unbearable torture. For the more acquainted he became with her, the more he found to love. She was so much more than the comely face and curvaceous figure that had attracted him when he'd first seen her. Why hadn't he seen past her outward beauty a year ago? Had he been that shallow?

Opening his eyes, Kent surveyed his ship, her trim, firm lines, the sturdy oak of her deck, the taut shrouds and ratlines strung upward in a tight web, her thick masts and yards upon which rose mountainous peaks of white canvas. Off her bow as far as he could see, nothing save turquoise sea billowed, sprinkled with caps of white that stretched to the blue horizon. Perhaps the *Restitution* would remain his one and only true love.

The pounding of a hammer broke through the normal creaks and moans of the ship, and Kent looked down to see his crew repairing the shattered bulwark—his crew, his men. This was his fortress, his castle, and he was in command. He'd achieved the power and success he'd fought for his whole life. The only dream he still had left to achieve was to become the new admiral of the Brethren of the Coast. That would entail, however, getting rid of Captain Morgan, and that was no small feat. But in the meantime, he was indeed a formidable pirate, and he possessed a hold full of treasure fit for a king. Had he done it only to impress a dead father, or was he proving to himself that his father had been wrong when he'd called him a disappointment, a frail halfwit? What did it matter? He'd proven himself either way. Yet why did he feel so empty? None of his accomplishments brought him the satisfaction he craved.

And what of Isabel's God? How could he deny that God existed after what Kent had seen today? She had to merely bow her head and appeal to Him, and He came to her aid. Raising his gaze, Kent peered past the bursting white of the sails into the vast sky. Did this God ever take notice of him? And if He did, did He turn his face quickly away, or did He see anything of measure? Perhaps it was too late to hope for that.

Isabel sat on the ledge of the window in her cabin, gazing out over the brilliant ribbons of crimson, peach, and violet adorning the sky as the sun sank past the line of dark blue sea. With each passing day, they drew closer to Frederick, and her heart soared.

As promised, the captain had sent a tub of hot water, and after discarding her bloodstained gown, she'd washed and donned a fresh one. Afterward, Isabel had tried to lie down and rest, but despite the miracle of the morning, a heavy despondency shrouded her. Grabbing her Bible, she'd flown to the window and opened it to find Proverbs 11:21: *"Though*

hand join in hand, the wicked shall not be unpunished: but the seed of the righteous shall be delivered." Her spirit had leaped within her as the quiet voice of God reassured her that Frederick would be saved.

The reverend had told her how important it was to read God's Word every day—for comfort, guidance, and strength, and also because it was a way to get to know the Lord and to become more like Him. And oh, she needed that. But more often than not, especially on this pirate ship, she despaired of finding a quiet moment alone to spend with her Father. Bowing her head in prayer, she vowed to make time with God a part of her daily routine.

She raised her hand to the window, her skin still raw from the harsh scrubbing it had taken to remove the blood. Yet Hann was alive! With a smile, Isabel closed her eyes as a warm breeze drifted over her, the tangy scent of rain floating upon it. God had not only delivered them from the Spanish fleet but had saved Hann, as well.

When her thoughts drifted to the captain, Isabel opened her eyes and scratched a rising itch on her arms, wondering at the new, intense feelings that battled within her. Even when surrounded by a fleet of Spanish warships, he'd displayed naught but courage and sagacity. She touched her hand and could still feel the strength of the muscles in his arms as he'd escorted her to her cabin.

A rap at the door sent Isabel jumping from her seat. Thinking it must be Kent, she rushed and flung the heavy oak aside to see Sawkins's handsome features and slick smile. Disappointment tugged at her heart.

"May I come in?"

Hesitating, Isabel stepped aside, allowing him entrance. Throwing his hat onto the table, he lit a lantern and led her to a chair before shutting the door.

Shifting uncomfortably, Isabel cast a glance at the oak barrier blocking her exit. A sudden unease welled within her. Surely, she'd be safe alone with Lord Sawkins.

His blond hair hung unfettered to his shoulders. The clean strong lines of his jaw flexed as he smiled at her. "After the day's harrowing events, I wanted to make sure you were safe and well, milady."

"Yes, thank you. I'm quite all right." Isabel nearly laughed, remembering how terrified Sawkins had been earlier that day. Perhaps she should ask him how he fared.

Fishing in his pocket, he pulled out a small velvet sack. "I have a gift for you." He held it out to her.

"A gift?" Isabel took it and gave it a shake. She had not received a gift in years, especially from a gentleman. Excitement swept away all her fears and embarrassment, and she untied the gold ribbon and peeked inside. A flash of white caught her eye as she poured the contents into her hand. A beautiful pearl necklace glimmered like beads of cream in her palm.

"Oh, Lord Sawkins, 'tis beautiful." Clutching it, she held it up before her eyes, delighting in the way the pearls shimmered in the lantern light. She ran her fingers over the beads and felt the weight of them in her hand. "But I cannot accept this." Even as she said it, she longed to keep it. She'd not had such an exquisite piece of jewelry since she'd lived in Hertfordshire, and it brought back fond memories of her life of wealth and privilege.

She glanced up at Lord Sawkins, who was beaming at her response. "Thank you for your generosity, milord—"

"Richard, if you please," he interrupted and clasped her hand between his.

"Richard." Isabel's skin crawled. She glanced toward the door. "But 'twould be most improper for me to accept this."

Moving a chair close to hers—too close—Sawkins perched on the edge and leaned toward her. "Not if we are engaged."

"Indeed." Isabel gave him a knowing glance. "But we are not."

"I realize this may not be the best time, milady, but I'm sick with love for you. I cannot eat, I cannot sleep for thinking of you. All you need say is yes, Isabel. Then you can have not only these pearls, but my title, my wealth, my undying devotion, and more jewels than you can ever imagine."

His honey-drenched words flowed around her like tantalizing sweets. She glanced toward the window, seeing only the darkness left by the retreating sun. Thunder rumbled in the distance, and a blast of chilled air swirled through the cabin. Unease seethed in her stomach. Was he trying to bribe her or was he sincere in his affections? Perhaps both.

Isabel patted the combs in her hair.

Sawkins's blue eyes glared expectantly into hers. "I thought these pearls would match the ones in those exquisite combs you wear."

Isabel eyed him, amazed at his thoughtfulness. The combs had been a gift from her fiancé, William Herbert, earl of Pembroke, the last remnant of their promised union. She had clung to them over the years—worn them every day. They represented hope for the future she craved. Now, she had another promise, another symbol of a devotion that would surely bring her and Frederick happiness and security. Easing the necklace back and forth in her hands, she listened to the clicking of the pearls as they rubbed against one another—like beads of hope giggling and urging her to accept.

Sawkins's lips curled in a confident grin. "Please say you'll become my wife, milady, and keep them as a token of my sincere intentions." He straightened the lace bursting from his blue doublet.

With a sigh, Isabel regarded him, his strong, stately features, the shimmer of lantern light in his golden hair, the elegance of his doublet and breeches trimmed in metallic braid, the gold-hilted rapier hanging at his side. She searched for any stirring of emotion or flutter of desire within her, but instead found only queasiness churning in her stomach. What did it matter? Here was a man of wealth and title, offering her everything she had ever wanted. And hadn't her mother told her many a time that love had nothing to do with marriage?

Oh Lord, what shall I do?

Her thoughts drifted to Frederick. Regardless of her feelings, she must consider his future her top priority.

Sawkins dropped to his knees and grabbed her hands. "Oh, Isabel, pray do not keep me in this agony any longer. Your silence will be the death of me. I must have your answer now."

Sawkins gazed into Isabel's green eyes. She still had the pearls clasped within her hands. He'd known she would love them. And with luck, neither the captain nor the crew would miss them from the chest in the hold. It was only pirates' booty absconded from the slave ship, anyway. And from Sawkins's brief perusal of the treasure stored below, his brother had acquired more than enough to last a lifetime. Greed bubbled within him. Soon it would all belong to him.

He squeezed her hands and put on his most handsome smile. How many other times had he used these very tactics to win the heart of the woman he pursued: a gift of jewels, lavish compliments, his most amorous glance, and a promise of commitment? The women had melted in his lap, and he'd enjoyed every ounce of the pleasures they offered him. Of course, he'd had to be much cleverer with Lady Ashton. Isabel was an intelligent woman and not so easily swayed, but as he gazed into her eyes and sensed her softening, he knew she would be well worth the trouble— especially since his brother also desired her. How Sawkins loved to prove himself the better man, not the illegitimate accident resulting from his mother's wanton behavior.

Isabel's gaze dropped as if she was pondering the best way to accept his offer, and Sawkins allowed his eyes to rove over her. What a delicious morsel. The red streaks glinting in her hair hinted at fiery passions beneath her frosty exterior. Her silken skin, the curves bounding beneath her gown, her delicate hands, and those exquisite green eyes enclosed by a forest of thick, dark lashes, all combined to create a tasty treat. He licked his lips in anticipation of having her as his own. He must have her. She looked up at him, and he flashed his gaze to her pink lips, anxiously awaiting her assent so he could posses them with his.

"I cannot in good conscience give you my answer yet, milord. We hardly know one another. Consider this my informal acceptance of your offer." She smiled, but her voice carried neither the excitement nor the joy he'd expected from a woman accepting the privilege of becoming his wife. After all, he was doing her a favor. No other gentleman would consider marrying her.

Lifting her hands to his lips, he placed a kiss upon them. "So we are promised?" He had to ensure he'd heard her correctly.

"If. . .I mean, *when* we rescue my son"—Isabel withdrew her hands from his—"and survive this ordeal, yes, then I will marry you."

"I am overcome, milady. I'm quite ecstatic." The exuberant joy welling within him surprised even Sawkins. No other woman had affected him so ardently. Yet as he watched Isabel, he wondered why she did not seem to share his excitement.

"Until then, milord, I'll return these to you." Isabel held up the string of pearls.

"I insist you keep them, milady"—he took the opportunity to embrace

her hands again—"as a token of my affection and our promise to one another."

A flicker of hesitation passed across her eyes; then she nodded.

Her sweet scent swirled around him. Surely she would not deny him a kiss now that they were betrothed. Moistening his lips, he inched toward her. From the corner of his eye, he saw her flinch, but he could not stop himself. He had to kiss her. She let out a gasp and tried to twist herself from the chair, managing to free one of her hands. "You take far too many liberties, milord."

Sawkins continued toward her. "Forgive me, Isabel. I'm simply mad with affections toward you, and I cannot contain them another minute."

Isabel forced a hand against his chest. "I beg you to try harder, milord."

Just one kiss. It was so little to ask of her.

A loud *slap* cracked against his left cheek, followed by a stinging burn. Sawkins jumped to his feet, holding his hand over the inflamed area, too shocked to utter a word.

With heaving chest, Isabel sprang from the chair, darted to the door, and flung it open. She turned to glare at him. "If you think to take liberties with me simply because I have consented to marry you, you may think again, milord. Though I have a son, I'll thank you to remember that he was conceived against my will. I am not a common strumpet whose affections you may purchase with a string of pearls." She pushed the necklace at him. "You may take your leave."

Sawkins squared his shoulders. How dare this pompous woman reject his advances—and strike him as well! He'd never let a woman hit him without suffering the consequences, and he wasn't about to start with this one, no matter how special she was. But he must wait for the proper time. Swallowing his pride, he feigned his most apologetic smile and bowed.

"I hope you'll accept my sincere apologies, Isabel. I only hoped for a simple kiss. But alas, I see you are a woman of great principle." He sauntered to the door and stopped beside her, pleased when he noticed a tremble pass over her. Cupping his hand over the pearls, he enclosed them in her hand. "I beg you to keep them—a symbol, I still trust, of our engagement?"

Thrusting her chin in the air, she gave him a petulant gaze that spoke of a strength he doubted she possessed—certainly not strength enough to shun his offer. Tugging her hand from his, she dropped it to her side, still clutching the pearls, but no denial of their betrothal fell from her lips.

Sawkins left, heard the door slam behind him, and smiled. He'd accomplished what he'd come to do, though the kiss would have been cream on the pudding. Leaping onto the main deck, he let the evening breeze cool his feverish passions. He'd make her his own soon enough. He just didn't know if he could wait for her puritan shield of ice to thaw.

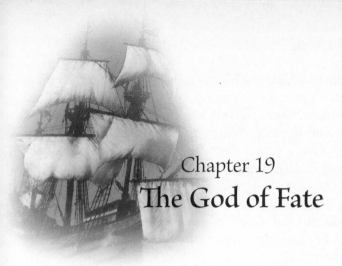

Chapter 19
The God of Fate

Searing pain jabbed Hann in her side and spread out like arrows throughout her body. She tried to lift her hand, but it weighed like a cannonball. Spicy pipe smoke drifted by her nose. Hearing a sigh, she pried her eyelids apart just enough to see Cutter sitting beside her, but unable to keep them open, she let her heavy lids drop. Warmth spread across her, becalming her pain and bringing her comfort. Cutter was here. He must care for her in some way. Her heart soared, but that effort alone sent a wave of dizziness crashing through her head, only compounded by the swaying of the hammock she lay in.

She heard the creak of the door and boot steps clomping across the floor.

"Cap'n, good to see you," Cutter said.

Kent. Hann cringed.

"How is he doing?"

"Much better," Cutter whispered. "Sh–he just needs his sleep. He should be up and about tomorrow, but it might take a week or two for a full recovery."

Did Cutter just nearly say she? *Does he know?* Hann tried to silence the beating of her heart to better hear what they were saying.

"A close call. I would have hated to lose such a good pirate."

"Indeed."

A moment of silence passed. "Well, I'll leave you to care for him." The floor creaked.

187

"Cap'n?" Cutter said, and the boot steps halted. "Do you truly think we'll be able to find your son?"

"Why do you ask?" Kent's deep voice spiked down Hann's spine.

"I've grown fond of Lady Ashton. I would hate to see her child harmed."

"No more than I." Kent sighed. "I've never seen my own son, but I fear what Morris might do."

"Did you really kill his son?"

"That he believes I did is all that matters, I suppose. But truth be told, I don't think I caused that explosion. I was nowhere near the barrels of gunpowder that night."

"I see."

Hann heard Cutter take a puff from his pipe. "Good night to you then, Cap'n."

"Good night."

A rat scurried past her feet as Isabel groped her way through the dark hallway the next morning on her way to Cutter's cabin. Stifling a scream, she jumped aside, allowing the filthy beast to pass. She wondered if it was Hoornes's rat. The putrid creatures all looked alike to her. The *Restitution* lurched, flinging her to the other side of the corridor, and she clutched the damp wall, bracing her shoes on the wooden planks of the floor. Thunder quaked across the morning sky, agitating both the sea and Isabel's nerves. With each roar of the storm, the ship shuddered in an eerie cacophony of creaks and groans that threatened to tear apart its timbers. Mighty ocean swells pounded the hull. Isabel hated storms nearly as much as she hated ships. No wonder she grew agitated when she found herself in the midst of both.

Lord Sawkins's attempt to kiss her loomed in her mind. Perhaps she had been too harsh with him. After all, she'd just agreed to marry him. An innocent kiss was a reasonable expectation. Yet the thought of it sickened her. Why? Certainly, his noble features would please any woman. But no matter. Marrying him was the best thing for Frederick, and it would also be in her best interest in the long run.

Grunts and guffaws drifted to her from the pirates' main berth below, where most of the men must be taking shelter from the storm. Thankful she didn't have to descend to that level, she rapped on Cutter's door, hoping he was there and would let her in quickly. When his smiling face came into view, Isabel uttered a sigh of relief.

With a gleeful gesture, he motioned her inside. "Good morning. 'Tis good to see you, milady. Hann has been asking for you."

Isabel took in the tiny room. Half the size of her cabin, it had barely enough space in which to move. Three wooden trunks lined one wall, overflowing with clothes, books, and weapons. A table strewn with medical equipment crowded the corner. Two chairs stood on either side. Hanging by ropes from the rafters, three hammocks swung in harmony with the ship—one of them rounded with Hann's small figure.

Hurrying to her friend, Isabel took her hand and pressed it between hers. Warmth radiated from it, and Isabel smiled, remembering how cold these same hands had been the day before.

With a flutter of lashes, Hann peered through half-open lids and offered Isabel a timid smile. "Milady."

"Hann, you had me—" Isabel glanced up at Cutter as he took a position on the other side of the hammock. "You had us so worried." Tears blurred Isabel's vision.

Hann's forehead creased. "Why are you crying?"

Isabel gave her a sideways glance. "I suppose I've become fond of you, 'tis all."

"You can't kill a tough pirate like me." Hann's chuckle was quickly strangled by a cough.

"Be still, Hann." Cutter laid a palm on her forehead. "You must rest."

"Don't coddle me," Hann snapped, a playful gleam in her eye. She turned to Isabel. "Did I not tell you this would happen? Once they discover you are a woman, they feel the need to treat you as though you are a fragile flower that will wilt under the first rays of the sun."

"When does caring become coddling?" Cutter snorted and lifted her hand to his lips, placing a kiss upon it.

"So I see your secret is out." Isabel raised a gleeful brow at Hann.

With a smile, Hann shifted her gaze back to Cutter.

As the ship careened over another swell, the lantern reeled back and forth above them, casting shifting patches of light and shadow over the hammock, but it did not hide the loving glance that drifted between Hann and Cutter.

Isabel warmed from head to toe. "It would seem you two have declared your affections for one another."

"That we have." Cutter smiled, his eyes never leaving Hann's. "And I would have done so long ago if I'd known the truth. As it is"—he balled his hands on his waist—"you two allowed me to wallow in shame at my misplaced sentiments. I daresay, I thought I'd gone mad."

Hann giggled.

"I don't see how I missed it before. 'Tis so obvious now when I look at you." Cutter brushed a lock of Hann's hair from her forehead. "No man could ever be as beautiful as you."

As he dropped his hands to his sides, a shadow dragged his features down. "I still don't know what you see in this grotesque body." He cast an uncertain glance at Hann.

Hann reached out and touched the sleeve of his shirt. "I see the most honorable, wise, kind man I have ever known."

Cutter cleared his throat and turned his face away.

Isabel wondered if she should leave. Did they even remember she was standing there? She averted her gaze to the wall where a baldric, hanging from a rusty nail, jostled back and forth against the wood with each move of the ship.

Facing Isabel, Hann gave her hand a squeeze. "The good doctor refuses to tell me how he discovered my gender. Did you tell him?"

"Nay." Isabel looked at Cutter, whose face blossomed into a deep purple that matched his scars. "I kept my promise." Realizing the truth would embarrass everyone, especially Hann, Isabel thought it best to change the subject. "Perhaps now that you do know, Doctor, 'tis not proper for Hann to remain in your cabin."

"Alas, but where else to send her?" Cutter rubbed his chin. "Certainly not to your cabin—though that would be the most proper place for her. The rest of the crew still considers her a man—a notion I have every intention they continue to believe."

Isabel cringed, remembering the way some of the men had gawked at Hann when they thought she was a boy. Heaven forbid what they'd attempt now. "Perhaps move her back to her own cabin, and—"

"I'll not have her sharing quarters with those pirates!" Cutter broke in with an incredulous tone.

Hann laid a hand on his. "I've kept my gender a secret from this entire crew—including you, I might add—for nigh six months. 'Twould seem suspicious if I did not return to my cabin now."

Cutter huffed. "I suppose you are right. As soon as you regain your strength, I'll escort you back." He gave her a complying grin.

Hann shifted her gaze back to Isabel. "But what of the Spanish fleet? Last I recall, they fired upon us."

"We have outrun them," Isabel reassured her, looking down at Hann's side, covered now with a burlap blanket. "Are you still in pain?"

"Aye, a bit."

"What a miracle that escape was." Cutter shook his head. "But it still troubles me." He paused and patted his pockets as if looking for his pipe, then gave up and examined Isabel's eyes. "Your God, milady. He comes quickly to your aid. He controls not only the wind but the minds of a whole fleet of Spaniards. Is there naught He is incapable of?"

"He is the Creator. He can do what He wishes with His creation." Isabel masked her excitement at Cutter's question and prayed silently for the right words to say.

"This evidence of His existence causes me great discomfort," Cutter stated.

"But why?" Hann wrinkled her nose.

Cutter crossed his arms over his chest, the withered limb lying atop the strong one. "If He is the creator and does what He wishes, then He must have intended for me to become so hideously disfigured that I need hide myself from society."

Isabel stared at the pain in his eyes, and a lump formed in her throat, preventing her from speaking.

"Cutter, would you tell us what happened?" Hann asked.

Sighing, the doctor glanced away. " 'Tis a simple tale, really. 'Twould be ironic and even satirical if it hadn't happened to me." He scratched his head. "You see, I spent my life saving people, healing them. At the ripe age of five and twenty I was handsome, yes"—with raised brow, he chuckled—"I was handsome once. A handsome, wealthy doctor with important friends and a beautiful fiancée. But one night, fate—or perhaps 'twas your God, milady—led me past the Lady's Harvest Inn on High Street in Canterbury. Flames burst from her doors, and thick, black smoke poured from her windows. A crowd of people formed in the street and pointed toward the structure. Upon questioning them, I discovered a family was still trapped inside."

Isabel raised a hand to her chest. "How horrible. What did you do?"

Cutter shrugged. "I rushed in and saved them. That is what I do. I save people. But alas. . ." He glanced down. "I could not save myself. The roof caved in on top of me in a mass of flaming wood. That's the last I remember until I woke up in the hospital"—he pointed at his gnarled lip and shook his withered hand—"like this."

Hann's eyes moistened, and Isabel remained silent, unsure of what to say to comfort him.

"So you see"—he grinned—"if God does exist, then He is naught but a cruel God who punished me for risking my life to save others. Aye, 'tis much easier to believe fate is in control than a God who hates me thus."

Hann squeezed his hand and stared at him with concern.

Isabel swallowed. *Lord, what do I say?* She opened her mouth. " 'The thief cometh not, but for to steal, and to kill, and to destroy: I am come that they might have life, and that they might have it more abundantly.' " The words flew from her lips before she had time to consider them. She'd just read them that morning.

"What did you say?" Cutter's gaze shot to hers.

Excitement prickled Isabel's skin. " 'Tis from the Bible—the Gospel of John. I suppose what I'm trying to say is, are you so unhappy now? You told me yourself you put no value on wealth or position. And you are still saving lives." Isabel smiled at Hann. "And would you have met Hann if you had not run into that building and been burned?"

Cutter narrowed his eyes.

"Do you really think you would have been happy married to a woman who valued you only for your outward appearance?" Isabel raised her brows.

Cutter glanced at Hann, then back at Isabel, realization sparking in his gray eyes.

"Doctor, perhaps God has done you a favor. Perhaps what seemed like a tragedy, He has transformed into a blessing." Isabel bit her lip and

silently thanked God for His wisdom.

Hann reached up and clasped Cutter's arm, then nodded.

Cutter tightened his gnarled lips. "You have given me much to consider."

Kent took off his hat and slapped it against his thigh, sending a shower of droplets over the floor of his cabin. Slamming the door behind him, he ran a hand through his dripping hair and stomped to his desk. The worst of the storm had passed. Exhausted, he slumped into a chair and leaned his head back with a sigh. He'd not seen Isabel since he'd escorted her to her cabin yesterday. He'd hoped she had fared well and not been frightened during the tempest, but the demands of the storm had kept him on deck. With Hann injured and Cutter attending to him, Kent could think of no one he trusted to check on Isabel. Despite the torment her presence inflicted on him, he determined to see her as soon as he donned some dry clothes. His eyes landed on an old bottle of rum taunting him from the shelf. Licking his lips, he longed for a sip, or two or three—anything to dull the pain carving a trail across his heart.

Someone pounded on his door.

"Enter." He looked up, daring to hope it might be Isabel, but when the sneering face of Sawkins snaked around the open slab, Kent's insides coiled.

"State your business and be gone." Kent leaned forward to remove his wet boots.

"Ah, brother, how discourteous." Sawkins entered and closed the door. "But you always were the savage."

Tossing his boots aside, Kent leaned back in his chair, glaring at Sawkins. "Do not call me *brother*."

"Well, stab me if you aren't an ornery fellow. No wonder she chose me."

A knot formed in Kent's throat. What mischief was the scamp up to now? "I have no time for games. Now if you please." He gestured toward the door. All Kent wanted was to check on Isabel and then get a warm meal and some sleep.

Sawkins sauntered toward the desk. With one hand alighting upon his waist, he picked up a parchment with the other and, after a cursory glance, dropped it. "I've come to inform you that congratulations are in order."

"Indeed?" Kent stood, circling the desk, and glanced at the bottle of rum that suddenly looked even more appealing.

"Lady Ashton has agreed to marry me."

The words formed a rope of agony that strung itself around Kent's throat, squeezing the life from him. Unable to speak, he stared at Sawkins as the cad's face broke into a devious grin.

"I see you're quite overcome with joy." Sawkins tugged on the lace at his sleeves. "Yes, 'tis true. Last night in her cabin, she professed her ardent love for me. As soon as this heinous voyage is over, she will be mine."

"You are lying."

"Nay, ask the lady yourself," Sawkins said with a chuckle. "I must say I've ne'er seen a woman so ecstatic about a betrothal. Swounds, for propriety's sake, I had to insist she keep her passions at bay, lest she tarnish her already somewhat tainted reputation."

Fury pounded through Kent like a searing ember, igniting all the vile cravings within him. He charged toward Sawkins and hammered a blow across his jaw. Shock widened Sawkins's eyes before he tumbled backward, arms flailing as he tried to grab the corner of the desk. He thumped to the floor.

Clutching Sawkins by his satin cravat, Kent lifted him and dragged his writhing body to the wall, where he pounded it against the hard wood. "I'll kill you if you touch her again." Lightning flashed, emblazoning the shadows of madmen on the wall. Kent grimaced as hatred flamed hot up his neck.

A wave crashed onto the window. A roar of thunder shook the panes.

Sawkins's hair loosened from its tie and flared against the wall with each thrust. Bumbling, he caught his breath. Fear skittered across his eyes. "You forget yourself, brother. You cannot kill me," he sputtered.

"Nay, but I can beat you senseless and throw you in the hold." Kent struck him again.

Sawkins rammed his knee into Kent's groin. "Not if you wish to find your son."

Doubling over, Kent gasped for breath. Before he could recover, Sawkins jumped on him, forcing him onto the desk and sending charts, pens, and sextant crashing to the floor.

With a grunt, Kent pounded his forehead into Sawkins's skull, stunning him, and then with a shove of his feet, sent him careening to the shelves behind him.

Struggling to his feet, Sawkins stared at Kent, gasping.

Kent stormed toward him, grabbed the lapels of his waistcoat, and raised a fist to strike him again. Wincing, Sawkins squeezed his eyes shut. Kent's fist hung in the air as he stared at his half brother. The rasping of their breaths filled the silence between them.

Kent let his hand fall. He tossed Sawkins into a chair, then stomped away, grabbed the bottle of rum, uncorked it, and took a swig. Slamming it down, he wiped his mouth with the back of his hand and leaned back on the desk, arms over his chest.

A vision of their father swarmed before him—his deeply lined face pale as he wheezed his last breaths. "Promise me, son. . . ," he had gasped. "Promise me you won't lay a hand on your brother." He'd known of the hatred between his two boys and didn't want his precious brat, Richard, harmed. Of course he hadn't forced Sawkins to vow the same on Kent's behalf.

His whole life, Kent had longed to close forever those frigid blue eyes that glared so vehemently at him now, to silence that insolent tongue, but his promise to a dying man who had done naught but berate Kent had kept him from it. Now curiously, as he stared at the ruthless shell of a man before him, he found he could not kill him, promise or no promise. The realization stunned him.

Sawkins eyed him cautiously, rubbing his jaw. "So this is the way of things between us?" A brief glimmer of sorrow softened his harsh look.

"I find you are worth neither my energy nor my time. If Lady Ashton is foolish enough not to see beyond your mawkish facade, there's naught I can do." A spire of pain wrenched through Kent at the thought of Isabel in this foppish man's arms. "You sicken me. You use people to further your own cause, gnaw all the good from them, and then toss them aside like dry bones." Kent stood and gestured to the door. "Get out."

Sawkins lumbered to his feet and threw back his shoulders. "You're no better than I. How many men have you killed out of anger or greed? How many women have you ravished to satisfy your lust?"

Memories of Lady Charlisse Hyde stabbed Kent's conscience. Hadn't he tried to steal her from Merrick just as Sawkins had done with Isabel? Hadn't he spent his entire life murdering and pillaging? His stomach curdled, and bile rose in his throat. Sawkins was right. Kent *was* no different.

Sawkins slid a finger across his slick mustache, a smug look on his face. "I will take my leave then." He bowed and strode toward the door, casting a glance over his shoulder. "I hope someday you will be happy for Lady Ashton and me. I am the best choice for her, after all."

Kent faced the window and swallowed hard. The *bang* of the door echoed across the cabin.

Grabbing the bottle of rum, Kent pressed it to his lips and took a full draught.

Isabel laughed. Cutter's and Hann's chuckles joined hers and filled the tiny room. It felt good to laugh again and to see the joy and love warming Cutter's and Hann's eyes, despite the pings of jealousy that pricked Isabel. How she longed for this kind of love.

Cutter had gone for some dried biscuits and tea, and when he'd returned, the three had spent the stormy afternoon enjoying each other's company. As Isabel nibbled on her meal, she couldn't help but wonder what her father would think of her newfound friends: a deformed doctor and a lady pretending to be a pirate. Giggling, she pictured the earl's aged features scrunched in a reddening knot.

A knock on the door interrupted their revelry, and Cutter opened it to allow entrance to a pirate Isabel remembered as Murdock.

"Milady." The sopping pirate removed his hat, spilling water onto the floor from its brim.

"Yes?" Isabel stood, alarmed at the nervous expression etching his tanned face.

"I thought ye should know, miss." He shifted his glance over the room.

"Know what?"

" 'Tis the cap'n, miss. He done found out 'bout yer marryin' Sawkins. He's turned the ship around and is headin' back to Port Royal."

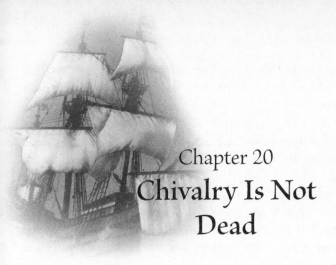

Chapter 20
Chivalry Is Not Dead

Anger hammered through Isabel. Going back to Port Royal? She had not felt the ship turn, but perhaps she wouldn't have sensed its movements in the throes of the storm. Surely Kent would not be so cruel as to abandon the search for his son?

In one leap, Cutter bounded from his chair. The warmth of his strong hand on her shoulder quelled her rising ire. "Marrying Sawkins, of all the preposterous notions. What foolery is this?" The scar on his upper lip curled as a snicker escaped his mouth.

Embarrassment stung Isabel's face. "I'm afraid it is true."

Cutter frowned, his brows pinching.

"I'll explain later." Isabel faced Murdock. "Surely you are misinformed. Who told you this?"

"Lord Sawkins, milady." His eyes shifted from Cutter to Isabel. "He sent me to tell ye. Said he thought ye should know."

Confusion and anger battled within her. The only way the captain could have found out about her betrothal would have been from Sawkins's own lips. Why would he purposely cause such discord? "Why didn't his lordship come here himself?"

"He's been busy convincin' the cap'n not t' abandon the search for yer son." Murdock looked away and rubbed the back of his neck.

"Oh he has?" Isabel found that hard to believe. "And where is the captain now?" She would have it out with the traitorous knave herself.

"Last I heard, he be down in the hold, milady, drinkin' and carryin' on like a crazy man."

Isabel nodded. "True to character." She'd known the news of her engagement would not sit well with Kent, but she had no idea he would stoop so low as to put her son's life in danger. "I believe I'll have a word with the captain."

Cutter clasped her arm. "Nay, milady, you can't go down there alone."

Isabel's legs trembled at the memories of the pirates' berth, but she had no choice. Frederick's life was at stake. "I'll be fine." She offered Cutter a reassuring grin. "With Sawkins and the captain down below, there will be no danger."

"I don't think that's a good idea, milady," Hann interjected. "Allow Cutter to escort you."

"It'd be me pleasure to escort ye, miss." Murdock twisted his hat in his hands. "Sawkins hisself bade me bring ye to the cap'n if ye desired."

"Very well." Isabel raised her brows at Cutter and Hann. "That settles it. Hann needs you more than I do, Doctor."

A grin twisted Murdock's lips, giving her pause. He headed out the door.

Ignoring Cutter's protests, Isabel followed Murdock into the dark hallway. Dread sank its teeth into her resolve. Could Murdock be trusted? Wasn't he the one who'd attacked Hann? But surely if Lord Sawkins had sent him, she would be safe. Thoughts of Frederick spurred her on— especially now that with each passing second they sailed farther away from him.

Darkness enveloped her as Murdock led her down a steep stairway.

"Shouldn't we have a lantern?" She clung to the railing, scuffing her shoes across the steps to ensure she didn't miss one and go tumbling down upon the filthy pirate.

"Naw, miss, I can sees fine."

Wonderful. They passed the gun deck where the massive shadows of sleeping cannons stood poised like snakes ready to strike. The smell of gunpowder still lingered in the acrid air, biting at Isabel's nose.

Snores, laughter, and curses swirled around her as they descended to the berth where most of the men slept and ate—save a few who were

housed in the forecastle above. Hammocks swayed in midair like a herd of manatees lumbering through a shallow cay. Clusters of slaves huddled in the corners. Isabel's heart sank. She doubted they were being treated very well, though any place would be better than a slave ship.

Eerie lantern light drifted over the hideous faces of the men as each one raised his gaze to watch the intruders. Some lay in their hammocks, others clustered around tables, playing cards amidst mugs of grog, while the unconscious bodies of several were strewn over the floor like refuse. The stench of feces, sweat, and rum smothered her, and she flung a hand to her nose and coughed.

The ship lurched. Isabel tightened her grip on the railing as she stumbled and nearly careened down the remaining stairs. The creaks and groans of the hull matched the catcalls and guffaws from the crew.

"Well, sink me sails. Look what Murdock done caught. A tasty morsel from the sea."

"Har, give us a bite there, mate," another pirate said, licking his lips.

Coarse chuckles blared through the murky room. Murdock grunted but offered them no response, and Isabel found herself suddenly thankful for his escort.

To her left, the table where Cutter had saved Hann's life sat alone in the shadows. A chill scraped down Isabel as the bloody scene replayed in her mind.

Grateful to leave the lecherous crew behind, she followed Murdock as he snagged a lantern from a hook on the wall and continued his descent past the berth. If not for the light he now carried, the darkness would have swallowed him up whole, for Isabel could see naught but the tiny circle the lantern chose to shed its light upon. When they reached the bottom, she released her tight grip on the railing and rubbed her aching fingers.

"This way." The scuffle of Murdock's boots sounded as he lumbered off toward the aft of the ship.

Isabel drew a shaky breath, desperate for a whiff of fresh air amidst the rank humidity saturating her skin and gown. Following Murdock's light, Isabel inched along, peering into the inky blackness. Nebulous shadows loomed all around her. Her shoe struck something hard. Pain spiked up her toes. She eased her hands over what felt like a barrel. Sidestepping it, she continued to follow the pirate, who had quickened his pace. The squeals of rats sent shivers up her legs. The ship groaned under the strain of the sea.

Abruptly, Murdock stopped and held the lantern up to his face. A devious grin upturned his lips, made more sinister in the dim light. Drawing a breath, he turned his head toward the lantern, and with a puff, Isabel's world disappeared. Darkness enveloped her.

Boot steps sounded. A door creaked open, and then a coarse chuckle echoed over the room.

"Murdock?" Isabel's quavering voice bounced off the walls and was quickly swallowed up by the darkness. Terror crept over her as an ominous silence tore away the remains of her courage. No sounds reached her ears save the creak and moan of timbers and the screeching of rats.

"Captain?" Her voice sounded so small and insignificant in the deep bowels of the ship. Terror clenched every nerve.

"Murdock, I insist you show yourself at once!" She bellowed in one last surge of bravery.

The patter of tiny feet answered her from all around. Pairs of red eyes peered at her from the corners. Isabel's breath came in rapid bursts. Afraid to step forward, she glanced over her shoulder. A flicker of light shone from where the stairway ended. Turning, she sped toward that tiny glimmer of hope.

She must keep her eye on the light.

Then it was gone. She ran into something warm and solid. With a scream, she stumbled backward. A chuckle grated over her nerves, and two strong hands clutched her arms, slamming pain through her injured shoulder.

She pounded her fists on the man's chest. "Let me go this instant!" He was tall and muscular, but the darkness hid his face.

He shoved her.

Isabel's blood pounded into her head. Her heart crashed against her ribs. "Who are you? What do you want?"

The man remained silent, but she could feel his wicked grin upon her. Her mind reeled. Where was the captain? Where was Lord Sawkins? She'd come down into a trap. Why had she been so foolish? A wave of panic crashed over her.

Stumbling, Isabel retreated, flailing her arms behind her to guide her way. She tumbled into a barrel, a crate, and tripped over a sack, toppling to the hard sodden floor.

Boot steps, confident and menacing, followed her—the outline of a man barely discernable in the thick shadows.

A light suddenly appeared from her left.

The man halted. The scent of cedar crashed through the stench of the bilge that permeated the hold.

"Lady Ashton?" Kent's commanding voice filled the darkness like a beacon of hope.

Isabel heard the creak of a door and the pounding of boots fading away.

Struggling to sit up, she held her hand to her chest, hoping to still the wild thrashing of her heart. Tears swarmed into her eyes.

"Isabel?" The captain's voice echoed. "Are you down here?"

"Over here," she managed to utter in a scratchy voice.

Light advanced upon the scene, sending the darkness cowering to the corners. Isabel looked up to see Kent emerge from the black shroud, lantern in hand. When he saw her, he set the light down on a cask and rushed to her side.

"Milady, are you hurt?" He knelt, putting one arm around her waist, and assisted her to her feet. "Who did this to you?"

Isabel fell into him, burying her face in his chest. His powerful arms encircled her and held her in a tight embrace. "Kent," she sobbed, unable to say anything further. The strength and warmth of him seeped through her like a soothing ointment, becalming her heart, and settled like a blanket over her fears.

Pulling back, he gazed down at her, his brow creased. "How did you get down here? Who was here with you?"

"I don't know." Isabel sobbed. "I couldn't see him. Murdock—Murdock told me you were here. I came to talk to you."

"Murdock. Why would he say that? Why, I'll have his lying heart for supper," Kent stormed. "Where is he now?"

"I don't know." Isabel swayed and clutched onto Kent's arm to keep from falling.

"I'll kill him!" Kent stomped to a barrel, gripped the hilt of his cutlass

201

and peered into the darkness.

"Nay. It wasn't him." Sniffing, Isabel dropped her gaze. "The other man was much taller."

Grabbing the lantern, Kent held it above his head. The light revealed a large room filled with crates and sacks and a half-open door to her right. "He must have gone this way." He shoved the door farther open with a *creak* and took a step inside.

The darkness emerged from the corners and crept toward Isabel. "Please don't leave me!" she called after Kent, ashamed at her weakness but overcome by fears more powerful than her dignity.

Poking his head back into the room, Kent gave her a half smile. "I have no intention of doing so, milady." He approached her and set the lantern down again. "Pray tell, why were you seeking me?"

"Murdock told me you'd turned the ship around—that you were no longer going to search for Frederick." Despair muddled her voice.

"Why would I do that?" Kent gave her a questioning look.

Isabel bit her lip and swallowed resurging fear. Perhaps he didn't know about her betrothal. She thought it better not to tell him now and risk his fury. "So you haven't turned the ship back to Port Royal?"

Kent shook his head. "Of course not." His eyes softened and he reached for her. "Are you hurt? Did he touch you?"

"Nay." Tears spilled down her cheeks. "Just a bit frightened."

Pulling her toward him, he wrapped his arms around her and slid his fingers through her hair. "You are safe now, milady." He kissed her forehead. "Come, allow me to take you back to your cabin."

With a nod, she took his arm, amazed at how safe she felt with him. Kent grabbed the lantern and escorted her up the stairway, opened the door to her cabin, and led her inside.

Isabel entered on shaky legs as Kent helped her to a chair and eased her into it. Setting the lantern on the table, he shut the door and marched to the window. The rain had ceased, leaving a gray haze to mark its passing, brightened only by a swath of orange over the bottom of the window. The sun was setting. What had started out being such a joyous day with her friends had ended in horror.

Snatching her handkerchief from the table, Isabel dabbed her cheeks. "How did you know where I was?"

"Cutter." Kent glanced at her over his shoulder. "He came to my cabin and told me you'd gone down to the hold, looking for me. He was concerned for your safety." He trudged toward her. "Seems he was correct."

New tears burned in Isabel's eyes. If it hadn't been for Cutter's wisdom and concern, she'd not be sitting here safe in her cabin. Silently, she thanked God for the doctor's friendship, and raised her gaze to meet Kent's. He stared at her, his dark eyes burning with concern.

"It would please me greatly, milady, if you would not be so daft as to follow any old pirate around my ship." He raised his scarred brow and gave her a sardonic grin.

"Daft?" Isabel's ire pricked, yet how could she deny how foolish she'd been? "My only thought was for Frederick." She folded her shaky hands together on her lap.

"What little faith you have in me. Do you really believe I would give up the search for our son?" He snapped his hair behind him and crossed his arms over his chest. "For any reason," he added sternly.

Isabel studied him. Did he know about her and Sawkins? His upper lip twitched as it always did when he was either furious or nervous—or both.

Sudden warmth blossomed over Isabel as she envisioned the moment when she'd thrown herself into his arms down in the hold. She'd been so frightened, so happy to see him that she'd tossed all propriety aside. Yet it wasn't so much the action itself that bothered her—an action of gratitude certainly understandable from a woman in her situation—it was the warm tingle now fluttering in her stomach as she remembered the feel of his arms around her.

Rising to her feet, Isabel patted the combs still clinging to her tousled hair and met his gaze. How could she have felt so safe and comforted in the arms of a man who'd once ravished her? Yet as she searched his eyes, she did not see the same man within them. Where before there had been fury, lust, and a callous evil shimmering in their depths, now all she saw was concern, devotion, and something else—remorse?

Her stomach churned in a whirlwind of confusion, and she laid a weary hand upon it.

"You gave our son my middle name," Kent announced, his voice cracking.

Isabel shifted her feet and looked down. So he'd noticed. She couldn't say why she'd done it, really. But somehow, she thought the boy should carry forth some part of his heritage. Kent's middle name was not often used or well known. But still. . . " 'Tis but a coincidence, I assure you. I simply like the name Frederick." She didn't dare raise her gaze to his, lest her eyes betray her turmoil.

He took a step toward her, and her breath quickened. The smell of spice and leather wafted around her, setting her senses aflame. "If you please, Captain. 'Tis been a trying day, and I fear I'm not feeling well."

Reaching up, he brushed a tendril of her hair away from her face. His lips curved in a gentle smile. "Then I will leave you to your rest."

The room swirled around Isabel, and she felt her legs give way beneath her.

Catching her by the waist, Kent led her to the bed and eased her down onto the quilt. "May I get you something? Water, perhaps?"

Raising a hand to her neck, Isabel shook her head. What was wrong with her? Nausea and elation clamored together in her stomach, creating havoc with her senses. The heat from Kent's body steamed over her. "Nay, I am quite all right. Thank you, Captain." She gazed into his eyes, just inches from hers, and her breath caught in her throat. His sultry gaze lowered to her mouth.

He leaned toward her and hesitated. His warm, rum-laced breath wafted over her. Isabel's heart flopped in her chest. He leaned nearer. Isabel closed her eyes, unable to move. His lips touched hers. The room exploded in a burst of heat as his kiss, gentle at first, grew hungrier, searching, exploring—like a parched lion drinking from a newfound spring. Wrapping his arms around her, he pressed her against him, and for a moment, Isabel melted into him, unable to resist.

Withdrawing his lips, he hovered near her face and tilted his forehead against hers. Their heavy breaths intermingled in the air between them.

Isabel's senses jolted back to reality. She pushed away from him, dashed a hand to her mouth, and stared at him aghast.

A sensuous grin played on his handsome lips. "Was it so horrifying?"

Icy fingers of shame raked over her, stomping out the flames of passion. She turned away. "I shouldn't have done that."

"Why not? Because you are promised to Sawkins?"

Her gaze snapped to his. "You knew?"

Kent nodded.

"And you didn't turn the ship around?" Isabel studied him.

Kent's sorrowful eyes swept over her. "Again, your low opinion of me cuts me to the quick."

"What do you expect? Where were my opinions of you born?" Isabel glared at him, and he flinched, a pained look in his eyes. Suddenly, she regretted her harsh words.

With a hard swallow, Kent clasped her hand. "But tell me, does his lordship invoke such strong passions within you?"

"Why, you insolent cur." Isabel jerked her hand from his. "There's more to draw a woman than a passionate feeling that is here one minute and gone the next." Although she had to admit her body still tingled with warmth from his kiss.

"How did you discover our betrothal?" Isabel got up, brushed past him, and sauntered to the bookshelves, trying to escape the intense feelings that swarmed over her.

"Sawkins was quick to lord his new conquest over me." Kent gave a bitter laugh.

"A conquest?" Isabel swung about abruptly. "I daresay, is that all you think I am—a prize to be won by the best man?"

Kent faced her and rubbed the stubble on his chin. "Nay, milady, but I fear Lord Sawkins considers you so."

She snorted. "You two have no doubt been battling for dominance since childhood. Be advised, Captain, I will not be the spoils of your personal war."

Kent narrowed his eyes, his upper lip twitching.

Isabel scratched her arms. "Was your kiss just another tactic to win my affections?" She averted her gaze as tears burned behind her eyes, confusing her. "I have no doubt, Captain, that it was no different from the multitudes of kisses you've had before."

"Truth be told, milady, there has been no woman since you." Anguish devoured the usual sternness in Kent's voice.

Isabel ran a wary gaze over him. "Since you ravished me, you mean?"

Kent eyes filled with remorse, and he shifted his stance.

"I don't believe you. Not a man like you." She turned her back to him, not wanting to see the regret on his face—afraid it would melt the shield around her heart, afraid of the outpouring of her feelings when that shield was gone.

"Believe what you will. 'Tis true, nonetheless. There can be none other for me but you."

"Then I fear you face a life of celibacy, for I am promised to Lord Sawkins."

"Perchance I have misjudged you, milady, for if you are fool enough to marry that ninny simply for his title, then I must say you are deserving of each other."

Isabel wheeled around. "I, too, have misjudged you, Captain, for I almost believed an ounce of honor had sprouted within your villainous heart." Biting her lip, Isabel fought back tears, unsure from whence they came. "You may take your leave."

With a sweep of his hand, Kent gave her a mocking bow and stormed from the cabin.

Darting a quick glance around the room, Isabel grabbed a teacup sitting on the table and threw it at the door as it slammed shut. The cup shattered, littering the floor. She marched to the door, avoiding the glass, and bolted it before the knave could return, then swung around and leaned her head back on the oak slab. Tears filled her eyes and slid down her cheeks. Why was she so furious? Kent not only maintained his course to find Frederick, but had rescued her from certain ravishment. It was obvious he'd been drinking and that her betrothal angered him. Yet he'd been naught but kind to her.

Isabel rubbed her temples, hoping to quell the confusion and fury that churned through her. She trudged to the bed and fell onto it in a heap, clutched her pillows to her chest, and prayed for the Lord to make her path clear.

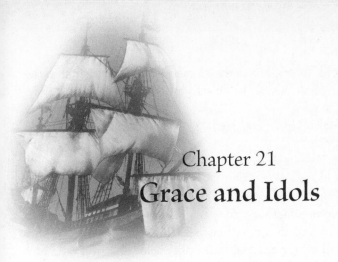

Chapter 21
Grace and Idols

Charging through the door of his cabin, Kent scanned the darkness, then grabbed the bottle of rum from his desk and headed up on deck. He marched onto the foredeck, ignoring the clusters of pirates littering the ship, well into their drink.

Darkness cast its shroud over the vessel, hovering like a demon over the waterlogged wood. Though the storm had ceased its assault upon the sea, it seemed only to be intensifying within Kent. A sudden chill seeped through his leather vest. Planting his boots on the sodden deck by the main head rail, Kent raised the bottle to his lips and poured a full draught down his parched throat in an effort to ward off the icy mist.

A sail snapped in the wind, drawing his gaze upward. Not the faintest glimmer of the moon or the twinkle of a star penetrated the heavy darkness that clung to the sky.

Boot steps approached, and Kent turned to see the doctor, pipe betwixt his lips, sauntering toward him. Blast. All Kent wanted at the moment was to be left alone.

The doctor withdrew his pipe. "Did you find Lady Ashton?"

Kent nodded but said nothing, hoping Cutter would leave.

"I find it hard to believe she is indeed betrothed to Lord Sawkins." Cutter shook his head and gave Kent a look of dismay.

Just hearing the words again sent pain lancing through Kent, followed by a cauldron of jealous rage that boiled over with fear for her safety.

Cutter puffed on his pipe and exhaled the sweet smoke in little ringlets that floated up into the night. "I cannot imagine what she sees in the man."

"Wealth and title."

"But at what cost?" Cutter chuckled. "Sorry, Captain, I know he's your brother."

"Half brother, if you please. And I'd be obliged if you didn't remind me." Kent gritted his teeth.

"I trust you found Lady Ashton unharmed?"

"Yes, but some mischief was afoot as you suspected. If you ask me, I'd say Sawkins had something to do with it." Kent knew what Sawkins was capable of, but why would he lure Isabel below? Why would any man steal something that would soon be his anyway? Sawkins had never possessed a great deal of patience—especially with women—but this was beyond the limits of even his deranged mind. Perhaps Isabel had scorned him in some way or injured his pride. Nausea curdled in Kent's stomach as he remembered his own acts of revenge on those who had dared to injure his inflated ego.

"Hmm," Cutter mused. "I'm sure she was grateful for your rescue."

Grateful? Kent's thoughts flooded with visions of the kiss he'd shared with Lady Ashton, and heat flushed over him as he remembered her flaming response. Such a passionate reaction could not have risen purely from the physical attraction between them. She held affections toward him. He saw it in her eyes, those lustrous green eyes that could melt his heart one minute and shoot arrows into it the next. "Yes, you could say she was grateful. Unfortunately, it didn't last long before her usual peevish temperament returned."

Cutter raised his scarred lips in a grin. "Do not discount intensity of feelings in whatever form they take."

The *Restitution* surged over a rising swell, and Kent braced himself. A shower of salty spray stung his face. He took in a deep breath of the tangy air as the breeze tugged upon his hair, and he willed it to cool his temper. "That she loathes me is a good sign?" Kent shook his head at the doctor. "I suppose I deserve nothing less than Lady Ashton's scorn. Yet to see her marry Sawkins—" Kent clamped his hands around the bottle of rum, nearly crushing it in his grip. Perhaps he deserved to lose her for what he'd done. Guilt pulled Kent's gaze down to the swirling black sea.

How could he blame Sawkins for doing the same vile things Kent had done most of his life? Neither of them deserved a woman like Isabel.

Cutter thrust his pipe back into his mouth and clasped his hands behind his back.

A ballad drifted on the wind from the pirates behind him:

> *"Where'er we roam*
> *We call it our home*
> *We plunder and pillage and feast.*
> *'Tis treasure we're after*
> *'Tis all that matters*
> *Some call us naught but beasts."*

Tipping the bottle to his lips, Kent took another swig and wiped his mouth on his sleeve. He watched the amber liquid slosh in the bottle as the liquor burned a trail down his throat, numbing his mind but heightening his pain. With a disgusted grunt, he heaved the half-empty bottle into the sea. It landed with a feeble *splash*. He gripped the railing.

They stood in silence for a moment, gazing out into the night. "Now, if you don't mind, Doctor. I'm in no mood for company."

Cutter faced him. "I'm beginning to believe in Lady Ashton's God."

Annoyance flared within Kent. Hadn't the man heard him? Yet curiosity begged the question. "You? I thought you believed in the god of fate."

"Ah yes, fate. I've found her to be very fickle and unforgiving. Not so with the true God. I used to deny His existence, but conscience and reason prevail upon me to do so no longer."

Kent could not argue with the things he, too, had seen. Truth be told, he'd avoided thinking about God. Somehow the idea that there was an all-powerful, holy Creator watching him made Kent feel dirty and worthless. And afraid, if he dared admit it. "I'll not deny He may exist, but either way, it makes no difference to me."

Cutter's brows pinched together. "Why wouldn't it?"

The words of Kent's father floated into the corners of his mind, taunting him. *"You're worthless. You'll never amount to anything."* His father belched, wiped rum-laced drool from his lips, and kicked young

Kent in the ribs.

Shaking the memory from his thoughts, Kent bunched his fists. He had proven his father wrong. He had amounted to something. But now as he faced the possibility of a holy God, he realized the cost of his success might have been too high. "If God is real, He gave up on me a long time ago."

"Hmm, perhaps, but Lady Ashton told me her God is willing not only to forgive all the wicked things we've done but to forget them, as well, as long as we truly repent and come to Him through Christ, His Son."

Kent chuckled. "Seems you've been spending too much time with Lady Ashton. You begin to sound like her."

"Aye, she's been assisting me with Hann." Cutter smiled.

"How is the lad?"

"Remarkably well, thank you, Captain."

Silence overtook them, all save the flap of sails on the yards and rustle of sea against the bow. Grabbing the bridge of his nose, Kent squeezed his eyes shut, forcing back a rising headache. Was it possible God indeed forgave all sins? He opened his eyes and glanced at Cutter. "This God forgives even murder, rape, and thievery?"

Cutter pursed his lips. "Aye, from what I am told."

"Kidnapping?"

Cutter nodded.

"Torture?"

"All sins, Captain." Cutter grinned.

"But why would He?" It didn't make sense. Kent had authority over others. When one of his men defied him, Kent's punishments came swift and harsh. Why would God be any different? Without fear of penalty, all discipline aboard the ship would be lost. Fear was the way to keep order and control, not forgiveness.

Cutter puffed his pipe. "I suppose He does it for love. He is our Father, after all, and what father would not forgive his children if they truly were sorry?"

Father? A clump of nausea rose in Kent's throat. His vision of a father was far from a loving one. Yet even as he pondered the thought, a sudden warmth blanketed him, stirring his heart with a longing he could not name.

"How can you say this? If this God loved you so much, why did He cause such a catastrophe to occur in your life?" Kent motioned toward Cutter's withered hand.

The flicker of a star appeared on the horizon where the thick clouds were beginning to dissipate.

Cutter shrugged. "What we consider a misfortune may turn out to be a blessing in disguise." His gaze landed upon the star, and its light twinkled in his eyes. "I discover I am not so unhappy here aboard your ship, Captain, and I would have never joined your crew if I had not been burned in that fire."

"I cannot accept that." Kent crossed his arms over his chest. "I'm in control of my life. I make my own plans."

Leaning toward him, Cutter raised a brow. "And pray tell, has that brought you the happiness you seek?" He slapped Kent on the back and strode away, leaving only the sweet scent of his tobacco swirling through the humid air.

Kent scanned the dark sea. His gaze drifted upward. "God," he began, then swallowed, not knowing what to say or even how to talk to the Almighty. Would God listen to him? The clouds above him broke, allowing a shaft of moonlight to fall on the railing in front of him. Was that a sign? He shook his head and continued, feeling suddenly foolish. "I've done many terrible things. I am not worthy of a single glance from You, but if You are there, if You're listening, I'm sorry for all the things I've done, and I ask Your forgiveness in Christ's name." He gripped the railing and hung his head. Below him, the moonlight shimmered over the foam churning against the hull. Crystalline bubbles chuckled up at Kent, matching the newfound joy suddenly surging within him.

A sense of value melted over him—an unfamiliar feeling of approval and love. It rippled down his back. He looked up. Sterling fingers pushed back the clouds that had captured the brilliance of a full moon, framing their dark masses in silver lace. Pearly light draped over the *Restitution*, covering Kent in its glow. He swallowed a burst of emotion that threatened to fill his eyes with tears. "Father?" The shame, the horror of all the wicked things he had done seemed to be lifted from his shoulders, and he sank to his knees on the deck.

Some time later, the vulgar chortles of pirates jarred Kent back to the reality of the ship. He stood and clasped the railing as a splash of sea spray doused him in a baptism of his new faith. Bowing his head, he prayed for the safety and quick rescue of his son, and for Isabel. He dared not ask God for her hand, but at least he could pray for her safety and happiness. Raising his gaze, he vowed to do everything in his power to keep her from marrying Sawkins.

Isabel emerged onto the main deck to a blast of hot air laden with the scent of fish, salt, and spicy tobacco. Raising her nose, she followed the aroma of the pipe until her gaze found Cutter, standing up on the foredeck. Hann sat on a barrel next to him. The two lovers engaged in a conversation full of grins and laughter as if they existed alone in the universe. Isabel couldn't help but smile despite the sleepless night she had spent pacing her cabin. Hann seemed much improved, and though Isabel longed to spend time with her new friends, she didn't want to sour their happiness with her foul mood. Besides, she hoped to find a solitary place to pray. Though the sun had only risen an hour ago, the heat in her cabin had quickly transformed the tiny room into an oven, baking her within and making it difficult to breathe, let alone pray.

One quick scan of the ship told her the captain was not on deck—much to her relief. She wasn't sure how she could face him after the kiss they'd shared last night. Lord Sawkins was nowhere to be seen either, but then he often slept late into the morning. Where had he been last night? Surely he had heard of her attack. News spread rapidly on a pirate ship, yet he had not come to ensure her safety.

Isabel skirted past a cluster of pirates and made her way up the stairs to the quarterdeck, heading toward the stern. Watching the ivory foam bubbling off the back of the ship always calmed her spirit.

Hoornes, manning the whipstaff, gave her a nod. "Good day to you, miss."

"And to you, Mr. Hoornes," she replied, causing a red hue to rise on the pirate's hardened features. The rat squealed at her from his shoulder.

Smithy, Zeke, Gibbons, and two other pirates loitered up on the poop deck. Isabel halted, deciding not to advance to the stern after all.

Their gazes raked over her. Isabel's stomach clenched, and she pressed a hand upon it and darted to the starboard railing, ignoring the snickers behind her.

Isabel turned back around and gripped the railing, wondering if it had been one of them who had attacked her last night. Silently, she thanked God again for His deliverance even if it was in the form of Captain Carlton.

"Shorten the main." The captain's imperious voice drew her view to the main deck, where he stood, hands on his hips, staring up into the shrouds of the mainmast. He lowered his face, and their gazes locked. A gust of wind sent his white shirt flapping and his dark hair dancing wildly about him. His lips curved in a sultry smile, and Isabel turned to face the sea again, her heart fluttering in her chest. *Oh Lord, keep my focus on Frederick and what's best for him.*

The sun, now a handbreadth over the horizon, flung its glittering gold onto the turquoise waves, setting the sea ablaze like a sparkling jewel. Isabel observed the chaotic jostle of each ocean swell—enslaved to the fickle blasts of wind. She clutched the railing, wringing her hands over the moist, weathered wood. A twinge of pain blazed in her shoulder. *Lord, I don't want to be tossed to and fro like these waves by each feeling or notion that comes my way. Make me as sturdy as this ship, and keep me set on the right course.*

"Milady." Kent's deep voice startled Isabel from her thoughts and quickened her breath. Hoping to hide the effect he had on her, she avoided his gaze. "Captain."

"I trust you slept well."

"I did not, thank you." She glanced up at him.

His mouth curved in a teasing smile, and his gaze dropped to her lips. "Perhaps the excitement of our kiss kept you awake?"

Isabel snorted. Yet he was right. It was his kiss—or rather her reaction to it—that had stolen her sleep. Why, when she was betrothed to Sawkins, did Kent fill her thoughts day and night? Though she had searched the pages of the Bible and sought God in prayer, she had found neither answers nor comfort. "You assume too much, Captain." She faced the sea again, amazed at his audacity but unable to stop the grin forming on her mouth.

Apparently, he noticed her smile as well, for he cupped his warm hand over hers on the railing. "I need not assume when I have the memory of your ardor burning upon my lips."

"You forget," Isabel said, jerking her hand from under his, "I am betrothed."

"Rest assured, I have not forgotten." He raised his right brow, his tiny scar reddening in the sunlight.

Sorrow darkened his eyes, and Isabel longed to brighten them again. Was this a trick of Satan to keep her from God's will? She rubbed her temples, weary of her tormenting thoughts. She'd finally decided last night that she must keep her mind and heart entirely on Frederick—on finding him and securing his future. Surely, they were nearing the end of their journey, and soon her son would be back in her arms. When he was, marrying Sawkins would be the best thing for Frederick.

But when she stared into Kent's brown eyes and felt her heartbeat quicken and her body warm, all sense of reason vanished like mist before the sun's hot rays. Last night in her anger and confusion, she had told him he was without honor. Yet he'd displayed naught but honor these past weeks. How deep that insult must have sliced into his heart. Even so, here he was, behaving the gentleman.

"You are rather solicitous this morning after the cruel things I said to you."

"I am learning forgiveness these days, and I find it quite freeing."

"You?" Isabel snapped. Something new flickered within his eyes. Confusion dove into the already chaotic stew of her mind. "Forgiveness? You surprise me, Captain."

"That I can still do so pleases me." He grinned and shifted his gaze to the sea. "You were thinking of Frederick when I approached you."

"Yes." Just the sound of his name awakened the ache in Isabel's chest. "Not a minute passes in which I do not think of him."

Nodding, Kent rubbed the back of his neck. "He has been on my mind, as well. I wish to know my son."

Wrinkling her brow, Isabel searched his eyes, expecting to see sarcasm or insincerity lurking in their depths. Instead, a sheen of moisture covered them.

"I prayed for him last night." He offered her a guarded smile.

"You? Prayed?"

Boots thundered across the deck behind them. "Ah, there you are, my love." Sawkins approached. "Trying to steal my fiancée, Captain?"

Kent turned to face him. "Nay, I believe that is your specialty."

The ship dipped over a wave, and Kent flung a possessive hand to Isabel's back to steady her.

Pushing Kent's arm aside, Sawkins squeezed in between them and grabbed Isabel's hand. "Word has come to me that you were attacked last night." He placed a wet kiss upon her cheek. "Tell me you are unharmed."

Isabel took a step back. "I am fine, thank you." The scent of cedar washed over her, pricking at her memory. "Where were you last night?"

"I am ashamed to say that I felt a bit under the weather and retired early, my love." His shoulders drooped. "And I am horrified that I was not there to save you, although I'm told the captain did a reasonable job as my second." Sawkins's eyes glinted with amusement.

Kent returned his stare with a fiery gaze and fingered the hilt of his cutlass.

Isabel felt a sudden desire to defend the man who had saved her. "The captain was quite gallant."

"Ah pish," Sawkins stammered. " 'Twould be a first, to be sure. But Captain, where is this Murdock? I trust you have dealt with the scoundrel?" Sawkins's eyelid twitched.

Kent narrowed his eyes. "He has found a new home, locked in the hold for now. I have questioned him, but he was not forthcoming with information."

"He should be hung at once from the yardarm." Sawkins waved his hand in the air. "What kind of pirate captain are you?"

"There is a bigger player in this, your lordship. 'Tis the shark we want, not the minnows who swim beneath his shadow." Kent's stern gaze bore into Sawkins.

A trickle of sweat slid down Sawkins's cheek as he lowered his hand next to his cutlass, stretched his fingers, and glowered at the captain.

"Captain, pray tell how far are we from Cartagena?" Isabel thrust between them, hoping to arrest the developing skirmish. "Surely we are near our destination by now."

"Aye, milady, we are but three days out," Kent answered her without removing his gaze from Sawkins. "At which time, your betrothed has promised to enlighten us as to our son's whereabouts."

A grin squirmed upon Sawkins's lips.

"Of course"—Isabel turned and smiled sweetly at Sawkins—"Lord Sawkins will do so, Captain. He is a man of his word, and he cares deeply for my son."

"That I do, my love." Leaning down, he kissed her on the cheek again, while darting a taunting glance at Kent.

"A sail!" A shout blasted from above.

"I beg your pardon, milady. I must attend to my duties." Kent bowed. "I will not be far should you need me." He regarded Sawkins with disdain, then turning, he gazed upward. "Where away?"

"Two points off the larboard quarter."

Marching across the quarterdeck, Kent plucked his spyglass from his belt and held it to his eye.

Sawkins stiffened beside her as he craned his neck for a view of the ship.

Shielding her eyes from the sun, Isabel, too, squinted for a glimpse over Kent's shoulder but could see naught but a speck on the horizon. Whoever it was, the ship was too far away to be bothered with.

Frowning, Sawkins took a step forward. His eyes flickered when he spotted Smithy and the other pirates up on the poop deck. Smithy nodded in his direction. Sawkins's face twisted into a tight knot. He seemed to have forgotten Isabel.

"Milord?" Isabel peered up at him.

Sawkins bit his lip and returned his gaze to the ship on the horizon.

"Milord? Are you all right?"

He glanced down at her, a sudden smile replacing his scowl. "Ah yes, my love, forgive me. I'm simply concerned for your safety."

"Not every ship in the Caribbean means us harm," she said, despite a niggling doubt that his thoughts were truly focused on her protection.

"Yes, never you fear." He patted her hand nervously between his. "Now, I beg your pardon, milady, but I have some business to attend to." He scrambled off before Isabel could inquire what possible business he could have on board Captain Carlton's ship.

She backed against the railing, steering clear of the pirates rushing about in response to Kent's bellowed orders. The captain lowered his

spyglass and marched down to the main deck, Smithy on his heels. Several men flung themselves into the ratlines and clambered aloft.

Isabel shifted her gaze to the ship on the horizon. Its silhouette had grown larger. Perhaps it was a threat, after all.

Sawkins's tall frame came into view, huddling with a group of pirates up on the poop deck—including Gibbons, Wolcott, and Zeke. Whispers hissed between them like snakes, and Isabel took a step in their direction, curious to know what they were discussing that had Lord Sawkins so intently involved. He slid his hand over the cutlass hanging at his side, and uneasiness slithered over Isabel.

Unable to make out what they were saying, she shifted her gaze to the captain as he studied the oncoming ship with Smithy, Caleb, and Sparks by his side. She searched her heart for the bitterness that normally flooded her when she looked at Kent, but could no longer find a trace of it. He was not the same man who had ravished her over a year ago. What had changed him? Forcing down her rising admiration, Isabel tried to pull her gaze from him but found she could not and instead chided herself, for she could no longer deny the strong feelings burning within her.

Several more pirates sprang up on deck and scrambled to the railings for a view of the pursuing ship. Her sails burst like white clouds against the horizon. Whoever she was, she had set a course directly for the *Restitution*.

Hann's vibrant chuckle caught Isabel's attention. With a hand clutching her side, the pirate girl descended the foredeck stairs. At the bottom, Cutter eased beside her, his hand grazing Hann's in a gentle touch that he quickly snapped away. Isabel glanced over the ship, wondering if anyone else noticed their playful dalliance, but all the pirates' gazes were glued to the horizon where the frame of the oncoming ship continued to grow.

Dashing down the stairs, Isabel rushed to her friends. "I'm happy to see you are feeling better, Hann."

"Aye, milady." Hann winked. "Must be the good doctoring." She smiled up at Cutter. "I'm still a bit sore, however."

"I'm taking her down to her cabin to get some rest." Cutter's stern gaze drifted over Hann.

"Against my wishes," Hann snapped.

Kent leaped down the quarterdeck stairs, glanced in their direction, then faced his first mate, who now stood on the foredeck. "Signal for a show of colors, Mr. Smithy."

"See? I am needed here." Hann scanned her comrades scattered across the ship and adjusted her waistcoat. "I must have my weapons."

"You'll have no such thing," Cutter stormed. "You will be of no use in your condition. I insist you go below."

"You insist, do you?" Hann crossed her arms over her chest and winced.

Chuckling, Cutter shook his head. "And it is not because you are a woman," he whispered. "An adorable one at that, I might add, but because you are my patient. And as my patient, you must do what I say until you are well."

Hann stared at him for a minute, then grinned. "Very well." She turned to Isabel. "I'm glad to see you are safe, milady. I warned you not to go below."

Isabel nodded and gestured toward Cutter. "I have the doctor here to thank for that."

"My pleasure." Cutter's gnarled lips curved in a smile. "But I hear 'twas the captain who saved you." His sandy hair flopped in the breeze as he glanced nervously toward the other ship. "Now you'd best get below too, miss. Looks as though we're to have company soon."

Isabel studied the ship. The tip of her bowsprit charged toward them like a sword amidst the spray of white foam. "Yes, but we don't know whether they are hostile."

"Not to alarm you"—Cutter's brow wrinkled—"but rarely have I seen a ship take a course directly toward another out of friendly intentions."

Isabel's gaze landed on Kent, who leveled the spyglass to his eye once again. His calm demeanor had previously sufficed to belay all her fears, yet now she sensed a tension in his stance. She offered Hann and Cutter a weak smile. "I'll be fine."

With an anxious nod, Cutter led Hann away, and Isabel watched them disappear down the companionway, envying their happiness. At one time, they had both possessed title and wealth. Now they had neither. Yet what they did have was far more precious than all the treasure in the world.

Tension buzzed over the ship as pirates scrambled up from below, their arms filled with pistols, knives, and boarding axes. Dread weighed on Isabel. Were they to engage in another sea battle?

Lifting her skirts, she marched toward Kent. "Who is it, Captain?"

As he lowered his glass, his brown eyes narrowed. "Morris."

Elation claimed Isabel's heart. She raised a hand to her chest to steady its fervent beating. Frederick. They had found Morris. But why was he heading toward them? What did it matter? With every wave he passed, with every swell he crested, Morris brought Frederick back into her arms. .

She darted to the railing for a closer look, straining her eyes for a glimpse of anyone on the deck. If she could see Frederick—just to know he was all right. Hope brought tears of joy to her eyes.

A plume of gray smoke erupted from the bow of Morris's ship. Instantly, strong arms forced her to the deck. Kent's warm body covered hers as the air exploded around them.

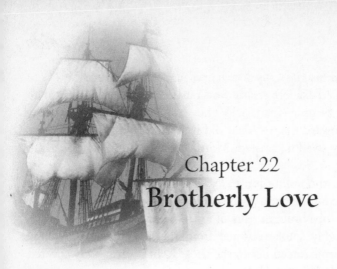

Chapter 22
Brotherly Love

The *Restitution* shook from bow to stern, sending a shudder through Isabel that rattled her bones along with her nerves. The *snap* of taut cords and the splitting of wood filled the air, followed by a barrage of angry curses that spewed from the pirates' lips.

Kent's weight lifted from her. "Osborn, damage report, if you please." His unruffled, commanding tone held no hint of panic.

"Minor, Captain, just a crack in the foretop," came the quick reply.

Isabel staggered to her feet, the blast still ringing in her ears. Terror sent her heart into her throat.

Frederick was on that ship.

Her son was now in the middle of a sea battle. She glanced at the angry vessel still charging straight for them. The smoke curled around the black muzzle of a swivel gun perched on her bow.

Isabel spun back around to see the captain stomping across the deck amidst an agitated sea of pirates rushing to their stations.

"Bring her to the wind, Mr. Hoornes!" he yelled, then turned to Smithy. "Have Logan run out the starboard battery."

"Aye, Cap'n." Smithy's shaggy hair disappeared below.

Hordes of pirates poured from the hatches. Dressed in flashy waistcoats adorned with sashes, and bright scarves tied around their heads, they strapped on knifes, axes, and swords. Pistols, tied to ribbons draped over their shoulders, bounced against their chests as they darted across the deck.

The *Restitution* swung about, and Isabel clung to the railing to keep from falling. Sails cracked like whips as the mighty frigate listed heavily to starboard. A surge of wind crashed over her, loosening strands of hair from her combs. Shielding her eyes from the glaring sun, she watched Morris's relentless pursuit. Men skittered across her decks, but there was no sign of Frederick. Panic clamped her heart. Why had Morris attacked them? Did he still have her son?

She scanned the chaotic mob of pirates speeding across the deck of the *Restitution* and spotted Kent handing out weapons to a cluster of ex-slaves. Taking a deep breath, she weaved her way though the crowd toward him. Men bumped into her from all sides in their frenzy to prepare for battle. Rubbing her arm from one such encounter, she approached the captain.

"Surely you don't intend to fire upon the ship with Frederick on board!" she shouted over the din and wrung her hands.

Kent handed out the last pistol, then nodded at the slaves before his gaze snapped to hers. "I assure you, milady, I shall take every precaution." His eyes were ablaze with the fervor of battle as he glanced over her shoulder.

"Take precautions?" Isabel clutched his arm, drawing his attention back to her. "You must not harm him!"

His jaw flexed as he narrowed his eyes upon her. "He is my son, too." The anger in his voice startled Isabel.

With a sigh, Kent pulled her hand from his arm and squeezed it between his. "Trust me." He nodded, raising his brows. "Will you trust me for once?"

Isabel didn't have time to answer before a clamor of obscenities erupted behind her.

"He's running out 'is guns, Cap'n!" Mac shouted from the crosstrees.

"Please go below." Kent gave her hand a final squeeze and strode away.

Isabel turned to see the captain storm up to Sawkins, who stood with unusual repose by the capstan. "You said Captain Morris was in Cartagena."

Sawkins shrugged. "Perhaps he was delayed." He eased a finger over his mustache. " 'Tis not my fault he happened upon you when he did."

A thunderous *boom* pounded the sky like a hammer. Covering her head, Isabel dropped to the deck. A cannon shot split the air above her, sending a crackle down her spine. She squeezed her eyes shut, expecting to be struck and torn asunder at any moment. The crunch of wood, followed by an ominous *splash*, told her she'd been spared. *Thank You, Lord.*

That second brazen attack ignited a fire beneath the pirates. They swarmed upon the railings and into the shrouds like a horde of wasps, slashing their swords out before them and pouring out a string of curses that inflamed Isabel's ears.

"Sparks, musketeers to the tops!" Kent bellowed as he made his way to the quarterdeck. Men brandishing muskets nearly as tall as themselves clambered into the ratlines.

Isabel backed into the main deck railing. Biting her lip, she allowed her gaze to wander over the scene of impending battle. Sunlight glinted in flashes off swords and knifes hefted about by pirates who growled and cursed and spat onto the deck. Smoke lingered in the air from Morris's cannon fire. Off the starboard side, his ship plummeted toward them, rising and plunging through the sea. Suddenly, the vessel veered sharply and brought all her guns to bear. Isabel cringed in horror. How far had she fallen from the privileged comforts of her parents' estate at Hertfordshire!

Captain Carlton, hands planted on his waist, stared resolutely at their oncoming enemy. She'd seen him fight many battles. If nothing else, he was a good pirate captain, and her confidence in his abilities gave her some solace. But her comfort quickly dissolved as she remembered his predicament. How could he subdue Morris without harming the pirate's ship and the precious child inside?

Sawkins cast a curious look at her over his shoulder. His eyes twinkled as if he held some grand secret. She wondered at his sudden brave demeanor.

The *Restitution* thrust boldly into a rolling swell. Her crowded sails snapped in the wind. The vessel dipped to starboard, and Isabel clung to the railing as seawater flooded the deck. The ship righted, and the salty water slid back through the scuppers to the ocean below. In a burst of speed, the *Restitution* swept athwart Morris's larboard beam.

Thumps and clanks off their starboard side reached Isabel's ears. She

dashed toward the railing and leaned over the side. Below, all twenty of the *Restitution*'s gun ports flew open. Blackened muzzles poked their heads through the gaping holes.

"No!" Isabel shouted. Lifting her skirts, she raced across the deck, took the quarterdeck stairs in two leaps, and barreled into the captain.

"No! Frederick might be hurt." Isabel jerked his arm.

"Stand fast, gentlemen." Kent laid a strong arm around her shoulder and held her in place. "Steady now."

Isabel struggled in his grasp.

"Never fear, milady. I'm aiming for her gun decks." Kent glance at her, then returned his gaze to Morris's ship. "Our son would not be there."

"But what if you miss?" Tears burned in her eyes. Terror forced them down her cheeks at the thought of Frederick being injured.

"Logan is the best gunner I've seen. He won't miss." Kent eyed his adversary. Ten gun ports snapped open with threatening clanks on the starboard side of Morris's ship.

"Fire!" Kent's shout clamored in her ears.

The world collapsed around Isabel as the reverberating thunder of guns cracked the sky. One by one, their powerful explosions roared like angry dragons awakened from their sleep.

Isabel covered her ears, and Kent drew her against his chest, holding her tightly. The *Restitution* rocked and staggered with each blast. The deafening sound lingered long after the last cannon fired. Backing away from Kent, Isabel peered into the smoky haze. She drew a hand to her mouth as the gunpowder stung her nose and stole her breath.

Desperate to see the damage, she dashed to the railing, swiping away the smoke as a deathly silence took over the ship. Perspiration beaded on the back of her neck and slid inside her gown. She leaned over, coughing, and tried to quell the rising nausea in her stomach. Kent appeared beside her. Even the pirates were silent as they waited to see the outcome of their broadside.

The smoke began to clear. Isabel's breath caught in her throat as bit by bit of Morris's retreating ship appeared. Several charred, smoking holes lined his hull—all at the gun deck. Relief washed over her in waves. As Morris's ship veered sharply away, Isabel read the name *Johnny's Revenge* painted in bold red letters across the stern. Was Johnny his son—the one whom Morris believed Kent had murdered? A sudden ache clamped her heart as a swell of empathy rose to join the anger she felt for this pirate captain. Losing a son was something she could understand.

She gazed at Kent—his eyes focused on the name, as well. He winced and drew a heavy breath.

Renewed anger burned through Isabel. Regardless of Kent's obvious remorse, he was the cause of Morris's hatred and all the tragedies that had followed. But she didn't have time to pour out her frustration upon him before a blast of small shot from Morris's demi-cannons swept the deck like a hailstorm. Isabel dropped and crouched by the railing. Kent covered her head with his arms until the roar of the cannons ceased and Morris's ship was out of range.

Assisting Isabel to her feet, Kent gazed after his enemy, then turned and crossed the deck, bellowing orders. "Hard to larboard, Mr. Hoornes. Trim the sails."

Smithy repeated the last order, and a mob of pirates leaped into the shrouds.

Isabel clutched the railing as the ship lurched to the left, sending a spray of white foam off her starboard quarter. Why were they turning away from Morris? The flap of sails drew her gaze upward. White canvas floundered, searching for a gust of wind. For a moment, silence overtook the *Restitution*. Even the purling of the sea fell into a gentle hush.

Isabel glanced behind her. Morris was getting away. Fury tore her grip from the railing, and she started toward Kent to demand an explanation. Instantly the sails caught the wind and their white bellies swelled. The ship jerked backward. Isabel tumbled to the deck, scraping her palms.

A hand extended down to her, and she looked up to see Cutter, a fretful grin on his lips. "Best to hang on during these skirmishes. Allow me to escort you below? Hann could use the company."

Taking his hand, Isabel stood, swiping at her gown, heat blossoming on her face. "Thank you, Doctor, but I must see if Frederick is on that ship."

"Bring her about!" Kent yelled.

Cutter grabbed Isabel as the *Restitution* veered once again to larboard. He led her back to the railing. "If you insist on putting yourself in danger, at least try not to injure yourself in a fall, milady."

Isabel gave him a curt smile, then gazed over the ship. Off their larboard quarter, the *Johnny's Revenge* had angled toward the right, sails flapping, as the *Restitution* made her final turn to bear down upon Morris on his damaged side.

They charged toward their enemy, all sails bursting. The *Restitution's* booms and blocks creaked and moaned under the force of wind and sea. Isabel stared ahead at the *Johnny's Revenge*, its frame growing larger with each swell they rode. Sea spray showered over her as she braced her boots on the deck and clutched the railing. Her gaze found Kent up on the foredeck, arms crossed over his chest. The wind blew his hair behind him.

Out of the corner of her eye, she saw Murdock, holding a pistol in one hand and a cutlass in the other, racing up the foredeck stairs. Hadn't he been locked up below?

Kent approached the railing. "Alongside their starboard beam!" he roared to Hoornes, still manning the whipstaff behind Isabel. "And ready the langrel shot!" he yelled to Smithy.

Isabel turned to Cutter, fear sparking within her. "What is langrel?"

"A type of cannon shot meant to damage sails and masts. Never fear, milady. He means only to cripple them."

Isabel studied Morris's ship. The *Restitution* was coming up on her damaged side. Could it be? Could she dare hope they would defeat Morris without bloodshed and Frederick could be in her arms within the hour? Elation soared through her. Bracing herself as the ship plummeted over a wave, Isabel squared her shoulders into the wind, caught up in the exhilaration of the chase. She smiled, remembering the last time she'd been on this ship during a sea battle and how she had cowered below, shivering in fear.

"Never fear! The captain's quite skilled in battle! If he weren't a pirate, he'd be an asset in His Royal Majesty's Navy!" Cutter shouted over the pounding crash of the waves.

Isabel could only nod as the wind stole her voice. She glanced over at Kent, but something caught her eye down on the main deck. Sawkins huddled amongst a group of pirates, strapped with a brace of pistols, a cutlass, and two massive knives. She'd never seen him so well armed, nor had he dared before to come on deck during a fight. Perhaps she had indeed misjudged him.

With the wind behind them, the *Restitution* flew through the turquoise waters, swooping over rolling swells to her prey. The *Johnny's Revenge*, unable to catch the full wind, wallowed in the breeze until the *Restitution* came athwart her starboard quarter.

Bowing her head, Isabel prayed, "Oh Lord, please help us subdue our enemies without bloodshed. Please give Frederick back to me."

"Amen." Cutter squeezed her hand, and she smiled up at him.

Kent leaped down the foredeck stairs and marched across the main deck. "Fire!"

Isabel cupped her ears.

Nothing. No sound save the grunts of the pirates and the rush of water against the hull as the *Restitution* came abreast of the *Johnny's Revenge*.

Kent stormed to the main hatchway. "I said fire, Mr. Logan!"

Still nothing.

Isabel darted to the quarterdeck railing, Cutter on her heels. The cock of pistols and muskets cracked from above where musketeers were perched in the shrouds like colorful parrots. An equal number of pirates hung from the ratlines of the *Johnny's Revenge*, both sides itching for the command to fire.

Scanning the deck of the *Johnny's Revenge*, Isabel squinted, desperate for a glimpse of Frederick, but only the brutal faces of sneering pirates glared back at her.

Smithy emerged from the hatch, a smirk tangling his lips.

"Swounds man, I told you to fire!" Kent charged toward him. "Do it now, or I'll toss you to the sharks!"

Tilting his head, Smithy scratched his thick sideburns and grinned—an icy, evil grin that sent a shiver through Isabel.

The cock of a pistol sounded next to her. Spikes of alarm fired up her spine, and she turned to see Lord Sawkins holding a pistol to Cutter's head.

"You'll leave Mr. Smithy be, Captain!" Sawkins shouted, drawing Kent's gaze to him.

A throng of pirates stormed onto the deck from below. Swords drawn and pistols cocked, they leveled their weapons upon Kent's crew.

Smithy plucked out his pistol and aimed it at Kent's heart.

Fury smoldered in Kent's narrowing eyes.

Caleb charged toward Smithy, but Wolcott slammed the butt of his pistol on the black man's head. He slumped to the deck.

Kent gripped the hilt of his cutlass. "What is the meaning of this, Sawkins?"

"The meaning, dear brother," Sawkins sneered, "is that I'm taking over your ship. Now, be a good boy and tell your men to drop their weapons, or I'm afraid I'll be forced to blast the good doctor's brains all over the deck."

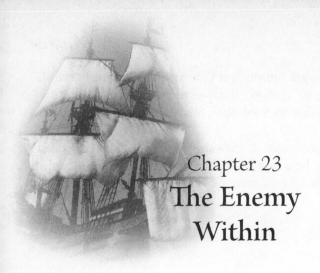

Chapter 23
The Enemy Within

Isabel clutched Sawkins's arm. "What are you doing, you fool?" Shock crashed into her reason.

Sawkins gave her a cursory glance. "I'm sorry, my love. But 'tis for the best. I will explain later."

"Have you gone mad?" Isabel yanked on his sleeve, trying to pry his aim away from Cutter's head. She dared not touch the weapon for fear it would fire accidentally.

"Wolcott, if you please." Sawkins addressed a man on the main deck as he gestured toward Isabel. The corpulent man lowered his pistol, lumbered up the stairs, and grabbed Isabel, wrenching her away from Sawkins.

"Let me go!" Isabel struggled against his tightening clamp. Pain seared up her arm and across her shoulders, bringing tears to her eyes.

Kent took a step forward, his fists clenching at his sides. "Lay a finger on her, and so help me God, I'll kill you, oath or no oath!"

"You are not in a position to give orders, Captain." Sawkins's eyes glimmered with amusement; then he glanced over his shoulder at Wolcott. "Keep her quiet, but do not harm her."

Wolcott dragged Isabel to the aft railing and forced her against it. She remembered him as the pirate who'd attacked Hann, and disgust rose in her throat. He crossed his arms over his prominent belly and thrust out his long, crooked nose.

Isabel scanned the ship. Her gaze scoured over Sawkins, still holding a gun to Cutter's head, then at the other pirates frozen in a standoff like powder kegs ready to explode. The *Johnny's Revenge* drifted by their larboard quarter. A tall man wearing a plumed bicorn stood staunchly upon the quarterdeck, a vicious smirk on his face. A fountain of curses poured from the lips of his pirates, but no shots were fired. Why? Did they see the mutiny taking place? Alarm clamored through Isabel as she watched the ship slip away—and Frederick with it.

"No!" she screamed. "Frederick!" Shoving Wolcott aside, she stormed across the deck, her eyes locked onto the man wearing the bicorn. "Give me my son!" All reason gave way to desperation as she dashed toward the railing with every intention of jumping into the sea and somehow making her way to Morris's ship.

She would not let another span of water keep her from her child.

But Wolcott quickly recovered his stance and raced after her. His thick fingers coiled around her arm again, jerking her toward him. Spasms fired through her shoulder. "No," she sobbed as he forced her back against the railing with a sneer.

Cutter stared straight ahead, his face like stone. "Let him shoot me, Captain. But whatever you do, don't let this peacock take over the ship."

Sawkins shifted his pistol to his left hand, drew his right arm back, and punched Cutter in the stomach.

Isabel gasped as her friend doubled over, groaning.

"I've been wanting to do that for some time." Sawkins shook his hand, then returned the pistol's aim upon Cutter.

Kent glared at his half brother.

"I said lower your weapons, Captain. If you have no care for your own life, surely you have some concern for the life of the doctor, beastly as he is, and"—his devious gaze shifted to Isabel—"sweet Lady Ashton."

A rush of heat swept over Isabel. Fury prodded her toward Sawkins, but Wolcott's burly arm blocked her way. "Why you lying snake," she spat, chiding herself for thinking him a gentleman, for trusting him, and especially for agreeing to marry him. What a fool she had been.

A wicked chortle rolled over the pirates.

Kent grimaced. "Do as he says." He glanced over his men. "Drop your weapons."

Moaning, the pirates and slaves lowered their guns and swords and tossed them onto the deck, each *clank* and *clink* grating over Isabel. She knew Kent had no choice—not with Cutter's life at stake.

"Now, if you please, Captain"—Sawkins gestured toward Kent's hip where his cutlass still rested—"your weapons, as well." He glanced up. "And order your shooters down from the tops."

Kent's distressed gaze drifted to Isabel, then over at the *Johnny's Revenge*, which kept pace with them just off the *Restitution*'s stern. His fingers clenched over the hilt of his cutlass as if he were considering drawing it and taking on the mutineers by himself. Finally, he plucked it from its scabbard and flung it, along with his pistols and knives, onto the growing mound of weapons. He looked above him. "Musketeers down."

As the men labored down from the shrouds and tossed their muskets onto the heap centering the deck, Kent turned a hard glare upon Sawkins. "Are you planning to battle Captain Morris all by yourself? I doubt you are up to the task."

Sawkins's only reply was a wicked chuckle as he directed two of his men to take the weapons and store them below. He lowered his pistol from Cutter's head, and the doctor let out a ragged sigh and wiped the sweat from his brow.

Strutting to the quarterdeck railing, Sawkins gazed down at the band of twenty pirates who'd sided with him. "Keep your weapons upon them, men." He studied the rest of the pirates, their eyes still wide with shock at this sudden turn of events. "Put the helm over. Reef all sails," he ordered.

Kent's pirates hesitated, shifting their glances between Sawkins and their captain.

"Do as he says!" Smithy bellowed and glowered over the men.

"By the laws of the sea, I have beaten your captain!" Anger flew like spittle from Sawkins's lips. "You'll take your orders from me now!"

"You have not bested me man to man." A smirk played on Kent's lips. "Come down. Bring your sword. It's time you learned how to fight like a real pirate."

Sawkins pressed a strand of hair behind his ear. "Some other time, perhaps, dear brother." He nodded toward Smithy. "Tie him up. And watch him. We wouldn't want him getting any heroic ideas."

Although Sawkins's tone was caustic, Isabel detected a quiver running

through him. He wiped the sweat from the back of his neck and then tore off his violet doublet and hung it on the railing. His white satin shirt shimmered in the blaring sun.

Smithy and another pirate inched toward Kent, rope in hand. The captain glanced at Isabel, and she knew by the look in his eyes that he would allow himself to be bound rather than risk her safety. As the men yanked his arms behind him and knotted his wrists together, Kent stared straight ahead.

Sawkins scanned the crew with fury in his eyes. "Now put the helm over and furl the sails or"—he leveled his pistol at Kent—"I'll kill him where he stands!"

Isabel gasped and raked her nails over the itch burning on her arms. Her eyes darted to Kent, and a sudden burst of fear gripped her. Would Sawkins kill his own brother?

The pirates still did not move.

Withdrawing a handkerchief from his pocket, Sawkins flapped it in the breeze and wiped his brow with a shaky hand. He gritted his teeth. "Do as I say, or I'll tie the lot of you to the rudder and drag your rotting carcasses across the Caribbean!" He glanced over his shoulder at the *Johnny's Revenge*. "With Captain Morris's compliments, I assure you." His lips curled in a wicked sneer.

Kent's crew shifted their dauntless gazes from Sawkins to Morris's ship. Expressions of terror twisted upon their faces.

Shock coursed through Isabel. What association did Lord Sawkins have with Morris?

As if in answer to her silent question, Sawkins crossed his arms over his swelling chest. "Yes, gentlemen, Captain Morris is with me, so I'd be obeying my orders if I were you."

Moaning, the pirates scuffled off to do their new captain's bidding.

Fury smoldered within Isabel as she realized the depth of Sawkins's deception. Had he taken part in Frederick's kidnapping, as well?

Clenching her jaw, she resisted the urge to run and push him over the railing. Besides, Wolcott still hunched over her like a guard dog. Cutter was right. Sawkins was naught but a peacock strutting about in his fancy clothes.

Cutter edged beside her and fumbled in his pocket. His usual calm demeanor had given way to a wrinkled look of anxiety. Isabel had to agree. She could not see how things could turn out well, and her heart kept a rapid pace in her chest. *Lord, forgive my lack of faith. Please help us. Please let no harm come to Kent or any of the rest of us, and please save Frederick.*

In minutes, with all sails shortened, the *Restitution* eased into a quiet drift. The *Johnny's Revenge* abruptly slipped from behind and sailed beside them off their larboard beam.

Frederick was on that vessel. Isabel knew it—could feel it in her mother's heart.

Sawkins flew down the quarterdeck stairs, passed Kent with a sneer, and waved to the man with the plumed bicorn. "Hail, Captain Morris. Good day to you."

The man grunted in return and motioned to his crew. Ten men tossed ropes over to the *Restitution*, where Sawkins's men caught them, and with groans and straining backs, they heaved the two ships together in a stammering *crunch*.

Wolcott abandoned his post and followed Sawkins to the main deck, allowing Cutter and Isabel to do the same. They inched behind Kent, who stood flanked by two pirates.

Tension seeped from the captain and saturated the air around him. He toiled at the ropes binding his wrists and shot an anxious glance over his shoulder at Isabel. "Stay behind me." He looked at Cutter. "Watch over her."

Gibbons and another pirate standing nearby chuckled. "Don't be worryin' none, Cap'n. They ain't goin' no wheres."

Sawkins's men stationed themselves across the main deck, up on the fore- and quarterdecks, and up in the ratlines, where they aimed their weapons at Kent and his pirates.

A baby cried—a tiny wail at first that soon heightened into a blubbering howl.

Clutching her chest, Isabel pushed past Kent, ignoring his warning for her to stay back. "Frederick!" Weaving through the mob of pirates, she dashed to the railing and scanned the deck of the *Johnny's Revenge*. Tears pooled in her eyes. "Frederick!" She saw nothing save ropes, tackles, barrels, and a throng of brutal pirates laughing at her.

She spun on her heels, desperation gripping every nerve. Kent wrestled in the grasp of two pirates. The tip of a sword held Cutter in place, and Lord Sawkins strutted toward her, a malicious grin dripping on his lips.

The *thump* of a plank drew Isabel's attention, and she turned to see a pathway of wood had been laid between the two ships—a pathway to her son. Lifting her skirts, she raced toward it just as Sawkins seized her by the waist and yanked her aside. "No you don't, my love."

Isabel tried to pry his thick fingers from her gown as she twisted in his grip. "Let me go, you beast."

"Is that any way to speak to your betrothed?"

"I wouldn't marry you if you were the king of England."

"Let her go!" Kent shouted. Wrenching from the two pirates' grips, he knocked them to the deck and charged toward Sawkins. With hands still tied behind his back, he struck his brother with the full impact of his muscular chest. Sawkins's clasp on Isabel snapped, and he toppled backward.

Captain Morris jumped onto the plank, his heavy boots pounding on the wood. "Is this the way you control your men, Captain Sawkins?"

Regaining his footing, Sawkins muttered under his breath, his face aflame, and snarled at Morris. "Mr. Kent was just on his way to the hold." He gestured toward Smithy.

"Nay, not yet. I have something for him to see." Morris stomped over the plank and jumped onto the deck, followed by five of his crew.

Isabel raised her gaze to a pair of icy blue eyes. Her stomach lurched. They were the same beady eyes of the pirate who'd approached her on the streets of Port Royal—the one who'd had an obsessive interest in her son. His salt-and-pepper hair coiled around his broad face like the snakes on Medusa. Beneath a rich damask waistcoat, his bulging stomach swelled.

"Lady Ashton." He donned his hat and swept it before him, the feathers fluttering in the breeze. "A pleasure to see you again."

"You"—Isabel stammered—"you took my son."

"That I did. And I must say, he's been quite the brat."

Isabel rushed toward him, the instinct to protect her baby overpowering her fear. "Where is he?"

One of Morris's men grabbed her, and she winced. "I demand you return my son at once!"

"You do? Why I admire your pluck, milady." He turned to Sawkins. "I can see why you are fond of her."

Throwing his shoulders back, Sawkins came and stood beside Morris. "Yes, you and I share the same fine taste in—"

"Such soft skin." Morris ignored him and slid the back of a finger over Isabel's cheek.

She flinched and turned her face away.

"And such exquisite eyes and hair." He reached up to stroke a lock of her hair.

Kent threw himself between them. "Take what you came for, Morris, but leave the lady alone."

The pirate released Isabel. Brushing past Kent, she whisked tears from her face. "I want my son."

The mob on Morris's ship parted for a dark-skinned woman holding a bundle to her chest. She halted before the plank.

"Ask and ye shall receive." Morris grinned and made a gesture toward his ship.

Isabel's heart burst. "Frederick!" She dashed toward the woman, nearly tripping over her skirts.

Frederick let out a sniveling wail as if he recognized his mother's voice.

"Ah-ah-ah, miss," Morris said as two of his men stepped in her way. She charged into them, the moisture from their sweaty shirts greasing her palms. The stench of dried urine and fish assailed her. Shifting to the side, she tried to dart around them, but one caught her by the wrist and yanked her back.

Kent lunged toward Morris.

In a flash of glimmering steel, Morris drew his sword and staved him off with the tip. He swaggered toward Kent. "Captain, I see you've grown quite fond of Lady Ashton. If I'd known, I would have kidnapped her, as well. Nonetheless, this grand event has been staged solely for your benefit." He waved a hand over the scene. "Aren't you pleased? For this is all your doing, you know."

Frederick bawled, and Kent's gaze flickered to the dark-skinned woman and then to Isabel.

"Ah, but you have yet to meet your son, am I right?" Morris glanced

234

over his shoulder. "Darla, bring him here." He motioned with two jeweled fingers. " 'Tis only fitting you should see him—at least once before you die."

Isabel sobbed, struggling in the pirate's clutches. The woman inched past her, pain clouding her expression. Isabel's gaze darted to the bundle, but all she could see was one lock of curly umber hair—enough to assure her, however, that it was indeed Frederick. Desperate to touch him, she wrenched against the fierce clamp on her arms until pain shot down to her fingers. "My baby," she sobbed, nausea choking in her throat.

The woman stopped before Kent and held back the blanket. Kent gazed down upon the baby. A quick flutter of his eyelids was the only indication the sight of his son affected him. When he lifted his face, his expression remained stoic, although moisture gleamed in his eyes.

"Why should I care about this child?" Kent shrugged his shoulders. "Why, I've fathered an army of brats across the Caribbean. This one is nothing special."

His declaration pierced Isabel's heart. How could he say such a thing? Heaviness settled on her, tugging her down. Had she been such a fool as to fall for both Sawkins's and Kent's trickery?

Morris cocked his head and eyed Kent with suspicion.

"Give him to his mother." Kent gestured toward Isabel. "He means nothing to me."

Morris sighed, then his eyes began to sparkle. "Egad man, you had me going for a moment." He chuckled. "But I don't believe you. Otherwise, why would you have taken the lady and come after me?"

"I came after you"—Kent narrowed his eyes upon Morris—"because I heard you had a fair amount of treasure aboard, and I took the lady because she pleases me in bed."

Isabel let out a deep breath. Well at least she knew the latter wasn't true. Heat sizzled up her neck as the pirates' chortles filled the air. Even Morris turned around to leer at her. Beyond him, Kent's face came into view. He winked at Isabel.

"We shall see," Morris said.

Sawkins marched up to Morris, one hand on his waist. "Captain Morris, I've done what you asked. What of our bargain?"

"Our accord remains," Morris said with annoyance. "The ship is

235

yours. At least you were able to do that successfully."

"This ship will never be his!" Kent spat through gritted teeth.

"I daresay." Morris glanced across the deck, sarcasm dripping in his voice. "Why, it appears you are mistaken, Captain."

Sawkins took a step closer, a nervous gulp gliding down his throat. "And you'll introduce me to Captain Morgan as we agreed?"

"Do you doubt my word?" Morris snapped. "I assure you, I've arranged for you to meet Morgan very soon." A hint of a smile lifted his curled mustache.

"Why, you spineless snake." Kent rushed toward Sawkins. "You think joining Morgan will make you a man? He'll not put up with the likes of you for long." Morris threw out an arm to block Kent's path, halting him before he reached Sawkins.

"Sorry, brother, but I fear you are mistaken. I do, however, apologize for the way things turned out. I needed a ship." He raised his cultured brows. "Yours seemed the easiest to come by. All I had to do was inform Captain Morris of your son's whereabouts and convince you to bring me aboard. 'Twas much easier than I thought." He ran a hand through his golden hair, his eyes glinting with humor.

"Well, let's get on with it, then, shall we?" Morris rubbed his hands together and faced Darla, who slowly backed away from him. She bumped into a wall of pirates, and Morris snatched the bundle from her.

Gasping, Isabel freed one arm and reached for her son. Arms and legs flailing, he let out a tiny yelp as the blanket fell from his body. "Frederick!" she screamed, struggling to free herself from the pirate. Despite his soiled nightdress, her son looked well and in one piece.

Frederick's tear-streaked face darted to hers. His eyes widened and he reached out both chubby arms toward her. His moist pink lips drew into a tight knot before he let out a shriek that tore her heart in two.

"I told you he was a brat!" Morris yelled over the screeching. "Does nothing but cry all the time. Rather annoying on a ship." Clutching Frederick by his nightdress, he held him at arm's length as if the boy had a disease, then ambled over to the plank and leaped upon it.

In a burst of strength, Isabel turned to the pirate holding her and kicked him in the shin. He released her and bent to rub his leg, cursing. She raced toward Frederick, knocking men out of the way as she went.

Although still bound, Kent joined her in a mad dash to rescue their son, but one word from Morris sent a swarm of his men to block their paths.

"Grab them both. And bring them to the railing. I want them to see every minute of this." Fury seethed in Morris's eyes.

Balancing himself with the swaying of the ships, Morris stepped to the center of the plank and held Frederick over the side. "Now we shall see how much you care for your son, Captain."

Kent let out a deep howl as he wrestled against the grip of three pirates. "Mark my words, Morris. If you harm a hair on his head, I'll hunt you down and kill you." He lunged, the sweaty strands of his hair flinging before him.

"I thought as much." Morris smirked, then glanced at Isabel. "Did Captain Carlton tell you what he did to *my* son?" His eyes flared. "He blew him to pieces aboard Morgan's flagship. My boy was only one and twenty." Dropping his gaze, Morris swallowed, then looked down at the choppy water below.

"No, please," Isabel begged, her voice screeching in agony. "Please. He's just a baby. He's done you no harm." Tears sped down her cheeks and dripped onto her gown. "I beg you." She tugged against the pirate's hold, agony squeezing her heart. She looked at her son. He had stopped crying and was pointing at the gurgling water below. Then his gaze rose, and his innocent eyes locked upon Isabel's. He reached out for her, legs kicking in the wind. His face scrunched, his eyes pooled, and his nose reddened. He began to whimper.

Isabel's heart shriveled. "Mother's here, darling."

"Your fight is with me," Kent said, "not an innocent babe." He took in a deep breath. "Morris, I know you. You're not the kind of man to hurt a baby. Give the child back to his mother, and let's you and I settle this with a duel."

Isabel glanced at Kent, his figure blurry through her tears. He was willing to fight Morris to save their child? Or was it only his ship he sought to regain?

Morris shot Kent a smoldering gaze. "That's been your error from the beginning. You don't know what kind of man I am, or you wouldn't have considered Johnny's life so frivolous a thing to tamper with." He scanned the crowd as if giving a speech. "As I see it, he killed my son, so I will kill his. Johnny had a cruel death at sea, and so will his son." Clutching Frederick's gown, he dangled him farther over the murky waters. The nightdress tightened over Frederick's small chest and pinched beneath his arms, eliciting another gut-wrenching wail.

"Any last words for the little whelp?" Morris asked with a sneer.

Terror clamped Isabel as tears blurred her vision. "No! No!" She held out a hand toward Frederick, unable to believe she was about to watch her son plummet to his death. "Please, please don't." She writhed against the pirate's strong clasp. Her body convulsed in agony.

"I have some words to say, Father."

All eyes shot to the source of the high-pitched voice bellowing from behind them. Hann hobbled onto the deck from the companionway stairs, her ardent stare focused upon Captain Morris.

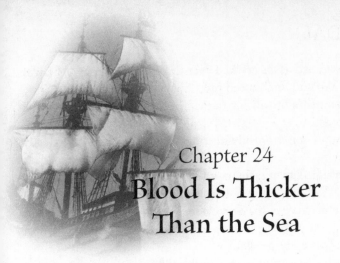

Chapter 24
Blood Is Thicker
Than the Sea

Kent watched his young quartermaster shuffle across the deck. He'd thought he heard him call Captain Morris *Father*, but that was not possible. Morris had only one son, and Kent had watched the boy die. Yet when Kent glanced back at Morris, the old pirate stood, frozen in place, confusion furrowing his brow.

"What did you call me, lad?" Morris still held Frederick teetering over the water.

The ships staggered upon a wave, sending one side of the plank tugging on its lashes and floating in midair before it clapped back to the railing. Isabel gasped, and Morris swayed and scuffed his boots against the wood to brace himself.

Hann snagged his hat from his head and halted before the plank. Tilting his chin, he presented a full view of his face to Morris.

"Annie?" Morris chuckled and drew Frederick back to his chest.

Relief assuaged Kent's rapid heartbeat, and he faced Hann, or Annie, as he tried to make sense of the miracle that had momentarily saved his son. Over Hann's shoulder, Isabel's reddened eyes darted to his, hope sparkling within them.

Morris shifted Frederick to his other hand as the boy began to whimper. "Faith, girl, whatever are you doing aboard this scallywag's vessel? And egad, what have you done with your hair?"

A volley of stunned gasps crashed over the pirates. "I know'd he was a girl all along," Wolcott announced proudly.

"Why, I'll be a slimy toad!" exclaimed Smithy, scratching his thick sideburns.

Catcalls flew at Hann from all directions, quickly silenced by a steady glare from Morris.

Girl? Kent studied Hann, the boy who'd been on his ship for nigh six months now. With his hat removed, traces of femininity—his lashes, his lips, the graceful curve of his chin evident in the bright sun—taunted Kent's stupidity. How could he have been so fooled? And the daughter of his enemy? He'd trusted him—her.

Hann flashed a placating glance at Kent before facing her father again. "Come down here with the child, and I'll explain everything."

"I'm still your father, girl!" Morris bellowed. "I'll not be taking orders from you!"

Frederick bunched his fists into tiny red knots. His face swelled like a blowfish, and he let out a screeching wail.

Isabel moaned, and Captain Morris grabbed the baby and held him away from him with both hands as if the child's fit were contagious. Frederick continued screaming, stopping only to draw a breath for the next outburst. His glassy eyes landed on his mother, but no sooner did he recognize her than another deafening yowl erupted from his mouth.

Pride swelled within Kent. His son had a good set of lungs and a fighting spirit. *Oh God, let him live.*

Hann crinkled her nose. "Father, please. I beg you to talk to me before you do something you regret."

"I rarely do anything I regret," Morris said, still holding the writhing baby at arm's length. He gestured toward Kent. "And killing this murderer's son will not be one of them. Are you forgetting your brother so soon?"

" 'Tis for my brother's sake that I am here." Hann cast a glance over her shoulder at Cutter, still held in place by the tip of a sword. His gaze widened upon her, filled more with concern than surprise.

Kent struggled against the rope that bound his hands. He clamped his teeth as the coarse twine grated against his skin. Had Cutter known Hann was a lady all this time? Humiliated, Kent glared at his crew. How many of them had played him for a fool? He'd expected treachery from

Sawkins, but not from Hann or Cutter—or Isabel. He studied her as she looked with yearning upon Frederick. If she'd known about Hann, it would certainly explain why the two of them had appeared so close.

The sun whipped hot lashes over them from its throne in the sky, sending waves of heat curling up from the deck. A light breeze teased the flaccid sails into a flutter against the masts, drawing Morris's attention upward.

"Very well." He cringed as Frederick, with arms and legs thrashing, let out another wail. "I can delay me plans for a moment. Besides, I must silence this brat, or I fear I'll throw meself into the sea just to gain a moment of peace." He thundered over the plank and down onto the deck, tossing Frederick into Darla's waiting arms. "I daresay I'll enjoy prolonging your agony as well, Captain." His petulant blue gaze flickered over Kent.

Gathering the child up in her arms, Darla rubbed his back and peered at Isabel across the deck. Frederick's howling soon diminished to a whimper. He snuggled his face into Darla's neck and grabbed a lock of her hair, his body still convulsing.

Kent inched across the deck, hoping to move closer to his son, but two pirates blocked his way.

"Explain yourself, girl, before me patience runs out." Morris's head twitched. He stared at Hann, but Kent detected no hostility in his gaze. If anything, he looked at her as a loving parent would an unruly child.

Sawkins's red cheeks swelled with annoyance. He blew out a sigh, whipped off his neckerchief, and wiped the sweat from his brow. With chin aloft, he sneered at Hann.

Isabel continued struggling against Murdock's fast grip. Wayward locks of hair blew across her face as her pleading eyes shifted to Kent's. He would do anything to answer the desperate call for help shooting from within them. But how could he, bound, helpless, and outnumbered? Continuing his battle with the ropes on his wrists, he studied his crew. Most appeared no happier than he was with the change in command. If he could just free himself.

Hann shifted her stance and pressed a hand to her side. "I came aboard Captain Carlton's ship to kill him"—she bit her lip and glanced at Kent—"to avenge Johnny's death."

The statement sped through Kent, causing both pain and anger. He'd taken the boy—girl—under his wing, protected her, trusted her. If she'd truly sought to kill him, she'd had many opportunities to do so. He glanced toward Isabel. By the shocked look on her face, at least she had not been privy to the plot to end his life—a token that brought Kent a smidgen of comfort amidst the deception rising around him.

"Ah, finally something sensible from your lips, Hann, or should I say *Annie*." Sawkins glowered. "I daresay I did think you were too effeminate for a boy."

"Still your tongue, man," Morris snapped, jerking his head toward Sawkins. He faced Hann again. "If your intent was to kill him, then why, pray tell, do I see Captain Carlton standing here, unscathed and ever the insidious bore?"

"He is not guilty of Johnny's death, Father. Please, you must not kill his son."

A spark of hope flared within Kent. Hann's violet gaze swept over his and then to Isabel, who returned her glance with a weak smile.

"Is that so? And how did you come by this conclusion?" Morris crossed his arms over his portly belly.

Hann swallowed and let out a deep sigh. She opened her mouth to answer when Morris leaned toward her with a scowl. "By the way, where is your husband? Or should I say, what have you done with him?"

"He is dead." Hann gave Morris a wary look. "Not by my hand, Father. I heard he fell sick and died shortly after I left him."

"Hmm." Morris studied her as a wheezing cough sounded from behind Hann.

Cutter lurched forward, nearly plowing into the pirate's sword pointed at his chest. Confusion and hurt marred his features. Hann stole a glance his way, then turned toward Sawkins. "Order your men to stand down."

"I will not," Sawkins replied with an insolent quiver, then faced Morris. "Captain, I must protest. The ship is mine. Can you not conduct your business aboard your own vessel so I may be on my way?"

In a flash, Morris drew his pistol and aimed it at Sawkins. The snap of the cock echoed over the ship. "I'll conduct me business wherever I please. If it vexes you so, just say the word, and I'll cancel the agreement

betwixt us and throw you overboard with the babe."

"Toss 'im to the sharks," Hoornes brayed, eliciting chortles from the others.

Horror bloated Sawkins's sweat-streaked face as he took a step back.

Morris scanned the mob. "Aye, lower your weapons."

The pirate who guarded Cutter lowered his sword, and the doctor pushed through the crowd and halted behind Hann.

Isabel flattened her lips and yanked her arm, still firmly in Murdock's grip. "Let me go!" Grinning at her, the pirate wiped his nose on his sleeve.

"Frederick, Mother's here!" she called across the deck.

Frederick lifted his head from Darla's shoulder and gazed over the crowd.

"Frederick," Isabel wept. His gaze locked on hers, and a grin lifted his pink lips. He stretched his hand toward her and spread his chubby fingers wide, then began to whimper.

The affection between mother and son swirled through the air like a sweet fragrance, weaving its way through the vile mob and bridging the distance between Isabel and Frederick. Kent envied such intense devotion—would do anything to place Frederick back in his mother's arms. Up until now, he'd really had no idea the horror Isabel had suffered being separated from her child. Continuing to toil with the ropes, sweat dripped down Kent's arms and stung the raw skin on his wrists. The sea gurgled against the hull as the ships tottered over the waves.

Morris snorted at Isabel. "Curb your tongue, woman." Then he started toward Darla while flinging a glance over his shoulder at Hann. "Get your mischievous little bones over to the ship, Annie. We'll discuss this later, as well as what I'm to do with you now."

"No, Father. Please." Hann laid a hand on his arm, stopping him, and for a split second Kent saw the resemblance between them—the same large oval eyes, the same triangular jaw and golden skin.

"I have spent six months aboard this ship," she continued, "asking, listening, learning. I had to make sure of the captain's guilt before I killed him. But he has no recollection of setting that ship afire. It could have been any number of pirates on board—even Morgan himself. 'Tis not news that the lot of you were drunk. Who's to say who caused it?"

Morris glanced toward Kent, his face like stone.

"I've found Captain Carlton," Hann continued, "to be a man of honor, trustworthy, and courageous."

Kent's eyes latched upon Isabel's. Her eyelids fluttered, and a tear slid down her cheek. Frederick whimpered, and her glance quickly shifted back to Darla, then over to Morris. "Please let me hold my son! Have you no decency?"

"Decency?" Morris chuckled. "This pirate's whore talks to me of decency?" His face tightened into firm lines. "I'll have you gagged if you can't keep your mouth shut, milady."

The ships lurched over a swell, then dove down the other side, sending beams grinding and a splash showering over them. Droplets landed on Kent's face, offering a brief reprieve from the assault of the sun. In the distance, dark clouds rose from the horizon like monsters from the deep—like the fury rising within him. He studied his son cradled in Darla's embrace. His curly hair danced in the breeze as he sucked on his thumb, oblivious to the danger around him. An overpowering sense to protect him came over Kent, and to protect Isabel—his family. He must stop Morris.

Morris doffed his hat and wiped the sweat from his brow. "So you expect me to believe that this scoundrel had naught to do with the incident? Why, he's just playing on your feminine emotions, girl. He's always been skilled with the ladies."

"But he didn't know who I was." Hann let out a sigh and again grabbed her side with a wince. "Father, you know me. I would have killed him if I thought for one minute he was responsible for Johnny's death. I loved my brother as much as you did." Hann's eyes moistened under her wrinkled brow.

Morris swung about, his gaze wandering to the *Johnny's Revenge* and the horde of men lumbering on her decks, awaiting his command. He hung his head for a moment. "Why can't you behave like a normal lady, Annie?" He glanced over his shoulder at her before turning back around. "Why couldn't you stay with the rich husband I painstakingly arranged to take care of you? Egad. Instead, I find you dressed like a pirate and on board me enemy's ship."

" 'Twas you who taught me to be a pirate, Father. Or do you forget?"

Hann grinned. "After Mother died, 'twas you who raised me on board your ship like I was one of your crew. Surely you can't expect me to sit adorned in satin and lace like a china doll—not after I've tasted the thrill of the sea?"

A faint smirk broke on Morris's lips before he forced them into a firm line. "That is exactly what I expect of you." A hint of pride swelled above the sternness in his voice. "You are a lady. I'll have a better life for you than pirating and an early death."

"*You'll* have? 'Tis my life, Father, and I believe I'll be the one choosing the course of it."

"Captain, the seas grow restless!" a pirate yelled from the *Johnny's Revenge*. "We cannot stay lashed together much longer!"

Morris nodded and studied the horizon as the ships pitched and the timbers creaked.

Gritting his teeth, Kent surveyed his weaponless crew. Caleb had labored to his feet, rubbing his head. Hoornes's eyes locked with Kent's. Loyalty and determination burned within them. Even his rat seemed to give Kent an affirming nod. Smokes, Graves, Mac, Sparks, and Osborn, along with other pirates, stood nearby. He knew he could count on their allegiance. Yet two dozen armed men surrounded them. Even if Kent could manage to get loose, what could they do? His only hope was to snag one of the pirates' pistols, level it at Morris, and demand the release of Isabel and his son. And of course, avoid being shot by one of the musketeers still positioned in the top yards of the *Johnny's Revenge*. With renewed effort, he twisted against his bonds and gave Morris his most conciliatory look. "I didn't kill your son, Morris. We all were responsible that night for those that died."

Morris's face took on the fury of a storm.

"But I am sorry for your loss," Kent added with all sincerity.

"Sorry for me loss, are you?" Morris raged. "Not as sorry as you're going to be."

Darla paced, bouncing Frederick in her arms in an effort to quiet his rising wail.

Hann raised a hand to her forehead and swayed. A red blotch appeared on the doublet above her right hip. Placing his hands on her shoulders, Cutter steadied her.

Morris drew his cutlass in a glittering scrape of metal. "Who are you to be laying your putrid hands on me daughter?" The tip of the sword pierced Cutter's brown shirt. The doctor didn't budge.

"It's all right, Fa. . ." Hann fell into Cutter's arms, and the crowd parted as he led her to a nearby barrel. She sat down and drew a deep breath, still clinging to Cutter's arm.

Morris followed them, his sword leveled upon the doctor. "I said unhand her."

"I am her doctor, Captain." Cutter straightened his stance and faced Morris, unflinching. "I've been taking care of her."

"I bet you have, you mangled beast," Morris snapped. "Now, step aside before I slice you in two. I'm in a killing mood. And if I decide not to kill the child, you'll do quite nicely in his place."

Not kill the child? Kent's hopes both surged for his son and plummeted for Cutter. The overconfident doctor had no idea who he was up against.

"No. Leave him be. He saved her life!" Isabel shouted, drawing all eyes toward her.

"Saved her life from what?" Morris leaned over and studied the growing bloodstain on Hann's side.

" 'Twas only cannon shot, Father. I'll live."

Morris stormed toward Kent, his sword parting a path before him. "You allowed me daughter to be shot aboard your ship?"

Ceasing his struggling, Kent faced Morris's angry glance with one of his own. "A risk any man—or woman—takes on board a pirate ship, as well you know, Captain."

Morris's eyes narrowed into tiny blue slits; then with a jerk of his head he turned around.

Cutter knelt by Hann and held both her hands in his. Whispers flew between them.

Morris charged toward them, sword flinging through the air. Positioning the tip of his blade beneath Cutter's chin, he raised him from his spot. "How dare you touch me daughter so intimately and right in front of me, as well. 'Tis a crime worth hanging in me book."

"Aye, aye," several pirates chimed.

"No, Father, please." Straining, Hann rose from the barrel and tugged on the hilt in Morris's hand. "He hasn't hurt me. He's a good man."

Blood trickled beneath Cutter's chin, yet he stared at Morris with a calm certitude that seemed to set the captain aback. Morris wrinkled his angry brow. "You leave a man with money and title and all the comforts and luxuries you could ever want for this deformed beast?"

"I love him, Father," Hann stated with a huff as she dropped to the barrel again.

Cutter's gnarled lips rose in a grin despite the sword biting into his neck.

The declaration sent a stunned silence over the two ships. The sea clapped against the hull as a blast of wind swirled around them, cooling the sweat on Kent's arms. Love? Incredible. What other surprises could he expect from his two closest friends?

Lowering his sword, Morris stared at his daughter. "What do you know of love, child?"

Hann shook her head and raised her swimming gaze to his. "I learned it from watching you and Mother."

Morris swallowed and looked away.

Dark clouds growled on the horizon.

Kent continued wrestling against the ropes, ignoring the pain. They gradually loosened.

Murdock leaned down to scratch his leg, and Isabel barreled into him, knocking him to the deck, and tore from his grasp. She darted toward Darla.

The ship bucked.

Kent freed himself. He clung to the ropes and waited for the right moment to make his move.

"No you don't, missy!" Morris nodded for Smithy to grab Isabel. The pirate stepped in front of her, wearing a sly grin, and blocked her way just a foot short of Frederick.

Isabel faced Morris and threw her trembling hands to her hips. "You will allow me to hold my son, sir." The impact of her stern command shriveled beneath the quaver in her voice. Sniffing, she wiped the tears from her cheeks. "We are but innocent pawns in this preposterous game of power and revenge." Her tone softened. "I know you understand the love between a parent and child."

Morris's shoulders slumped. "On that we do agree, milady, but then, you also understand that I must avenge me son's death. 'Tis the only thing that will put him to rest in me soul." Morris tore his gaze from Isabel's. "Bring the boy here, Darla. Enough of this dallying. The weather worsens, and we must be on our way."

Gasping, Isabel pounded on Smithy's chest in a vain attempt to push past him.

Kent clenched his fists behind him and scanned for a weapon within reach.

With Cutter's assistance, Hann stood. "Father, Captain Carlton hardly knows his son. If you throw him into the sea, he'll mourn him, yes, but only for a week at most. What sort of punishment is that? Keep the boy alive. Hide him somewhere where he'll never be found." Her eyes darted to Kent, and he thought he saw the flash of a wink. "Then Captain Carlton will live in torment all his days. Now that's a fitting punishment for Johnny's death, wouldn't you say?"

Morris rubbed his chin. "Aye, you have your mother's brains, to be sure. Makes sense to me." He glanced over his shoulder at Isabel. "But I'll be taking the babe's pretty mother, too. I see the way the captain looks at her. That'll settle his debt for sure." His wicked chuckle sped over the ship, bouncing off masts and railings, and shot straight into Kent's heart. No, he could not lose Isabel, too! Blood raced through him, surging through each muscle. To Kent's right, one of Morris's men lumbered against the railing. Stifling a yawn, he looked out over the horizon.

"No need to take the lady, Captain." Sawkins stepped forward, his upper lip trembling. He fumbled with the hilt of his cutlass.

"It's none of your concern." Morris growled. "You should be pleased we're finally leaving."

Darla inched past Isabel, a look of understanding on her face.

Isabel reached for her son.

Smithy held her back.

"Come here, girl," Morris motioned to Darla with his sword. "Be quick about it." He sheathed his weapon.

Kent plowed into the pirate by the railing, snatched his pistol from his baldric, shoved him to the deck, then turned, cocked the weapon, and pointed it at Morris's head. "Order your men to stand down and leave my ship or I'll shoot you where you stand."

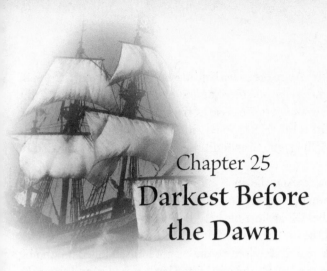

Chapter 25
Darkest Before
the Dawn

Isabel stared at Kent as he aimed a pistol at Morris's head. Armed enemies surrounded him. He was either the bravest man she'd known or the most foolish. As a pinprick of hope tingled within her, she opted for the former. He risked his life for her—for her son—and that alone made him golden in her eyes.

Morris narrowed his gaze while a grin tugged at his lips. "You plan to stop more than a hundred men with that one little pistol?"

"No. I plan to stop you." Kent tossed sweaty strands of hair from his face. "After that, it won't matter." He glanced behind him at the pirates inching toward him. "You know I'm a good shot, Morris, and it'll take only one bullet to pierce that thick skull of yours."

Wiping the sweat from his brow, Morris swept his glance across the top yards of his ship. His eyelids fluttered in a silent nod, and Isabel looked up to see a man aiming his musket at Kent. Alarm raged through her heart at the thought of losing him. The reaction surprised her. Surely her fear must stem from her need of him. After all, who would rescue them if Morris followed through with his threats? She couldn't lose the one man courageous enough to risk his life for the sake of her son.

"One more step and I'll shoot your captain!" Kent barked over his shoulder to the men creeping behind him. They halted.

Smithy loosened his hold on Isabel and ran a hand over the back of his neck. She jerked from his grasp and dashed toward Kent. No plan formed in her mind except to somehow save his life. Charging straight toward him, she saw a look of surprise in the corner of his eye just as she shoved her body into his. He toppled sideways, one arm reaching out to keep her from falling, the other still holding the pistol, as he tried to maintain his balance.

A musket shot cracked the air.

"Swounds, woman, what are you do—" Kent stammered and reached for the railing. Isabel fell against his hard body and wondered what to do next. He still held the gun, and she didn't have strength enough to knock him down. But she had to stop him before he got himself killed. Grabbing a belaying pin from the railing, she took a step back, raised it, and slammed it down onto his head. His gaze met hers in a confused stare of pain that nearly broke her heart. Then he slumped to the deck, unconscious.

A cacophony of cackles erupted all around her.

"You showed 'im!" one pirate chortled.

"Why did you do that?" Hann's wary voice bounced over the deck.

" 'Tis about time," Sawkins stated.

Dropping the oak pin beside Kent, Isabel stared at his silent form, praying she hadn't struck him too hard. Exhaling a deep breath, she quieted her hammering heart and turned to face Morris. "How did you expect to satisfy your quest for revenge with Captain Carlton dead?"

"I didn't intend to kill him, milady." Morris laughed. "Just knock him down with a shot to his leg, 'tis all, but I thank you for saving me the trouble. I found your display far more amusing." He snickered and directed his gaze across the still chuckling crew.

Heat crept up Isabel's neck. She pursed her lips and looked back at Kent. Hopefully, a head wound would heal more quickly than a musket shot to the leg. Either way, he would not have been a player in the final round of this heinous game.

"Well, that'll be the end of it, then." Morris rubbed his hands together. He snapped his fingers. "Darla, bring the babe." He nodded toward a pirate standing by Isabel. "Miss Ashton, as well." Then, facing Hann, he raised a brow. "And you, young lady, you'll be coming with me."

"No, Father, I am staying." Hann backed into Cutter.

"You will not. I'll not have a daughter of mine pirating these seas,

especially not under a captain like Sawkins."

Sawkins stretched his neck and thrust out his chin but kept his jaw clamped shut.

"Then allow Cutter to come with us," Hann pleaded.

Morris examined Cutter, disgust souring his features. "I'll not have some mangled freak on my ship."

"He is not. . . !" Hann's face inflamed into a shade of purple that matched her eyes. "If he doesn't come, then neither will I."

Cutter touched her arm. "Go with your father." He gave her a reassuring wink. "I promise I'll find you."

"You will do no such thing, sir." Morris plucked his pistol from his brace and aimed it at Cutter's head. "My daughter is off limits to the likes of you. Why, I ought to shoot you where you stand just for laying a finger on her."

Hann gasped and pressed a hand to her side. "No, Father. Don't hurt him. I'll do whatever you say."

Isabel's heart thumped in her throat, but Morris's eyes twinkled as he looked at his daughter. "Will you come with me willingly then, if I leave this monster alive?"

Hann gazed at Cutter, then faced her father. "Aye."

Morris took her arm, pulled her away from the doctor, and led her across the deck. "You'll thank me later, girl. But for now, I'll have a real doctor attend to you."

Cutter leveled his stormy eyes on Morris's back.

Stopping before Sawkins, Morris sneered. "The ship is yours, your lordship." He doffed his hat in a mocking bow. "Do take care of her. You're likely not to see another in your lifetime."

"I beg you one last time to leave Lady Ashton." Sawkins's voice held a slight quaver. "She was not part of the bargain." His blue eyes shifted to Isabel, concern flickering in them. Concern for her? No, she would not be made a fool of again—not for the likes of him.

"And I beg you, Captain," Morris said through gritted teeth, "to be content that I have the courtesy to honor your half of our bargain—a man who would betray his own brother!"

Darla skirted the crowd and approached the plank, followed by several pirates.

M. L. TYNDALL

"Allow me at least to carry my son," Isabel pleaded.

Donning his hat, he sighed. "Very well, give the child to her." He motioned, and Darla stopped and turned around. Lifting Frederick from her shoulder, she smiled shyly and held him out to Isabel.

Isabel rushed toward her son. Gently taking him from Darla, she drew him against her chest, wrapped her arms around him, and squeezed him. Tears of joy streamed down her cheeks. "Oh, Frederick, it's Mother. Frederick, I'm here." His innocent baby scent filled her nostrils like a bouquet of flowers. *Oh, thank You, Lord. Thank You.* Showering his forehead with kisses, she leaned back to get a good look at him and ran her fingers over his soft cheeks.

Frederick lifted his gaze to hers, and a giggle passed through his lips before they broke into a beaming smile. He reached his chubby hand up to touch her face as if he didn't believe she were real. Grinning, Isabel kissed his fingers.

"How touching," Morris declared. "Now come along." He led Hann through the throng of pirates, bellowing orders as he leaped up onto the plank. Hann glanced at Cutter before she yanked her pain-filled gaze away and followed her father.

Prodded from behind, Isabel trudged forward, casting one last glance at the doctor, whose sorrowful eyes were fixed upon Hann. As Isabel halted before the plank, Sawkins's gaze caught hers for a moment. Pain seeped from his eyes. But hadn't he caused this? Wasn't this what he wanted?

Holding Frederick with one hand, she raised her chin away from Sawkins. A pirate extended a hand to her from the plank. Rejecting it, she tried to hoist herself up, but the ship swayed and she nearly fell.

A glowing spire shot across the darkening sky, followed almost instantly by another one. Isabel quivered.

Thunder roared in the distance as if God Himself protested the happenings He witnessed below. *Lord, please help us. Please do not allow Frederick and me to be taken by this pirate.*

Hann retreated over the plank and offered her hand to Isabel. Isabel gave her a weak smile as she climbed onto the wooden bridge and gazed over at Morris's ship. Hordes of ill-kempt pirates buzzed across the deck, curses spewing from their foul mouths, as they prepared the ship to sail. Swallowing hard, she drew Frederick tighter to her chest. He whimpered.

Another pirate ship awaited her. But this time, its captain harbored no infatuation for her that would aid in her safety. He wished only to harm her and her son. Hann gave Isabel's hand a comforting squeeze as if she could read her mind. At least she'd have a friend on board—or would she? Isabel released Hann and wondered how deep her friend's treachery went. She was the daughter of a pirate, after all.

As Isabel inched over the plank, she gazed at the black sea swirling below her. Frederick would have drowned in minutes in that treacherous water. Even if someone had dived in after him, they would never have found him. She clung to her son and quelled a rising sob, then glanced over at Kent's still form lying on the deck. Surprising grief overcame her. Would she ever see him again? *Oh Lord, help him. Please be with him.*

"Throw him in the hold," Isabel heard Sawkins order. Two pirates lumbered over to Kent and hoisted his limp body.

Taking the final steps across the plank, Isabel kissed Frederick's forehead and stepped down onto the main deck of the *Johnny's Revenge*.

Biting pain gnawed through Kent's head, springing from one spot, then spreading out in waves. Grating squeals flew at him from all around, luring him from his dark repose. But he didn't want to come out. Something terrible had happened. He couldn't remember what, but he knew it was so horrible he didn't wish to face it again. Cutting pain struck him once more as if someone poked a knife into his skull. Something warm and furry scurried across his chest, and Kent raised his arm to his forehead, sending a hundred little feet pattering away.

He pried his eyes open to the same charcoal void that had existed behind them, but slowly, as they adjusted to the darkness, his eyes made out a rake of iron bars standing like black spires against the dim light of a distant lantern. That and the rush and gurgle of water against the hull told him he was imprisoned in the hold.

The tap of little feet sounded, and another sharp pain dove into his head. Kent sprang to his feet. The room spun, and he grabbed onto the rusty bars lest he tumble back down to the rats and the sludge. Leaning his head against the hard, cold iron, he waited for the timbers to stop swirling while he tried to remember how he came to this place.

Isabel. He pictured the beautiful features of her face twisted in concern as she'd rammed into him. Why had she done that? He'd been trying to save her and their son! Kent reached up and slid his fingers over his hair. A slick, wet blotch covered a swollen mound on the top of his head. Drawing his finger to his nose, he took a whiff. Blood. He could smell it even over the fetid stench of the bilge. Now he remembered. His precious Isabel—that infuriating woman—had struck him. Why?

The ship lurched to port, and Kent clung to the bars, hearing the rats squealing as they slid across the floor. The hull creaked in sharp snaps as the wood groaned under the strain. The lantern flickered, and Kent prayed it would not go out and leave him alone in this ebony hell. He'd been locked in a hold before, and he knew this darkness well. It was the kind of black slime that could swallow a man whole if he allowed it to seep within him.

Terror sliced through him as more of his memory returned. Sawkins had taken over the ship. Why had he been so daft as to let his brother come on board? Kent pounded his head against the bars, not caring when the chipped metal bit into his skin. And Isabel. She was either dead or in Captain Morris's hands, along with their son. Frederick. What would become of them now? "Oh God." He rattled the cage until flakes of rust rained down on him. "I gave my life to You. Was it only so You could torture me?"

Jerking away from the rods, Kent paced his cell, his boots sinking into the sodden wood. His son's face loomed before him, that tiny, chubby face with the shock of curly hair. His wide, dark eyes had sparkled when they locked on Kent's, and at that moment, the boy had stolen his heart. His son. His blood. For the first time, Kent began to understand Captain Morris's agony.

The grating of a latch and the thump of boots alerted Kent that someone was coming down the stairs. The burgeoning lantern light cast shadows of deformed creatures over crates and barrels and onto the dark hull of the ship.

"Get on wit' ye now," a sinister voice echoed off the walls.

A tall, dark figure emerged from the stairway, descending the final steps. The lantern held by the man behind him shone over his gray waistcoat and sandy hair—Cutter. The pirate shoved the doctor, sending

him toppling down the final steps. "I said hurry, ye spineless toad."

Righting himself, Cutter brushed the dirt from his jacket and gave the man a solemn grin before he rounded a stack of barrels and headed toward the cells.

Kent dashed to the front bars.

"I daresay you're looking well, Captain." Cutter's woeful eyes flashed at Kent as the lantern revealed Gibbons ambling behind him.

The light struck Cutter's face, revealing a swollen, purple eye. "I'd like to say the same for you, Doctor." Kent grimaced. "But it appears your face has collided with something—something hard from the looks of it."

"Ah yes. A fist."

"That'll be enough chatterin' out of ye both." Gibbons nudged Cutter toward the cell next to Kent's, grabbed a set of keys from his belt, and unlocked the door. It swung open with a *clank*. He pushed the doctor inside, then slammed and locked it.

Holding the lantern up beside his face, Gibbons sneered at them through brown teeth. He snorted.

Kent thrust his hand between the bars and nearly snagged Gibbons's sleeve. The pirate jumped back, his grin tumbling from his lips.

"When I get out of here, Gibbons," Kent hissed, "you'll wish you'd never seen this ship or the ocean it sails upon."

Cutter cleared his throat and gave Kent a disapproving glance, then faced Gibbons, who had continued to retreat, his wide eyes riveted on Kent. "Gibbons," Cutter started, drawing the man's attention to him, "we'd like our supper served promptly at seven, if you please."

Gibbons scratched the hair on his chest and raised his bushy eyebrows. Chuckling, he turned and plodded toward the stairs. "Supper. Ha. Crazy as a sun-baked turtle, the both of ye."

As soon as Gibbons and his lantern were gone, darkness folded over them, and if not for Cutter's deep breathing, Kent would have thought he'd just had a vivid dream. But soon, with the aid of the distant lantern, he made out the doctor's tall frame in the cell next to him.

"What news of Isabel?" Kent was afraid to ask, but he had to know. Even so, his heart teetered on the edge of a cliff, waiting for Cutter's reply.

"Captain Morris took her." Cutter sighed. "And Hann as well."

Kent let out the breath he'd been holding. "Does my son still live?" Fear coiled through him as he pictured Morris holding the child over the water.

"Yes, never fear, Captain. He's with his mother. Hann may be able to save them both," Cutter said. "The lady astounds me."

Kent shook his head and folded his arms across his chest. "How long have you known?"

"About Hann? Only a few days, I assure you. I discovered her secret while attending her injury."

"Yes, of course." Kent envisioned the scene of Hann's surgery. "That would account for your strange behavior when I came down to inquire after him. . .her. Egad, I still can't grasp the idea." Kent uttered a harsh chuckle. "And her father, did you know who he was, as well?"

Cutter shook his head and patted his pockets. "Blast! They took my pipe. Barbarians!" He glanced up at Kent. "No. I assure you, Captain, I had no idea."

"Yet you don't fault Hann in this treachery?"

"Nay, Captain. I'll admit to being surprised, but I cannot believe she meant any deception other than what she stated. You saw Morris's face as clearly as I did. He did not know she was on board. Nor did Sawkins know who she was. Therefore she could not have been privy to their agreement." A rat climbed onto Cutter's boot, and he kicked it aside. "Besides, if it weren't for her, your son would be at the bottom of the ocean right now."

The ship pitched, throwing Kent against the bars and sending the dim lantern light undulating over the dismal scene. Indeed. Hann had no reason to have come on deck and reveal herself to her father. She had every reason not to. Had she done it just to save Frederick?

"You place much confidence in this would-be pirate lady who has deceived everyone on board this ship."

"I have confidence in her character, with which I have become acquainted these past months, both as the man and the woman." Even in the shadows, Kent saw the gleam in Cutter's eyes.

"What is it between you two?"

Cutter released a deep breath. "I fear I love her."

Love? Kent rubbed the sweat from the back of his neck and couldn't

help the bitter chuckle that spilled from his lips. "That you fear it leads me to believe you are indeed in love, for I have found it to be a terrifying thing."

"But also as sweet as fine wine." Cutter grinned.

Kent fingered the bump on his head. "I have yet to experience that side of it."

"Ah yes, how is your head, Captain?"

Kent gave him a peevish look. "Sore and bloody."

"She was trying to save you, you know."

"Save me? Egad. I'm not so daft as to believe that."

"She thought Morris's pirates were going to shoot you."

The crack of sails and the groans of masts and yards under strain filtered down from above. Bracing himself against the heaving ship, Kent paced the cell. "Why wouldn't she just let them?" Isabel no longer needed Kent's ship to find Frederick, and she'd made her feelings toward him plain from the beginning.

Cutter snorted. " 'Tis obvious to me, even if you cannot see it—or even if *she* cannot see it, for that matter."

"And what, pray tell, are you referring to?"

"She cares for you."

"Hmm." Yet Cutter's words sparked a glimmer of hope through Kent's doubts. "At least she finally knows Sawkins for the rat that he is." He booted one of the furry devils across his cell, imagining with glee that it was his brother.

The ship pitched, then bolted in a violent shudder. Grabbing the bars, Kent clung to them as his feet nearly left the floor. Cutter did not fare as well. His large body tumbled across the cell. What caused the ship to careen so sharply? A storm? It didn't feel like a storm. No, it was the speed—they sailed at full speed. "Did Sawkins indicate his heading?"

"He intends to rendezvous with Morgan at Panama." Cutter picked himself up from the floor and brushed off his coat.

Alarm spired through Kent. "We must break out of here before then." He had to reach Isabel and Frederick before Morris could put into action whatever dreadful plans he had for them.

Cutter grunted. "I am of the same mind, Captain."

The *Restitution* lunged to starboard, and the lantern light flickered, then disappeared. Darkness fell on them like a death shroud.

"Perhaps we should pray." Cutter's voice was naught but a whisper, but the impact of his words struck Kent like a cannon blast.

Pray? Of course. That's what people did who believed in God. Hadn't he given his life to the Almighty just last night? Now, in the roasting stench and murky blackness, it seemed like a glorious dream—that feeling of worth, approval, and love. "I'm afraid I wouldn't know how."

"Allow me, then," Cutter said.

Kent shuffled over to where Cutter's voice emanated, and bowed his head against the bars.

Cutter cleared his throat. "Lord, please hear the prayer of two pirates who deserve neither Your time nor an inkling of Your regard. We do, however, come in the name of Your Son, Jesus, and ask that You protect Hann, Lady Ashton, and Frederick and that You free us from this prison in order that we may rescue them. Amen."

"Amen." Kent added the only thing he knew to say and then stood in the darkness, listening to Cutter's breathing and the scampering of rats.

A deep, pulsating *boom* shook the sea around the hull and sent a tremble through the keel. Despite the heat, a chill raised the hairs on Kent's arms. Ghostly silence consumed them.

Bam! An enormous crash split the darkness with the cracking of wood and clanking of metal.

Saltwater blasted over Kent. He crashed to the floor, arms and legs flailing under the force of the ocean. Grabbing onto the bars, he clawed his way upward, gasping for air. Water gorged his mouth and lungs.

Chapter 26
Double Cross

He couldn't see. He couldn't breathe. Kent's fingers ached from their tight grip on the iron rods. Cutter's muffled shout bounced over the hold, but Kent could not respond, could barely move against the force of the surge. Inching his fingers up the bars, he struggled to stand and finally pulled himself up as the cascade of water flattened him against his cage. He gasped for air and inched his way out from the center of the torrent.

The ship lunged to port and Kent hung on as he tried to focus on the cell next to his. "Cutter!" he shouted above the mad rush of water, praying the doctor had not been injured. No response. Muted light shone from behind Kent, and he swerved to see the ocean pouring through a breach in the hull, sunlight along with it. It was still day.

Who had fired upon them? What in the name of Davy Jones was Sawkins doing? Anger pumped through Kent at the thought of his ship in the hands of that pompous incompetent.

Following the direction of the deluge, he saw where the shot had blasted a hole through the bars of his cell. Darting over, he leaned his shoulder into the gushing spray and fingered the opening to see if it was large enough to pass through. The water pummeled his shoulder like a hundred fists, the pain only matched by the sting that shot through his hand as the slivered iron sliced his skin.

The opening wasn't big enough. He'd be skewered if he tried to squeeze through. Wrenching himself out of the water's path, he stood, panting and watched as the Caribbean poured into his ship. Water pooled at his feet. If the hole wasn't patched soon, they would sink, and he and Cutter would drown in these iron tombs.

God, if You're there, I could use some help.

"Captain." Cutter's faint voice drifted to Kent.

"Yes. I'm here!" Kent yelled over the din and sloshed through the water to the edge of the cell. He peered into the shadows, where he could barely see Cutter lumbering to his feet. Water dripped from his coat and slid down his face and neck.

"Are you hurt?" Kent asked.

"No. What happened?"

"Cannon shot. Can you get out of your cell?"

Cutter slapped his head with the palm of his hand as if to knock his brain back in place, then plodded around his cell, testing each iron shaft. He gave Kent a daunting look. "No."

"Blast!" Kent clutched the rods and rattled them as hard as he could.

The sea continued its thunderous gush through the hole, pounding on Kent's nerves and smothering his hopes. Rats screeched as the flood carried them across the hold.

He could not die like this—not imprisoned on his own ship. He could not die without knowing if Isabel and Frederick were safe.

As he seized the bars once more, repeated booms roared through the ship, sending a violent tremble through her hull that shook his cell and the wood beneath Kent's boots.

Sawkins had fired a broadside.

At least he was fighting back. Gritting his teeth, Kent flung his saturated hair from his face. He had to get above deck or that madman would kill them all.

Inhaling a deep breath, Kent dashed into the deluge once again, determined to force himself through the opening in his cell. It was their only hope. Saltwater flooded his nose and ears and thrashed against his body. He thrust his head through the gap, but instantly the shattered iron speared his shoulders and sides. Burning spasms of pain shot through him. He backed up and crumpled to the floor of his cell. Gasping for air, he spit saltwater from his mouth. Even if he made it through the hole, he would not live long enough to save Cutter.

Light glowed by the stairs, illuminating the water swirling at the base.

"Cap'n!"

"Over here!" Kent answered.

The light brightened, and Caleb and Hoornes appeared at the bottom of the stairway. They sloshed toward him through at least eight inches of water, looks of concern on their faces. Another eight inches and the ship would begin to sink. Hoornes lifted his lantern and nearly slid on a fish flopping in the shallow water in front of Kent's cell. His rat poked his head from the pocket on Hoornes's waistcoat as Caleb unlocked Kent's door and forced it open through the rushing water.

Bracing himself against the torrent, Kent darted across his cell and through the door. He clasped Hoornes's hand as Caleb went to release Cutter. "What's happening?"

" 'Tis Morgan. He attacks us," Hoornes answered, fear quivering in his voice.

"Morgan?" Alarm raked over Kent. Morgan was an expert at sea battle. Why was he attacking Sawkins when the deal had been to rendezvous with him?

Cutter emerged from his cell.

"Find some sailcloth," Kent ordered. "We must patch this hole."

Hoornes hooked the lantern on a beam and joined the others as they plodded through the water in all directions, opening crates and chests. They soon retrieved mounds of white canvas. Bunching it together, they each grabbed an armful and charged toward the incoming flood. The force of the sea knocked them down, but they quickly got up and rushed it again until finally, after several attempts, they managed to stuff the bulk of the cloth into the hole and reduce the gush to a trickle. Drenched and exhausted, the men backed away while Kent added more sail and made final adjustments to ensure the temporary patch would hold.

Motioning to the others, he raced for the stairs, frowning at the water sloshing back and forth across the floor. It needed to be pumped out, but that must wait.

The thunder of a distant cannon bellowed, and Kent halted, waiting for another explosion to rip through the ship's timbers. A scream and the snap of wood told him the shot had landed up on deck.

"Is Sawkins in command?" Kent asked as he darted up the stairs.

"Aye, ye might call it that." Hoornes grabbed the lantern and followed behind him.

"What damage to the ship?"

" 'Sides the hole we just patched? There be another one toward the bow above the waterline and we lost the mizzen topsail and some riggings, and the taffrail be shattered," Hoornes panted.

Shouts, curses, and the frenzied thudding of boots filled the air.

Kent growled. That impudent whelp was going to tear his ship to pieces! And how could he stop him? "How many are with us?"

Another cannon blasted in the distance. Someone yelled, "Fire!" and thunder rolled through the ship as the *Restitution*'s guns spit their reply. The ship staggered, and a rat fell down from above and landed on the steps in front of Kent before scampering away in screeching protest.

"The slaves be with us, Cap'n." Caleb's husky voice sounded from below him. "But I dunno who else we can count on. I can tell ye, though, the crew don't much like Sawkins."

Kent took the stairs two at a time. The sharp scent of gunpowder stung his nose. That would make thirty-four men against more than a hundred—not exactly great odds for a mutiny. Then again, Kent knew if he could subdue Sawkins, most of his men would side with him.

Suddenly, the ship lurched to starboard, and Kent grabbed the railing. The hull creaked and groaned under the strain, and the cuts on his hands from the iron rods throbbed against the rough wood. When the vessel righted again, he continued past the berth. A horde of men brandishing weapons emerged from the shadows—the slaves. He nodded to them as they fell in line behind Caleb. Sawkins must have allowed them to arm themselves for the battle.

At the gun deck, a frenzied throng of pirates sped back and forth across the crowded room. Gun crews hovered over the cannons, loading, priming, and running the mighty guns forward until their muzzles pushed through the gun ports. Men carrying powder buckets scrambled from gun to gun, distributing charges and shot. Sunlight and seawater spilled through a jagged hole in the hull. The shot had taken out one of the guns. Blood stained the deck.

Logan's anxious glance landed on Kent. The captain returned his firm gaze, wondering where his master gunner's loyalty lay, but with only a moment's hesitation, Logan nodded before resuming his duties.

"Steady men!" Kent shouted. The gun crew glanced in his direction. Their eyes flickered in surprise but held no defiance. Power surged through him—the power of command. He threw his shoulders back and eyed each man with authority. Some nodded and grinned. Others grunted in approval. "Good to 'ave ye back!" one man yelled. A few "ayes" shot his way before the men returned to their duties.

Kent warmed at their loyalty. He was the captain of this ship, and he intended to take it back. From the looks in these men's eyes, his old crew would give him no quarrel.

A few steps to the right, Kent shouldered through a door and burst into the gunroom. Scanning the weapons, he chose two pistols, charges, a dagger, and a cutlass and began to strap them on. Cutter followed him in and did the same. They primed and loaded their pistols while Hoornes, Caleb, and the slaves waited outside the door. When Kent emerged, he looked confidently over his men. "Let's save the ship, gentlemen!" he bellowed, and growls of affirmation sped over the slaves.

"Aye, Cap'n," Hoornes said. "We're with ye."

Kent darted past them and continued up the stairs. Turning a corner just before the companionway, he slammed into a pirate carrying a man over his shoulder. The tangy scent of blood filled the air.

"Out o' me way!" the pirate yelled without looking up. Then he raised his gaze. "Ah, Cap'n, didn't see ye." His eyes widened. "What're ye—"

"Never mind, Osborn," Kent said. "Who's this?" He gestured toward the pirate flung over Osborn's shoulder.

"Zeke." His gaze held the panicked look of a man in the midst of a battle. "D'ye know where the doc is?"

Cutter pushed past the crowd and grabbed Zeke's dangling hand, fingering his wrist.

"Ah, there ye are, Doc," Osborn said. "Zeke's hurt real bad."

Lifting Zeke's bloodied jacket, Cutter studied the wound beneath it, then glanced at Kent.

"Go ahead." Kent gestured. "Attend to him."

"God be with you." Cutter nodded, then headed down the stairs. "Follow me!" he yelled back to Osborn.

"Murdock's hurt pretty bad, too, Doc," Osborn added as he squeezed past Kent. Strands of damp hair dangled from Zeke's limp head as it swung like pendulum across Osborn's back.

Kent took the rest of the stairs in two giant leaps and burst onto the main deck. A blast of warm air struck him, cooling the sweat that covered his body and tearing the stench of bilge and blood from his nose. He drew his cutlass and surveyed the chaotic scene. Pirates raced across the deck. Several clung to the shrouds and ratlines, adjusting sails and brandishing muskets. Two feet of railing on the larboard quarter had been blown into shattered splinters that littered the deck. Some of the men stopped when they saw him, mouths agape, but they quickly continued on their way.

No resistance so far. Good.

Kent scanned the horizon and shielded his eyes from the sun, which hung just above the blue divide.

"He's comin' straight fer us agin', Cap'n!" a pirate yelled from the crosstrees, and Kent turned to see the larboard quarter of Morgan's ship, the *Jamaica Merchant*, spewing foamy spray into the air as she veered to port. White canvas swelled above her decks like angry clouds as she caught the wind and made a swift turn. Ten minutes at most. That's all Kent had.

"What are yer orders, Cap'n?" Kent heard a man ask.

He turned to answer him, but saw the question had not been directed to him. Instead, several of his crew thronged together up on the quarterdeck.

Kent leaped up the stairs, hearing Caleb, Hoornes, and the slaves on his heels, and pushed his way through the crowd. A few brows rose at the sight of him, but most of the men's gazes were focused on the deck. The stench of sweat, blood, and something else—fear—assailed him.

Sawkins stood, ashen-faced, staring down at where Wolcott and Gibbons attended to Murdock. Blood ran in rivulets from where the pirate lay writhing in agony, his arm ripped off at the elbow. Gibbons cinched a rope around Murdock's upper arm to quell the bleeding. Sawkins's face tightened in horror, his eyes locked onto the bloody stump as if it were a gun pointed at his heart.

The men nudged him. "What are yer orders? Morgan's nearly on us!"

Smokes's eyes landed on Kent. "Cap'n!" he exclaimed, drawing the gazes of several men.

Sawkins continued to stare blankly at the wounded Murdock.

Kent took a step forward. "Wolcott, Gibbons, take Murdock below to the doctor."

The two pirates gaped in his direction, then over at Sawkins, whose eyes were still glazed over in fear. "Aye, aye," they said in unison and quickly hoisted the moaning Murdock from the deck. The crowd parted for them as they lumbered away.

As soon as Murdock had been removed, Sawkins found his voice and the remainder of his sanity. "What is the meaning of this?" He swung his blazing eyes to Kent. He reached for his gun. "How did you get out of the hold?"

The cocking of two dozen pistols snapped through the air like firecrackers, and Sawkins's hand froze on the butt of his weapon. The pirates flung their wide gazes over the armed slaves surrounding them.

"I'll be taking back command of my ship, if you please, brother. Now, out of my way." Kent shouldered the gawking Sawkins aside and marched to the railing. "I see you've gotten us into a bit of a mess." The *Jamaica Merchant* charged straight for them, her bowsprit bobbing over the churning swells of the sea. She would be within firing range within minutes. He turned toward his brother.

"Seize this man at once!" Sawkins stormed with quivering lip. "I'm the captain of this ship." His frantic eyes darted across the crowd. "Smithy, disarm these men or you'll answer to me!"

The crew hesitated and glanced amidships where more pirates had left their posts and congregated below, glaring with interest at the proceedings. Smithy was nowhere to be seen.

Kent swallowed hard and glanced across his crew. He wouldn't stand a chance if they decided to remain loyal to Sawkins, but he'd seen no loyalty toward his brother so far.

The scrape of steel and snap of pistols exposed Kent's premature supposition.

Still aiming their weapons forward, the slaves glanced over their shoulders, then faced Kent, the whites of their eyes stark against their dark skin. They moved aside. Thirty men pointed weapons in their direction, some on the quarterdeck, some below on the main deck. The rest of the pirates either remained loyal to Kent or didn't care enough what the outcome was to risk their lives.

Smithy sauntered forward, waving his cutlass through the air. "What're ye plannin' on doin', takin' over the ship with just these darkies to fight with ye?" He chuckled.

"Why, you little lying, thiev—" Kent started toward Smithy but something sharp bit into his skin. He turned to see Sawkins pointing the tip of his knife at Kent's chest. The malicious grin twisting his lips belied the tremble in his hand. "Having a hard time accepting your defeat, brother?" Sawkins shook his head, clicking his tongue. "You always were a poor loser. Back to the hold with him." He gestured with his knife.

Kent gazed out to sea toward the oncoming ship, then back over his crew. "If you wish to die, side with this man!" he bellowed in his loudest voice. "For he will surely allow Morgan to sink you to the depths of the sea! But if you wish to live, follow me!"

A blast from Morgan's cannons sounded, drawing all gazes off the starboard side and reaffirming Kent's declaration. The shot plummeted into the sea just short of the starboard bow. Water splashed over the railing.

"Captain Morgan will be on us in seconds!" Kent continued. "Do you want this buffoon to command you in a battle against the best seamen on the Caribbean?"

The crew's tremulous gazes swung to the fast approaching enemy. Shaking their heads, they muttered amongst themselves.

"Long live Captain Carlton!" one pirate trumpeted over the murmuring crowd. A moment's silence ensued, then another, "Long live Captain Carlton!" followed by several "Ayes!" blaring across the ship. One by one, each man drew either blade or pistol and leveled them upon Sawkins and his men.

With a curse, Smithy sheathed his cutlass and gestured for the others to follow. Groaning, the mutineers housed their weapons.

Kent exhaled a deep breath and silently thanked God, then gripped Sawkins's wrist and squeezed it until the knife clanked to the deck.

Sawkins's expression transformed from one of brazen ineptitude to sheer terror. He backed against the railing and gripped the hilt of his cutlass as if it were his lifeline.

Smithy stepped forward from the crowd, raised his chapped lips, and giggled nervously. "Good to 'ave ye back, Cap'n."

Sawkins grunted and glared at Smithy.

The weasel-faced first mate shrugged. "Sorry, I goes where fortune dictates."

"And fortune dictates you are locked below." Kent replied, then nodded to Smokes, who stood beside Sawkins. "Escort his lordship and Smithy below, if you please." He scanned the slaves still surrounding them. "And take all the men who sided with Sawkins below as well."

Kent swung his gaze to the horizon where the *Jamaica Merchant* bore down upon them, all guns blazing. "Bring her about, Mr. Hoornes. Twenty degrees to starboard." Hoornes sped to the whipstaff, knocking aside the pirate who manned it.

"Morgan wasn't supposed to fire upon me," Sawkins blubbered as two pirates grabbed his pistols, knives, and cutlass and dragged him off. "It wasn't my fault."

" 'Tis what you get for bargaining with a man as deceitful as you are," Kent replied, then stormed across the deck. "I want every swivel and culverin manned, armed, and ready to fire!" he roared. "Now!"

The men darted off, glimmers of hope replacing the despondency previously ingrained on their features.

"Musketeers, remain at your posts!" Kent yelled aloft, then lowered his gaze and glared at the *Jamaica Merchant*. How was he going to defeat a pirate like Morgan? Even with an undamaged ship, it would be a daunting task. Yet he had no choice. He must save his ship, his men, and himself. For if he died, who would rescue Isabel and Frederick? Fear sent his heart crashing against his ribs as he thought of what they must be enduring at the hands of Morris.

God, help me.

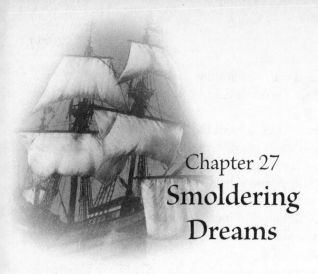

Chapter 27
Smoldering Dreams

Isabel clambered out of the wobbling longboat and dipped her feet into the warm water. Sand oozed between her toes as they sank into the soft silt fanning out from the inlet. Holding Frederick with one hand and her shoes in the other, she gave up trying to lift her skirts. Frederick nuzzled against her chest, snug in the sling Hann had fashioned for him. Isabel envied his ability to sleep so peacefully, especially with their future so uncertain. But why wouldn't he? He was back in his mother's arms. She knew she should be trusting in God with the same peace and assurance of a child in her Father's embrace, but after the events of the past few days on board the *Johnny's Revenge*, Isabel's faith teetered just like the small boat she stepped from.

The first rays of the sun spilled over a natural jetty to her left and spread out over the cove, setting the golden sand glittering, the turquoise water sparkling, and the forest beyond glowing in a myriad of greens. Dragging her sodden skirts through the water, she headed toward shore, where Captain Morris and two of his men were already trudging onto the beach. They turned and waited for her with piercing gazes.

Tiny colorful fish darted out of her way with each step. If she weren't so anxious for Frederick's safety, she'd be enjoying the beautiful, pristine beach and be thankful to finally be on land again after weeks at sea. Even as she emerged from the water and stood on the dry sand, her legs

wobbled, still expecting the pitch and plunge of the ship beneath them.

Frederick whimpered, and Isabel glanced up at Morris, his hands balled at his hips, his plumed hat whisking in the breeze. He would not meet her gaze. This morning was the first time she'd seen her captor since she'd boarded his ship two days ago. Locked below in a cabin so small Isabel could barely take two strides from bunk to door, she and Frederick had not seen a soul save for an aged pirate who brought her meals and emptied her chamber pot twice a day.

Hann had not paid her a single visit, and Isabel had begun to worry for her friend's safety. But when the girl popped up on deck that morning, unharmed and unfettered, Isabel's fears were quickly replaced with doubts. With Captain John Morris as her father, no wonder Hann was such a good pirate, woman or not. But had she known about the plot between her father and Sawkins? Had she known all along where Frederick was? Isabel's stomach clenched. Sawkins's deception was one thing, but surely Isabel was not so bad a judge of character that she'd been duped by Hann, as well.

Isabel kissed Frederick's moist forehead. He giggled and smiled up at her, revealing a new sparkling tooth—one that had sprouted during her absence. She hated that she had not been there to witness it. The sunlight struck his eyes, and he winced and looked away. Isabel squeezed him, thanking God for the time they'd had alone. She'd spent every minute holding him, playing with him, and singing to him, and when he slept, she'd pressed him close beside her and breathed in his sweet scent. Though Isabel's faith had wavered, God had been faithful to return her son. Why should she doubt Him now?

Sloshing sounded behind her, and Isabel turned to see Hann trudging through the water, followed by three more pirates. They'd been prevented from speaking in the longboat, but as the girl's gaze met Isabel's, a flicker of a smile lifted her lips. She wiped the perspiration from her brow and came to stand beside her.

"Ian, Meyers!" Morris yelled toward two men who were still sitting in the boat. "Meet us at this spot in a week. And there'll be hell to pay if you're not here."

Fear darted through Isabel, setting her heart drumming in her chest. A week—only a week for Morris to put in place his grisly plans for them. Her mind reeled with gruesome possibilities. Would Morris leave them alone in the jungle to die? Would he sell them to a passing Spanish ship?

The pirates in the boat nodded, then grabbed the oars and shoved off into the calm, glassy sea back to the *Johnny's Revenge*. Anchored just fifty yards from the beach, the vessel was hidden behind the curve of an inlet where she drifted idly, awaiting her master's return.

Morris turned to discuss something with his first mate—a robust young man named Akers.

Isabel gave Hann a worried glance. "Where is he taking us?" she whispered.

Hann glanced down at the sand, kicking it with her soggy boot. She eyed Isabel, agony wrestling in her gaze, then looked away and shook her head. Expelling a deep breath, she pinched the bridge of her nose.

Isabel gulped. Hann's silence confirmed her worst fears.

"I'm sorry, milady," Hann said without facing her.

Terror clamped every nerve. "Please tell me. I must know, no matter how dreadful it is."

Hann glanced at her father, still busy talking with Akers and another pirate. She tightened her jaw.

Isabel clutched Hann's arm. "Please. Surely, 'tis better for me to know beforehand."

"He aims to sell you to the Caribs," Hann said. "A small band of Indians he often trades with."

Alarm choked Isabel. *Sold to Indians?* She'd heard stories of the brutality of the savage beasts inhabiting the Spanish Main. A chill coursed through her. What would become of her—of Frederick?

Another bright ray of sun hit Frederick's face, and he began to fuss. Bouncing him up and down, Isabel gazed over the deserted beach. "Where are we?"

"Somewhere south of Cartagena."

Isabel snapped her pleading gaze to Hann. "Can I still count on your friendship?" Though she sensed the same rapport between them, she didn't know if Hann would be willing to defy her father.

"Aye, as always, milady." Hann glanced at her from the corner of her eyes—eyes that sparkled with sincerity.

Isabel bit her lip. "Please help me escape."

Hann nodded and opened her mouth to say something when Morris's

booming voice thundered over them. "That'll be enough. I'll have no conspiring between you two, do you hear me, Annie? I brought you along 'cause I need to keep me eye on you."

Hann shrugged and returned her father's stare. "We were only talking, Father. Besides, what could two women possibly do against five strapping pirates?" She cocked her head and grinned.

One of the men chuckled.

Morris snorted and gave her a wry look. "Come along, then, daylight's wasting." He motioned toward the forest, and the two pirates beside him hoisted packs onto their backs, withdrew machetes, and headed toward the wall of tangled green that circled the cove like an impenetrable fortress. With snaps and cracks they hacked away at the vines and branches, forcing their way into the thicket.

"Warren!" Morris shouted to one of the pirates. A skinny man with hair the color of the sun strode up from behind Isabel. In addition to the pack on his back, his chest was crisscrossed with two baldrics loaded with pistols and axes, and Isabel wondered how such a small frame could hold all that weight.

"Walk between these two cackling hens and keep 'em quiet," Morris ordered, then gestured for Hann to follow him.

Hann gave Isabel's hand a squeeze before trudging after her father.

Warren fell in line behind Hann, and Isabel dropped her shoes onto the sand, lifted her dripping skirts, and slid her feet into them, positive the silver embroidery and velvet shoes wouldn't fare well scraping over the forest floor.

A pirate nudged her from behind, prompting her forward. Wiping beads of perspiration from Frederick's forehead, she slogged through the sand and hesitated at the threshold of the jungle as she watched Warren's lanky body swallowed whole in the tangled web of green. Vines whipped out from where he'd disappeared, trying to latch onto Isabel and drag her inside. "Lord, help me," she prayed. Taking a deep breath, she shielded Frederick with her arms and dove into the brush.

The *Jamaica Merchant* sped toward the *Restitution* in an angry fume of boiling waves.

Kent gestured to Caleb. "Take a few men. Go below and get the chest of treasure we acquired from that Dutch merchantman. You know the one?"

"Aye, Cap'n."

"Dump out half the gold and bring the chest to me along with two empty ones."

The dark man gathered a few of the slaves and disappeared below just as the ship veered to starboard. The sails snapped in the wind. Kent glanced over his shoulder at the setting sun.

The blazing golden orb licked the horizon, flinging hundreds of crimson and orange tongues across sky and sea. It would be dark within an hour. If Kent could just stave off Morgan's attack, the *Restitution* could slip away in the darkness.

Kent turned to Smokes. "Bring up some gunpowder," he ordered, sending the singed man leaping down the companionway.

The band of ex-slaves circled Kent, determination and courage in their gazes. He needed to give them something to do. "Position yourselves over the ship and be ready to fight if we're boarded."

With nods and grunts, they scattered across the deck.

Logan popped his head through the main hatch and grinned when he saw Kent. "Your orders, Cap'n?"

"Ready both batteries and await my command."

With an "aye," he dove below again.

Kent eyed Morgan's ship. A burst of orange from the setting sun transformed her sails into snorts of fiery breath from a dragon's mouth. She angled to larboard, bringing her guns to bear, and raised and lowered her flag.

"She signals for surrender, Cap'n!" a pirate yelled down from the crosstrees.

Yes, Morgan would not expect Sawkins to put up much of a fight—which was why he'd probably come alone. No sense in wasting good ships and gunpowder to subdue a pirate as inept as Sawkins.

But Sawkins was no longer in command. "Head straight for her, Hoornes."

"Straight for her, Cap'n."

Not only would the bold charge throw Morgan into confusion,

but the *Restitution* would present a smaller target, and Kent hoped the combination would allow him the extra minutes he needed.

Caleb returned with the three chests and set them on the deck just as Smokes and Graves heaved the barrel of gunpowder up the companionway stairs.

"Listen up, men!" Kent bellowed across the deck, drawing the attention of the crew. A few ambled closer to hear. "Shall we offer our good friend Morgan a gift—a small token of our affection?" He grinned.

"Our treasure, Cap'n?" Osborn scratched his head.

Grumbles rolled through the crowd. "Have ye taken leave of yer senses?" Sparks crowed. "I'll not be givin' me share of the gold to that dog!"

Ignoring him, Kent turned to Smokes. "Fill the chests with gunpowder," he ordered. "Caleb, top them with the gold and load them into a cockboat with their lids open."

"But, Cap'n, the gold!" Graves protested.

"Do as I say, man!"

Cursing under his breath, Graves pried open the barrel and carefully scooped out the powder.

Caleb's frown lifted. "I sees where yer goin' wit' this, Cap'n."

Kent pointed to two pirates. "When they're finished, lower the cockboat and tie a white flag to its bow." He scanned the men, their crinkled looks of confusion smoothing into wide-eyed comprehension.

Kent raised his brows. "What say you to a gift for our dear friend now?"

"Aye, let 'im have it, Cap'n," one man said, followed by chortles of agreement.

"Who is my best swimmer?" Kent marched across the deck.

"I am, Cap'n." Blake rushed forward.

"I need you to deliver our gift to the *Jamaica Merchant*. Can you do that?"

Blake studied the cockboat. "Aye." He gave a toothless smile and pushed his headscarf further down on his head. Tall and scrawny, he appeared unfit for the task, but Kent had once seen him swim fifty yards underwater without coming up for air.

A thunderous *boom* shook the air, and a volcano of grapeshot erupted over them. A shot punched through the outer jib, leaving a ragged hole in the sail, while others ricocheted over the ship, tearing through timber, masts, sails, and riggings. A scream joined the clamorous uproar. Curses flew.

Kent faced Blake with a stern look. "When you get within five yards, jump. Then swim back to the ship as fast as you can."

"Aye." He nodded. Kent detected no fear in his blue eyes. He clapped him on the back and ordered the boat lowered, then marched across the deck, nearly tripping over an injured pirate. Kneeling, Kent saw the wound was not serious and motioned for two of the slaves to take him below.

"Sparks." Kent scanned the mob, looking for the boy with the eye patch. The pirate darted up beside him. "Aye, Cap'n."

Kent leaned and whispered in his ear. A jeering smile widened upon the boy's lips, and he raced across the deck and flung himself into the ratlines.

"Strike tops and mains!" Kent shouted aloft. He must slow the ship to a near stop.

"Why is we slowin'?" one pirate asked.

"We'll be sittin' ducks!" another man yelled.

"Steady, men." Kent hoped to calm them with his confident tone but heard fear seep into his voice.

He jumped up onto the foredeck, ignoring further grumblings behind him. It would take Blake at least five minutes to row halfway between the ships—close enough for Morgan to take an interest. He glared at the *Jamaica Merchant*. She'd be in position to loose a broadside upon them in under three. He must try to delay them. "Fire the swivels!"

The thundering of guns cracked through the darkening skies. Kent's ears rang and smoke clouded the bow. He snapped his gaze to the *Jamaica Merchant*. Her pirates bolted over the decks. Lifting his spyglass, he leveled it across the sails. Only the fore course had been struck. Not enough to deter Morgan. The ship abruptly swerved to larboard so as to come up on the leeward side of the *Restitution*. Morgan lowered his sails as two of his big guns roared and flung their deadly shot into the sea just beyond the *Restitution*'s bow.

The pirates gaped at the oncoming ship as she slowed and came up beside them. Another minute, and they would be within range of her broadside. "Raise our whites!" Kent shouted aloft.

"Raisin' the white," came the sharp reply.

Graves appeared at Kent's side. "We're not surrenderin', are we, Cap'n?"

"No." Kent stormed to the railing and peered over. Blake had rowed nearly twenty yards from the *Restitution* and was nearing the midpoint betwixt the two enemies. The gold in the chests glittered as the sun cast its farewell rays over the sea. Kent prayed it would not set before the reflection glinted in Morgan's eye.

The black muzzles of ten cannons thrust from the holes of the *Jamaica Merchant* as her bow crossed within range. If Kent opened his gun ports, Morgan would consider it a hostile act and begin firing. He turned to Graves. "Go below and tell Logan not to open the ports until my command."

"Aye, Cap'n." Graves sped away.

Dear God, please. Kent hung his head. *Please protect Blake and allow Morgan's lust for treasure to overcome his senses.*

The *Jamaica Merchant* swung beside the *Restitution*. Kent waited for the thunderous cannons to belch, but the giant muzzles only stared at them in silence. Blake continued his furious rowing and now drifted within twenty yards of Morgan's ship.

Still no thunderous boom.

Kent leveled the glass upon his eye and scanned the ship. He spotted Morgan. He'd know him anywhere. His tall, corpulent frame swaggered across his deck as if he owned the world—or the seas at least. Kent supposed he had earned the right, being commodore of his own fleet, albeit a pirate fleet. The commodore strutted to the railing and lifted a glass toward Blake in the cockboat. He hesitated for a moment, lowered his scope, then turned and spoke to a man beside him. He waved Blake toward the ship.

The prey had taken the bait.

Kent could almost see the drool dripping from Morgan's lips as he eyed the treasure.

The sun fled below the horizon, transforming the remaining blue of the sky to gray. Water gushed against the hull, and the ship creaked with each passing wave.

Ten yards.

Kent clenched his fists. The shadows of night crept out of hiding and hovered over the sea.

Seven yards.

Kent rubbed the back of his neck. Caleb came and stood beside him.

Five yards.

Blake plunged into the sea, the motion of his body pushing the cockboat even farther toward Morgan's ship. Morgan stared at the treasure for a moment, then glanced over the water where Blake had disappeared.

"Now, Sparks!" Kent yelled. And Sparks fired his musket from the main top. The sound of the blast echoed across the sky. What seemed like minutes passed, and Kent thought perhaps the boy had missed and they were doomed. Instantly, the cockboat exploded in a fiery ball of red and orange. Chunks of wood and gold shot high into the sky. A billowing cloud of smoke and flames enveloped the *Jamaica Merchant*.

The pirates cheered and hurled themselves into the ratlines, making obscene gestures toward their enemy.

Kent stomped down onto the main deck and peered across the water looking for Blake. Had he survived? There was no sign of him. He swept his gaze over the choppy waves littered with flaming debris.

Nothing. *God, please don't let me have sent him to his death.*

Finally, a dark head popped above the dark water, and he glanced over his shoulder at the burning ship, then smiled back at Kent and continued swimming toward him.

As they waited for Blake to board, Kent peered through the smoke at the *Jamaica Merchant*. Her larboard beam was on fire. Flames licked up toward the main sails, and Morgan's men raced back and forth dipping buckets into the sea and pouring them over the blaze. Gray smoke curled into the darkening sky. Seven of the cannons had disappeared from the ports, the others sat impotent in their caves. Kent found Morgan, unscathed, up on the foredeck, barking orders to his men.

Osborn and Logan appeared next to Kent. "Ye can finish him off, Cap'n," Osborn said.

"Yeah, takin' Morgan would make ye the new commodore, wouldn't it?" Logan spouted proudly. "The new leader of the Brethren, eh?"

The leader of the Brethren of the Coast. It was what Kent had always wanted—to be the best of the best. He had never presumed he'd have the opportunity to take down Morgan. But it would require time to finish him off, and drag him and his men to the Brethren as proof—time that

Kent didn't have. Every minute he spent here, Isabel and Frederick were getting farther away. Every minute meant less time to find them and more time in which they suffered.

Yet he doubted he'd ever have another chance to fulfill the dream he'd pursued his whole life.

Gritting his teeth, Kent eyed his prey, lusting for the power that was within his reach.

What do I do, Lord? He glanced up into the dark gray sky, where tiny stars were beginning to twinkle.

"You know, My son."

Son. He gripped the railing and gazed at the burning embers of the *Jamaica Merchant* and at her pirates shaking fists and weapons in his direction—daring him to finish the job.

He spun around. "Make all sail!" He nodded to two men hovering over the railing. "You men there, assist Blake on board." Then turning, "Caleb, you're the new first mate. Gather men to repair the mizzen top."

Caleb's shocked expression gave way to a beaming white smile before he turned and began barking orders.

"But, Cap'n," Mac protested.

"What 'bout Morgan?" another complained.

"I says we blast him to the depths!" Osborn added.

"Leave Morgan." Kent marched across the deck and barreled up the foredeck stairs. "We've done him enough damage!" he yelled over his shoulder. "After all, 'twas Captain Morris who put him up to this. He's the one we want."

"I says we put it to a vote," Graves said, scanning the pirates. "Morgan may have treasure aboard."

Kent had feared this would happen. But how could he convince his crew to go after Isabel? How could he convince them to follow his lead when suddenly all the wealth and power in the world meant nothing to him without her? Bracing his hands on his hips, he looked down from the foredeck railing upon the crowd of men forming on the main deck. "Even if we took the *Jamaica Merchant*, do you think the Brethren will allow us to join their fleet again when word gets out that we were swindled by that fool, Sawkins, and allowed Captain Morris to steal a woman and a baby from our ship?" Murmurs spread throughout the mob. It was a dangerous game he played, this affront to their pride—and to their esteem of him as their leader.

"Egad, men," Kent continued, "we've been made fools of, and we must regain our respect should we ever hope to be considered one of the Brethren. I say we go after Morris and prove ourselves. What say you to that?"

"All in favor of goin' after Morris, say aye!" Hoornes shouted.

A chorus of "ayes" rang across the ship.

"All opposed, say nay!"

Two "nays" bellowed forth.

"Then after Morris it is." Hoornes turned and winked at Kent.

Kent nodded. Relief washed over him as the sails caught the evening breeze in a billowing *snap* and the ship lurched forward. Dripping, Blake clambered over the railing and plopped onto the deck, puddles forming at his feet. His gaze locked with Kent's and he grinned. Beyond him, the dying embers on board Morgan's ship flickered before finally fading to black. Just like Kent's dreams of power and success.

"I told you, you'd never amount to nothing. Weakling. Fool." His father's voice grated over his heart. *"Giving up everything for a silly woman."*

Turning his back on the past, Kent planted his boots firmly on the foredeck and thrust his face into the wind. Perhaps his father was right. Perhaps Kent would never amount to anything this world deemed important, but somewhere deep inside, Kent now knew the things his father had valued were not the true measure of success—or of a man.

The last traces of gray faded on the horizon, blanketing the world in darkness. The *Restitution* picked up speed and surged over a charcoal swell, tumbling down the other side and spraying foam upon the deck.

A chill pricked Kent's skin. Balling his hands on his waist, he clenched his jaw. He must find Isabel. But how? Where?

Lord, help me find Isabel and my son before it's too late.

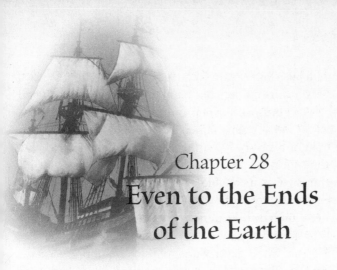

Chapter 28
Even to the Ends
of the Earth

Isabel stepped into the steamy jungle. Instantly, her world transformed from one of brisk, salty breezes and sweeping horizons to muggy, stagnant air and a shroud of confining green. An orchestra of birds scolded her as they fluttered from branch to branch, squawking their protests at the intruders who dared to invade their domain.

Up ahead, the plume on Morris's bicorn no longer ruffled in the breeze but merely bobbed up and down with each step of his boots. In front of him, the pirates continued swinging their machetes. Each chop and hack grated over Isabel like the lash of a whip. She wondered how far away these Indians lived. Would they arrive at their camp today? Tomorrow? Apprehension seized her.

Perspiration beaded on the back of Isabel's neck and slid behind her gown. Reaching up, she tucked her wayward curls into her combs and fingered their inlaid pearls—the only thing of value she still owned. Her thoughts drifted to her ex-fiancé, William—Lord Pembroke, as he liked to be called even by his friends—and wondered how he would respond if he could see her now: filthy, sweaty, tramping through the jungle without a shilling to her name, and about to be sold as a slave. A chuckle escaped her lips, followed by the surprising realization that she no longer felt any pain when she thought of him. Naught but pity lingered around his memory.

Frederick raised his chubby hand and grabbed her chin. With a gurgle, he tapped his fingers on her cheek and grinned, jumping up and down in his sling. Isabel brushed his hair from his forehead. His brown curls reminded her so much of his father. Fear tore at her heart. Was Kent still in the hold of his ship? What had Sawkins done to him? She pictured the last time she'd seen Kent as he aimed his pistol at Morris's head, risking his life against incredible odds. Courage and desperation had filled his eyes—the same eyes of the boy who looked so lovingly at her now. She rubbed her thumb over Frederick's cheek and smiled. Had Kent risked himself only to save his precious ship or did he really care about her and their son? *Their* son. She'd never willingly used the phrase *their son* before. Surprisingly, the sound of it no longer repulsed her. It had quite the opposite effect.

Lord, please watch over Kent.

Hours passed. Isabel caught glimpses of the sun as it peeked through narrow gaps in the canopy above. Heat sweltered around her. Even the thick shrubs, ferns, and trees drooped under its oppressive weight. Insects—some too small to see—sped past her, whining in her ears and stinging her skin. Frederick wailed and squirmed to be free of his sling, which had become a prison of perspiration. Isabel tried to calm him as best she could and swat the bugs from around his face but found she could no more comfort him than she could herself. The heavy air squeezed the breath from her lungs, and each step shot arrows of pain across her feet as the dried sand in her shoes scraped her tender skin. Her neck and back ached from the weight of Frederick's sling, sending burning spasms through her injured shoulder.

Thorny branches gripped her gown, ripping holes in her sleeves and tearing her skirt. Birds cackled at her from their thrones in the sky as if enjoying her agony. She looked up in time to see a monkey scamper up the trunk of a tall tree to her right. Life teemed all around her, yet she felt as though she were dying.

The toe of her shoe rammed into something hard, and she stumbled and nearly fell, clinging to Frederick. Throbbing pain radiated up her foot. She glanced over her shoulder to see a massive root crawling across the trail. Frederick broke into a piercing scream, and Isabel paused to becalm him along with the frantic beating of her heart, but the pirate behind her soon gave her a nudge. When she didn't move, he swatted her

behind with a wicked chortle.

"I'll be happy to carry ye if ye'd like, yer ladyship."

She threw a fierce look over her shoulder that belied the quiver in her belly. Tall, muscular, and hairy, he resembled a gorilla she'd seen once in the London Zoo. "You will keep your hands to yourself, sir, or. . .or. . ." Isabel stammered and searched for some champion she could summon who would swoop down to defend her honor.

"Or yer lover, Captain Carlton, will come to yer rescue, mebbe?" he snarled through sullied teeth. "I doubts he's able to do much o' anything anymore."

"He is not my lo—"

"Hurry up there!" Morris bellowed, and Isabel smirked at the pirate and stumbled forward. Hugging Frederick, she fought back tears burning behind her eyes. She'd always had someone to protect her. Her father, Reverend Thomas, even Kent. Now, no one was there to stop these brutes from doing whatever they wanted with her.

No one besides God.

The thought poured into her mind like a tonic—an antidote for fear— and she allowed it to spread through her, dispelling the poisons of doubt and anxiety. Yes, she did indeed have a protector—and one who would never leave her.

With renewed faith, Isabel continued her trek through the green labyrinth, trying to keep her eyes off her surroundings and focused instead on her Father above. But as the day progressed and the heat and insects persisted, her body languished. She marveled at the pirates' stamina— and Hann's—for they seemed not to tire after hours of tromping through the jungle. They stopped only twice and for only a few minutes, during which time Isabel pulled Frederick from his sling and allowed him to crawl through the leaves littering the trail. Tin canteens filled with water were passed amongst them, along with chunks of dried pork and plantains that one of the men had picked along the path.

As the afternoon waned, the trail widened, and the pirates reduced their hacking to the few branches and vines that intruded upon the path. The hard-packed dirt indicated a well-traveled trail, and a shudder ran through Isabel, for she knew they were too deep within the forest for any civilized wayfarers.

Her velvet shoes were a faint semblance of their former elegance. Tattered and soiled, their silk embroidery hung in shreds. Each step set Isabel's feet ablaze. Unable to bear the pain anymore, she kicked them off and tossed them into the greenery lining the trail. Where she was going, she doubted she would need shoes anyway.

As the light in the forest began to dim, the sound of rushing water filtered through the cacophony of chirps and buzzes, and they soon emerged into a small clearing. A sparkling creek flowed down one side with fruit trees lining its edge. A strange green fruit striped with black lines hung from the branches.

Much to Isabel's relief, Morris ordered the men to stop, and she dragged her bleeding, muddy feet into the clearing. Pulling Frederick from his sling, she set him on the mossy creek bank and plopped down beside him. She removed the brace from around her neck, then sighed as the light breeze cooled her damp gown. Rubbing her sore shoulder, she plunged her aching feet into the rippling water.

Frederick flapped his arms and giggled, reveling in his freedom. He grabbed a handful of leaves and crammed them into his mouth.

"No, no." Isabel shook Frederick's hand and ran a finger over his gums, pulling out the foliage. She laid him on his back and removed the sodden cloth from his bottom, cringing at the rash beneath it. After washing the cloth in the creek, she hung it over a branch to dry, hoping she could find something else with which to diaper him. In the meantime, the fresh air would do him good.

On Morris's order, the pirates scattered in search of wood, and soon a fire centered the camp. The men began unpacking dried meat and rum. They filled their canteens with water from the creek and splashed the liquid onto their faces, then hunkered by the fire to eat their meal. Isabel's stomach growled, and she wondered whether they intended to let her starve. Thankfully, Frederick was too enamored with his surroundings to notice he hadn't eaten in a few hours. But his silence wouldn't last long.

Thunder cracked the sky with an enormous roar, startling Isabel. Frederick shifted his wide eyes to her, and then his face wrinkled as a scream blared from his lips.

"There, there, Freddy." She picked him up and held him close, rubbing his back until he quieted.

Light sprinkles, almost like a mist, floated down upon them, and Isabel watched as Hann stood, hands on her hips, speaking to her father across camp.

The pirate who'd walked behind her—Miles, she'd discovered his name was—perched on a log across the creek from where she sat. He chomped on a plantain and leered at her, and for a minute, Isabel thought he might pound his chest and confirm her suspicions of his heritage.

Ignoring him, she sat Frederick beside her and splashed water from the creek over his arms and legs and then onto her neck. Though the sun retreated, the heat refused to give up its reign. Her gown clung to her, and she yanked on a rip in the fabric at her shoulder and tore off her sleeve. Then ripping off the other sleeve, she splashed some water from the creek onto her bare arms. The cool liquid sponged the heat from her skin, leaving it tingling. Wait. She looked down at her arms in surprise. Her rash had cleared. When had it stopped itching? She couldn't remember.

Isabel dipped the torn fabric into the water and ran it over Frederick's forehead and neck and then inside his nightdress. He cooed and gurgled and clutched the cloth, bringing it to his mouth.

Morris howled an obscenity and threw himself down beside his men. He glared Isabel's way as he bit into a hunk of meat and took a swig of rum. Hann sat a short distance away from the men and nodded toward Isabel.

Isabel attempted a smile, battling feelings of mistrust for the pirate's daughter. She had to speak with her. Hann had said she'd help Isabel. Had she meant it?

Soon the sun sank behind the thicket of shrubbery, and the forest darkened to a canvas of sinister shadows. The mist had stopped falling, but thunder still threatened in the distance. The pirates were well into their drinks, shouting boastful tales of their conquests at sea and on land. Isabel thought of covering Frederick's ears and hoped his innocent mind wouldn't remember the obscenities spewing from their rum-laden lips.

Hann slipped from her seat and crept over to Isabel, her arms full of fruit. She sat beside her and handed her one of the green melons and a clean cloth for Frederick's bottom.

"Can you talk?" Isabel asked

"Aye, just keep it to a whisper." Hann glanced at her father, who was engrossed in the telling of a recent sea battle. "You can trust me, milady." She gave Isabel a reassuring look as if she knew what Isabel had been thinking.

"Heavens, he's your father. All this time you knew he'd kidnapped my son?" Isabel hissed through clenched teeth, and began to peel the fruit. It looked like a giant green pinecone.

"I didn't know that he'd taken your son until it was too late." Hann drew her knees up, wrapping her arms around them, and looked down. "By then, it would have only invoked further suspicions if I'd revealed my identity."

Isabel gave some of the moist white pulp to Frederick, who opened his mouth, allowing her to plop it inside. His eyes sparkled as they gazed at her, and Isabel felt tears rising. She had missed him so. Terror struck her. Would he be taken from her again?

"You had no idea Lord Sawkins and your father had an accord?" she asked Hann.

Frederick got on all fours, a chunk of fruit sliding down his chin, and headed toward the creek. Isabel grabbed him by the waist and set him on her lap. He began to whimper, stretching his arms out toward the bubbling water, now a slick glaze in the fading light.

Hann shook her head, her eyes clouding. "Nay, milady. I did not. I assure you I would have told you had I known. Especially with that vermin Sawkins involved."

"Yes, he fooled us all, I'm afraid." A chill gripped Isabel as she thought of their brief engagement.

"Please believe me," Hann said, sincerity and concern flowing from her gaze.

"I do believe you. You've been a good friend to me. And you saved my Frederick"—Isabel hugged him and leaned her chin atop his head— "when you didn't have to."

Hann snorted. " 'Twas the least I could do." She faced Isabel. "He's not a cruel man, my father."

"At the moment, you'll forgive me if I don't agree."

Nodding, Hann looked away.

"So you intended to kill Captain Carlton?" Isabel asked, still shocked by Hann's confession.

"Aye, at first." Hann gave a crooked grin, then swallowed. "I loved my brother. Someone had to pay for his death."

"And now?"

"Someone still must pay. But it shouldn't be the captain—or you."

Isabel gave Frederick another chunk of fruit, thinking about revenge. Although she had not sought after it for what Kent had done to her, her heart had been filled with the same kind of hatred that fueled it. Frederick took the juicy pulp in his hands and squeezed it through his fingers before shoving it into his mouth.

"How long before we get to the Indian camp?" Isabel darted her gaze to the pirates.

"Tomorrow." Hann glanced at her father. He took a swig of rum, slapped his knee, and then spewed out a spray of liquor in a fit of laughter.

"I'm going to try and talk to my father tonight. If he won't listen to reason, we will wait until the rum knocks them unconscious and make our escape." Hann grabbed a twig and flipped it in her fingers. "Once they are deep in slumber, we will leave."

"Do you know the way back?"

"Aye."

"In the dark?" Isabel asked as Frederick batted his arms up and down and grabbed her gown.

Hann sighed. "Let's hope so."

Isabel pulled her gown from Frederick's grip lest he tear it further. The last thing she needed was to expose any more bare skin to these pirates. "It cannot be that simple. Surely he will post a guard." Frederick let out a wail and squirmed, and Isabel plopped more fruit into his mouth.

"No doubt, milady, but you forget I, too, am a pirate." Hann raised a sly brow. "I know how to handle myself."

Isabel dipped her sleeve into the water and ran the cloth over Frederick's forehead and neck. Dunking it again, she washed his mouth. He flung his arms and legs through the air, then reached up and grabbed a lock of her wayward hair and tugged on it. Isabel raised her gaze to Hann's.

Hann cocked her head, and a hint of a smile played on her lips.

"Why do you stare at me?" Isabel asked.

"Where is the fearful, trembling lady I knew aboard the *Restitution*?

285

You are in more dire straights than ever, yet there is a peace about you I cannot deny."

Isabel blinked, taken aback by the compliment. "I *am* afraid, to be sure." She doused her sleeve into the gurgling water again and handed it to Frederick. He grabbed it, threw it into his mouth, and began to suck the water from it. "But I am trying to trust God. I know He is with me. He has delivered my son into my arms out of an impossible situation. There's naught He cannot do." Declaring her faith aloud seemed only to strengthen it in her heart.

Minutes passed in silence. Isabel glanced at the pirates, so absorbed in their drinking and boasting that they seemed to have forgotten the women. The firelight contorted their features in hideous shadows, and Isabel looked away.

Even if they got lost in the dark, it would be a better fate than the one Morris had planned for her and Frederick. "You risk your life for me—and you defy your father." Isabel turned to Hann. "Thank you. You wouldn't even be in this jungle if it weren't for me."

"As far as risking my life, I do not. And I've defied my father before." Hann swatted a mosquito that landed on her neck. "The sooner we get out of this bug-infested oven, the better. I miss the sea." Wincing, she placed a hand over her side.

"How is your wound?"

" 'Tis better every day. Cutter is a good doctor." Hann stared into the shadows of the jungle and seemed lost in another place.

"You're thinking of him." Isabel wiped the fruit drool sliding down Frederick's chin and gave him another chunk.

"Aye, I was." A flicker of a smile tilted her lips. "How did you know?"

"By the gleam in your eye."

"I fear I'll never see him again."

"Of course, you will." Isabel laid a gentle hand on her arm. "He said he'd find you. He's a man of his word."

"Perhaps he'll change his mind now that he knows I'm Morris's daughter, and"—Hann hung her head—"that I was married."

"If I recall, 'twas after those two facts were revealed that he promised to come after you, was it not?"

Hann scrunched her nose and nodded.

"You'll see him again. I'm sure of it." Isabel plopped some fruit in her mouth and chuckled. "It's not so bad being a woman when you have a man like Cutter to love, is it?"

Hann's face reddened.

"Do you still despise your gender?" Isabel gave her a coy look. "For if you had remained a man, I can assure you Cutter would have kept his distance."

Hann snickered, drawing the attention of her father, who peered into the darkness, then shrugged and threw another log on the fire. Hann's face fell and she looked away. "My apologies, milady, here I go on about my misfortune when yours is far worse."

Isabel scanned the pirates, chortling and chugging rum. "So it would seem."

"Do you think of the captain?"

"Captain Carlton?" Isabel threw her shoulders back. "Why should I?" But she could not deny the man had consumed her thoughts the entire day.

"You do not lie very well, milady."

Isabel tried to conceal a smile. "I only fear for his safety." That much was true. Her heart froze at the thought of him hurt or dying, but it also froze at another thought, one she dared not admit: the thought of never seeing him again. But why? Wasn't he the reason she and Frederick were enduring this torturous trek in the first place? Whether or not he was innocent of killing Johnny, it was his vile escapades that had brought disaster into her life.

"So you forgive him for—for. . ." Hann cast a sheepish glance at Frederick.

"For ravishing me?"

"Aye," Hann said. "Though I can't imagine him committing such an act—not the man I have come to know, anyway."

"I must admit he *has* changed." Isabel brushed the dirt from Frederick's hand as he drew his fingers to his mouth. She searched her heart for the hatred that had burned there for so long. "Truth be told, I suppose I do forgive him." She swallowed as the memory of that night stormed through her mind. " 'Twas a horrible thing he did. Yet who am I not to forgive, when I have been forgiven so much?"

"What have you been forgiven for?" Hann scrunched her nose.

"Though I've not committed the same outward acts of a pirate, my heart ofttimes has been just as dark: filled with envy, selfishness, and pride. God considers those things no better than murder, rape, and thievery."

Hann shrugged. "Then everyone is guilty."

"Indeed."

The darkness fell so suddenly it was as if a blanket had been tossed over the jungle. Save for the light from the fire that flickered over Hann's face, Isabel could barely see the girl.

Morris stumbled to his feet and took another swig of rum. "Get over here, Annie!" he bellowed, then let out a belch. "What did I tell you about speaking to that wench?"

Hann gave Isabel a confident wink before struggling to her feet. Isabel fed the rest of the fruit to Frederick and gave him another wet sleeve to suck on while she diapered him. Tossing the sling around her neck, she placed him inside it and sang a lullaby. Soon, much to her relief, he drifted off to sleep.

Hours passed, and the fire dwindled to a sizzling crackle, leaving the camp in complete darkness. Yet with her eyes closed, Isabel forced her mind to stay alert.

She heard footsteps and opened her eyelids a crack to see a dark frame approaching. *Oh Lord, let it be Hann and not that lecherous Miles.* But as the shadow approached, she realized it wasn't tall enough to be one of the men, and she released a sigh. Frederick lay asleep, snuggled against her chest. His deep breaths reminded Isabel of how thankful she was to have him so close.

Hann knelt beside her. "It's time."

Isabel wrapped her arms around Frederick, tight in his sling, and struggled to her feet. Hann stood beside her, barely a shadow in the consuming darkness. She leaned toward Isabel.

"Miles was standing guard on the trail to the coast," she whispered. "I waited as long as I could, hoping he'd fall asleep, but the stubborn oaf has the vigilance of a jaguar."

Isabel peered across the gloomy camp. Dark, bulky shapes lay haphazardly around the remaining embers of the fire. Rhythmic snores rose to accompany the chirp of crickets. "Is he still there?"

"Aye, but no longer standing." Hann grinned.

"What did you do?" Isabel whispered as Frederick stirred slightly. Rubbing his back, she prayed he would stay asleep. He made a gurgling noise, then snuggled his head into her neck.

"I didn't kill him, if that's what you mean," Hann replied. "Let's just say he should have a good night's sleep."

Isabel followed Hann across the dark camp. Every crunch of the leaves beneath her bare feet sent her nerves quivering. Halting, she glanced toward the sleeping men. They didn't move.

At the head of the pathway, Hann disappeared into the brush, and Isabel took a deep breath of the muggy air and tiptoed after her. The damp soil clung to her feet. The hum of insects vibrated from all directions. Up ahead, a mammoth shape lay across the trail. A chill raked over her.

" 'Tis just Miles." Grabbing Isabel's hand, Hann helped her step over the unconscious pirate. "Quick, this way."

With a sigh of relief, Isabel followed Hann's shadow down the trail. They were free! *Thank You, Lord.* She kissed the top of Frederick's head, refusing to worry about how two women were going to traverse the jungle and make it to shore.

Hann gasped and halted.

Isabel crashed into her.

"Not so fast, Annie." A familiar voice snaked over them. "Where d'you think you're going?"

"Father." For the first time, Isabel heard fear in Hann's voice.

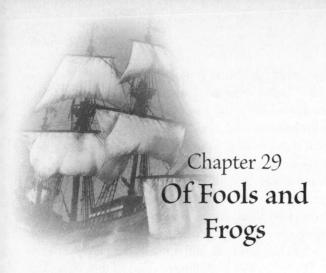

Chapter 29
Of Fools and
Frogs

Kent tore off his bicorn, wiped the sweat from his brow, and gazed up at the sun nearly straight above his head. He didn't know if it was better to keep the hat on for shade or allow the breeze to run through his damp hair. He decided on the latter and tossed the brown hat to the bottom of the longboat.

The oars struck the water in unison, sending the craft speeding across the choppy sea toward the coast of the Spanish Main—land under the jurisdiction of the Viceroyalty of New Spain. Kent studied the shoreline, looking for enemy ships, but saw nothing save a ribbon of brown and green extending in both directions.

Sawkins's loud grunts drifted back to Kent from where he'd placed the scoundrel at the front of the boat and ordered him to row.

Cutter grinned. "I fear his lordship is not accustomed to physical labor."

Kent chuckled. "If I am forced to bring him along, he will earn his keep, which I believe, for him, will be a first."

After defeating Morgan, Kent had wanted nothing more than to toss Sawkins and his traitorous followers into the sea and allow the Caribbean to have its way with them, but Kent's determination to keep his promise to his father had been further emboldened by his new allegiance to a God who always kept His.

Cutter raised a single brow. "Remind me, Captain, why exactly did you bring him along?"

"He informs me that he knows where Morris has taken Isabel, Frederick, and Hann."

"And you believe him?"

"No, but I cannot afford to ignore his assertion, for without it, I have nothing to go on." Kent hated it that he was forced to depend on the word of a man who made more efficient work of lying than any other endeavor, but what choice did he have? Without Sawkins and the half-truth Kent prayed existed within his lie, Kent had no idea where to start searching for Isabel. Sawkins had been able to describe with extreme accuracy the layout of the coast, the inlets, the natural harbors, and the mountainous regions south of Cartagena, informing Kent he had accidentally seen a map Morris had in his possession. Whether the bumbling lout could actually find the spot and whether it was where Morris had taken his captives were two other matters altogether. Yet after Kent had spent all night in prayer, he had an inner peace that, despite Sawkins's possible treachery, led him to believe he was on the right course.

Kent swung a glance over his shoulder. The white sails of the *Restitution* floated like balls of cotton on the horizon. Not knowing how long they would be gone, Kent didn't want his ship tarrying along the Spanish Main where *los guardacostas* roamed, ready to attack any vessel daring to venture into Spanish waters. He'd put Caleb and Logan in charge, trusting them to sail by the coast every few days to check for his return.

Facing forward again, Kent grimaced. He'd never trusted anyone before—especially not with his ship. Yet what choice did he have? Isabel's and Frederick's lives were at stake, and he trusted their fate to no one else.

A gleaming white beach fanned out from a fortress of green, then dove into the turquoise waters. Beyond the towering walls of the jungle, mounds of ascending treetops stretched as far as the eye could see. Were Isabel and his son somewhere within that prison of green? Fear clipped his heart. Morris had two days' lead on him. They could be anywhere by now.

The longboat rode on the swell of an incoming wave, and the men flicked the oars and angled the craft to keep it upright. Water splashed over Kent, failing to cool his ill humor, as more waves carried them to shore. Hoornes and Sparks tumbled out of the boat and sloshed through the frothy water, dragging the vessel onto the sand. Kent jumped over the side with a *splash*. A wave struck him from behind, soaking his breeches. He trudged onto the dry sand, Cutter behind him. Sawkins lumbered to his feet and, with much grunting, followed.

"Help the men stow the boat behind that thicket of palms," Kent ordered Sawkins.

"I will not." Sawkins pressed a strand of hair behind his ear and smirked, refusing to look at Kent. "Such tasks are not for men of high station, but for these men." He pointed with disdain to Hoornes and Sparks. "They were born for it."

"We don't want his lordship's help anyways, do we?" Hoornes spat and slid a finger over his rat's head before setting him on his shoulder. Then grabbing Sparks, he and the young sharpshooter hauled the boat over the beach and hid it in a clump of trees.

Kent swung a stern gaze to Sawkins. " 'Tis bad enough I must suffer your company, but I'll thank you to not bore us with your insolent opinions."

"Perhaps I should cut his tongue out," Cutter offered.

Sawkins snarled at the doctor. "Then how shall I tell you where your precious little pirate girl is? Though why you'd want to seek her after she betrayed you is beyond me."

"She didn't—"

"Enough! Half the day is gone. Let's be on our way," Kent ordered. "Sparks, Hoornes, grab the packs." Drawing his cutlass, he plunged into the jungle. Cutter pushed Sawkins in after Kent and fell in line behind him. Hoornes and Sparks took up the rear.

After hacking through a web of thick vines for nearly fifty feet, Kent emerged onto a narrow trail that ran parallel to the coast. At least Sawkins had been right about the location of the path. He faced his brother. "Which way?"

Sawkins's expression soured as he swatted a bug from his face. "Who's to say you won't kill me after I've led you to Lady Ashton?"

"As I told you, if you indeed find Isabel and my son, I'll set you free. If you do not, I'll tie you to a post in the center of the nearest Spanish town with the words BRITISH PIRATE burned into your chest."

Cutter's laughter echoed across the trees.

"You wouldn't dare." Terror quaked in Sawkins's voice. "You know they would kill me."

"Kill? Egad, no, my daft brother." Kent ran an arm over the sweat on his forehead. "They will torture you for months until you will beg for death."

"If not for the precious lives at stake," Cutter said, "I would be praying you had lied to us once again, your lordship."

Hoornes chuckled.

"Fortunately, the wishes of a mangled doctor mean nothing to me," Sawkins spat.

Kent clutched his brother by the sleeve and yanked him to the front of the group. "Now lead the way, brother, for you know what's at stake."

Sawkins inched beside him with a groan. "I'll need an ax to chop away the branches."

"But you'll not get one, so I suggest you use your traitorous body to forge through the greenery."

"But what of snakes and poisonous bugs?" Sawkins shifted his eyes over the shrubbery. "I hear these savage jungles are teeming with them."

"Why do you think you're in front?" Kent grinned.

Cutter snickered, and Sawkins glared at him, then swung about and stormed down the trail, mumbling curses in his wake.

Sawkins threw up his arm to push aside a vine dangling in the midst of the path, careful not to touch it with his hands lest some creeping beast slither upon him. He hated bugs—had always hated bugs. He'd known a man once who had been bitten by a poisonous spider that had left him paralyzed from his waist down. Sawkins cringed, remembering the last time he'd seen Lord Riley being carried into his mansion by a servant as though he were but a child. Sawkins would rather be dead. And now his brother forced him to be the first amongst them to encounter any noxious creature hidden in the foliage.

His brother. Hatred bubbled in the pit of Sawkins's stomach, driving a rancid taste to his mouth. Why did the blasted man always have to beat him at everything? Sawkins cursed as he tripped over a root, eliciting snickers behind him. Faith, he'd had Kent's ship, his woman, and all the treasure in the hold. If it hadn't been for that lying cur

Morris double-crossing him, he'd be the new captain of the *Restitution* and a member of the Brethren of the Coast.

A vision of his father's gruff, swollen face swirled in his mind. "Ye've got noble blood in ye, boy," he had said as he took Sawkins aside one day. "Yer brother's naught but a whoreson. Yer smarter than he is and stronger, too. I'm counting on you to make somethin' of yerself—show the world who the son of James Carlton Bristol is. Power and wealth, boy. That's what ye needs to gain respect—power and wealth."

Withdrawing a handkerchief from his pocket, Sawkins wiped the sweat off his brow and moaned. An earl's son should not have to endure this infernal heat. His rank and title afforded him certain considerations, ones which Kent had never granted him. Even after their father had sent Sawkins overseas for a noble education, upon his return, his brother had never bowed to him—never deferred to his status.

Soon after their father died, Kent had left home to make his fortune in the Caribbean. Sawkins remembered how he'd shoved him out the door, shouting after him that he would never amount to anything—that he'd soon return with his tail betwixt his legs.

As it was, Kent acquired the ships, the wealth, and the women, while an unfortunate streak of bad luck at the gambling tables had relieved Sawkins of their father's shipping business. Kent had also become a coveted member of the Brethren of the Coast—that was up until the fateful night when Sawkins had hired a man to kill him aboard Henry Morgan's flagship, the HMS *Oxford*. Sawkins hadn't instructed the assassin to blow up the entire ship—the fool. Only ten people had survived, and of course Kent had been amongst them. Pity about the hundreds who had died that night, but how was Sawkins to know the man he'd hired was a buffoon? It wasn't his fault. A chuckle crossed Sawkins's lips as he skirted the trunk of an enormous tree. If Captain Morris only knew who'd really killed his son.

But Sawkins had been able to use the incident to his advantage by spreading rumors that Captain Carlton had been at fault. Hence, his brother had not only been ejected from the Brethren of the Coast but had to constantly keep a weather eye out for Captains Morgan and Morris, who both sought him for revenge. Sawkins grinned. It had been a brilliant way to recover from a plan gone awry.

Yet still Kent had succeeded. While his power and fame spread throughout the Caribbean, Sawkins's reputation had been reduced to that of a drunken gambler. And each time his brother had paid off his debts, Sawkins's fury had burned more intensely.

Things would have turned out differently if Sawkins's luck hadn't gone awry. Instead, his thieving brother had stolen the life that rightfully belonged to him.

He halted, his breath coming in quick spurts. "I must have some water." He turned, and Kent nearly barreled into him, his mind obviously elsewhere.

Grabbing the pouch hanging from his belt, Kent handed it to Sawkins. "How far is it?"

"A few days." Sawkins tipped the water bag and guzzled the warm liquid.

"Hold up there," Hoornes complained. "Save some fer the rest o' us."

Cutter grabbed the pouch, wiped the nozzle on his sleeve, and took a sip, then passed it behind him. "Are you sure you know where you're going?" He smirked. "If I recall, you had trouble discerning the stern from the bow on the ship."

Sawkins frowned. "Of course I know where I'm going." What he wouldn't do to be rid of that malformed doctor and his caustic quips.

Turning, he scanned the jungle—a tangled labyrinth of greens and browns that wove together into an indistinguishable mass. He had no idea where he was or in what direction he should head. Only from bits and pieces of remembered conversations with Morris had Sawkins been able to recall some mention of an Indian tribe that lived inland south of Cartagena. And to that vague destination, he now led these men. If they found Morris, all the better, for he knew Kent would enforce a strict enough punishment on the treasonous captain to satisfy Sawkins's own need for revenge. If they did not find him, Sawkins would still have a better chance of escaping his brother out in the jungle than locked in the hold of a ship.

"Get going." Kent poked him in the back with his knife.

Lifting his gaze in a pretense of gathering his bearings, Sawkins plodded down the trail, keeping a keen eye out for slithering creatures dangling from the treetops.

If he did manage to get away, Sawkins's only regret would be not having the chance to see Lady Ashton again. Ah, the beautiful Isabel. What a delightful surprise she had been. It was no wonder Kent had become so enamored with her. Sawkins's own feelings had taken him quite by surprise—and she would be his if not for that blackguard Morris. If he ever saw her again, Sawkins hoped to make it up to her, hoped to persuade her of his sincere devotion and absolve himself of any involvement with Morris that might cause harm to her and her son. Part of that was true, after all. But despite the hideous fate that awaited her, if he was presented with a chance to escape, he intended to take it.

Only a fool would risk everything for a woman.

Kent gazed into the canopy stretched above him like a massive web of green. Monkeys scampered across branches and flung their warning chatters down upon them. Multicolored birds of all sizes flitted between the branches, their ear-piercing twitters raking over him. Patches of dark blue broke through the maze as the sun stole the light from the sky in its descent. It had been a long day. Kent's feet ached. Sweat saturated his shirt, and the bites from a multitude of bugs spotted his bare skin and began to itch. He was hungry, thirsty, and miserable, but all he could think about was how Isabel and Frederick were faring under these conditions, or if they were faring at all. Terror spiked through him with each step he took, and he prayed God would keep them safe and lead him to them.

Besides Kent's nagging fear, the worst part of the journey had been having to stare at Sawkins's back. If Kent had his way, he'd never have to gaze at any part of his brother again. The man had done naught but blubber and complain all day long—a constant annoying whine that matched the buzz of the mosquitoes in Kent's ears.

Thunder growled in the distance, and a light mist sprinkled over them as they entered a small clearing. "We'll stay here tonight," Kent ordered, hearing the sighs of relief behind him.

"Egad, 'tis about time." Sawkins stormed to a nearby log and plopped down. "I thought I would be reduced to a puddle of sweat."

"One can only hope," Cutter said, swatting at a bug fluttering about his head.

Sawkins stood and took a step toward the doctor, his hand grabbing for the cutlass that no longer hung by his side. His face reddened as he fumbled through his clothes for any other weapons; then he blew out a sigh.

Cutter raised his brows, amusement glinting in his eyes. "Not so tough without your sword, are you, your lordship?"

Kent stepped between them. "Sparks, Sawkins, gather wood for the fire."

"I beg your pardon?" Sawkins thrust his chin out.

"Do you wish to eat?" Kent asked.

With a flex of his angular jaw, Sawkins turned and followed Sparks into the brush, both men soon returning with armloads of wood. While Kent knelt to start the fire, Hoornes and Cutter laid out the water pouches—recently topped off at a creek that had crossed the trail—some dried meat, and an assortment of fruit the men had foraged along the way.

Hoornes rubbed his hands together and plucked his rat from his pocket. "I'm starvin'."

Dragging a dead log to the fire, Kent sat and tugged off his boots, stretching his toes in the stagnant air. A bright, red and orange bird flew overhead, drawing his attention, and he watched as it landed with ease on a nearby branch, turned its head, and stared down at him with one eye. He half wondered if the fowl were a spy sent by Morris to see who dared follow him. Kent wished it were so, because that would mean Isabel was close by. His heart jumped at the thought. His whole body yearned to leap up and find her. But the men were tired, and the jungle too treacherous at night to traverse.

Sawkins brushed off another log and sat down, grabbing some meat. Cutter took his place beside Kent, while Hoornes and Sparks settled upon the leaf-strewn ground.

Sawkins scowled and pointed to Hoornes's rat scampering over the pirate's shoulder. "Why don't you let the filthy beast go free?"

"Because we need you to lead us to Morris." A slight grin twisted Cutter's lips as he snatched a piece of meat.

Sawkins narrowed his eyes. "I meant the rat, you fool."

Glaring at Sawkins, Hoornes took the creature into his hands and began stroking its back.

The men dove into the food, giving Kent a moment of silence save for the smacking of their lips as they ate and the buzzing of the forest. Taking a swig of water, Kent scanned the jungle as dark shadows draped over the trees and shrubs. The scent of moist earth and fragrant flowers surrounded him.

Kent plucked a yellow fruit from the pile and bit into its sweet, juicy pulp.

Sawkins tossed a laugh toward Kent. "Do you really believe, Captain, that your men will return for you? They have your ship and your treasure. Why if I were them, I'd be long gone by now."

"Lucky for me they possess higher morals than you ever did." Kent offered him a jeering grin, but behind his smile, the pain of Sawkins's statement cut deeper than Kent wanted to admit. All he'd worked so hard to achieve these past years could be gone. Without his ship, his treasure, and the power they gave him, he would be reduced to nothing. Then even if he found Isabel, what could he offer her?

Thou shalt have no other gods before me. The words of the first commandment fired through Kent's mind.

"Morals amongst pirates?" Sawkins's laughter interrupted his thoughts. "My dear, naive brother, how have you managed to remain captain of your own vessel all these years?"

Kent flung his hair behind him. "I don't see your ship anywhere."

Cutter chuckled, and Sawkins curled his lip.

"Don't listen to 'im, Cap'n." Sparks adjusted his eye patch. "The men be wit' ye to be sure."

Kent nodded as gray smoke from the fire spiraled upward and disappeared into the darkness. The woodsy, charred scent filled Kent's nostrils.

Hoornes rose and rummaged through one of the packs, pulling out a bottle of rum. Uncorking it, he sat and took a swig before passing it to Sparks.

"So we shall arrive tomorrow?" Kent turned a suspicious eye toward Sawkins.

"Yes, though I cannot promise they will still be there." He shifted his gaze away from Kent. "But I can bring you to the place Morris intended to take them."

"Hmm." Cutter grabbed the bottle from Sparks and took a sip, then held it to Kent.

Kent shook his head. He needed to remain alert. Besides, he had a notion God did not approve of his overindulgence in the pungent liquid, and he intended to curb his appetite for it from now on.

Thunder rumbled, sending a growl rolling through the forest.

Kent wiped the sweat from the back of his neck and prayed the evening would assuage the stifling heat.

The fire flickered over Cutter's face. "I hope they are unharmed."

"Rest assured, your lover is quite safe," Sawkins taunted. "She's been in on this from the beginning."

Kent gave the doctor a level stare. "You know that's not true."

Ignoring Sawkins, Cutter swallowed. "I am still baffled that she declared her love for me before her father. What audacity that girl has." He grinned and shook his head.

Sawkins flapped his stained silk shirt against his skin. "Do you truly believe any woman would want to live her whole life looking at your hideous face? Faith, she was only being kind—a fickle emotion oft found amongst females."

Frowning, Cutter plucked his pipe from a pocket, filled it with tobacco from his pouch, and stuck it in his mouth. Grabbing a burning twig from the fire, he plunged it into the bowl and lit it. As the smoke coiled upward, a shroud of gloom seemed to wrap around him.

"Don't listen to him," Kent said, his stern gaze shooting from Sawkins to Cutter. "He's an impudent fool who has no understanding of women. Otherwise, he'd be able to keep one for himself."

Sawkins blew out a gasp.

"Hard to believe Hann be a girl," Hoornes piped in, tipping the bottle of rum to his lips.

"Indeed. She had me fooled." Kent rubbed the stubble on his chin.

"A common occurrence since your birth." Sawkins smirked.

"Yet who was foolish enough to be tricked by both Morris and Morgan, and who now is naught but an imprisoned guide?" Cutter raised his brows toward Sawkins and puffed his pipe.

A chortle arose from Sparks that was quickly silenced by Sawkins's fierce gaze.

Kent stretched his feet toward the fire and crossed his arms over his chest. "My half brother has always suffered from an overconfidence unhindered by his many limitations."

"Indeed?" Sawkins face swelled red. "We shall see who has limitations."

Shaking his head, Kent gazed into the jungle. A black curtain had dropped over the scene, leaving only dark shadows in its place. He could make out nothing save what the circle of firelight afforded him.

Hoornes drew a pack beneath his head and lay down upon it, setting his rat on his chest. Taking one last swig of rum, Sparks corked the bottle, set it aside, and eased to the ground in a heap. Soon, their snores rose to match the drone of the night insects.

"Perhaps you should get some sleep as well," Kent said to Sawkins, hoping he'd take the hint and spare them his annoying company.

A frog hopped into the firelight next to Sawkins, and without hesitation, he raised his boot and crushed it, chortling.

"Cruel." Cutter shook his head.

Kent groaned. "You didn't have to do that."

"Pish, that's the difference between you and me." Sawkins ground his boot into the frog's remains and looked up, his eyes aglow with mischief. "You're too soft. Don't you remember what Father taught us? Control and power—that's the way to succeed."

Kent threw a log into the fire. Yes, he did remember his father's words all too well. They haunted him day and night. Had Kent been that cruel? Had he crushed the weak and defenseless beneath his boot just as Sawkins had done to that poor frog? Kent hung his head. *Forgive me, Lord. Make me a new man.* Even as he silently breathed the words, he knew the change in him had already begun.

With a grunt, Sawkins stood, shifted his log away from the fire, and stretched out on the ground beside it, closing his eyes.

Kent snatched a stick and poked at the wood in the fire.

Cutter seemed lost in his own thoughts as he smoked his pipe and stared into the flames. Finally, he said, "I fear I may not find sleep tonight. I am worried for Hann and Lady Ashton."

Kent's eyes met his. "As am I."

"What do you suppose Morris intends to do with them—especially Lady Ashton?"

"I prefer not to consider it." Kent rubbed his eyes.

"Do you think of her often?"

Often? She consumed his thoughts day and night, and even more since he'd gotten to know her and love her. He didn't know what he would do if he lost her. But he wasn't ready to admit such weakness to his friend. His thoughts drifted to Frederick. "Did you see my son?"

"A fine boy, to be sure." Cutter nodded.

"Fine? Why, he's magnificent." Kent grinned. "A true pirate's son."

Sawkins cleared his throat from where he lay. "You're a bigger fool than I assumed you to be if you think that fine lady will ever want a common pirate like yourself. Why, you have nothing to offer her."

"And you do?" Kent replied curtly, cursing under his breath. Why hadn't the villain fallen asleep and given them some peace?

"I have noble blood." Sawkins kept his eyes shut but crossed his arms against his chest. "And the title that goes with it—something you can never boast of—and if I'm not mistaken, something the lady highly values, especially for her son."

"So that's the bait with which you trapped her."

" 'Twas no trap, brother. Why, she nearly gave herself to me in the hold of your ship." Sawkins propped himself on his elbows. "If you hadn't come along. . ." He sighed, shaking his head, then grinned with malicious delight.

"That was you!" Kent lunged toward him. He clutched the collar of Sawkins's shirt and nearly lifted him off his feet. "You frightened her half to death!"

"Frightened?" Sawkins managed to sputter, despite the clamp Kent had on his neck. "I assure you, hers were screams of delight, rather than fear."

Kent tossed him to the ground and began searching the camp.

Laboring to sit, Sawkins rubbed his throat. "We shall see where her affections lie when we find her." A hint of a grin played on his lips.

Fury tore through Kent. He'd had enough. Must he suffer this man's impertinent tongue all night as well as all day? Grabbing a bundle of rope from the pack, he stormed toward him. Sawkins's eyes widened, and he fumbled to stand. Kent flipped him over and wrenched his arms behind him, binding his wrists together.

"What is the meaning of—" Sawkins's protest was stifled by the handkerchief Kent thrust inside his mouth.

Wide-eyed and groaning, Sawkins scrambled to his feet. Kent shoved him toward a tree lining the clearing. Forcing him to the ground, Kent wrapped the rope about his waist and yanked it tight, knotting it to the tree.

Panting, Kent stood before him. "Now, will you go to sleep?"

Ignoring Sawkins's muffled curses, Kent returned to his place by the fire and joined Cutter. One look at each other sent them both rolling in laughter.

Hours later, after Cutter had drifted off to sleep and Sawkins's groans had faded, Kent stretched back onto a log and laced his hands behind his head. He stared up at the patches of stars sparkling amidst the trees and wondered if God was looking down on him. Doubts flooded him. Had his encounter with God on board the *Restitution* been real? Did the God of the universe truly love him and care for him as a father does a child? Then why had Isabel and his son been taken from him? He sighed. Perhaps he deserved no less for the crimes he had committed. But not Isabel. She had done nothing wrong. *I don't understand, God, but if You're there, please help me find them.*

The hint of a glow brightened behind Kent's eyelids. The chirping of birds called to him in his slumber, but another noise rose to prick his nerves— footsteps, then the swoosh of leaves. Feeling for the knife strapped to his thigh, Kent grabbed it and sprang to his feet. Muttering, Cutter labored to sit, while Sawkins groaned from the tree that held him captive. Hoornes and Sparks still snored in the distance. Hoornes's rat curled up beside him.

The birds stopped chattering.

Kent scanned the jungle, just a faint blend of green in the early dawn. Nothing. But he knew someone or something was out there. Holding his knife before him, he lowered his gaze and searched for his baldric and pistols on the ground. Spotting them, he stooped to grab a pistol when the jungle exploded around him.

Slowly, Kent straightened. The camp was surrounded by a dozen half-naked men brandishing spears.

Chapter 30
Agony of Loss

Isabel trudged back into the pirate camp, dragging her feet through the mud along with her trodden hope. Morris and Hann marched behind her.

"I knew you weren't to be trusted, girl," Morris spat as he pushed past Isabel and stomped into the clearing.

Isabel's heart clenched. What would Captain Morris do to Hann now that she had openly disobeyed him?

"I didn't wish to defy you, Father, but the lady has done nothing to deserve the punishment you intend."

"That is for me to decide." Grabbing a stick, Morris squatted and poked at the fire, igniting the coals. "Egad, sit down." He gestured toward the logs the pirates had dragged around the fire. " 'Tis my guess none of us will be sleeping tonight." He threw more sticks onto the rising flames.

With care, Isabel lifted the sling from around her neck. Cradling Frederick against her chest, she sat on a log. His eyelids fluttered, but he did not awaken. Nor did the four pirates who remained lost in their slumber, strewn across the ground like sacks of stale meal.

With a shaky sigh, Hann dropped beside Isabel.

Morris stood and warmed his hands over the blaze, although Isabel couldn't imagine why. Prying her damp gown from her body, she prayed for a whiff of a breeze to cool her roasting skin. Smoke filled her nostrils, and she turned her head and coughed, tightening her grip on Frederick.

M. L. TYNDALL

Snatching an open bottle of rum, Morris raised it to his lips and downed several gulps. Wiping his mouth on his sleeve, he leveled a piercing gaze at Hann. "I thought better of you for your brother's sake."

Hann shook her head. "You haven't been listening to me."

" 'Tis you who should be listening to me!" he stormed, purple veins bulging in his thick neck. "I'm your father."

The fire popped, and Isabel jumped, thinking a pistol had been fired. She squeezed Frederick, trying to still her frantic heart, but then glanced at Hann, who hadn't even flinched at her father's outburst.

Morris sank onto a rock and leaned the bottle on his thigh, staring into the flames. He seemed more disappointed than angry, and Isabel's nerves uncoiled from the knot they had formed.

Sadness clung to him as heavy as the air, and despite his threats, a tender spot for him bloomed in Isabel's heart. He had suffered a tremendous loss—one she'd only been threatened with thus far. Perhaps if he spoke about his son, it would help ease his pain, not to mention diminish his need for revenge.

"Captain Morris." Isabel gulped. "Tell me about Johnny."

"I'll not be telling the likes of you about my son." Morris scowled and gnawed his lip.

"If I'm to suffer for his sake, I beg you, do not deny me the comfort of knowing what type of man he was."

Morris grunted and poured another draught down his throat. He lowered his gaze and kicked his boot into the dirt. The silver in his hair gleamed in the firelight, and Isabel noticed for the first time that a corner of his right ear was missing—an injury normally hidden beneath his hat.

Finally, he raised his moist gaze to Hann. "Johnny was a fine lad, wasn't he, Annie?"

Hann smiled. "That he was, Father—the finest."

"He was only one and twenty." His fiery eyes landed on Isabel. "About your age, and already a pirate captain." Despite his anger, pride rang in his voice. "A good captain he was."

"Who's to blame him, with you for a father?" Hann declared.

Isabel gazed down at Frederick. She could not imagine loving him for twenty-one years only to lose him in a horrific mishap.

"He sailed with Morgan and the Brethren in the raids on Porto Bello

304

and Maracaibo," Morris continued, staring into the fire. Then he lifted his bottle in a salute. "A fine pirate." He took another swig.

"He sounds like an exceptional man." Isabel dared to interject her opinion, then braced herself for Morris's angry retort, but "Aye" was all he uttered in reply.

"He was very handsome." Hann's violet eyes danced in the firelight. "And funny. What a sense of humor." She paused, her eyes welling. "He had a good heart." She gazed at Isabel. "You would have liked him."

Isabel smiled, but inside, her heart melted as she realized how deep the blade of Johnny's loss had cut into both Hann and her father.

Morris swayed on his seat. His eyes glistened in the firelight.

Hann stretched out her legs. "Mother would have been proud of him."

Morris chuckled. "Well, she weren't too pleased when he followed in me footsteps and became a pirate, to be sure, but aye, lass, I think she'd have been proud of him."

Frederick murmured and shifted in Isabel's arms. She faced Hann. "What happened to your mother?"

Clutching his bottle, Morris jumped to his feet and turned his back to them.

A log tumbled in the fire with a crackle, shooting out sparks onto the moist dirt.

Hann shifted her sorrowful eyes to Isabel. "Yellow fever."

Morris swung about and cursed. His face swelled into a red ball, and he seemed to have aged ten years. "I shouldn't have brought her to the Spanish Main."

Hann gazed up at him. "She wanted to come."

"I couldn't save her." Morris shook his head.

Tears burned behind Isabel's eyes as her gaze shifted between father and daughter. Agony folded over them both, suffocating them. This family had suffered far too much. *Oh Lord, please bring them the comfort that only You can bring.*

Hann rose to her feet. " 'Twas not your fault, Father."

"What is a man if he can't protect his own family?" He thrust the bottle toward Hann, anger fuming in his blue eyes. "First your mother, then Johnny." He dropped his gaze. "At least she weren't around to watch her son die." He grunted. "I can thank God for that."

"Father, you take too much on yourself. Only God can control who lives and who dies."

"Perhaps." He stumbled, threw his arms out, then regained himself. His glazed eyes landed on Frederick, still asleep in Isabel's arms. "But I can avenge their deaths—at least Johnny's, so he can rest in peace."

Hann rushed to her father's side. "Johnny wouldn't want an innocent woman and her babe to suffer for his sake." Morris studied her and blew out a sigh, the lines in his face softening. "Leave your vengeance to God, Father. If you cling to it, it will poison your heart." Hann cast a knowing smile at Isabel, who returned it with one of her own. Hann had been listening to her after all.

A slight glow began to lift the heavy shroud of night as dawn broke over the jungle. Was that a sign that Isabel's nightmare was over? A single bird twittered. One of the pirates rolled over with a groan. She held her breath. Would Morris change his mind? Would he let her and Frederick go? *Oh touch his heart, Lord. Please touch his heart.*

Morris swayed, then rubbed his eyes before his hesitant gaze landed back on his daughter.

Hann gripped his arm, her expression alight with anticipation.

Frederick whimpered, drawing Morris's attention, and the softness instantly faded from his face. With darkened brow, he tore his arm from his daughter's grasp. "Nay, I will not suffer it, nor will I bear your defiance any longer." He held out his hand. "Your weapons, Annie. And if you so much as look at Lady Ashton, I'll have her bound and gagged."

"But, Fa—"

"Enough!" His bellow silenced the fading chirps of the crickets. Akers stirred in his sleep.

Isabel hung her head. Drawing Frederick close, she wondered what would happen to them now.

With a snort, Hann reluctantly handed her father her sword, knives, and pistols.

Grabbing them, Morris turned and started across the camp, then spun back around. "It'll be on your head if I am forced to tie and gag Lady Ashton. You'll do well to remember that, girl."

Morris lumbered about the camp in his drunken state, booting the sleeping pirates awake. "Pack up. Let's be on our way. The quicker I get

this over with, the better." His guilty gaze flickered over Isabel.

Thunder cracked the morning sky, and Isabel squeezed her eyes shut. *Father, why aren't You answering my prayers any longer? Where are You?* She gazed down at Frederick. His dark lashes fluttered over his cheeks like tiny fans, and her heart swelled with love for him. There was nothing she wouldn't do for him, no sacrifice too big. With a sigh, she brushed a curled lock of hair from his cheek and remembered that God considered her and Frederick His own children.

If God loved her even half as much as she loved this little boy, she had nothing to fear. *"Perfect love casteth out fear."* And God's love for His children was perfect—the kind of love that prompted Him to sacrifice His only Son to save them.

After changing Frederick's diaper—to his extreme agitation at being forced from his sleep—Isabel returned him to the sling and gave him a piece of fruit.

As the pirates tossed bits of leftover food, canteens, and bottles of rum into their packs, Miles wandered into the camp, rubbing his head, and Morris laid into him with a barrage of insults regarding the heritage of his mother. After flinging an angry scowl toward Hann, the pirate grabbed his pack and took his place in line.

Clinging to Frederick, Isabel dove once again into the green maze, breathing in the warm, musty scent of earth and life. Massive leaves hanging from the canopy sank low under their weight of morning dew and splayed beside her like outstretched palms offering their gifts of water. Instead, they only soaked her gown as she brushed past them, sending a chill through her. Above, an orchestra of colorful birds tuned their melodious warble for the day's ensemble as more light lifted the dark curtain on their performance.

Fully awake, Frederick bunched his knees and clutched Isabel's gown, trying to crawl from his brace, then sobbed when he found himself once again confined.

" 'Tis all right, Freddy." Isabel kissed his forehead and rubbed his back, but found she no longer had the energy to console him. With every step of her bruised feet, pain lanced her legs. An agonizing spike drove from the sling at her neck down her back. Her injured shoulder burned. Hunger gnawed at her belly, and exhaustion sat upon her like a weight, forcing her down.

She stopped to adjust Frederick in the sling, and Miles's hot, rancid breath curdled down her neck as he crept close behind her and nudged her back.

Plodding forward, she couldn't imagine how things could get much worse, when in an instant the sky opened and a cascade of rain dumped upon them. Sheet after sheet pounded over Isabel. Frederick wailed, and she wrapped her arms around him and tried to shelter him with her head.

"Keep going!" she heard Morris shout as the deluge intensified, obscuring him from view.

Within minutes, the path transformed into a river of mud, bubbling over her feet and leeching away her strength. Thrusting into the downpour, Isabel slogged up the trail as hope seeped from her with each step. Captain Morris was determined to sell her to the Indians, and she could no longer count on Hann's help. The poor girl was as much a prisoner as she was. Even if Kent managed to escape Sawkins's clutches, he had no idea where she was. Her heart shriveled at the realization that she would never see him again.

The rain continued for what seemed like an eternity but finally ceased as abruptly as it had come. By then, it had done its damage. Isabel's hair hung in saturated strands. Mud clung to the bottom of her gown, weighing it down as she dragged it through the mire. Frederick had fared no better. She did her best to wipe the water from his eyes and face. When he fussed to get out of his wet sling, she finally complied, wringing the rain from his soaked nightdress. Steam rose from the hot forest floor, and her sodden gown chafed her skin. The *pitter-patter* of drops on leaves surrounded her like a rhythmic march, lulling her exhausted mind into delirium. Slogging forward, she braced Frederick in her arms and prayed.

All she'd ever wanted as long as she could remember had been wealth and title and the comfort and respect that came with them. The more she had craved them, the more they had slipped from her grasp. The more she had turned her nose up at common people, the more like them she had become, until she had been reduced to this: a mud-encrusted, soggy, hungry woman with naught but the ragged clothes on her back and two silver combs. She gazed lovingly at Frederick and kissed his cheek. But she had her beloved son. And she had the love of God. And

somehow, as she trudged through the mud on her way to becoming a slave, none of those other things mattered anymore.

At midday, a band of savages sprang out of the greenery.

Naked save for loincloths, the men surrounded Isabel and the pirates, brandishing clubs and spears in their hands and looks of hostility on their faces. They stood at medium height, clean-shaven, with long black hair. Streaks of black paint lined their brown faces.

The pirates instantly drew their pistols.

"House your weapons, men," Morris said in as calm a voice as Isabel had heard from the pirate. Turning to the natives, he said something in a language unfamiliar to Isabel.

The man Isabel assumed to be the leader, due to the number of feathers and teeth hanging around his neck, nodded at Morris, said something to his men, and then took the lead.

Several of the natives glanced at Isabel with interest, and she clung tighter to Frederick. Terror squeezed her heart.

This can't be happening.

Frederick whimpered, and Isabel plodded forward, eyeing the Indian on her right. A white bone, perhaps from a fish, pierced his nose. He wore bracelets and a necklace lined with shells and what looked like human teeth. Nausea churned in Isabel's stomach, and she darted her gaze forward.

She began to pray silently. She must keep her focus on God. He was with her. He would not leave her.

After nearly an hour, the natives led them around the flank of a mountain and past a waterfall that plunged into a crystalline lake. Pushing aside a thicket of dense brush, they led the way into their camp. Small huts thatched with palms encircled the clearing, in the center of which blazed a crackling fire. Isabel examined the roasting pit that was certainly large enough for a human body and wondered how the natives obtained the teeth hanging around their necks. Shuddering, she clung to Frederick.

No sooner had the troop entered the camp than dozens of Indians swept upon them, chattering unintelligibly. They greeted their fellow natives and clawed at the newcomers as if they were merchandise in a store. Several women and children descended upon Isabel, running their hands over her wet gown, tugging at her hair, and fingering Frederick.

Dressed no more modestly than the men were, they wore rings of gold and silver in their nose and ears. Isabel cringed and tried to escape their mad clutches, but they only followed her. One woman tried to grab Frederick, another Isabel's combs, but one emphatic "No!" from Isabel sent them cowering backward.

A man wearing a thin cotton robe that reached to his ankles approached. A crown of white reeds sat atop his head. Three ostrich feathers protruded from it. Next to him walked a shorter man sporting a similar crown but without the feathers. A plate of gold in the shape of a half moon jutted from his nose, and two golden rings hung from his ears.

Captain Morris addressed the men and nodded toward Isabel. Their gazes raked over her, and she looked down, trying to stop her legs from trembling.

The chief led them to an open-sided hut with a fire in its center and motioned for them to sit. Hann dared cast a glance at Isabel, sorrow spilling from her eyes, before her father jerked her aside and forced her to sit beside him. The pirates took their spots around the fire, but Isabel sensed from their stiff, silent demeanors that they felt no safer in the presence of these savages than she did.

Plopping Frederick in her lap, she removed the sling from around her neck and gave it to him to play with, hoping it would keep him occupied. At one snap of the chief's fingers, the women rushed off and soon returned carrying plates of strange food: large yellow eggs, mashed fruit on leaves, and some type of fish that smelled like the bilge on the ship.

The pirates gobbled down the food with their usual gusto, removing bottles of rum from their packs and offering some to the chief and the other Indians.

Captain Morris continued his exchange with the chief, surprising Isabel with his fluent use of their language. Yet Isabel didn't have to understand what they were saying to know Morris was making a deal with theses savages that involved her. As the conversation continued, more of the Indians' gazes found their way to her and Frederick—especially the shorter chief, whose lips curled in a sinister smile beneath the golden plate projecting from his nose.

Some of the teeth on his necklace were very small.

Unease curdled in Isabel's belly. The smoke from the fire rose and drifted through a tiny hole above them. It began to rain again, and the droplets sounded like evil laughter as they splattered on the leaves thatching the roof. Smoke stung Isabel's nose along with the stench of the food. Frederick whined, and she laid a kiss on the top of his head and said a prayer over him as alarm took over her senses. Her desperate gaze scanned the surrounding jungle, and she wondered how far she would get if she made a dash for it. Not far with so many natives on her heels.

The little chief leaned toward Morris, said something, and pointed toward Isabel.

Tossing a piece of fruit into his mouth, Morris glanced at her. "He wants the babe."

Isabel shook her head, wondering if she'd heard him correctly. "I beg your pardon?" She clung to Frederick. "He will not touch my son!"

"Aye, but he will, seeing as I just sold the brat to him."

"You didn't, Father!" Hann protested.

Isabel's heart thundered in her chest. "Sold him! What do you mean?"

"Murato here has just purchased wee Frederick for a sack of cacao beans. Fair trade if I say so meself." Morris chuckled.

Murato rose and headed toward Isabel, motioning for her to hand over her son.

Hann tried to get up, but Morris yanked her down and held a tight grip on her arm.

Isabel jumped to her feet. Alarm surged through her. *This can't be happening. Lord, I can't lose my son again!* She backed up, casting a glance over the darkening jungle. Perhaps she could make it if she ran fast enough. Murato narrowed his dark eyes upon her as he crept forward. Isabel lurched toward the trees. Strong arms clutched her from behind, holding her in place. A wicked chortle blasted down her neck: Miles.

"I won't let you take him!" A flood of tears cascaded down Isabel's cheeks. Frederick began to scream.

Murato stopped within a few feet of her, examined her curiously, then turned and shouted something back at Morris. An odor of putrid fish and sweat gushed from his body.

With a grunt, Morris lumbered to his feet, followed by the tall chief. The three men conversed in angry tones, and Isabel thought for a minute a fight would break out between them, but then the parley soon came to a

311

close. The tall chief returned to his dinner while Murato snorted, turned on his heels, and joined Morris.

"I've done you a favor, milady." Morris grinned maliciously. "I've convinced Murato you should not be separated from your son."

Isabel stared aghast at him, wondering why his kind words did not match the evil glint in his eyes. Swiping the tears from her face, she rubbed Frederick's back, trying to calm him as renewed dread crept up her spine.

Morris sat and grabbed a chunk of fish. "Chief Murato is from another village far deeper in the jungle—a place where no white man has ever been." His blue eyes twinkled with mischief as he nodded toward the smaller chief next to him.

Hann jumped to her feet and faced Morris. "What have you done, Father?"

"Faith, girl!" Morris bellowed. "I'll thank you to quit interfering!"

Murato licked his lips and leered at Isabel through brown, pointy teeth.

Morris's gaze shifted to Isabel. "Oh, where are me manners?" He feigned a pretense of distress. "Lady Ashton"—he doffed his hat and gestured toward Murato—"meet your new husband."

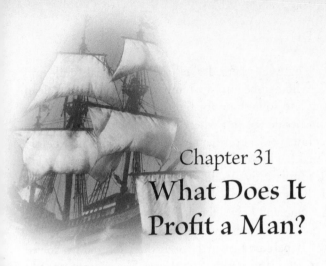

Chapter 31
What Does It Profit a Man?

The twitter of myriad birds beckoned Isabel, drawing her from the half-conscious state she had thankfully slipped into sometime during the long night. A musky scent filled her nostrils as moist grains of dirt scratched her cheek. Pulling the rough woven blanket over her head, she felt Frederick's warm body cradled against her chest, breathed a sigh of relief, and then fought to keep yesterday's memories from bursting forth. Just a few more minutes—a few more precious moments of drifting on the calm sea of slumber where she and Frederick were safe and free. But that was not to be. Voices in an unknown tongue shot like arrows around her, their intensity exceeded only by Morris's angry commands.

Pushing against the dirty ground on which she'd slept—because slaves didn't sleep in huts with their masters—Isabel rose, rubbed her eyes, and scanned the Indian camp. Captain Morris stood near the place where they had entered the village, speaking with Akers, while the other pirates stuffed their packs with fruit and meat that Isabel assumed the Caribs had given them for their journey. The women circled the fire, cooking something on massive leaves that sent a putrid smoke curling into the gray light of dawn. A group of children laughed and shouted as they played a game in the far corner, and most of the men she could see lumbered about talking or sharpening their weapons.

Hann gazed at Isabel from beside her father. The concern in her eyes breeched the distance between them. Isabel gave her a weak smile and picked up Frederick, who had begun to whimper. She must find a clean diaper for his bottom and something for him to eat. Rising to her feet, she stepped out from beside the hut where she'd been tossed a blanket and told to sleep. A chill raked across her shoulders, and she knew before she looked his way that her betrothed—Murato—was staring at her. He stood with five other Indians by a trailhead on the other side of camp. His long black hair hung in a tangled mass to his shoulders. He had armed himself with a club and knives for their journey, which made him look even fiercer, if possible, than he had yesterday.

Averting her gaze, Isabel stumbled in the other direction and swallowed the clot of terror that had clambered up her throat. She did not want to consider what atrocities awaited her as the wife of that savage. "Oh Jesus," she whispered and took no more than two steps when a sudden feeling of peace folded around her—so strong that she lifted her gaze, expecting to see an angel of light come to rescue her. But she saw nothing save pirates and Indians and the hostile world that was about to devour her and Frederick alive. Taking in a deep breath of the moist forest air, she gazed around the camp and knew—despite the horror of her circumstances—that God was with her. *"For we walk by faith, not by sight."*

Deep in prayer, Isabel ambled forward and bumped into one of the Indian women scurrying away from the fire. She glanced at Isabel and smiled. Frederick began to wail and thrash his arms in the air, and Isabel pointed toward him and gave the woman a pleading look. Her brows scrunched as she stared at the cloth on Frederick's bottom as if it were the strangest thing she'd ever seen; then her eyes lit up and she sped off. Moments later, she returned with several loincloths and some fruit and coconut milk. Her own child, no older than four, clung to her leg.

Isabel thanked her and found a clean spot where she could lay Frederick down. The woman followed, watching curiously as Isabel changed his soiled cloth. When she finished, she sat Frederick in her lap and stared at the Indian woman. Her long black hair ran down to her waist, and her brown eyes warmed in innocence. Despite the red stripes painted on her face and the silver ring in her nose, she had a beauty about her. Isabel recognized her as the same woman who'd shown an interest in Isabel's silver combs when they'd first arrived.

"Kura," the woman said, pointing toward herself. She smiled, then glanced at the little girl beside her. "Mekita."

"Pleased to meet you, Kura, Mekita." Isabel nodded at them both, and the little girl snuggled her face into her mother's hair, peeking at Isabel through the strands.

Isabel gestured to herself. "Isabel," she said, and then to Frederick, "Freddy."

Kura tried to say their names, and both women laughed at her fumbled attempts. Conviction nipped at Isabel's conscience. Kura was not a savage. She was a woman just like Isabel; only she had grown up in a different land and culture. Isabel had been born to privilege and raised with excess. But what good had it done her—what happiness had it brought her? Kura had lived in poverty her entire life and seemed content and happy.

Reaching up, Isabel plucked the combs from either side of her head, allowing her hair to tumble down her back. Holding them in her hands, she watched the firelight sparkle over the silver and set the pearls aglow. Why had she held on to them for so long? She'd thought they were her only link to the wealth and title of her past, but as she stared at them now, she realized they were meaningless trinkets from a man who didn't know the first thing about love.

Isabel held them out to Kura, who, after a moment's hesitation, took them, her eyes sparkling with delight. Giggling, she ran her delicate brown fingers over the combs and then flipped them back and forth in her hands.

Isabel smiled at the woman's exuberance, feeling suddenly lighter, as if the combs in some way had held her down. Then she realized all the treasure she needed, all the treasure she would ever need, she had found already in the storehouses of her Father, in His love, His provision, and His protection.

Kura laid down the combs and took a shell necklace from around her neck and put it around Isabel's. Isabel examined the glossy shells and thanked her. A very fair exchange indeed.

Out of the corner of her eye, she spotted Miles heading her way and grabbed Frederick just as the pirate clutched her arm and hoisted her up. Pain shot through her shoulder, and she cried out.

"Time fer ye to go, milady. Yer husband's awaitin'." He slurped up the spittle that threatened to dribble from his mouth. Tightening her lips, Isabel yanked her arm from his grasp and followed him toward Morris and Hann.

"No, you can't do this, Father. I'll never forgive you." Hann stood before her father, pleading with him.

"I'll have to bear that burden, Annie. For Johnny's sake."

Miles shoved Isabel, and she inched closer to Morris and Hann. Hann's anxious gaze met hers. The girl swallowed hard and dropped her arms in exasperation, then rushed to Isabel.

"I'm so sorry, Isabel," Hann said, tears moistening her eyes.

" 'Tis not your fault." Isabel squeezed her hand. "I'll be all right. Pray for me."

"I don't know how."

"I'm sure you'll find a way." Isabel grinned, then looked over Hann's shoulder at Morris. She felt the smile slip from her face. "Captain."

Morris would not turn around.

"Captain, are you not man enough to face the innocent woman and child you send to a gruesome fate?" Isabel heard the tremble in her voice but wanted Morris to look her in the eye as she and Frederick were led away. She wanted him to see what he was doing, not for revenge's sake, but because she knew this was not an easy choice for him. She knew there was still a chance he might change his mind.

He swerved around and jerked his chin in the air.

A volley of guttural, angry words pelted Isabel's back, and she turned to see Murato motioning for her to join him. He and his five companions waited at the head of the trail, ready to leave. His fierce gaze raked over her, the gold from his nose plate reflecting like fire in his eyes. Though he stood no more than five-feet tall, he appeared as solid as a tree. Isabel was sure if anything struck him, it would be crushed. He continued his perusal of her and grunted another word. There was something cold and harsh behind his savage stare.

Isabel slowly turned back around. Frederick screamed, fighting to be free of her grasp. Alarm stung like tiny bees over her skin, and her legs went numb. *I can't do this, Lord. Where are You?*

"Is this truly what Johnny would have wanted?" Hann sobbed, glancing at her father.

Morris's gaze dropped to Frederick, and a glimmer of sorrow flashed in his eyes. He swiped at the sweat forming on his brow, then narrowed his eyes upon Hann, avoiding Isabel's gaze. "It must be done, girl. It's the only way." He clenched his jaw, nodded at Murato, then turned his face away.

Footsteps sounded behind Isabel, and she squeezed her eyes shut. Strong fingers clamped around her arm and dragged her over the dirt.

A shrill whistle pierced the air.

Isabel opened her eyes. Murato released his grip on her as he and the other men grabbed spears and stood on alert, scanning the surrounding jungle. One of them cupped a hand around his mouth and piped the trill of a bird in reply. Another whistle answered, and the Indians lowered their spears.

The green thicket parted, and three natives emerged from the jungle, followed by Hoornes, Sawkins, and another Indian.

Isabel's breath froze and her eyes widened. What were Hoornes and Sawkins doing here? Sawkins's blue eyes met hers, and he gave her a pained look of appeal.

The leaves rustled again, and Cutter appeared. Hann gasped and threw a hand to her mouth, then ran into his arms, nearly knocking him over. He wrapped his good arm around her, relief softening the taut lines on his face. He glanced at Isabel.

Hope sparked in Isabel's heart. If Cutter and Sawkins were here, maybe. . . ?

She focused on the spot from which the others had emerged and tried to peer through the crowd of Indians forming around the newcomers. Her heart thundered in her chest. Frederick had stopped his fussing and plugged his thumb into his mouth. The hair on Isabel's arms stood on end.

Hann gazed up at the doctor. "What? How?"

" 'Tis a long story." Cutter brushed the hair from her forehead and lowered his lips to hers.

"What in the devil is going on here?" Morris headed toward the couple with the fury of a wild boar. "How dare you touch my daughter?" He shoved his face into Cutter's. "I knew I shoulda killed—"

The captain's threats were instantly silenced when the foliage again parted in a swoosh of leaves.

Kent marched into the clearing.

Wearing nothing but breeches, his bare chest dotted with perspiration, he stormed into the camp bearing the same confidence with which he strutted across the deck of his ship. His glance passed over Morris and his pirates with no more than a flicker of interest, then over the mob of Indians, until his gaze finally locked upon Isabel's. A grin lifted one corner of his mouth, and he headed her way.

Isabel's heart flipped in her chest.

"Not so fast!" Morris drew his sword and rushed to thrust it in Kent's path.

Sparks and another Indian sprang from the greenery. The Indian wore Kent's shirt and baldric.

Kent halted before Morris's shiny blade, his eyes never leaving Isabel. She lowered her gaze as heat blossomed up her neck and onto her face at the intensity, the depth of feeling that flowed from his dark eyes. *He's alive! He came to rescue me.* Her heart struggled to believe it. Raising her gaze again, she found his eyes still focused upon her, and the realization blossomed over her. She loved him—she truly loved him.

The men from the tribe began conversing with the newcomers. The chief, decked in his long white robe, came charging out of his hut, his eyes puffy with sleep. He spoke briefly with the Indians who had arrived with Kent, and then approached Morris with shouts and loud gestures.

Still holding his sword to Kent's chest, Morris responded with equal intensity, then turned to Kent. "The chief says his hunting party found you sleeping like babes in the woods. And thinking you were perhaps on my trail, they brought you to me." He pushed the blade of his sword against Kent, forcing him back.

"Then I should thank them for their assistance," Kent said.

Morris frowned and glared over his shoulder at Sawkins. "I figured you and your ship—along with this mongrel—would be at the bottom of the Caribbean by now."

Sawkins wiped the back of his neck with his handkerchief and grunted. Jagged red stripes circled his wrists. "Perhaps next time you'll not send that minnow Morgan to silence the shark you have swindled."

Morris laughed. "Shark? Egad, Sawkins, does your ego never falter? Has it come to me for more beatings, perhaps?"

"Don't believe 'im," Hoornes piped up. " 'Twas Captain Carlton who bested ole Morgan." His rat poked its head out from the pocket in his breeches.

Morris swung his gaze back to Kent. "Odd's fish, you released this scalawag, Sawkins? You're a bigger fool than I thought."

Sawkins squeezed the bridge of his nose and inhaled a deep breath. "Morgan's cannons released him." His gaze swept over Isabel, and a sour taste rose in her mouth.

"More like Captain Carlton's loyal crew," Cutter interjected.

Hann gave Kent a timid smile. "Good to see you, Captain."

Kent nodded in her direction. Even though Hann had originally intended to betray Kent, Isabel detected no animosity in his eyes.

The chief barked something else at Morris, drawing the captain's furious gaze away from Cutter.

"He's asking if I need any help. Can you imagine? To subdue the likes of you?" Morris chuckled and spit at Kent's feet, then responded to the chief.

The tall, lanky chief nodded. His intense gaze shifted over Kent and then over the other pirates before he turned and issued further orders to some of his people. The Indians who had just arrived were led to the fire, where the women waited on them, all the while shooting wary glances toward the ensuing altercation and keeping their children close by their sides.

"So you see, Captain"—Morris eyed Kent with disdain—"your plan to rescue your fair maiden has only brought you to a camp where, with one command from me, these natives will flay you and your companions alive."

Kent curled his lips in a sardonic grin. "My plan to rescue my fair lady has only just begun, Captain. And as for your power to destroy me and my crew, it will be given to you only if God allows it."

"Humph," Morris grunted. "The jungle has made you mad."

Isabel studied Kent, amazed at his declaration of God and his cavalier attitude under such precarious circumstances. Yet, truth be told, she'd never seen him unsure and distraught over anything or anyone—save her.

Most of the Indians stood in clusters, watching with interest and muttering amongst themselves. The chief snapped his fingers, and a wooden stool was set on the ground behind him. Flinging back his robe, he sat as if preparing to watch a play, and Isabel got the impression he would not get involved unless called upon to do so.

Whispers passed between Cutter and Hann, drawing Morris's attention. Morris stormed toward Cutter. "I told you to keep your hands off me daughter, you freak." He aimed the tip of his sword at Cutter's chest. "How many times must I threaten your life, boy?"

A sinister laugh came from Sawkins's direction.

Cutter didn't flinch.

Morris pushed the blade and broke Cutter's skin. A rivulet of blood flowed down his chest, leaving a trail of red down his shirt.

In a flash, Hann plucked Warren's cutlass from its scabbard before the pirate could react. "Stop, Father." Knocking her father's sword aside, she leveled her own at his chest.

Morris's brow furrowed, and shock and sorrow burned in his eyes. "You'd hurt your own father?"

"Don't do this, Hann." Cutter stepped beside her and laid a hand on her wrist, trying to force the blade down.

Hann moved away from him, her intense violet eyes focused on her father.

Kent started toward Hann and Cutter, and Isabel wondered what he intended to do.

A pirate behind Cutter drew his sword in a gleam of sunlight. Miles and Akers grabbed their pistols and leveled them upon Hann.

Kent froze.

Frederick whined. Isabel's heart sank like a stone in her chest. The lives of all the people she loved stood in the balance.

Out of the corner of her eye, she saw Sawkins inch toward the violent standoff while swatting at bugs circling his head. Odd—he usually ran away from a fight, not toward one.

Hann gave the pirates no more than a sideways glance. "I'm sorry, Father, but I can't let you hurt the man I love."

Morris blew out a sigh and lowered his sword, his face reddening. Then his gaze swept over his men. "Lower your weapons," he spit with contempt. "And don't ever aim them at me daughter again, or there'll be hell to pay." He shook his head as they complied. "I'll deal with you later, girl."

Kent turned and rushed to Isabel. His gaze swept over Frederick and then landed on hers, unsure and hesitant. Isabel smiled and fell against him. Releasing a sigh, he wrapped his arms around her and Frederick. Isabel sank into his chest, allowing his warmth and strength to wash over her. Wood and spice filled her nostrils, and she took a deep breath of him. Frederick reached up and grabbed his father's chin. Kent smiled and kissed him on the cheek, then moved his lips to Isabel's. His stubble scratched her face as he tenderly caressed her lips with his own. Isabel's breath quickened, and a burst of warmth tingled in her belly.

Tears filled her eyes. "You came for us," she whispered, gazing up at him.

He lightly kissed the tip of her nose. "I love you, Isabel. I always have."

Morris sped toward them like a madman, fury twisting his lips into a devilish grin. "How touching. The family reunited," he panted, halting before them. "Because of you, my family will never be together again, so enjoy this moment, Captain Carlton. It will be your last." He shouted over Isabel's shoulder, and she knew without turning that he had summoned Murato. The Indian's stench of sweat and filth assaulted her.

As Morris's and Murato's words fired back and forth, Isabel closed her eyes and leaned her head on Kent's chest, fighting back tears and trying to lengthen the moment she knew would soon be torn from her. But a strong arm clamped around Isabel's waist and tore her from Kent's arms.

Frederick wailed, and she tried to cling to him as Murato nearly lifted her off the ground and carried her toward the trailhead.

She heard Kent shout and start after her. Murato swung her around and tossed her to the ground. She turned. Morris had shoved a pistol beneath Kent's chin, immobilizing him. Kent's fierce gaze darted to hers.

Morris glanced over his shoulder at Sawkins, who had made his way over to where Morris's pirates stood. "I must congratulate your incompetence, for it has served my purpose well. I never dreamed to be fortunate enough to have Captain Carlton witness Lady Ashton's betrothal."

"Betrothal?" Kent growled as Morris lowered the pistol to his chest.

"Yes, to Murato here." Morris gestured toward the Indian holding Isabel. "They make a lovely couple, wouldn't you say? And your son will make a fine addition to his household slaves."

Kent's guttural moan roiled through the camp. He tossed strands of hair from his face and clenched his fists. His hard gaze bore into Morris. Muscles twitched in his chest and arms, and he reminded Isabel of a loaded cannon whose fuse was about to be lit.

When he looked her way, Isabel shook her head, trying to dissuade him from doing something foolish. She didn't want her last vision of him to be of his death.

Frederick's wail softened to a sob, and Isabel patted his back. He glanced up at Isabel, then over at the Indian next to her before tossing his thumb back into his mouth.

Rage seared in Kent's eyes as he lunged toward Isabel. "No. I will not allow it!"

Isabel's heart stopped.

With one nod from Morris, Akers and Miles sped from their spots and jumped onto Kent. The three men tumbled to the ground in a heap of thrashing legs and arms amidst groans and curses. Soon Warren and Grayson joined the fray, each taking a limb until finally the four men subdued Kent.

Murato grunted and pulled Isabel back. "No, please don't hurt him!" She snapped her pleading gaze to Morris. "I'll go quietly. Just please let him live." Tears filled her eyes as she struggled toward Kent. *Oh Lord, it hurts so much. Why did you bring Kent here if I must still be taken from him? Please protect him.*

"You'll go either way. 'Tis no matter to me whether you're quiet." Morris scratched his chin and gave her a curt smile. "But never you fear. I'll let Kent live. And 'tis a long life I'll be wishing for him, a life filled with the agony of what he's done to you and his son."

Murato yanked on her arm again. He shouted something to his companions and turned to start down the path.

"Isabel!" Kent yelled, and one of Morris's men slammed a boot onto his head, forcing it into the dirt. The last thing Isabel saw was Kent's distraught gaze as he raised his head from the ground to watch her leave.

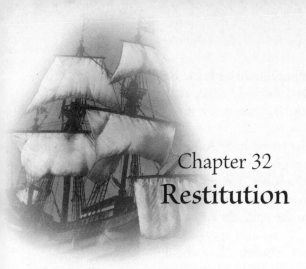

Chapter 32
Restitution

W ait!" Kent shouted. "Tell him to wait!" He threw a demanding look at Morris, who crossed his brawny arms over his chest and smirked. "Take me," Kent said.

"What did you say?" Morris cupped a hand around his injured ear. "I don't think I heard you."

"Myself instead of her and the babe," Kent panted, writhing in the pirates' clutches. He'd uttered the words without thinking but knew no amount of thought would bring him to any other conclusion.

Morris bent over in a loud chortle that shook his belly. "Why I'll be a half-masted monkey. I never thought I'd see the day."

Jerking himself free from one pirate, Kent kicked the next one, sending the man tumbling to the ground several feet away, and then slugged the third pirate with his free hand. The fourth man lunged on top of Kent, grinding his face into the dirt.

"Blast! Can't the four of you hold down one man? Let him up," Morris said, shaking his head. "He's not going anywhere."

The pirate on top of Kent hastily complied. Another pirate dabbed at the blood spilling from his mouth.

Morris shouted, and Murato stopped and turned around, pulling Isabel with him. Tears streamed down her face.

" 'Tis me you want," Kent said, rising to his feet. "I'll suffer for Johnny's death. They've done nothing to deserve such a fate." He glanced at Isabel. A flicker of surprise, then fear crossed her gaze. Frederick, still crying, grabbed one of her auburn curls and brought it to his mouth.

"At last, some sense to be had," Sawkins chimed in.

"No, Cap'n," Sparks said, adjusting his eye patch. "Don't be doin' that."

Morris scratched his coarse hair. "Am I to be understanding that the great Captain Carlton is giving up his ship, his treasure, and his very life for a mere woman and a babe?" He jerked his head toward Kent. "And what's to stop me from selling you both?"

Cutter took a step forward, his eyes wide with alarm, yet he said nothing.

Hann stormed toward Morris. "You wouldn't, Father!"

Kent examined Morris. Would he? Yes, he didn't doubt the depth this father would go to ease the pain of his son's death, but Kent had known Captain Morris before the accident. He had been a good man. "I appeal to your honor, sir." Kent prayed his words sped to that decent part of Morris he hoped still existed.

"Me honor, is it? Egad. I'm afraid what little I had sank to the depths along with my son." Morris planted his fists on his hips. " 'Tis a noble sacrifice, I'll admit." He narrowed his eyes upon Kent. "And one which I never thought to hear from the likes of you. But now I know how much you care for the wench and her son. And though 'twould certainly be a more fitting punishment for you to know they are suffering in your stead, I'm not a man without some shred of compassion. I'll see if Murato would consider taking you instead—that is as long as you'll go willingly?"

Kent swallowed. His glance swept over Cutter, Hann, Hoornes, and Sparks. The looks in their eyes told him not to go through with it. Could he give up everything he'd worked so hard to achieve, even for Isabel? Even for their son? His stomach churned.

He turned to Murato, who stood waiting, still holding Isabel's arm, his features like stone. Could he submit to this savage's authority and become a slave the rest of his life, stripped of all his power, weak—just like his father had always told him he was?

Kent's gaze landed on Isabel. Tears pooled in her beautiful green eyes. Was she crying for him or out of fear for herself and Frederick? Yet hadn't she allowed him to kiss her? Hadn't he seen affection in her eyes? It didn't matter. He would give up everything to save her whether she

returned his love or not. He sighed, longing to hear from God. Suddenly the futility of all the things he'd valued flashed before him—the power, the wealth, the success. He raised a determined gaze to Morris. "Then give him my word I will offer him no resistance. I will do as he commands the rest of my days."

"No!" Isabel struggled in Murato's grip, sobbing. "No, Kent. You mustn't."

Hann moved beside her father. "This has gone too far."

"I think it's a fine idea," Sawkins interjected.

"No one asked you, you ignorant carp." Hann shot him a fierce look.

Sawkins raised his chin, his sweaty face swelling. He stood beside Akers, who leaned against a tree, eyes half closed in boredom.

Morris spoke to Murato. The Indian turned and conversed with his friends, then answered him.

Abruptly, Morris cocked his head toward Kent. "He says he'll take you instead of the woman. He has too many wives, anyway."

Murato released Isabel, and she dashed toward Kent. "I won't let you do this."

"You have no choice, milady." Kent gazed into her eyes, thrilled by the love pouring from them. He brushed a finger over her cheek, and she leaned her face into his hand, closing her eyes. Frederick looked up at him, and Kent kissed the top of his head, drawing in the scent of him—his son. Isabel smiled. Her green eyes stared at Kent's with admiration. He felt as though his heart would burst. Laying an arm over her shoulder, he drew her near. *'Tis so unfair, God, that just when I have her heart, I must lose her.*

Morris's face wrinkled in confusion as he watched Kent and Isabel. He turned and spit onto the dirt with a grunt. "If you try anything, Kent, I'll change me mind, and she and the babe will join you in your slavery."

Kent nodded. "Tell Murato he has my word."

Before Morris could relay the message, the Indian glanced at Sawkins and uttered a string of choppy words, sending Morris into a loud chortle. "He says he'll take the pretty man, too," he said between guffaws. The pirates joined in his laughter.

Sawkins lengthened his stance, a look of horror mangling his features. "Of all the. . . I will not go with that savage!"

"Well, I say 'tis a fitting end for a coward like you," Morris sputtered. "Faith, why didn't I think of it before? A very fitting end, indeed."

Hann nodded her approval. "Aye, give him Sawkins instead of the captain."

Sawkins scowled at Hann, then shifted his alarmed gaze over the camp and finally to Morris. "You are the coward, sir. A man who does not honor his word." He grimaced. "I will have my revenge."

"And yet"—Morris grinned—"I don't see how that is possible."

Kent flexed his jaw. The fate that awaited him was bad enough, but to have Sawkins join him would be a living hell. He slid his fingers over Isabel's arm, already missing the soft feel of her skin. Her intoxicating scent of vanilla and coconut swirled around his nose. These were the last moments he would ever spend with her and Frederick. Agony weighed heavily upon him.

Morris turned and spoke to Murato, who then relayed orders to his men. Two of them started toward Sawkins.

In a flash, Sawkins yanked a cutlass and pistol from Akers and then thrust his boot into the pirate's stomach, knocking him into the thicket of greenery behind him. The other pirates fumbled to retrieve their weapons as Sawkins rushed toward Morris, screaming, "I demand you stop this at once!"

The Indians grabbed spears and started toward Sawkins, but one gesture from their chief froze them in their tracks.

Kent eased Isabel and Frederick behind him.

Caught off guard, Morris stumbled backward, recoiling from the advance, and frantically searched for his weapons. Sawkins's charge came too fast. He aimed for Morris's heart. The captain shifted at the last moment, and Sawkins's blade thrust into Morris's shoulder.

He withdrew it in a spurt of blood, and Hann screamed. Cutter grabbed her as she started toward her father.

Morris's men drew pistols and leveled them upon Sawkins.

Isabel's body tensed, and Kent grabbed her hand, keeping his eyes on the Indians around them. The chief shot up from his seat and glared at Sawkins. At any minute, he could order his warriors down upon them all.

Kent's thoughts sped through a myriad of outcomes and how he could best protect Isabel and Frederick. It all depended on how Sawkins's foolhardy attack played out. Hope surged within him. Perhaps this was God's way of getting rid of both Sawkins and Morris.

Morris stumbled to the dirt, holding his shoulder. Blood oozed between his fingers. "I'll have your innards for breakfast! Kill him, men."

Lowering his bloody sword, Sawkins cocked his pistol, pointed it at Morris's head, and glanced over the pirates and Caribs now heading his way. "I'll shoot him if you dare come any closer." He glared at Morris. "Tell your savages that I will shoot you if they so much as move a muscle," he ordered, sweat beading on his brow.

Morris turned and spoke to the chief, then barked something to Murato. The chief narrowed his eyes upon Sawkins. Natives and pirates alike froze in place

"Milady"—Sawkins shifted his pleading gaze to Isabel as she stepped out from behind Kent—"I've done this for you. Come with me now. My offer still stands." His gaze flashed to Kent and back to her. "Let the man who ravished you go to the fate he deserves. Do what is best for Frederick."

Kent eyed Sawkins. Was he jesting? Did he still hope to win Isabel? He glanced at her. A furrow creased her delicate brow. She bit her lip, hesitating. Alarm sent his heart racing as doubt filled him. Perhaps he had misread her feelings toward him. She had, after all, agreed to marry Sawkins once. Why wouldn't she do it again?

"What life can you possibly hope for now?" Sawkins continued. "The boy will grow up poor and starving, the illegitimate child of a pirate—of a slave. Is that what you want for your son?"

Frederick released his mother's hair and reached a chubby hand out toward Kent. Kent smiled at his son, his heart melting within him. Truly he wanted the best for him. But not with Sawkins. *Not him, Lord.*

Isabel's moist eyes lowered to Frederick, and fear consumed Kent. What would happen to her now with Kent enslaved and no family left to care for her? How would she survive? How would she provide for Frederick? He knew she must be pondering the same things. Sawkins would be her best choice, and God forgive him, Kent hated his brother for it.

Isabel wove her free arm through Kent's and raised her tiny nose in the air. "Your wealth and title no longer hold any attraction for me, milord. Neither, I have come to realize, do they make a man." She shifted her brimming green eyes to Kent. "I would rather raise my son alone in poverty or in slavery with this pirate than"—she glared back at Sawkins—"in riches with you."

Kent's heart exploded within him. "You cannot. You would?"

"Aye, Captain." She smiled, and Kent swallowed a burst of emotion that threatened to moisten his eyes in front of the men.

Sawkins's lip quivered. His blue eyes turned to ice. "I see. Then you're as big a fool as my brother is." He swung the pistol to Kent's chest, still holding the bloody sword in his other hand. "I would rather see you dead, brother, than have you best me again." His regal nostrils flared as his finger twitched on the trigger.

Yanking from Cutter's grasp, Hann dashed toward Sawkins, cutlass in hand. "Stand down, you fool!" Her violet eyes stormed amidst her crimson face.

Cutter jerked into action and sped behind her, Hoornes and Sparks quick on his heels.

Morris, still holding his bloody shoulder, watched with wide eyes as his daughter threw herself in front of Kent and held her palm up to the barrel of Sawkins's loaded pistol and the tip of her sword to his belly.

Kent grabbed her from behind. "No, Hann." He tried to shove her aside just as Sawkins, his face a blubbering mass of sweat and fury, drove the tip of his cutlass toward her.

Cutter lunged into the path of the blade. He shoved Hann out of Kent's grasp and grabbed the sword from her hand. The full force of Sawkins's cutlass thrust into his side.

Isabel gasped, and Frederick broke into a wail. Shooting one glance over his shoulder to make sure Isabel was unscathed, Kent headed toward his injured friend. But before he could reach him, Cutter twirled around in a fit of rage and whipped his cutlass through the air, slicing Sawkins across the face. Then, coughing, the doctor gripped his side and folded to the ground.

"No!" Hann crawled beside him, grabbing his shoulders.

Screaming, Sawkins dropped the sword and pistol and flung his hands to his face.

"What have you done?" He lowered his fingers and moaned at the blood covering them. A deep gash ran from his forehead down the bridge of his nose, split his mustache, and sliced through his lips. "You've scarred me." He stared aghast at Cutter. "You've made me like you." His chest heaved. Alarm tightened his features. Then he spun around and darted across camp, weaving around pirates and Indians before he plunged into the jungle. Within seconds, the green web swallowed him up.

Clutching his shoulder, Morris labored to his feet, spouted something to Murato, and jerked his head toward the forest.

The Indian gestured toward Kent and replied in an angry tone.

Morris shook his head and again pointed toward where Sawkins had disappeared. He said something else and picked up Sawkins's pistol laying on the ground, then motioned with it toward the other weapons in his pirates' hands and baldrics. Hope began to climb back into Kent's heart.

Finally, Murato nodded, hefted his spear, and sped into the jungle, his men following.

"Hand me a cloth, you fool," Morris yelled at Akers, who sheepishly grabbed a rag from his pack and approached. " 'Tis your lazy fault all of this happened." Pursing his lips, Akers did not reply but handed his captain the brown cloth, which Morris immediately pressed onto his wound.

Morris glanced down at Cutter. "You saved me daughter's life," he stated as if he couldn't quite believe what he'd seen.

"I love her." Cutter faced Hann sitting beside him. Tears trickled down her cheeks. "Never fear." He pressed the bloody gash on his side. "I've survived worse wounds than this." He grinned. Hann grabbed his face and brought her gnarled lips to hers.

The pirates whistled, and Morris grunted and looked away.

"What did you tell Murato?" Kent asked Morris as he squeezed Isabel's hand and brought her beside him. Her quivering, moist palm gripped his in a tight embrace. Whatever it was, it had sent the savage away, and that, coupled with Morris's jovial attitude, further bolstered Kent's hope.

Morris pushed his saturated hair from his forehead and sighed. "I told him he could have Sawkins if he could catch him—which I have no doubt he'll soon do—and all our weapons when he returns. It seemed a fair exchange to him instead of the likes of you." He spit to the side and winced. "I believe he thinks you'll give him more trouble than you're worth. And speaking for meself, I've found that to be true."

Releasing Kent's hand, Isabel rushed to Morris's side. "Thank you, Captain. I knew you were an honorable man." She laid a hand on his arm. Frederick smiled up at him, revealing three baby teeth.

A red hue rose upon Morris's cheeks, and he swatted her away. "Enough of that, girl."

As Kent watched the scene unfolding before him, he shook his head in disbelief. They no longer were being sold as slaves? A moment ago, he would have thought that impossible. God truly was almighty.

Beaming, Isabel moved beside him and handed Frederick to him. Kent pressed his son against his chest and gave Morris a perplexed look.

Sorrow spilled from the old captain's eyes, but a look of understanding passed between them.

"Johnny is dead," Morris said matter-of-factly. "No matter whether you had a part in his death, I cannot change that, nor—I have come to realize—could I have prevented it, just as I cannot have stopped me daughter here from falling for some mangled doctor." He laughed, and Hann looked at him with playful scorn.

"Then are we free to go?" Kent asked, uneasy at the sudden turn of events.

"Aye." Morris tilted his head toward the jungle. "And ye best be goin' before I change me mind." His pained gaze landed on Hann. "Take me daughter, too. She done well on your ship, and I don't want her sailin' under me debased influence."

Hann sprang to her feet and clutched Morris's good arm. "Father, surely you aren't staying here. Let us help you get back to your ship."

"Quit your fussin'. I'm all right, girl." He tugged from her grasp, annoyance twisting his features, then his face softened and a slow smile formed on his lips. "But I wouldn't be mindin' your company along the way."

Hann cast a worried look toward Cutter.

Following her gaze, Morris snorted. "Patch 'im up. You can bring him along, if you must."

Hann kissed her father's cheek, then grinned at Kent and Isabel.

The warm Caribbean sun spilled around Isabel as she sat on the shore, its rays kissing the sea and setting the water aglow like sparkling diamonds. Frederick sat beside her, playfully swatting at the foamy waves that teased his chubby bare legs. His giggle was like music to her ears. She plunged her feet into the golden sand and closed her eyes as the grains folded around them like a warm blanket. Turquoise waves caressed the shore, gurgling in laughter. A bird squawked above her as the breeze danced through the palm fronds, setting them aflutter.

Kent's strong arms wrapped around her from behind. His warm breath caressed her ear. "I love you, Isabel."

A tingle ran through her, igniting sensations she'd never felt before, and she leaned back onto his firm, broad chest. Turning her head, she met his lips. Hot and strong, they devoured her like a man deprived of food for months. Her breath came heavy, and she pulled away and stared into his brown eyes. Tiny flecks of gold shone from within them. No longer did bitterness, lust, or pride rage in their depths. "What a miracle the Lord has wrought in you."

"So does that mean you forgive me?" One side of his mouth curled upward.

Smirking, Isabel faced the sea. "I haven't quite decided yet." She grinned mischievously.

"Perhaps you need more convincing." Laying a finger on her chin, he turned her face back around and took her lips in his again. Isabel lost her senses in the taste of him.

Frederick giggled, and sand showered over them. Pulling away from Kent, Isabel saw her son, his hand raised, about to toss another handful. Kent chuckled—a guttural sound that bounced over Isabel's heart like droplets of joy. She couldn't remember ever hearing him laugh so heartily.

"No, no, Freddy." She pushed his hand back down to the beach and brushed the grains from her gown.

"Seems our son doesn't approve of me kissing his mother."

Frederick tossed the sand onto a wave licking his feet and laughed, then turned to seek his mother's praise. "If he didn't approve of you, you

M. L. TYNDALL

would know it, I assure you." She cast him a furtive look from the corner of her eye.

"He's magnificent," Kent said. Leaning down, he propped an elbow in the sand and ran a finger over Frederick's arm.

"He has your temperament," Isabel said with annoyance.

Kent lifted a brow. "My apologies." Then he gazed at his son and leaned toward him. "You'll make a good pirate someday, boy."

Isabel tossed her chin in the air. "He will do no such thing."

Hann's laughter drew Isabel's gaze down the shore to where her friend sat beside Cutter. He stretched out upon the sand, one arm behind his head. As he'd assured them, his wound had been minor. Captain Morris had already made sail, giving his blessing to his daughter and her newfound love and planning to rendezvous with them for their wedding at Barbados in a month. Happiness gushed from the couple in bubbling waves that flowed over Isabel, warming her heart. Silently, she thanked God for bringing her friends together—a most unlikely pair, she had to admit. But then so were she and Kent.

Isabel turned to the crystalline sea and drew in a deep breath of the salty air laden with the scent of tropical flowers. A hint of Spanish cedar reminded her of Lord Sawkins.

Murato and his warriors had never returned to camp with him. A chill ran down her back as she wondered what had happened to his lordship. Visions of his bloody face drifted through her mind. His one greatest fear—the one thing he'd tried desperately to avoid—had found him in the end.

Kent sat up and ran his fingers through Isabel's hair. "Have I told you how beautiful you are?"

"Now I know you are truly mad"—she gave him a coy look—"for I'm naught but skin and bones covered in rags and dirt."

"And even more radiant than I remember."

Isabel gave him a sultry smile and lowered her lashes against his perusal. Feeling his gaze still upon her, she glanced at him again. A breeze lifted from the sea and toyed with his umber hair. Isabel ran her hand over the dark stubble littering his chin. He grabbed it and brought it to his lips, his eyes sparkling with unhindered affection. Isabel felt her heart would burst.

The Restitution

"I cannot believe you love me," he said.

"It is quite baffling, isn't it?" Isabel grinned. "God must have brought us together, for I certainly never would have chosen you myself."

Kent gave her a sideways glance. "And to Him I'll be eternally grateful. Not only for you"—he brushed a finger over her cheek, sending another warm tingle through her—"but for showing me the truth about myself and forgiving me for being such a rogue my whole life."

"I believe He's taught me a great deal, as well." Isabel lowered her gaze, remembering what a pompous, spoiled girl she had been. When she looked back up, Kent smiled and squeezed her hand.

"So where is this pirate ship of yours?" Isabel cast her gaze out to the sea. "Are you sure they'll be back for you?"

"Why wouldn't they?" Kent tossed back his shoulders.

No sooner had Isabel rolled her eyes at his tone than Cutter shouted, "A sail, Captain!" A glistening spritsail rounded the corner of the cove, followed by the three masts of a frigate. The *Restitution* rode, all sails brimming, on the swell of a wave, lowering and raising its flag in salute.

Struggling to her feet, Isabel brushed the sand from her torn gown and raised her hand to shield her eyes as she watched the ship lower its sails and throw its anchor into the waters with a splash. No fear welled within her, no terror spiked through her heart at the sight of the pirate ship or even at the thought of boarding it. She knew now that no matter what happened, God was in control. He had put things in the right order in her heart—and in Kent's—and fear no longer had a place.

Kent stood and tossed Frederick in the air, and the boy let out a loud belly laugh.

"Be careful." Isabel bit her lip at the sight of her son flying above Kent, arms flailing.

"He's a boy." Kent caught him firmly and brought him to his chest. "He doesn't need any more pampering. He needs a father to teach him to be a man."

Isabel threw her hands on her hips. "And who, pray tell, is going to take on that job?"

An impudent grin lifted Kent's lips as his eyes scoured over her. "Would you consider marrying a pirate?" He set Frederick down on the sand by their feet.

"It depends on which one." Isabel raised her chin.

He took a step toward her. "Can you never still that sharp tongue of yours?"

"I believe you have discovered a way, Captain."

Kent pulled Isabel toward him and placed his lips upon hers.

The sound of Hann's and Cutter's laughter warmed Isabel as she lost herself in Kent's arms. A sudden blast of sand struck her legs, and she pulled back and looked down to see Frederick, armed and ready with another handful. With a giggle, he glanced up at his parents.

Isabel raised her gaze to Kent's smiling face, and they fell into each other's arms, laughing.

AUTHOR'S HISTORICAL FOOTNOTE:

Richard Sawkins (British Pirate: Active 1679–80): It seems that Richard Sawkins escaped the clutches of Murato's band of Caribs, for he appeared in the records of piratical history some ten years later. In 1680, he commanded one of the pirate ships in a fleet of five who attacked the coast of Panama. This band of 330 buccaneers then crossed the Isthmus of Darien to the Pacific Coast, where Sawkins captured two small Spanish vessels before sailing toward Panama City. On the way, the pirates encountered a Spanish fleet of eight ships and engaged in a furious battle later known as the Battle of Perico. It is said that Sawkins's extreme bravery contributed largely to the pirates' victory. Sawkins then led a band of sixty men against the town of Puebla Nueva, but the Spaniards, having been forewarned, were well prepared. Leading the charge at the head of his men, Sawkins was killed by a musket shot. It was said Sawkins was loved by his men for his courage and valiancy and that he was known as a man who feared nothing. (Apparently, facing his biggest fear of disfigurement radically changed Sawkins forever. It is regrettable, however, that it seemed he never turned from his villainous ways.)

John Morris (British Pirate: Active 1663–72): A good friend of Henry Morgan's, John Morris participated in most of Morgan's famous raids, including the sack of Granada (1663) and the raids on Porto Bello (1668) and Maracaibo (1669). After the tragic death of his son and his encounter with Kent and Isabel, Morris returned to piracy, and in 1671, along with Lawrence Prince, led the attack on Panama. After Henry Morgan and the governor of Jamaica were sent to England to be tried for piracy, the new governor of Jamaica, Thomas Lynch, gave John Morris a frigate and ordered him to arrest pirates who refused to give up piracy. (It is this author's hope that at the end of his life, John Morris forgave those who wronged him and allowed God to heal his broken heart.)

John Morris Jr. (British Pirate: Active 1668–69): Son of John Morris, Johnny commanded his own ship in Henry Morgan's raids on both Porto Bello and Maracaibo. He was killed when Morgan's flagship, the HMS *Oxford*, blew up during a drunken party in January 1669.

ABOUT THE AUTHOR

M. L. TYNDALL

MaryLu Tyndall dreamt of pirates and ships during her childhood days on Florida's Atlantic Coast. She holds a degree in Math and worked as a software engineer for fifteen years before testing the waters as a writer. Her love of history and passion for story drew her to create the Legacy of the King's Pirates series. MaryLu now writes full-time and makes her home with her husband and six children on California's coast, where her imagination still surges with the sea. For more information on MaryLu and her upcoming releases, please visit www.mltyndall.com.